**FIERCE, FORMIDABLE FIGHTING FEIN
FORCES FEARLESSLY FOLLOW FAIR
FUNDAN FORWARD FOR FENRILLE'S
FREEDOM . . .**

Amid the chaos of battle, Fair signalled the Fein forward. Her command group began to move up the tangled heaps of trash and busted equipment that cloaked the mountain. Flashes of light from the battle threw stark shadows on the garbage.

There was a huge flash from the airstrip and a crackling thud. A cloud of white smoke billowed up from the fuel station. Fair urged the Fein to move faster.

They came on a small EASU strong point in the uppermost moraine of garbage, a handful of troops dug into a narrow trench. They were standing, watching the fireworks. In front of them was an open stretch, fifty yards on either side—a potential killing ground.

Fair hesitated, then told N'kobi to smother the position without firearms. The Fein moved forward with bodies close to the ground, on all fours like leopards stalking antelope . . .

By Christopher Rowley
Published by Ballantine Books:

GOLDEN SUNLANDS
STARHAMMER
THE VANG: The Battlemaster
THE VANG: The Military Form

The Fenrille Books:
    THE WAR FOR ETERNITY
    THE BLACK SHIP
    THE FOUNDER
    TO A HIGHLAND NATION

TO A HIGHLAND NATION

Christopher Rowley

A Del Rey Book

BALLANTINE BOOKS • NEW YORK

A Del Rey Book
Published by Ballantine Books

Library of Congress Catalog Card Number: 92-97264

ISBN 0-345-35860-0

Manufactured in the United States of America

First Edition: May 1993

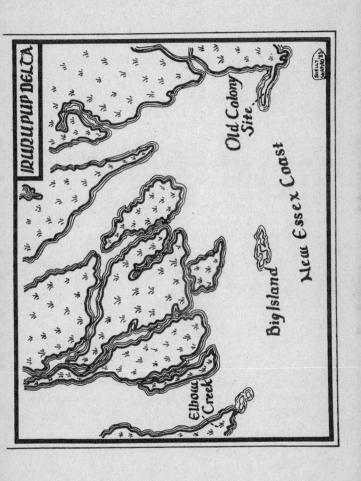

PUPUPUP DELTA

Old Colony Site.

Big Island

New Essex Coast

Elbow Creek

SHELLY CARMO '85

Part One

THE LAST FARMER

1

It was a most unusual day, bright and sunny, with a fresh breeze coming in off the ocean. The usual tropical mist was absent, the temperature was down in the high twenties centigrade, and no monsoon cloud masses loomed on the horizon.

It was a great day for a funeral, and it was a sizable crowd that showed up at the little cemetery behind Hospital Square on Big Island, as they called it now.

The man they'd come to bury had also been highly unusual, so it was a fitting day for the interment of one of the greatest minds the human diaspora had ever produced. Augustine Miflin was his name, and he'd been second-generation, born to parents who'd made the trip on the *Founder* to the New World. He was a bright kid, homosexual and sensitive about his sex preference, tall and good at basketball, fond of swimming and orchestral music. Most important of all, however, was his love of entomology. From an early age he took to the study of insects, and especially the study of the chitin insect, the New World's prolific hive builder. His studies launched the revolution in the production of longevity drugs for human consumption. For daily doses of the drugs that could be made from chitin communication proteins offered the cruel hope of vastly extended human life. These proteins came from the chitin's evolutionary edge, a vast, slow-moving "brain" made up of a class of "vizier" chitin that spent their lives exchanging chemicals with one another as they clustered in a great mass deep in their nests.

When Miflin began his work the production methods were messy, dangerous, and cruel. Huge nests were dynamited to obtain miserable quantities of the desired proteins. The drugs were then made in microgram amounts and were surrounded by secrecy, treachery, and murder among the colonists.

Augustine Miflin discovered how to tame the wild chitin and begin the process of communicating with the nests. From

3

his work came the era of production in grams and kilograms and an explosion in the use of longevity drugs.

It was no wonder that he was known as "The Saint." And since he was the one who had opened the doors to centuries of life for so many it was a sad irony that of all people it should be Miflin that they were gathered to bury, dead at sixty-four. Of course, back in the beginning, everyone had predicted an early death for him, but back then everyone had thought he was quite suicidal for wanting to climb into live chitin nests, stark naked, to try and communicate with the damned things. But it was not the horror death in the depths of a nest that had taken him. Instead he'd been knifed by a boy, a wharf rat kid Miflin had picked up for sex, but who turned out to prefer armed robbery.

To his enemies this squalid fate was a slight measure of justice, for they had hated this man with a passion. To his friends it seemed a desperately sad thing and a sign of the declining powers of civilization.

Friends, lovers, or enemies, they were all drawn to see him buried. And thus they had packed the little square cemetery, in which were buried all the early heroes of the colony. Everyone was there, everyone who counted in the colony on the New World of the Fundans. Not many still called it that. "Devil World" was popular with the second generation, and the common usage among third and fourth generations was "Fenrille"— a bastardization of the native Fein name for their world.

The crowd of notables was split into two clearly distinct groups. On one side were the older colonists, the Coastal folk. They were clad in synthetics, somber hues, the women in gowns, the men in wide-trousered suits and pseudo-silk shirts. Here and there some wore fragments of the old space suits, ultra-fashionable mementoes of the early heroic period. Many of these older colonists were pale and hunched, "domies" who lived indoors and ate kelp and synthetics: people in retreat from the planet they'd failed to conquer.

The other group was clearly not in retreat. They exuded a wild, confident air. They wore rumpled field suits of natural fiber along with wide bush hats, trail boots of gzan hide, and heavy knives and holstered sidearms on their belts. These people were heavily tanned, with a weathered look that came from a life lived mostly outdoors, sleeping under the stars on high mountain meadows. Here and there, they wore little flashes of color: bright yellow skrin feathers, a patch of scarlet skaw skin, some black and white Fein beads. These were the notes of happy savagery, signs of the nomad life-style of the chitin farmer who lived among the native Fein in their high valleys.

The Coastal people, in their tattered, oft-repaired, hand-me-down space suits and their synthetics, eyed the Highlanders with distaste and a certain respect. The Highlanders, for their part, simply exuded contempt for everyone else.

Anatol Koski, a tall, thin man who had been Miflin's lover once and had contributed to some of his early, greatest work, was reading a poem to the dead man while the urn was lowered into the slot in the ground. Anatol's voice was racked with emotion, and he broke down into sobs a couple of times. As he sobbed everyone looked up and stared angrily at the other side.

The fiercest looks of all came from the last farmers, the fanatical few who still struggled to survive on the mainland. Although they wore the ragged threads of old space suits, symbolizing their attachment to the old colony, they were just as rangy and weathered as the Highlanders. Furthermore, there was a wildness in their eyes, something that spoke of lives lived with endless hazard.

In this group was Gainer Fundan, a barrel-chested man with red hair and a round face trimmed with red beard. He stood there with an obvious truculence about him, as if he could barely restrain himself from bellowing insults across the grave. Gainer was the master of Elbow Creek Farm, the largest and most successful of the remaining agric colonies.

Across from him stood old Ervil Spreak, surrounded by other Spreaks, Highlanders all, in their bush hats with yellow feathers pinned to the brims. Ervil's granitic visage gave no hint of anything other than a wry amusement. The other Spreaks were less restrained, and some smirked back.

Gainer wore a much-patched space-suit top with equally ancient Fundan space overalls, neatly cleaned and pressed, underneath. Gainer had a right to the space suit; he had served his time in orbital duty in his youth, doing the work that was still performed by the old colony Fundans, keeping the skeleton of the old ship functional enough to stay in high orbit.

Gainer felt no love toward Augustine Miflin or his followers—he was only there because he wanted to see the bastard put into the ground at last. He wanted to be sure that no more damage could come from what he perceived as an evil genius. And every time he looked over at the Spreaks, he saw the traitor Fundans standing alongside them, and he felt the anger rise within him.

The Toronto-Fundans and the rest, they were all there, with Proud Fundan at their head. They were a group marked by an aristocratic bearing, the product of centuries of being Fundan. Beside them were friends and followers, a motley crew, though mostly Highlanders.

Then there was a gap, between the main group and a pair of young, attractive women standing together. One was hugely pregnant. The other, slim, blond, and handsome, he thought he recognized. She was a granddaughter of Adelaide Fundan, and after a moment's thought he had her name. Rowntree. He decided that she had her grandmother's looks to a quite astonishing degree.

The long, weepy poem came to an end at last, and Anatol was lead away, sobbing on a friend's shoulder.

Since Miflin had no close family, his closest aides now shoveled the small pile of sandy soil back into the little grave. The headstone, like the others in this cemetery, was only six inches long and a foot high. Augustine's name and the dates of his life were all that were molded in the marbleized pink puffcrete.

A few friends threw petals into the grave as the sand was returned. Then it was over and the crowd began milling as it struggled to get back onto Hospital Square through the two small gates. By the east gate Ervil Spreak and Gainer were pressed close together. Gainer could not resist speaking out.

"So," he said with a gesture, "your great man is gone for good."

"A great man, a very courageous man," Spreak said.

"But perhaps a foolish man, too, eh? Killed like that, gutted by some piece of street trash."

"The man's personal life was filled with tragedy, I'm afraid."

Gainer's bitterness came into the open. "The life of every one of you is a tragedy."

Ervil chuckled. "Long lives they are, too. Must be galling to you idiots down here." Ervil had been there since the beginning, since the day they'd first given proto-optimol to human guinea pigs. He'd been one of the first to volunteer.

"You people are taking the lifeblood of the colony, you're killing it. All for longevity drugs."

Ervil shrugged. "And you are content with a short life and a bloody dangerous one, too."

"It's what we're supposed to do here. We're not supposed to go native."

"Bah, you are a fool. What the hell are you risking your life for? Field-grown grain? Broccoli? You have to be crazy."

"We can do it." Gainer's voice had grown stark. "We're winning."

Ervil shook his head contemptuously. "You people have been fighting the same enemy for a hundred years, only you haven't got the message. The war is over; the enemy won. There's hardly any of you left alive."

Gainer was drawn, unable to hold his tongue. "But it isn't over and we're close to victory. We have the techniques now, we can beat them."

"You're stark raving mad, young man, that's all."

They were through the gate, and Ervil moved away from Gainer, leaving him standing there red-faced, gasping with anger. After a moment Gainer turned and found himself face-to-face with Rowntree Fundan and the very pregnant young woman with her, a dark-eyed beauty with glossy black hair and a prominent chin.

"Hello, Gainer," Rowntree said. "I don't know if you remember me."

"I do. You are Rowntree, Adelaide's granddaughter."

She smiled and tucked a wisp of pale yellow hair behind her ear. Gainer was struck by her beauty, that small-nosed, high-cheekboned look that was still called the "Minnesota" by the older generations.

The pregnant woman broke the short silence. "You're the last of the farmers, aren't you? I've heard so much about you. You know, you're a legend here on the Island."

His eyebrow shot up. "Legend, eh?"

Rowntree made the introduction. "Gainer, this is Edena Faxeen. She's been taking care of old Compton for several years now."

"Ah, yes," he said. So this was the little whore who had besotted the old man in his declining years. And so obviously pregnant, too. Well, it couldn't be Compton's, could it? "Nice to meet you, then." He looked down at her swollen belly with the question in his eyes.

She laughed, bright white teeth flashing in the rare sunlight. "Oh, yes, it's his. I know what you're thinking. But you shouldn't believe all the vicious gossip you hear. I always wanted to have his child."

His obvious surprise made her laugh some more.

"There are ways, you know, beyond the, uh, normal."

"Edena!" Rowntree said tautly.

"Well, that's nice," Gainer said. "Good for old Compton, begetting an heir in his final days."

"It's a girl," Edena said. "That's what I wanted. I'm going to call her Fair. Don't you think that's a nice name for a Fundan?"

"Well, yes, I suppose I do."

"She's going to be a princess, is my Fair, you'll see."

Then they were moving away, and he nodded, waved goodbye, and went on, feeling a strange mixture of emotions at war within his breast.

He left the square and made his way through the narrow, crooked streets in the center of Big Island Town. He stopped outside the Harbor Bar, then pushed into the cool, darkened interior. There was hardly anybody there, so he had a cold beer, exchanged a few words of chat with Kimme, the daytime bartender, then grew restless. He bought half a liter of rum and left to go down to the dockside, where he jumped aboard his boat, an old Fundan-made cruiser called the *Firefly*. The engines started with a solid growl, then thunked and grumbled as he reversed her out into the channel before turning and heading out onto the broad water of the delta.

As he went, he passed a row of older buildings, domes with big covered porches thrust out in front, looking seaward. On the nearest one the green paint was peeling. Gainer waved, knowing that the old man, old Compton Fundan, would be on his veranda watching the boats go by.

So old Compton was going to be a father again after what was it, forty years or something? For some reason this idea made Gainer feel better. He whistled a tune from a video show his daughter Helen watched every day. He hated the show, but the tune stuck in his head and wouldn't go away. If old Compton could become a father at the age of eighty-five, there was hope for everyone.

2

THE FUNDANS HAD ABANDONED BIG ISLAND, ALL EXCEPT FOR THE old man who lived alone in the green dome house. For the clan, it was just another footstep in the sand.

Except for his housekeeper, a dour sinic named Wong, Compton saw virtually no one. Which was not to say that he did not watch them, for he spent much of his time on the big veranda, observing the comings and goings of boats large and small. It was what he loved most—the sea and the boats he'd built to cross it—and it was fitting to sit and watch them as he prepared to die.

He never spoke with Edena, even though he knew that she carried his child. Artificial insemination, he had heard, and not in vitro. For some obscure reason this thought amused him greatly. He would rock from side to side and laugh about it for hours.

Edena, a beautiful child who could have been his legal wife, had refused him at the last and left. It was absurd to think that he could have held on to her for any length of time. It was just his luck and her good fortune that they had met as they had. And now there would be a child from his loins, albeit via the sperm bank. Nobody else had ever made use of his sperm samples in the Fundan Gene Bank. He chuckled at the thought. Now he would join his illustrious sire in that regard.

Sometimes these thoughts caused him to look up at the portrait of Claire, his first wife and the mother of his children. All dead now and dead for decades, causing a sadness from which he had never properly recovered. All lost to the sea, leaving him behind—a sad old man with memories and little else, sitting on the covered porch watching the tides roll in and out, waiting for the end.

To Rowntree Fundan the big house seemed sad and neglected as she approached it. She hadn't seen it in ten years, and the reality clashed badly with her memories. From where it perched up above the dockyard, facing the delta, it presented a rather forlorn appearance, and she felt for it.

The paint was peeling and there was discoloration on the roof windows. The big front yard was a mess, with knuckoo growing wild and the terrestrial flowers dying.

Rowntree sighed. Her memories of this place were bound up with her childhood, a happy time of friends and schools and parties on the beach. Now she realized that the place was smaller than she remembered and sadly divested of its former charm. The excitement she remembered was largely associated with Adelaide, her grandmother, and not with her mother, Clarisse. Her grandmother had filled this house with life; she had had more energy than five normal people. She drove herself and her husband, old Tobe, into activity on behalf of a thousand good causes. There were always meetings, parties, and events, an endless round of them. Rowntree smiled. Her own mother had been driven to distraction by Adelaide's constant demands. Throughout her life, Clarisse had wanted nothing more than to be free of her own mother. Unfortunately for her, that freedom came only with death, in a plane accident when Rowntree was twelve years old.

But that was all history now, and nobody lived here but old Compton Fundan. He was a living memorial to the early times, the last link to a vanished way of life. And, like a memorial that is ignored, he had grown rank and forbidding, focused on his memories, overgrown with the past.

The doorbell rang inside the hallway. She could hear it from outside the front door. It made an empty sound, as empty as the lives of the old domies. A window on an upper floor had been broken and covered with a sheet of wallboard. The front door was gouged where someone had tried to break in.

There was a long wait before Wong appeared. Then the door was abruptly cracked open a few inches and a suspicious pair of black eyes looked out.

"What you want?" Wong was not known for politeness. In fact, she had suffered brain damage from fly fever as a child.

"Hello, Wong, I'm Rowntree. You remember me, don't you?"

"No, no remember anyone. You go away now."

"No, Wong, I've come to see my Uncle Compton."

"Old man no see anyone. Go away."

"No, Wong, I've come a long way to see him. He knows I'm coming. You must let me in."

Wong remained expressionless.

"You are Rowntree? Clarisse's daughter?"

"That's right. I used to live here; you must remember."

"All dead now."

Rowntree swallowed. "Yes, they are. Now."

"You come in and wait, I will ask old man if he want to see you."

Wong cracked the door a trifle wider and let Rowntree slip inside. She waited in a gloomy green room. On the walls were pictures of Fundans of long ago and she recognized one of Edward Fundan sitting in a chair on a long green lawn. He had a cigar, unlit, in his hand and wore a red smoking jacket and black trousers. His beard was neatly trimmed, and his eyes sparkled with intelligence. Deer grazed on the shrubbery in the background. She studied the face of the last prince of the Fundans. He had begun the drive to leave the home system but had not lived to sail the vast deeps of interstellar space. How would this utterly civilized man have reacted to what his family had become on the New World? Rowntree had no answer for that.

Next to Edward was a picture of Dane Fundan. In contrast to his grandsire, Dane seemed far from patrician, dressed in a set of green overalls, holding a spanner in one hand. They had called him "the engineer" in those days, and his legacy still ran throughout the colony in its technology, much of which he had designed and built himself. Rowntree noticed that the artist had included oil stains on the overalls and grease on Dane's hands.

At the end of the room, in a central position above a long side table, was a portrait of the Princess Leila Khalifi. It had been done when she was fifty years old and showed a woman of formidable beauty, wearing a gown of green silk, sitting on a chair in this very room, beside the window that overlooked the front yard. How things had changed! Rowntree wondered what the Princess would have said about the new life in the mountains if she had lived to see it. Would she have left this island refuge for the nomadic freedom of the chitin farmers? Or would she have been like her son, too wedded to the big island to ever leave it?

Rowntree continued her tour of the walls, the portraits that she had not seen in a decade. The pirate, Peter Fundan, who had styled himself "Asteroid Prince," gazed out from a space suit of antique style and bulk. Next to him was Melanie

Fundan, inventor of the unique Fundan software system that had built the fortune of the Watermoon-Fundans.

Rowntree shivered. Melanie looked out from a holo effect, surrounded by an orange senso mist. Her eyes were green and artificially enlarged. Her entire face had been the product of surgery and bore a devastating, cold beauty. Such a strange way of life that seemed, the swirling sophisticated societies of the early Watermoon habitats. Rowntree was repulsed by the very idea of living in a space habitat. Nothing made by human hands could match the beauty of her home on the rooftop of the New World.

And then there were Emily and Talbot, the first Fundans to make it up the gravity well from Earth. They wore simple clothing, white T-shirts and shorts, and stood on a tiny lawn surrounded by yellow flowers. Their faces showed only a healthy solidity, a bland calmness born from comfortable, wealthy lives. And yet they had taken the great original risk, selling their business on Earth to buy space in the *Atlantis* habitat.

The door opened again. Wong was back, her features set in a slightly less ferocious expression of gloom.

"Old man he say he see you now. Right away."

"Why, thank you Wong."

"No need thanks."

Rowntree went down the long corridor, which smelled of polish and faintly of flowers. The place was spotless, but old and empty of life. She glanced through one door into a room filled with heavy pieces of furniture. Such pieces seemed utterly bizarre to her now. As a nomad, she owned nothing like this, none of these impediments to movement. All these things were part of the other life, a kind of life that she had forgotten just as the Fundans had forgotten the asteroids and, before that, Toronto.

Then she stepped out onto the veranda, where the old man was waiting to speak to her. He rose unsteadily from his chair and welcomed her to take another one. They were spindly rocking chairs built by Dane Fundan himself from a ceramaze mix known as Fundantal Five, which had originally been invented to make boats but had proved even better for furniture.

"How are you, dear?" Compton Fundan was a shrunken figure. His shirt and trousers hung loosely on his spindly frame.

"I'm very well, Uncle Compton. Everything has been going just great."

"You came down here for the funeral, I take it."

"Yes, of course. It was a big shock to all of us. Everyone who'd known him came, I think. The cemetery was packed."

"I would have expected it. Extraordinary man, was Augustine Miflin, extraordinary."

He heaved a sigh, a soft sound. Outside the veranda, down in the harbor, there was a big fishing boat in motion, chugging slowly out the channel into the delta. *Devilqueen*, read the name painted on her ceramic bow. Compton studied it a moment and the Fundan boatyard number swam into his mind. "Four-oh-sixty," he said to himself. As sure as there were fish in the ocean that was old 4060, a boat he had worked on himself.

"An odd man, a genius, of course. Things have been completely changed by his work. You realize that, don't you, girl? The colony is not what it was, not with most of the people gone." Old Compton was resigned to the turn of history, an old man waiting for death to release him. He had none of the bitterness of Gainer Fundan, out at Elbow Creek Farm.

"You know that's one reason I came to see you, Uncle. We're concerned that you're too alone down here."

Compton laughed. "Never alone with old Wong about. Oh, no, never alone."

"Nevertheless, you could see more people, you could take an interest in life again. You don't have to die."

Compton chuckled again. "But I don't want to live much longer. I really don't. I've seen enough of life and I know it's not going to get any better." He paused and rubbed his chin. Five days' stubble now—he really ought to shave soon.

"Anyway, enough of what I'm doing, which is nothing. Tell me what's happening with you younger folk."

"Well, that's the main reason for my coming. I have news for you from Edena."

"She was at the funeral. I saw. But she won't come here." He sighed. "Ah, well." At least he had the memories of a young woman's generosity.

"Edena's been living with us on Cinnabar Ridge. She doesn't work the chitin, but she helps with everything else. Of course she's very pregnant. It's going to be a girl. They estimate a birth weight of seven and a half pounds. She'll have dark hair, and Edena's going to call her Fair."

"A dark-haired girl called Fair. Well, Edena always had a contradictory side. Still, I'm gratified. She knows that I have no objections? Although, of course, I can't leave her anything much in my will: that would set a precedent that would upset the family council."

"Of course, Uncle Compton."

"And what about yourself, girl? Are you going to marry, or have children without the formalities like so many seem to be doing nowadays?"

Rowntree shrugged. "Marriage isn't something that interests me at the moment. My life is too busy."

"There isn't some fortunate young man?"

"No, there's no one." She suppressed any lingering bitterness. Of course there was no one, not with Steven gone from her life, living with that damned Gerine Butte down in Ghotaw Central. She looked up, her face determined. "But someday I want to have children, two or three, I think."

He smiled, then reached out and patted her hand. "I trust that you'll do that. I'm sure you'll make a good mother. Of course, I shan't be here to see them, but never mind."

"You know, you don't have to die. You could have another hundred years, another life entirely. Everyone would contribute for you."

Again came the sigh. "I could, but I don't think I'd enjoy all that time spent as a withered old man. No, child, I've had my time and I'll not regret its passing."

"But with optimol you'd never get cancer. And there's enough optimol now for everyone."

Compton's smile became wintry.

"So, you're not killing each other for it anymore, are you?" The dark days were a searing memory for everyone.

"No, that's all over and done with. We're in the era of peace now, no more killing and fighting."

His smile grew grimmer. "If you really believe that, then you are in for one hell of a shock, my dear. They know about it in the home system, there are ships on the way; some of them will be here in five years or less. You think it's going to be peaceful after that?"

Rowntree blinked, then brushed away doubt. "There'll be enough. We're producing so much now we could handle twice the load."

"Twice! Is that how many you think are coming?" He snorted and shook his head. "All right, it's your life and you'll probably find some solution, just like your grandmother. You know, you're very like her, Rowntree. You really remind me of Adelaide."

He was looking away, out the window.

"It will not become a utopia, this New World of ours." He chuckled. "But I'll be dead, and I won't have to worry about it anymore. One of the definite advantages in dying." He gestured feebly out the window. "Everything here will be gone. It'll be like Earth, you'll see it."

Now Rowntree laughed. "Like Earth? Now, Uncle Compton, that's just crazy. There'll never be that many people here, and we aren't communists, either."

"You think your wishes in the matter will be taken into consideration? Hark to my words, girl. The Social Synthesis will be here in all its awful power within fifty years—raw communism. They'll bring it from Earth."

Rowntree snorted in disbelief. Not only was Uncle Compton old, he was getting senile. Rowntree couldn't imagine anyone wanting to live under the rules of Social Synthesis, not once they had escaped the crushing crowding of Earth's teeming population zones.

Old Compton railed on for a while about the danger from Earth, then grew tired. She watched his eyelids droop and his hands fall into his lap. He was a very old man, after all. She left him to Wong and made her way out of the old house. She would report her failure to the family council. There was no way to make him change his mind; he would die, and soon, and he would die in his own house down here on the Coast.

Rowntree strolled through the streets of Big Island, noticing the changes that had occurred since her childhood. The place seemed shabby and run-down. There were a lot of empty windows. She had lived here as a little girl, and she remembered it as a good place, bustling with crowds of people. Now it seemed desolate, all its faults exposed by the unusual bright sunshine.

The sun slanted between the buildings as she strolled into Hospital Square. She was glad it was such a fine day; it made this visit more bearable. Still, she doubted that she would come back any time soon.

3

WHEN THE FOREST GAVE WAY TO FOODBEET THE CHANGE WAS startling. The wall of giant trees vanished and there was a spread of the brightest green leaves ever seen on this alien world. Foodbeet had the lushest leaves of any known plant, a sure sign of its origin in a human laboratory. Under the bright sun of the dry season it virtually glowed.

Gainer felt a good sensation in his gut whenever he saw that—the untidy, mountainous mass of the trees gone, the mark of the farmer placed on the land in its stead. And Gainer was that farmer, for he headed the crew of the Elbow Creek Farm and he identified utterly with the enterprise.

This particular field had been cleared years back and had been worked until the soil became weakened. Then they'd grown a number of crops of nitrofixing vetches on it, which had been ploughed in along with pulp from freshly cut trees. Now it was back in production, harnessed to humanity's needs.

The creek rounded a bend before turning inland to the landing dock. At the corner was the skeletal remains of a tracto-crawl, an early machine, smashed and destroyed long ago in an elemental battle with the enemy. They'd scavenged it for years, but there was still enough left to provide a landmark. At night they kept a two-hundred-watt light going at the top to help with inshore navigation for the fishing fleet.

He heard the reassuring mutter of the security tower in his earphones. He was cleared for the landing dock. All was quiet on the farm. The *Firefly* chugged briefly, then coasted as he cut the motor, expertly ran the boat in to the dock, and slotted her in beside the big barge used to ship machines and crops back and forth to the islands.

On the dock was a small welcoming committee. He recognized his youngest son, Ishmael, and his daughter, Helen. Ladbrook Lambeer was there, too, a tall, imposing presence. Ladbrook waved. Gainer waved back, then tossed his line across. Ishmael caught it and fed it into the wincher, which wrapped it tight and hauled it in until the *Firefly* was snugged nicely with its bows against the dock.

Short, dark, with a pageboy, Helen hugged him hard for a few moments. As always, he felt his strength renewed by the contact. Helen was his greatest support.

"We got the broccoli in, and you have to see what the tomato house did." Helen was wildly enthusiastic about the new vegetable operation.

"I'm looking forward to it," Gainer said. In truth, the vegetable crops were enormously welcome. The prices they could get for real vegetables on the islands were fantastic. People who'd spent their entire lives eating synthetics—slabs of this, chunks of that, all flavored and processed and made from biotank sludge—reacted very favorably to a real tomato, or a pineapple, or even broccoli and salad greens. Gainer had been quite surprised, in fact, by the fervor these things had aroused when they'd first taken them over to the island market. The first day had ended in something close to a riot!

"What was it like, Dad?" Ishmael asked quietly.

He looked up; Ladbrook was studying him intently. They were all curious about the funeral. That was why they were here to welcome him back, after all.

"It was crowded, biggest crowd I've ever seen. One of his friends read a poem and started to cry. A lot of them were crying, especially the men."

"Well, he was that way," Ishmael said.

"Yeah. Well, they were all there, and I saw our cousins. They all dress the same; some of them are wearing bones in their hats, though. I think it's getting to them, living the way they do."

"Bones in their hats?"

"Yes, and feathers and bits of skaw skin. They think they're Fein or something."

Helen laughed at this, and they all turned to the path and went up to the Fort.

At the Fort, his middle son, Elgin, was waiting in the control tower. Gainer sent the others on to the kitchen for lunch, then climbed the stairs to the small room, packed with screens and equipment. Elgin, taller than either Ish or Randy, was sitting in the middle of it.

"Hi, Dad." He stretched in the chair. Gainer gripped his

son's hand hard. This one, more than any of the others, this was the one he loved.

"Randolf?"

"Gone over to the flats, that camera is still inop."

"Defense?"

"Took twenty-two and twenty-five. They're both working pretty good."

"Okay, we'll just have to see. Still can't get anything from an aerial?"

"Nope. Just that sighting yesterday."

"Unconfirmed."

"Well, sure, but what the hell else do you think is going to move in those woods out there? Every tree in miles is zippered."

The screens provided quiet tableaus of tropical forest, in which nothing moved.

"You never can tell. Could be nothing, could be a flock of skrin or skaw, could be . . ."

"So, what was it like?" Elgin cut him off.

"Pretty much as expected: big crowd, lots of emotion, all the cousins were there. They're looking like savages, these days, all wear tags of feathers and bones and so on."

"Sure, I've seen that. They've been doing it for years now." Elgin seemed to accept the Highlanders' ways completely, and this chilled Gainer's heart, for he feared more than anything else that he might lose this boy to the Highlands. Ish and Randy would stay with him—they were farmers, no doubt of it—but El was not so convinced.

"Well, I don't know why they do it but it looks strange to me."

"Sure."

Gainer looked out the windows, over the roofs of the farm buildings to the nearby fields, lush with fresh vegetables. Far away, the monstrous alien trees formed a gray wall across the land, cutting off the bright terrestrial greens of his corn and foodbeet fields.

This was what they had built, what they shared, what they fought to preserve. This was what Gainer wished to bequeath to Elgin, who should be the leader after him. But Elgin didn't care about the farm. He was just going through the motions. Elgin was a traitor in his heart. This thought brought Gainer to the point of tears, it left him incoherent at night when he'd had a couple of whiskies and was alone with his memories. He would babble to himself of the woman he had loved, whom he still missed as if he had just lost her, the wife now dead these eleven years and the mother of these children. In a way, the farm's success was his response to her death. It was her monument. And Elgin didn't want it.

"You coming to lunch?" he asked.

"Not right now, not with Randy out there."

"Herbert will inform you if anything happens."

"I know, but when something moves out there you can't take chances. It's the rules, Dad. You know, you wrote them."

Gainer sighed. "Yeah, you're right."

"But I am coming in with you tonight. I'm doing the market this week with Helen. Randy's staying here."

"You got a taste for some high life, eh?"

Elgin grinned. "I'll be in the Beachcomber. Where are you going to be, Harbor Bar?"

Gainer laughed. "Beer is better in Harbor Bar, you know that. Those idiots at the Beachcomber have ruined old Mutu's beer. I heard they lost the yeast; a mutant got in and killed the whole fermentation dead. They still haven't got a good strain to settle down."

"Well, it's better than your beer, Dad, you'll admit that."

Gainer hugged him hard. "To think that my own flesh and blood would sit there and say such a wounding thing, why, it just breaks my heart . . ."

Gainer turned and descended the stairs. Elgin laughed, and Gainer felt a moment of joy in his heart. Perhaps, just perhaps, the tide could be turned.

Lunch was an affair of ten men and women, plus three kids, around a long table. The menu included lasagna with real tomatoes and a big salad of fresh lettuces and tasty greens from Helen's experimental garden; everyone tucked in heartily. Despite Elgin's complaints, bottles of GOB, or Gainer's Own Brew, were happily accepted from the chiller. The little ones drank chilled fruit-juice cocktails, also from the farm's own fruits. Conversation centered on the funeral and Augustine Miflin's importance in history.

Ishmael, ever the serious youth, was offended by something Paula Grudon said about Augustine's libertine streak.

"He was a genius! He was the only real genius this colony ever produced."

"Hey! What about Dane Fundan?" big Ladbrook growled.

"Dane Fundan was an eccentric engineer, not a scientific genius. Augustine Miflin was."

Gainer disliked such talk about the "saint" of chitin science, but he was drawn in anyway. "I don't know about that. He just worked out how to farm the damned insect."

"Not an easy thing to do."

"It was the goddamn Spreaks that did the hard work. They produced the first drugs."

"The Spreaks did the chemistry, but they never understood the insect. It took Miflin to come up with a solution to the real problem."

Gainer shook his head at his son's words. "You think there's such a thing as a solution? You're living in a dream world. There are no solutions. If everyone's gonna live forever then there's gonna be one helluva shortage of supply. There'll be nothing but war and killing to come out of it."

Ishmael had gone quiet. So had the table; everyone was munching their food and looking down. Gainer bit back his tirade and looked down, too. Why did he always explode so when this subject came up? What did it matter what anyone thought about goddamn Augustine Miflin?

After a silence, Helen spoke up. "Does anyone else want to come in to market tonight?"

Ladbrook nodded. "I'm coming. I have an appointment with a few beers at the Harbor Bar tonight."

"Oh, great," Helen groused. "Fat lot of good you'll be tomorrow, then. We start at dawn."

"I've never understood why. Everyone could wait just a little longer if they really tried."

"Listen to you! Nothing would get done around here if it wasn't for the women—nothing."

Ladbrook laughed happily. Gainer nodded, glad the difficult moment had passed. It seemed he couldn't hide it, this pain that he felt from the looming betrayal he knew was coming from Elgin. How long did he have, he wondered, how long did he have left of the happiness on Elbow Creek Farm?

That evening, as the sarmer mackees started to scream at the sunset, the *Firefly* towed the barge across the waters of the delta. On the barge, under Helen's constant care and supervision, were sixty boxes of broccoli under ice, two thousand heads of lettuce, eighty boxes of bright red tomatoes, a thousand bunches of arugula, five hundred heads of radicchio, a thousand bunches of scallions, twenty boxes of oranges, and a dozen boxes of ripe melons. It was going to be a heavy market stall this time.

Gainer sat in the bow, doing his utmost not to think while he watched the final throes of the sunset. Pink-flecked gray clouds still caught a trace of light far out to sea. The moons were up, the large Pale Moon riding above the horizon in the west and the small Red Moon hurtling by directly overhead. The water was smooth and quiet, though breakers gleamed on the shore far away to the west. Much closer were the lights of the islands. The red warning blinker of the radio mast on Little Island winked steadily in the gathering dusk.

Elgin was in the stern, sitting with Ladbrook, engaged in quiet conversation. Gainer tried not to think about him. Thank space and stars the boy would be in the Beachcomber that night. Gainer didn't want him around in case he drank a little too much and got into a mean one. He didn't want Elgin to see him like that, nor did he want to get into the kind of argument that he knew would spring up if he did. He just wouldn't be able to stop himself then.

He sighed. Happiness was such a fragile thing.

4

THE HARBOR BAR WAS A WARM, COZY PLACE. POLISHED WOOD surfaces, scuffed floors, and red checked tablecloths were its style. It had been standing on dockside for seventy years and had grown from a single twenty-by-fifteen room to two separate bars with a restaurant upstairs. On the ground floor was a large saloon and a rough bare-boards room for the fishermen at lunch. In the saloon, there were lamps made from permiad skulls and a huge fish tank set into one wall. In the tank swam a dozen or more exotics from the oceans of the New World: silvery viperfish, scurrying crakoons, and dwarf permiads with shining blue skins.

Gainer was in the saloon, as usual. He'd eaten a plate of spicy synthetics at the Mexical restaurant and was washing them down now with his second pint of the Harbor Bar's best ale. He didn't know why he gave in to the urge for junk food like this, but he did, most visits to the Island. It always made him burp, too, at least until he'd had a couple of beers. Every so often someone would go by and nod to him or exchange a few words. Gainer was an institution in this place on Saturday evenings.

Ladbrook was not in sight yet. Gainer expected the big man was down at the roast-fish place. He loved his seafood, did Ladbrook.

Gainer's gaze flicked across the screen up above the end of the bar. A surfer shot through a tube in brilliant sunlight and a crowd applauded. The surfing championships were being held in Coast City this year, and since CC was six thousand miles farther west the sun was still shining there. The shot shifted to surfers paddling for the next wave, and the cameras zeroed in for every nuance.

Gainer had never been much of a surfer, so he didn't tune in. Instead his thoughts wandered, a happy daze spreading out from his belly as the beer took effect. He liked this warm fuzziness; it was his only way of letting go nowadays. Indeed, it had been a tough ten days, what with harvesting all the broccoli and fixing the icemaker twice, but everything had come in on time in the end. There was some satisfaction in knowing that things were going well on the farm.

Market tomorrow was going to be a wild one. There were only two farm crews in this time, the Elbow Creek crew and one from Max Butte's Mission Farm. That meant a distinct shortage of supplies. By midmorning there'd be mob scenes around the stall as they started to run out of tomatoes and lettuce and the rest of Helen's goodies.

He was staring out at the sea when a woman passed through his line of vision and snapped him out of his reverie. There was a startling resemblance to someone he knew, but for a moment he could not place her. She was slender, quite tall, with pale blond hair that grew down to her shoulders. She was wearing a faded olive green bush jacket. She passed by without seeing him, looking off down the length of the saloon, checking for someone. Finally he realized it was his cousin Rowntree.

He turned to watch her reach the far end, then come back through the tables to take a stool not far from him.

"Hello," he said when she was settled. She looked up and gave a little start as she recognized him.

"You stayed down for market day, did you?" he suggested.

She shrugged. "Not really, though come to think of it I will show up there tomorrow morning. Everyone up at Ghotaw would love some fresh tomatoes."

"Better come early, then, there'll be a mob. There's only us and Max Butte's crew down here."

"Not many of you farmers left, I guess." Which was painfully true. They'd taken so many casualties in the early days. Now there just weren't that many crews still fighting for the land.

"They're good tomatoes but they're expensive." He smiled. "Real red and real tasty."

"I have a card on the Optimol Bank. There's plenty in the account." She smiled back, one prosperous farmer to another.

"Well, did he come?" he asked.

"Who?"

"Your friend."

She looked around, and he thought how lovely her neck was, how firm that square chin, and how round and desirable the breasts under the green bush jacket.

"No, it seems he didn't." She sounded quite cool to the whole idea.

"In that case, could I have the honor of buying you a drink?"

She stared at him for a moment. He thought he'd made a hash of it and that she was about to leave, but instead she gave him a little smile. "Why not? Yes, I'd like a drink. A whisky. Do they have Spreak Whisky here?"

He nodded. "Oh, sure, Spreaks come here and they always like to see their whisky available."

Chips, the Friday-night bartender, was already filling a small glass.

"No ice," she said.

"On me," Gainer said.

They raised their glasses and drank.

"So may I inquire as to what really kept you down here for another day?"

She pursed her lips, took a stimtube from her pocket, and opened it. She decided not to mention her visit to old Compton; she sensed that Gainer would not be sympathetic.

"Some business, the bank, you know, that sort of thing. We

don't get down here that often, so there are always a few errands to run."

She took a drag on the stimtube. Gainer felt the familiar irritation with his family rise to the surface. "Well, you're not exactly conveniently located for the shops, now, are you?"

She smiled. "No, I guess we're not. But we have other things to compensate."

He grunted, fighting to keep the animosity out of his voice, and failing nonetheless. "What, Fein villages? Sitting around with a bunch of Stone Age guys making stone tools?"

She looked at him with amused eyes.

"Now, that sounds as if you're jealous. Are you, Cousin Gainer?"

"Jealous?" Perish the thought.

She laughed, a pretty sound, and changed tack.

"You are a cousin, aren't you?"

He put a hand to his chin, glad of the change of direction, "Well, now, I must be, but it's a pretty distant connection. My mother was Melissa Fundan—she was a Martian Fundan—so they all came from the children of Natural Fundan."

"That's a long time ago, twenty-second century or something."

"Yeah. So we're cousins, but only just."

"And your father must have been old man Randolf Flecker."

"That's right."

"I remember him coming to visit my grandmother, when we lived here on Big Island."

"You lived down here then?" He seemed surprised.

"My childhood. We left later."

Gainer wondered if he'd ever seen her when she was a kid.

"I used to visit that house. When Adelaide was elected mayor, I remember we all went over there and had a tremendous party."

She giggled. "I wasn't born then."

"Oh." He hushed himself. The memory was from his own youth, and he was suddenly embarrassed by his age. What an ancient he must seem! Already. It didn't seem fair, somehow, except that he had raised four kids along the way, and now faced the quieter part of life, the downhill slope to the grave.

It was ridiculous. He wasn't an old man—he still felt young! In his heart he was still booming Gainer Fundan, captain of the Big Island football team.

"Anyway," she said with a smile, "I only remember my

grandmother from after that period, when she was retired. She was still the center of things, of course. There was always something going on."

"I remember that she was very important; my father thought the world of her."

"Yeah, well, they were all in it together, back in the earliest days. Your mother and father played a big part in it, didn't they?"

"Old Randolf never would talk about it much, and Mother, well, she didn't like to discuss it either. She wasn't involved much, anyway, since she lost a leg up in orbit."

"Oh, but wait a minute, she was a hero! We read her story in school. She was fighting right alongside Dane. She must have told you."

"Not really. I think they were tired of being legends in their own lifetime by the time I was born. I was their last and they had me pretty late in life. My mother had special medical just to conceive, it was right up there at menopause for her."

"I was wondering about that . . ."

"Funny thing, medical science."

She giggled. "Hardly need it now."

He looked at her again. Of course. He was nearly fifty and he had the look of a man that age, a man who worked hard at an outdoor job. But Rowntree had the look of one who had used the longevity drug from an early age. Who could know how old she was? She could be twenty-five or forty; she was an eternal youth, locked forever in her early twenties, not quite fresh enough to be a teenager but certainly no older than thirty. They were all like that now, except for the ones who'd started later.

Maybe he should forget his vow and take the optimol, accept a lifetime of three or four centuries. They said even the brain stayed good, you didn't lose anything. Gainer suddenly wondered if he was just being a selfish fool, condemning his kids to short lives when they could live very long ones if they wanted to, just to keep his romantic notion of the great farm going.

He deliberately refused to think about this. It was treachery to even consider it. Treachery to her.

"I'm afraid we still need medical skill down here," he said slowly.

"Not for long. We're getting production levels up so high

there'll be more than enough for everyone. Just think of that, no more cancer, no more unnecessary death."

He swallowed. Could it be possible? Was the immortality just going to wash up around him and take him, whether he wanted it or not? If it was going to become cheap and plentiful, then he would end up taking it, like everyone else, wouldn't he? How could he resist?

"That sounds wonderful." He made it sound anything but.

"Yes, it will be." She was very definite. She smiled again. He amused her, he could tell. She felt a little smug, perhaps, certainly a little superior to plain old dirt farmers down here on the jungle coast.

"Well, here's to bug farming or whatever you call it." He raised his glass.

She laughed. "That's what we call it, especially when we're tired and nervous."

"Nervous?"

"What do you think? You think it's easy? Believe me, it isn't. You're risking your life every time you go into a nest, and really, it's a terrible way to die."

"I bet."

"But you know something, I'd rather face that than deal with what you have to deal with." She shivered and sipped her whisky.

"Yeah, well, it's not so bad now. You know we figured out ways to deal with the damned things. We just dynamite them inside their zippers now. Don't hardly shake those trees, of course, and they start up another one, but we dynamite that, too."

"There's so many trees, though."

"Yes, there are, but not so many that zipper up. We have pretty good surveillance and we generally know well in advance. Nothing much happens beyond the ten-kilometer mark anyway, so that's about how far we push the robots out."

"So the supply of tomatoes is assured?"

"You bet."

"Everyone will be very relieved to know that." She toasted him and sipped the whisky.

There was still no sign of Ladbrook, and Gainer found that he was glad of it. This was a lot more interesting than swapping the same old stories with the big guy. "Tell me about how it is up there. I've often wondered."

"You've never been?" She tossed her head in astonishment. "I can't believe it, you've never even been up in the mountains?"

He shrugged. "Always been too busy, I think. I inherited the farm early and we built up the crew. You know we had some hard times for a while."

"Well, you should come up for a visit. Things are better now for you, right? Then you can take a few weeks and go see the Highlands. It's so beautiful, you can't imagine."

There was an evangelist's light burning in her face all of a sudden, and she launched into a passionate description of the great sweeping high valleys, the near-freezing mountain lakes, the vales of black-leaved jik, the scarlet bloodmenots that dappled the meadows of green arble. He was captivated despite himself. Chips put another pint of Harbor Ale on the bar top without being asked, and Gainer never even noticed. He'd seen a lot of these places on video, but he'd never visualized them so clearly as he did from listening to her. Vines glistened on the flanks of cliffs, vast mountains soared all around, snow shone on their impossible peaks. He could almost smell the pure mountain breeze blowing out of the jik forest.

"Amazing," he whispered, captured by that light in her eyes. He was almost ready to go see these mountains of hers. In fact, it was with an effort of will that he pulled back and turned his attention to his beer.

5

ROWNTREE WAS NEVER SURE JUST WHEN EXACTLY THE EVENING changed course. But change it did, and quite dramatically. Perhaps it was because she was feeling wounded over Steve, not to mention being stood up by that jerk from the airline. Perhaps it was just that she hadn't met anyone like Gainer before. Whatever it was, it turned her life in a new direction that was most unexpected.

They left the Harbor Bar together after a couple of hours, because neither wanted to drink any more, and went down to the shore side to walk on the sand and look at the moons. Neither wanted to sleep just yet, even though Gainer knew he had to be up and working at dawn. The long waves came rolling in to crash on the sand and flow hissing up toward them. The breeze off the ocean was warm and spicy and quite delicious.

Rowntree felt a sudden, appalling strike of concern for this man. He was so doomed, so hopelessly wedded to his outmoded dream, chained to it like Ahab to his white whale. There was something so strong and pure about his need to succeed that it made him dreadfully vulnerable. This fragile nobility drew her to him like a moth to the flame. What could she do to save him? Surely she could do something? In the next moment, she determined to try.

It would take time, she knew. A passion like his could not be diverted overnight, but there would be time. She would make allowance for it. In the meantime she could give herself to him, and in the process of giving feel some reward. He wanted her, that she knew. And his need and his wanting were on a level vastly more urgent, more important than any such need she had ever experienced before. The other men in her life had been just, well, men. This man was possessed by a force, and if she could save him, then at least she would have achieved something on this visit to the Coast. The thought was so astonishingly silly and egoistic that she burst into a happy laugh at her own stupid vanity.

He turned to her then, his broad, solid face sculpted in moonlight, and instinctively reached out to her. She melted into his arms and felt his lips on hers. Everything else seemed lost in the roar of the surf.

She held his hand as they walked along. He was riding the crest of a wave of wild emotion; she sensed the shifts of pride, gratitude, triumph, and something else—a sense of healing, of closing a great wound that had lain open for a long time.

Poor man, he was aging fast under the relentless tension of his life, all just to grow tomatoes and wheat. It was too crazy. Nobody needed those things, they could live out of the biotank and the ocean, there was plenty of food. But he had been programmed by the Fundan Colonization Plan; his farm was his mission in life.

When they came back from the sandy shore, she was carrying her shoes in her left hand and he had one arm around her waist. She liked the feeling.

They avoided the Harbor Bar now. Instead, they walked

aimlessly through the streets of Big Island and, somehow, magically almost, they found themselves outside the Island Hotel, the only real hotel there was.

"Where are you staying?" he asked.

"Third floor." She nodded to the hotel.

"We're all on the second floor. We always take the same rooms, I don't know why."

"Come up to mine, then," she said, accepting that discretion would be a good thing at this delicate moment.

He accepted this arrangement with a nod. In bed, she found him forceful but still gentle and quite aware of her own needs. Then she recalled that he was the father of adult children, an old married man who understood women, not a young stud like Steve with that precious, fragile intensity of young men so concerned with their potency and a need for immediate pleasure. Gainer was concerned with her pleasure as much as his own, and that was a trait she found irresistible.

It was the body that had confused her initially, she realized, because Gainer was as hard as any young man, with a flat belly and ropes of muscle on his arms and shoulders. A real farmer, she thought. And there were the scars. When his shirt came off she saw the ripple of scar tissue that ran up his back, along the shoulders, and ended just below the neck. It was an inch thick and two feet long. There was another one on his right buttock and several pocked circular scars on his left leg.

"I told you we needed a lot of medical attention" was all he would say, although her curiosity was piqued. And then the scars were forgotten, except when her fingertips brushed across them, which they did again and again.

Afterward, there was an exultation in her heart. This was something she had needed all her life—this rawness, this intensity, this passion.

Later they slept and awoke only because Gainer's wristunit began beeping plaintively. It was dawn, and he had to get down to help set up the stall. It was a tradition, they had to be first to set up; that showed the proper Elbow Creek spirit. She promised to join him right away but instead slept for another couple of hours, and when she awoke felt terribly guilty. She dressed at once and went down to the marketplace.

There were two large stalls set up close to each other near the entrance to the square that had been given over to the market. On the left was the Elbow Creek Farm and on the right was Max Butte's crew, each stall surrounded by a solid mob of customers. The Elbow Creek stall had three people at work: Gainer, a tall youth with pale brown hair, and a shorter, dark-haired girl. While arms writhed in front of them and voices babbled, they calmly bagged vegetables and exchanged them for credit. Their little portable credit machine rang shrilly for each transaction, and the sound was matched only by that coming from the other stall, across the square.

"Well, you're just in time," Gainer said with a smile and a brief hug before he turned back to the mob of customers and put a basket of tomatoes into a kelp-string carrybag. He weighed them and turned to the customer. "All right, that's forty-six point five."

The customer, a stout woman with short white hair and red sunglasses, paid and left.

"I'm sorry, I just went straight back to sleep," Rowntree said.

He smiled again. "I thought as much. Say, now you're here I hope you won't mind helping a little."

"Sure."

"Meet my daughter, Helen, my son, Elgin. My big layabout partner Ladbrook is down at the dock getting another load of broccoli."

She smiled at them, shook hands with the tall, gangling youth, who was older than she had at first thought, and then with the compact girl with the black hair in the pageboy.

"You bag, I'll take orders," Helen said, a firm take-charge sort of tone in her voice. Rowntree bristled slightly but agreed to bag tomatoes and mangoes as Helen took the customers' selections. She saw little of the young man, since he was working the lettuce and broccoli end of the stall and she was at the fruit and tomatoes end. A little later, however, she noticed a huge man come up with a heavy barrow laden with broccoli and ice. When he'd dropped his load and helped arrange it behind the stall, he came over to say hello.

"Ladbrook Lambeer," he announced in a hearty voice. He looked as strong as a Fein, and almost as big.

"Rowntree Fundan." She watched her slim brown hand disappear into his cavernous paw.

"You must be a cousin, then, of Gainer and the kids."

"Well, yes, but very distant. How about you?"

He laughed, a big, easy sound. "Yup, we're Fundan cousins, too, but illegitimate, from way back in the Asteroid days."

They worked on. The tomatoes were all gone by nine

o'clock and the fruit soon after that. The lettuce and arugula ran out at last at ten-thirty, the stall was closed down by eleven, and they all trooped into the Harbor Bar shortly thereafter. Gainer came over to her side.

"I forgot to mention your pay. We ought to work that out now, before we ask you to buy any drinks."

Helen turned around, deadly serious. "You pay up now, Dad, or we're on strike. No slave labor around here."

Rowntree giggled, but Gainer insisted and she gave him a card, which he charged up in the little portable machine—one hundred credits drawn on the Optimol Bank. Then came a round of beers and some sandwiches, crakoon and tomato slices. They were delicious and she realized how hungry she really was as she bit into the fragrant slices of roasted crakoon flesh and the luscious red tomatoes from Helen's tomato house.

At one point Elgin leaned across to say something to her. He'd had three beers, fast, and his face was contorted with emotion. She heard only part of what he said, catching only the phrase "not forever, that's for sure." She nodded and then laughed as Ladbrook Lambeer told another joke and Gainer and Helen guffawed together.

For a moment, however, her eyes met Elgin's and a strange feeling of unease ran down her spine. There was something here, some enormous latency. With an effort she turned away and made sure not to look toward Elgin again.

After a long lunch and one too many drinks she went back to the hotel to freshen up. She called Garth Fundan over the satlink and told him that Compton had shown no interest in leaving his house and trying the life in the Highlands. Nor had the old man expressed any interest in the plan to provide him with optimol treatment. Then she called the airline ticket machine and canceled her flight to Ghotaw that night. She had told Garth that she would be staying on the Coast for another week. She had some "business" to take care of.

When she hung up, she stood on the veranda and looked out over the ocean. The hot, sunny weather was still holding, and the ocean was blue and vast and beautiful. She felt at one with it, quite calm and ready for an enormous adventure.

6

***

"THESE WOUNDS!" SHE EXCLAIMED THAT NIGHT. "I DON'T KNOW how you survived."

"Well, I told you we needed a lot of medical attention."

Her fingers continued to explore the puckered holes in his leg where the scar tissue had grown into thick buttons. Moonlight fell through the window and across the bed. The wall video showed the lawn outside, where nocturnal skrin were hunting through the terrestrial grass for small insects.

"What happened?" she asked.

"Too much to tell."

"Go on, tell me." Her fingers probed at the buttons of dead flesh. "I want to know."

The moonlight cast his face into a somber mask. Suddenly he gave up. She'd asked him a dozen times now. With a slight irritation in his voice, he told her. "On my twentieth birthday, those holes in my leg. A defense robot went amok and I was in its way."

"One of your own robots?"

"Something scrambled it. Anyway, first I knew about it was when it targeted me and hit me with a burst from its nine-millimeter."

Her fingers had found the beginning of the big V-scar on his abdomen. "What about this? It looks like you had a cesarean to deliver triplets."

He didn't smile. "Well, that's a different matter. I got that, and these—" He gestured to the huge scar that ran up his back. "—about five years later. It's the closest I've ever been to death."

She said nothing, wanting more.

"You really want to know, don't you? Well, I was out on perimeter search. Back then we were in a hot war. Things got wild about once a week. All of our machines were banged up. Anyway, my lead probe went dead on me. Now, I should have

32

waited until I could get another up in front to get some video, but, what can I say? I was young and impatient. I wanted to get back early and go in on the *Firefly* to the Island. So I broke the rules and I went forward without any probe ahead. I was in a small crab-cab. That was another thing: I could outrun the bad ones, so I went in for lightweight equipment. Anyway, I never really saw the one that got me. It must have been standing behind a tree and when I went past it was right on top before I knew anything about it."

Her eyes were wide, her lips parted. This was a horror story as elemental as the planet they lived on. Caught in the open by the top predator animal in the forest of giants. Many people had died thus in the early years, and their appalling stories were the bedrock myths of the Fenrille colony.

"It smashed the cab of the crab like it was flattening a can of fish. I was still inside and it broke my shoulder and cut my back open from neck to hip. Then it knocked the crab over and sent it rolling down a slope until it slammed into a tree. That knocked me cold.

"Fortunately, all our crabs had this escape software, designed for just such a moment. The crab landed on its feet and its motors were still fine and it took off."

She was imagining the night and the chase, the little crab machine scuttling ahead of the monster that pursued it through the nightmarish forest of colossal trees.

"Well, we almost made it. The crab got back to the outroad we'd cut down that direction and really took off. I was about half dead, barely conscious then. I got to the perimeter and that's when the damned thing caught up. It went across the bend in the road at that point and made up the lead. Anyway, it caught the crab, tore its legs off, and hammered it flat. I was still inside, of course. That's when part of the seat mounting came up through the seat and cut me wide open, that's the V-scar. Both legs were broken along with some ribs, some hand bones, and my lower jaw. But the skull survived and so the docs in the old hospital were able to bring me back."

He paused to look at some of the smaller scars on his left wrist, then sighed and hung his head back.

"Most of these things were the result of that time, except for those holes down there on the leg."

She was silent, amazed that he carried on this life out here with that terrible threat just over the far side of the neat, geometric fields of foodbeet.

"I'm sorry. I don't know why, but I just had to know."

"Yes, well, now you do. This planet has chewed me up in just about every way it can, but I'm still here."

So it had, she concluded. And what had he gained in return? Outside, through the window that sealed them against the night heat and flying insects, she could see the flat fields, a pointillist expanse of black and green where the moonlight played on the leaves of foodbeet and lettuce, shrub peach and brussels sprout.

Elbow Creek Farm, a magnificent memorial to wrongheadedness, a monument to a lost obsession. It was an incredible spread. Hundreds of hectares of perfect fields, controlled with agrichem and fertilized naturally with super vetches and other nitrofixers. It was like one of the illustrations in the old Fundan colony manuals. And it was all Gainer's. Still, she could tell, it was not enough.

And when they made love, these questions kept returning. What was she doing here? And why? She realized she had no idea where it was leading her.

In the morning, she was up early and explored the downstairs in a robe and slippers she found in Gainer's closet. Gainer slept on, snoring softly.

The central house was an interesting structure. It had started as a thirty-foot dome. That dome was now a front hall for the main sixty-foot dome that had superseded it. From the center spread out three interconnected one-story wings, to which had been attached several sheds and other smaller laboratory structures. It was a maze of narrow rooms, workbenches and double-flap doors, all agriscience, and she found it alien, almost menacing. She soon retreated back into the central dome's atrium space.

There was a kitchen area with a dining table set close beside it. On a side table were plates, bowls, and forks. In the refrigerator she found breakfast foods among a mass of tomatoes and sundry fruits, many of which she had never seen before. At the bottom was a compartment filled with small beer bottles with homemade labels. In the door were breakfast synthetics and a flask of "milk."

She fixed herself a bowl of cold cereal, suspecting that the crunchy flakes were of actual wheat although the "milk" was a white fluid straight out of a biotank. She used it to wash down a tablet of alvosterine, the routine antifungal that everyone in the low-lying regions had to take to stave off the deadly blood fungus. Then she attacked the cereal.

She was eating and looking out the window, which offered a view down a lawn to a pair of terrestrial palm trees and a low wall of gray stones, when she heard someone else come down the stairs.

"Good morning." It was Helen. She sounded very much like someone who habitually woke up bright and cheerful and ready for the day.

Rowntree acknowledged that it was morning with a nod while working on a mouthful of cereal. It didn't taste as good as she'd imagined it might. Perhaps these kinds of things didn't travel so well out of childhood after all.

Helen was wearing black slacks, dirty white slippers, and a faded bush shirt. She went to the refrigerator, pulled out tomatoes and cucumbers and some other vegetables, and began making a salad.

"Salad for breakfast?"

"Best way to start the day," Helen answered in the same cheerful tone while downing her alvosterine with a sip of water.

Rowntree remembered Helen's laughing, happy eyes in the Harbor Bar. Either Helen was a real cheap drunk or she had very light hangovers. For some reason, it annoyed her.

"So, was my father good in the sack?"

Rowntree winced. So it was going to be like that, was it. "There's no need," she said.

Helen cut a tomato in half and ate a piece of it. She came over and sat across the table from Rowntree. "Why not? He's my father, after all, and he's been a lonely old father for a long time. Why shouldn't I, his only daughter, be interested in how he did with his glamorous conquest of the night?" She gave Rowntree a sharp glance. "Who also happens to be a distant cousin."

Oh, that. "Well, very distant indeed, if you want to know. I don't think we're breaking ancient genetic taboos."

Helen laughed. "And we're just twigs on the Martian Fundan tree, I guess. Trash from way back."

Rowntree's turn to smile. "Only if you say so."

"I do. You should have seen my grandmother drink. Shots of vodka, straight back. She never seemed to show it. Sure sign of trash status, that kind of tolerance."

"Well, we're both Fundans."

"But you folks don't really think of us as kin. And we're not the important Fundans."

Rowntree laughed. "Well, we're not the important Fundans, either. Aren't many left of those."

"But you're not trash, either."

Rowntree smiled, a little nervous. "We're all here now; those differences are over."

"So, there's no taint of the slums of Mars on us?"

"Nothing I know of. In fact, I don't even think I know what you're talking about."

"Well, the descendants of Natural Fundan went down in the world, you know that."

Rowntree shook her head. "Sorry, I didn't take a lot of the family history courses. All I know is that Natural went to Mars and that there are a lot of people called Fundan who live there still, but they aren't closely related to us at all."

"Us?"

"The other Fundans, then—the families who went on to the outer planets."

"I see. In any case, it's perfectly acceptable for you to sleep with my father; no genetic taboos there."

"Yes, it is."

But Helen did care, Rowntree could tell, and she wondered why. A moment later it came out.

"I'm so glad for him, you see, he's been so lonely lately."

Ah, concern for Daddy; that was it, was it?

"Perhaps the Harbor Bar isn't the best place to meet single women."

Helen made a face. "Well, that's true enough. Nasty, comfortable place full of old salts drinking beer, isn't it? I much prefer the Beachcomber. But Father won't go there and all the ladies his own age on the Island know him too well."

"Oh?" Gainer was a big ladies' man, was he? Her eyebrows rose involuntarily.

"There's only so many people here, you know. With all of you moving away, the Island only has about a quarter of the population it used to have."

Rowntree looked down at her cereal. "Yes, of course." Poor Gainer, she thought, and how difficult it must be to get people out here to visit at all. Fear was a big deterrent to romance.

"But you're different." Helen was very serious all of a sudden. "I can tell. You seem pretty open, if you don't mind my saying so."

"Open?"

"Not closed up like most people on the islands. You're open to new experiences, new life."

Rowntree finished the cereal and pushed away the bowl. "I could use some caffeine."

"In the cupboard." Helen pointed. Rowntree stood up.

"You know we're experimenting with coffee bushes?"

"No."

"Difficult to grow here; it may be the climate is all wrong but we'll persist. Real coffee would be wonderful, wouldn't it?"

"Can you really tell the difference?"

Helen shrugged. "If it's anything like the difference between biotank tomato flavor and real tomato flavor, it will be enormous. We'll be able to sell every bean we harvest. That is, if we can work out how to roast it properly. Apparently there's quite a technique to that."

There was some synthcaf in a cupboard above the work space. Rowntree pulled it out and boiled some water on the enormous stove, which had unfamiliar heat elements shaped like flowers with many small holes around the edges.

"Gas?" Rowntree hazarded a guess.

"Yes, Dad and Randy built a methane system under the house. We do all our cooking with gas; it's quicker and more convenient than solectric."

Helen finished her tomato and made a full bowl of salad, from which she filled two smaller bowls. "Try it?" she asked, offering one to Rowntree.

It didn't make sense following a bowl of cold cereal, but Rowntree's curiosity was piqued. Her taste buds were rocked by the first mouthful. The leaves and tomatoes and cucumbers exploded with flavor on her palate. The textures were all strong and interesting, like the wild foods she'd eaten in the Highlands in Fein villages. It was so different from textured synthetics.

"Very good," she said. "Very interesting."

"Better than all those damned synthetics, right?"

Rowntree had to agree that it was. She felt a barrier go down between them. They seemed to be getting along. She was relieved. The questions about Gainer in bed didn't come up again; it seemed that it'd been a test of some kind, and that maybe she had passed without knowing how.

Later they strolled outside together, no man of the house having yet put in an appearance. It was a rest day, after all, and Helen had warned her that the men of Elbow Creek were rarely early risers on the rest days. They crossed the front of the house and entered a yard area with a paved floor and sheds and granaries all around it. On one side hulked a robot machine with the look of a giant insect at the front and a truck at the back. A canopy was pulled up on one end, where it had been partly dismantled for cleaning and repair. Helen continued across the yard, through a gate, and into a garden.

"This is my garden," she said. There was no mistaking the strength in that "my."

Rowntree realized that it was a very scientific garden. There were rows of dozens of different plants, all with colored tags attached to their stems and their flowers and fruits.

"You're very serious about this."

Helen flashed her a look of puzzlement. "Of course. This is where we work out what we can grow commercially. Look at those tomatoes."

The vines were groaning with red spheres the size of a man's fist.

"Very, uh, impressive." Rowntree saw Helen look up to see if she was being mocked. "No, I mean it. You've put in a lot of work here."

"They're O'Henry Plush," Helen went on, "a variety we dug out of the archives."

The garden was cut into segments and each segment had a theme: berries here, cruciforms or carrots there.

"What are these?" Rowntree asked, pointing to a cluster of thick-stemmed plants with long, broad leaves.

"Banana trees, long-term project. Won't see anything there for a while yet. But they should find this climate ideal."

Eventually they stumbled out of the cabbage patch where seven varieties of brussels sprouts were being test grown, and went through a pair of double doors into a long, shedlike structure with a concrete floor and stacks of crates and packaging along one wall. Helen gestured to the boxes. "This is where we process everything."

There were metal-topped tables; the walls were white and cold. Streaks of dried vegetable crud covered the floor, and a few specialized robots stood by the tables. Helen patted one as she went by; it had two arms, shoulders, and a camera imaging system for a head. "This is Picker Two." The arms ended in a complex of grippers and pincers. The robot was not equipped with day-to-day software, and it remained silent and inanimate.

"We couldn't do it all without our metal crew. They're the real workers on Elbow Creek Farm. Those ones over there are

Server and Loader. That's Picker Three down there. Picker
One is a big fellow that works outside. Picker Two here has
been processing broccoli for the last few days."

"You believe in all this very much, don't you?" Rowntree
asked.

Helen flashed her that glance again. A challenge? "You
were at the market, you saw what people will do for good
food."

"Very worthwhile," Rowntree said.

Helen looked a little angry now. "Well, yes, if you say so.
More than what most folks are doing."

Implying? Rowntree felt moved to reply, even though she
didn't want to. "Well, what we do is make the means by which
we can all live a long time, if we want."

Helen snorted. "It's a drug. I'm sorry, but I believe that the
worst thing that could have happened to this colony was the
discovery of the chitin drugs. It's become an obsession, everyone wants more and more and more, and I don't think it's
right."

"Well, it's not going to stop, whatever it is." Rowntree was
sure of that. "Think of the longevity proteins as money in the
bank, sometime in the future. There'll be a lot more people
here then. This place will change."

"You foresee that? More and more coming?"

"Inevitable. Augustine let the thing loose, they've known in
the home system for a long time now. But there were ships on
their way long before that, more refugees like us. There was a
breakdown on Earth. Rebellions on three continents at once.
Several groups of spacers managed to make it out while the
World Government was paralyzed by the chaos."

Out there, rushing toward them at a high percentage of the
speed of light, were dozens of huge colony ships packed with
new people.

"Well, I guess I could be wrong, then. Maybe what you're
doing will help the colony long-term. If more come then it will
grow. One thing is, it might get crowded up there in those
hills, you thought about that?"

Rowntree nodded. "Yes, but there'll be enough for a long
time, the way we're boosting production with Miflin's methods. I think it's doubled in just the last three years."

They were out of the sheds and crossing a concrete yard liberally splattered with mud. They stopped on one side next to
a wire fence and looked out over a field of bright green plants.

"Carrots," Helen said. "Variety called 'Brightlees.' We found that in the Fundan Bioreserve."

Carrots! The domies would love them—fresh, orange, crunchy carrots that would snap off with a loud crack when you bit into them. Rowntree was left wondering; perhaps she was wrong, perhaps it was really worthwhile, what they did here at Elbow Creek Farm.

Carrots, tomatoes, broccoli. Rowntree felt a great confusion in her heart. It seemed so right, so beneficial, but she knew that it was forbidden, in the Highlands at least. Although what she and her people did with the chitin was a kind of agriculture, the Fein had never objected to the chitin gathering, only to efforts at growing nontraditional food crops. Even the sites where traditional crops could be grown were strictly controlled. What Helen was doing was completely banned in the Highlands. It was the primal contract with the Fein.

"And over there—" Helen pointed. "—are the tomatoes. Two acres are in full production this week. Picker One is in there somewhere."

Rowntree could see a humped thing of dark metal that moved slowly through the field. Her doubts continued. They had it all very nicely organized here. Completely unlike the somewhat haphazard ways of chitin farming.

They turned back toward the house. Rowntree looked back at the robot once more and noticed the alien forest in the distance for the first time. The gray-green mass loomed like a cliff wall along the far edge of the fields. It was miles away but enormous and menacing, once she focused on it. Out there dwelled the enemy, the stuff of nightmares. Deliberately, she turned her back. The things were out there, but they could not get at her. She was safe, and so she would not think about them.

They went back through the mud-coated yard, through Helen's experimental garden, and into the house. Elgin was in the atrium, breakfasting on some toast and grilled tomatoes. The greetings were pleasant but the tension was there again. There was something about this young man that was electrifying. His looks were different from the rest: a longer jaw, a leaner face, and no red to the light brown hair. When he looked at her she felt something run right through her, frightening in its intensity.

Helen and Elgin talked about the tomatoes and Picker One and moved on to discuss the state of the cold-storage sheds. Rowntree helped herself to a mango. It was not a fruit she'd ever eaten before, and it was quite an experience. While she cut and ate, she did her best not to stare at Elgin, but she wanted to. She felt herself acutely aware of where he was, as if he were the center of a magnetic field and she was a compass needle.

This had to stop! She could not entertain this, she could not do this. Not when things with Gainer had been so, well, perfect.

The mango was disturbing food, but that wasn't the reason her stomach was churning by the time Elgin finished his toast and went out to work on a broken baling device.

7

THE NEXT DAY THEY WENT OUT ON A PERIMETER PATROL. GAINER was very subdued, though irritable. He rode up front with Randolf; something had happened with Elgin, she knew.

The machine they rode in was an armored crawler, moving on six big legs, powered by an ancient nine-hundred-horsepower engine that burned methanol with a constant hacking roar like a giant with a bad cough.

The weather had returned to the usual misty, humid haze, the sun lost in it. Rowntree felt lost as well. Elgin had not come along and there had been some shouting. She'd heard it while she was downstairs with Helen after lunch, sitting in the living area. Then Gainer had come down, face white, shoulders hunched, and stalked out of the house. Elgin did not show at all after that, and an hour later Gainer called Rowntree to join him on this noisy crawl around the perimeter of the farm.

On their left, inside their track, rose the outermost fence, spylo link fencing sixty feet high. On their right, just a few meters away, were the damaged hulks of enormous trees. Beyond those were less damaged titans, and above them was the enormous gray-green canopy of the Fenrille forest. In the shadowy spaces past the damaged trees a tangled jungle of vines and megafungi crowded the forest floor between the enormous, twisted root systems.

Rowntree tried to avoid looking in that direction. Since she'd been a little girl she'd been afraid of this forest and of the demons that haunted it. The stories they told when she was little were terrifying. Just being here made her feel decidedly uncomfortable.

But the fields just inside the fence were uninteresting, filled with soil-improving crops of supermulch and nitrofix. Her thoughts kept going back unerringly to Elgin. He was so different from the others, from Randolf and Helen in particular; Ishmael, too, although Ish less blatantly inherited his traits from one parent or the other.

Randolf was virtually his father's clone. She'd met him at last just before lunchtime. He was short and burly, with an orange beard and the beginnings of a beer belly. He loved Elbow Creek Farm more than anything in the world, or so he informed Rowntree within twenty minutes of being introduced by Helen. There was an antipathy between them from the start. Where Gainer had aggression, Randolf had a bullying streak. The wrong things were overemphasized. Gainer had strong opinions, but Randolf was coarse, and called the Highland people "bug-suckers" to her face until Helen called him on it and he tendered a weak apology.

He didn't like her, either, that was plain. Perhaps he was jealous. Gainer, it seemed, loved Elgin the most and Randolf the least. Randolf worked extra hard to win his father's love, but could never change the order of things. When they were together, Rowntree found herself disliking the sight of them. They were too similar and Randolf's jokes were all sexual and misogynistic. Gainer rarely laughed at them, but unfortunately, Randolf liked to giggle at his own jokes.

Rowntree had never known people who produced such strong reactions in her. Elgin's spareness, his restraint, his graceful way of moving around provided a haunting counterpoint. No wonder Gainer loved him so much.

It was turning into a horrible day, in fact, and it helped her realize that she couldn't fit in here. For a while there she had actually entertained the thought of staying here on Elbow Creek Farm. Now she knew she wouldn't. Her own life called too strongly, up in the mountains where she lived wild and free.

And Elgin? She shivered a little, not wishing to complete

that thought. Ridiculous woman! she snapped at herself. She was going on like some lovesick teenager with a crush.

Suddenly the crawler jerked to a halt. Gainer and Randolf cracked the doors on either side and got out, Gainer signaling to her to follow. They were between two giant trees. One had been damaged, a huge section sheared off to lie in rotting ruins. There was a hole the size of a house ripped out of the main trunk. The other huge tree towered above them, untouched.

Randolf was pointing up at something—a broad streak of dark brown, deepening to black. From a distance it looked like a fuzzy zipper. "Shit, another one," Randolf snarled.

Rowntree saw that this tree, too, had wounds after all. There was a crater blasted in the tree's trunk not far from the ugly zipper mark. Gouts of resin had run out of the wound and pooled on the ground below.

"What do we have in the crawl?" Gainer asked.

"I think we have some GH. I'll look." Randolf went back to the crawler.

Rowntree stared up at the zipper with horrified awe. Gainer noticed her expression.

"Yeah, there's one in there. But it's not going to get the chance to get out and do anything. There's nothing to worry about."

She let herself be hugged, enjoying the comfort of it and yet somehow feeling unclean. This man had been so good, so strong, and so sweet, and how was she going to pay him back? By lusting after his favorite son.

And the thing coiled up there in the wood? It hated them and could do nothing. It was weeks away from hatching. What did it think, she wondered, if it could think at all?

Randolf came back with a heavy drill that he carried in a harness and some tubes of red plastic capped with black radio sensors. From a backpack he produced a climber's aide, opened it, and activated it. "Got everything we need."

Gainer nodded. "Then we'd better do it. See if any more have zippered up along the trail."

Rowntree went back to the crawler and sat inside while Randolf got up the side of the tree with the help of the climber's aide. The tool consisted of two small footrests connected to a motorized belt that moved them up the side of the tree.

Once he was positioned beside the zipper mark, he began drilling inch-wide holes in the bark. It took a while, but eventually he had drilled six holes. Into each he put a tube of the red plastic, activating the radio sensor on each. Then he climbed down and joined the others in the crawler, which started up and moved away a farther hundred yards.

Randolf aimed a power wand at the tree and pressed a stud. There was a startlingly loud *crack* and the zippered part of the tree erupted in a flash of light. Huge chunks of wood fell all around the enormous tree's base while a cloud of smoke hung in the air before slowly beginning to disperse.

Randolf was already out of the crawl and making his way back to the tree. The crawl activated and followed him, detouring around some pieces of wood, each longer than a man was tall, that had fallen in its path. Randolf moved around the fallen fragments, examining them carefully. He kicked a few.

"It's here all right," he finally shouted, "still wet, long way from hatching."

He held up something gray-brown, like a thick rope, then dropped it with evident distaste. The thing that had hated them was dead, its passion ended.

Gainer stayed in the crawler and so did Rowntree.

"Can we go back now?" she asked.

Their eyes met.

"Had enough, then?" he responded, sounding upset. She nodded.

"It's rare, you know, these days. We patrol all the time and we usually find them before they get this far."

She stared at him. Could he sense her treachery? What she thought of herself right then?

Self-hatred. It was a new experience for Rowntree Fundan.

8

ELGIN WAS TWENTY-FIVE AND RESTLESS. SO RESTLESS THAT HE was finding it difficult to hang on down on Elbow Creek Farm. He had this urge to get up and go. He had to concentrate hard to keep from speaking his mind, from seeing the truth come out and destroy the fragile peace surrounding him.

When he went to the Island and spoke to the drifters and chitin people in the bars, he longed to be off to the Highlands. That was the life for him, he was sure of it. And so the guilt was always there. If Dad ever found the secret subdirectory he'd built up in the house encyclopedia, boy, would there be a scene. If Gainer was ever forced to confront his favorite son's desperate fascination with the chitin insect, they were all in trouble.

But the truth kept gnawing at him and wouldn't leave him alone. Elgin had to leave, and he had to leave soon. He clenched his fists, cursed silently, and turned away from the window with his face contorted in a grimace.

His sister was watching him. Before he could speak, she said, "You ought to go, you know. Just do it, get it over with."

Anger rose in his chest, almost choking him. "You spying or something?"

A cool smile. "No, I was just passing through. Complete co-incidence."

He scowled at her but she persisted. "Doesn't change what I said. Dad knows, I know, even Randolf and Ish know. You should go, get it over with."

"I ..." He couldn't say it; the sense of betrayal was too great.

"Look, I understand. We've been brought up on the mother's milk of Elbow Creek since we were old enough to talk. Dad's obsessed. He's lucky because, Randolf and me, we love this place, too, and we'll never leave. You and Ish, though, well, who knows about Ish. He hasn't made up his mind yet. But I know what you want."

Elder sister sticking her nose in his business again. Elgin rebelled subconsciously.

"You always say stuff like that, I don't—"

"Hey, I'm sorry, but I know you as well as you know yourself, Elgin. I helped raise you, especially since Mama died."

It was true enough, but he wasn't going to admit it.

"And I know that you really want to be gone from here. I think you should leave."

"It's not just me, it's everything. You're all going to have to leave, if you want to live."

She frowned. "What?"

"If I'm right, and I think I am, there's a secondary forest reaction coming. We haven't a hope."

"What are you talking about?"

"We've had four incidents in the past two months, four adults, full-formed, dry and traveled. You can tell by the condition of their feet; anything that weighs thirty tons does stuff to its feet."

"Yes, well, so what?"

"So we never found the trees they came from."

"We're still looking, or you are. Aren't you in charge of that?"

"Yes, sister, I am. That's why I know what I know."

She still hadn't got it. He stabbed a forefinger at the floor for emphasis. "Four of them, adult, traveled a ways to get here. The year before that we had one. In the three years before that we had one. Before that, none since the one that killed Mother."

She didn't like the implications of this. "So?"

"So there's a secondary reaction in the forest system. We've exhausted the ability of the local forest to destroy us and prevent us from clearing trees."

"Yeah."

"We patrol constantly, dynamite two hundred zippers a year, maybe more."

"Yeah."

"But that's just the local reaction. Now there's a secondary reaction coming. Upcountry, there are more and more trees zippering up, more and more of them are going to come down here."

"You mean they can communicate?"

"Of course they communicate, we already know that. I'm saying that trees a long way off will zipper to help the trees in this locality. Altruism, or long-range planning, if you like."

"Nonsense, absolute bloody nonsense," she snorted.

"Yeah, well, that's how I expected you to react, so how am I going to tell Dad."

She was fighting the idea. "I mean, where would it end? If you're right? Every tree on the whole continent could zipper."

"Yeah, imagine a billion of the things, an army."

Helen met his gaze with fierce eyes. "I don't believe it."

"Yeah, I expected that."

The sound of the crawler coughing into the yard broke in.

"Back early," Helen said, turning away, not wanting to let him see the newfound fear in her eyes.

Elgin retreated to the control tower. Gainer and Randolf found him there. They seemed subdued, as if they'd been arguing.

"Found a new zip, on the three-fifty trail about six kloms out. Tree number one-oh-six-four-one-five by the tag."

Elgin opened the tree file and checked the tag number.

"We blew one there a year ago. And before that about five years back."

"Frequency picking up?" Randolf was uneasy. He was close to seeing it for himself, Elgin knew. The question was whether he would be able to admit it to himself even if he knew the truth.

"Well, yes, just as it did in the inner margin."

"We'll have to be more drastic; damned trees only understand one thing, eh?"

"Blow the fucking shit out of them!" Gainer snarled.

Gainer was angry. This business always got under his skin. Because of Elise, of course, they all knew it. Their father had never forgiven himself for her death, and his rage at the creatures had always been intensified by his anger with himself.

The angriest Gainer had ever been with Elgin was one time when he was fourteen and he suggested that the woodwose were just doing their job.

"Damn it, how many of them do I have to kill before they get it, before they get the fucking idea!"

Elgin sensed that his dad was also still angry at him for refusing to ride the perimeter with Randolf and Rowntree.

"How many?" Gainer was staring out of the window of the tower toward the distant trees.

For some reason Elgin couldn't stop himself. "No limit there," he said.

Gainer whirled around and stared at him. Elgin thought for a moment that his father was going to attack him.

"I've been working on the data I collected on the four recent ones," he said quietly. The moment had come, and whether they were ready or not he was going to give it to them. Randolf was looking at him, too, brow furrowed.

"Yes?"

"They had all come a long way, at least two hundred klicks."

"But where?" Gainer asked. "There's a pocket of zippers out there we don't know about?"

"Can't be!" Randolf said. "We checked everything in this region. No clearances anywhere except on the Coast, the other farms. There's nobody left inland, not since the Ikeuchis pulled out."

"No, it's not from around here. This is from farther away."

"Is somebody new doing something upriver, that's what you're trying to say?" Gainer was still furious.

Elgin shook his head. If only it were that simple.

"No, I'm afraid not. It's a new reaction, from the forest as a whole. It's an organism—you know that."

"Oh, shit, not that again!" Gainer was shaking his head angrily. "We went through that with Augustine Miflin and his boys fifteen years ago. I never believed it then and I don't believe it now."

"What didn't you believe? That the forest is an organism?"

"Yeah, damn right it ain't. It's just a lot of big trees. Sure, they've got this thing developed that keeps everything else from growing and competing, but don't try and convince me that the forest has a gestalt consciousness."

"The woodwose are like antibodies, the trees release them when they're threatened. The analogy is perfect."

"And stop using that dumb name for the fucking things."

"Why? Why does it matter? Seems dumber to me to keep calling them 'things' or 'monsters.' "

"Well, they are monsters, fucking demonic monsters that killed your mother, and don't you ever forget it!"

Worse than that, Elgin knew. One of them ate her. "Well, look at this projection." He hit a key and the screen in front of him showed the graphic he'd made. "Four in the last few months, a couple in the three years before that, and then just one in the twenty years before that."

"There've been more than that," protested Randolf.

"Not seasoned, not traveled like these. These had all been on their feet for a while. They'd come a distance. Not local hatch."

"Not local?"

"Next year there'll be twenty, the year after that a hundred, and if there's anything left here after that, there'll be thousands every year."

"What? Every fucking one of them!" Randolf gestured to the forest out there, biding its time, hating them.

"I don't know, maybe."

Gainer threw up his hands and his fury suddenly turned to contempt. "Stuff and nonsense, you'll see. You've got terminal fever, should get out of this place more, come out on the perimeter."

Gainer went down the stairs fast and heavy-footed. The door below slammed behind him.

Randolf was looking at Elgin as if he were a traitor, which he rather expected he was.

He shrugged. "Look, it fits the facts. But it's a hypothesis. We'll soon know if it's right because we're gonna see a lot more of them."

Randolf sighed. "It could just as easily be a random variation. A few of them hatch all the time; we've just been unlucky recently."

"If that's what you want to believe, go ahead."

"You are such a bastard kid. You know how important you are to him—why'd you go and hit him over the head with this?"

"Because he has to know!"

"Your hypothesis? You don't have enough data to support it. No, I think you're just sadistic. You're acting something out, like you blame him for Mom's death or something."

"For all I know, you're right, but this is what I see in the data and he has to know."

Randolf turned away with obvious disgust and left. Elgin spun in his chair and stared out the window at the distant forest. After an hour or so he logged off, left the observation port to the software, and headed down to the kitchen for a bite to eat.

He grabbed some salad and a sandwich and found Rowntree sitting alone in the living area. She had a family search on the screen, through the old Fundan Encyclopedia.

"That software is almost as old as this family," he said, taking a seat nearby.

"As the Fundan family?"

"Yeah, I studied Fundan Data Systems. The basis for the 'cyclopedia was something that Talbot and Emily brought with them from Toronto."

"Wow. That's old."

"A commercial thing on an ancient optical disk. Of course, it's been modified ever since. I think it's about seven times as large now."

He noticed that the three-dimensional slice of the family tree she was studying was of Martian Fundans. He could tell at once by the names: Turalina, Tural, Dmitri, Stephan, Vasily.

"Martians," he noted, gesturing vaguely toward the screen.

"Yes." She seemed a little embarrassed at being caught digging around in Gainer's family's heredity. "I want to know just where . . ."

"We come from? Melissa's roots, eh?"

"Right. I've gotten it back to Tural Fundan in Demosivina. Tural was a great-great-granddaughter of Natural herself, so that places it pretty much all the way."

"You know something, I've never dug into that. I guess I never thought of myself as much of a Fundan, you know?"

She turned to him with astonished eyes. "Why not?"

He shrugged. "I dunno, it didn't seem important to our way of life. I mean, it's different for you, you're all working together up there."

Elgin thought to himself, as he had before, that Rowntree was the most desirable woman he'd ever met. There was something quite electric going on between them. He could feel it, and he thought he saw something more in her eyes than just curiosity about the family roots.

"Down here, we're all alone, you see."

"Well, I guess."

He was suddenly uncomfortable with the subject. "Are you staying long?"

Her eyes grew guarded. "No, I have to get home." So it was just a fling, as he'd suspected. He felt sorry for Dad.

"But I'll be back. I want to see your father, you know."

For some reason he found this hard to believe. "They won't change, you know, they're too—" He groped for the words. "—involved here. Can't leave."

"Oh, I can see that. They've done a tremendous job. This place is nothing like what I imagined."

"Yeah, pretty impressive, isn't it?"

"Very."

He felt uncomfortable again. He was the traitor, after all. "And what's it like where you live?"

She was only slightly surprised at this, although, other than Gainer, he was the first person at Elbow Creek to show any curiosity about her own life.

"Well, it's not like this!" She laughed lightly.

"No, really, tell me."

"Well, I don't know where to start. I mean, it couldn't be more different. It's all so spacious, you know, open and wide and you can see for miles and miles. There's the mountains all around and the valley bottoms, covered in jik forest. It's nothing like this, nothing at all."

"And what do you do up there?"

"Well, I'm currently working six nests spread out on Ghotaw Ridge. So I generally camp on the ridgeline—there's a spring there, so we have great water. It's always cold in the mornings in the camp, real cold, but it warms up once the sun starts shining. And the water from our spring is just delicious, it's the best-tasting water in the world."

"You're so high up, the air must be real thin."

"Well, sure, there's only one-third as much oxygen in each volume of air, so you have to adjust. It takes a while but most people manage it quite easily."

He'd heard all this so many times. It roused again the urge to be there himself. "Who's taking care of your nests while you're down here."

"I work with a team, that's the way we do it. There's six of us, one for each nest, so right now they're taking turns making up for me. When I go back then someone else can take a break and we'll make up for them. The nests don't like it but we try and make it up to them."

"Possessive, huh?"

"Extremely."

"Dangerous, too."

"Of course."

"It must be great."

She stared at him. "Well, yes, I think it is."

"Yeah." There was a bitterness to his tone that she began to understand. Elgin did not want to stay here; unlike his brothers and sisters, he wasn't committed to Elbow Creek Farm.

"You don't understand us," he said. "You couldn't. They've got so much invested in this place. You know, my father, he inherited it. Of course there wasn't much here then, and they were fighting off woodwose every night. But he came out here with our mother."

"Yes, Elise van Kort. She was a Spreak cousin. New Transvaalers." Together she and Gainer had produced three more stocky Fundan children in the Mars mode and one replica of Elise herself—in the tall, willowy boy they called Elgin.

"I got to get out of here," he said thickly.

She stared at him. "You did four years on the Fundan Academicals, and agrisci. Why do that if you don't want to be here?"

He didn't seem to have heard her. "They're out there, all the time. It's not like it used to be, now that we dynamite the zippers early. But I can feel it, the damned forest hates us. All the time, relentless hatred, pulsing out of there."

"Do you think they communicate?"

"What? Oh, yeah." He waved a hand absently. "Look, terrestrial trees communicated, released chemicals when suffering predation. Some species could load their leaves with tannins and alkaloids just a few minutes from first being brushed with the alarm substance."

"What's this word 'woodwose' I hear you use?"

"Old druidic phrase, I think, from a religious pretech Earth cult that centered their worship norms around trees. Means 'tree protector,' I think. They're using it at the Academical Institute now. You know, makes a change from 'monsters.' "

"I see, I think."

"It was one of them that killed our mother, you see."

She nodded. She'd heard the grim story from Helen.

"Caught her out by the perimeter in a crab with no armor, no defense anywhere close enough." His eyes were staring. There was something at war inside him, something that made him profoundly uncomfortable. Her heart went out to him, but she was unable to move a muscle.

He gave her a tired-looking smile. "I've never felt the same about this place. Not since that day."

"You have to leave, I think."

He chuckled in a grim way. "No, you have to leave, you can't stay here. But the rest of us, we'll manage it, we'll keep Elbow Creek going."

This was the truth, then. It seemed that there was nothing she could do for Gainer. And if she stayed a moment longer she'd do things that would make her hate herself forever.

"Yes, you're right," she said, and she knew it was over.

9

Gainer's boat chugged back slowly from the airport. He missed her already, as he knew he would, and worse, he was sure he would not see her again. It was over. There was that feel, that indescribable lack of something that tells a man when a woman is no longer interested. He cursed and took a swig from a flask of whisky. It was his temper, he was always so close to losing it, and that frightened people who didn't know him.

People who knew him knew his bark was worse than his bite, but Rowntree didn't know him well enough yet to make allowances. She'd seen him lose control with Elgin and then watched him sulk the rest of the day. No wonder she'd left like that, with barely a kiss.

The whisky went down easily enough, and he stared out over the flat waters of the delta to the dark gray line of the distant shore. Out to sea, banks of mist rose up to erase the sky. The setting sun was lost in red haze westward. The temperature had dropped a few degrees, for which he was grateful, since it had been swelteringly muggy earlier, but there was no sign yet of the evening onshore breeze.

When thoughts of his son arose, he swigged again and froze them in their tracks. He wouldn't think about that just now.

But he knew that this couldn't last long; he knew those thoughts were going to return, orbiting back from the dead zone to the front of his mind.

"Elise," he whispered. His woman, perhaps the only woman who would ever be right for him in this life. The woman he could never recapture, never bring back from the dead. There were so many memories, and they were so warm and inviting that it was impossible not to linger among them.

For instance, there was the way Elise had predicted exactly how each of the kids was going to turn out when they were just squawling little babies. Randolf would look just like his grandfather, short, stout, and red of hair and beard. Helen would have Gainer's build and dark hair. Elgin would be Elise's own, tall, nearly blond, with the Dutch Afrikaaner looks of the van Kort family.

Elgin was so like his mother! Independent, secretive, stubborn—the similarities sometimes drove Gainer to wild places of the heart where he would weep and rage at the same time. The boy moved like her, had a way of shaking his head before speaking, and a sudden intensity on certain, deeply cared-about subjects. Gainer had often thought that he and Randolf were like burly bookends while Elgin occupied the graceful center.

Then there was Ish, a difficult one, there. He was young for his years, it seemed, slow to mature out of adolescence. And while he had the leanness of the van Korts he lacked the grace, the presence, all the things that had made Elise van Kort a magical person.

Gainer ached again, a familiar feeling.

Slowly the image of Rowntree surfaced in his thoughts. Another failure. Sourly he took a swig.

By the time the *Firefly* chugged up Elbow Creek and moored at the dock, night had fallen. The creatures that they called "fliers"—though they were as big as birds, they were more like feathered insects—were on the move, crisscrossing the air above the waters of the creek in pursuit of smaller insectlike creatures.

Far away, he heard a distant screaming. Gainer knew it was just the sarmer mackees, an amphibian lizard about the size of a terrier or a domestic cat. Out here on the farm you still heard them a lot. They always screamed, long haunting wails of what sounded like the tortures of the damned, just around dusk. Many early colonists had found the sound unnerving. It was just another reason why so many had never left the islands, where you never heard the damn things.

Tucking the flask away aboard the *Firefly*, he strolled up the path to the house under a traveling light. He passed below the control tower, where the lights were on. Elgin was up there, working with the computer as usual. Out on the tomato field the big picker machine was working, small red lights winking, engine grunting as it gathered O'Henry Plush. On the surface all was well here at Elbow Creek Farm.

Inside he found Helen watching something on the screen in the living area. He caught sight of Humphrey Bogart and

Lauren Bacall in a black-and-white movie from the prespace era. Gainer was fond of the period "films." They were so sparse, so edited, so quick-moving—all elements that had been lost in the modern era of video entertainments. The reality imposed by senso systems to heighten response to audiovid stim overwhelmed the viewer's critical faculties. They could make you feel as though you were bathing in a barnyard pig roll and you would love it. But these old things from the beginning of the technical era, they were "art" of another kind, employing the most rudimentary technological enhancements, depending on vanished human skills like "acting."

Helen blew him a kiss as he went by.

Miss Bacall was smoking a cigarette. Gainer shook his head at such outlandishness and went down to his study. He logged on, and then, troubled by what he'd been listening to in the Harbor Bar, he checked into the net and sought a download from the Fundan Encyclopedia over on the Island. It took a few seconds to get it ready for viewing, and then he studied the resultant screen with a furrow on his brow.

There was a colony ship due in less than a year with ten thousand people aboard. They were refugees from Earth itself, Eurotrash from the North Sea littoral states. Using positions of power in the centralized states, they had looted treasuries wholesale to build their ship and escape the home system.

Two more ships were just a few years behind them, each with six thousand aboard. After a gap of eight years another small ship, the *Hope of Ceres*, was due, with two thousand refugees from the former Queen of the Asteroid Belt. They'd been in space for a long, long time—centuries, in fact. All that was known about them was that they were mostly still alive in cryohibernation.

And behind them came the real armada, twelve ships from the inner planets, ships that brought people directly from Earth itself. The lucky, wealthy ones who made it out during the interregnum as the World Social Synthesis collapsed into the congealed World Social Union. In that brief time, a dozen great interstellar ships had been built and launched outward before the Social Union clampdown came in full force.

Gainer sat back with a thoughtful look. Within thirty years, the modest little settlement on the islands was going to expand to more than two hundred thousand people—a village turned into a large town overnight. The implications were enormous. His world would change completely. The market for fresh fruits and vegetables was going to grow immensely, and at the same time there would be so many people they would have no problem in finding recruits for the farm.

With that many people they would have the manpower to battle the forest and kill it. They would liberate the planet for human occupation. His dream would never die.

10

ROWNTREE FLEW BACK TO THE HIGHLANDS IN AN OLD FUNDAN turbo that had seating for twelve on top of the big cargo hold. The whole way, she pondered the strange dilemma that had developed in her emotional life.

At the airstrip on the Island, Gainer had refused to even discuss coming up for a visit to the Highlands. All he wanted was for her to "seriously think" about coming back to Elbow Creek. He wanted her to "try it for a month next time."

She didn't tell him what that might cost.

The old turbo juddered and wobbled through the turbulence when they hit the mountains. She glimpsed sparkling meadows and patches of jik forest like dark stains on the slopes of the stone peaks. The sights brought back the love of home; she was back where she belonged.

She resolved to put it all behind her. It had been an interlude in her life, no more. She was going to forget the whole thing, both the father and the mysterious son who had so abruptly done dangerous things to her emotions. Such weird passion was dangerous, and she had her life to lead.

On her return to Ghotaw Mountain, she was caught up in an immediate whirl of activity. Lesli and Draga Kubashvili were down from her ridgeline. The White Tree nest was ready to give birth to a new nest—all the signs were there. But the White Tree's primary keeper, Devan Leery, had broken a leg in a fall two days previously. It was out of the question for Devan to go in and perform the dangerous job of leading the colonists out of the nest. As backup, they had young Sinoia Katsuga, who had worked the nest with Devan several times. Her first approaches to the White Tree had met with grudging approval, but the nest was nervous; all such nests became testy and difficult at such a time. A tremendous effort was about to be made to reproduce a new nest. Queens and drones had been exchanged with three other nests and the right genetic mixture fixed for the new location. Assistance from the "humble servant creature," as the White Tree thought of Devan Leery, was essential. All around the White Tree there were other nests which would eagerly destroy the young, newly founded colony unless Devan were to guide it to reach an open area where it could develop for a few months without attack.

Devan had managed to communicate to the nest just how he might help. With artificial pheromones and a paintbrush to put fine scratch marks on the mud walls of the nest, he had indicated direction and his willingness to help. Of course, he could not perform a waggle dance, but with artificial pheromones he could approximate many of the appropriate cues.

The White Tree was ready, expectant, but unhappy with the absence of Devan Leery. It knew Sinoia but did not entirely trust her. As a result, Sinoia was very nervous and had received some bad bites already.

Rowntree flew directly up to the ridgeline with Lesli while Draga went to the Fundan stores for a number of supply items.

At the ridgeline they found an anxious Sinoia pacing around the center of the camp, angry with Devan.

"Why was he out walking on the slopes like that? At this time, when things are so critical here? He was asking for an injury." And now Sinoia was in a position where she could be killed. Trapped, naked, oiled, in the depths of an angry nest that could shred a human down to the bones in ten minutes. It was not a good way to die.

Rowntree took Sinoia aside.

"You don't have to do this," she said as they sat down in her tent, which was gritty with dust from her two-week absence. It was the fine dust of the dry season in the Ghotaw Valley, gray and silky to the touch.

"How could he? He's so thoughtless, so damned selfish."

"Devan is really sorry about this, you have to understand."

"Oh, I understand all right. I have to get down there in that nest tomorrow and risk my life."

"Sinoia, you don't have to do this."

"Well, someone has to. It's ready, and if we don't do it now we'll lose it. It'll turn feral."

Rowntree nodded. "I know. I'll go in."

Sinoia gulped at that. "You? But you haven't been in White Tree all season."

True, Rowntree thought. "I was Devan's backup last season. It will remember me."

Sinoia licked her lips. It might remember, but then again it might not, and it might get angry and kill Rowntree.

"No," she said quickly, "I won't let you do that. It's my job, my risk. I'll do it. If I didn't, I'd be finished. I could never work another nest again."

Of course, there was a contract with Sinoia's thumbprint on it filed in the Fundan Archives, but Rowntree never mentioned it. It was equally true that Sinoia would be finished with the group if she flunked out now. To be a chitin talker meant risking your life just like this. That was the way it had had to be ever since they'd first found that chitin communication protein was unique in the universe and impossible to replicate in a laboratory. No terrestrial organisms, not even lab-made assemblers, could produce this fantastically complex protein.

Sinoia knew that it was her task. A little later she came up to Rowntree. "Thank you," she said. "You really helped me get a grip on myself, I was in danger of losing control there."

"My job."

The next day Sinoia went into the White Tree nest, naked, oiled, painted with rune lines of pheromone R12 and the entire M series from 1a to 42. She carried succulent glob glob fruits as her gift to the fierce, paranoid entity under the ground.

There was a long, difficult moment. Rowntree felt her fingernails biting into the flesh of her palms as she waited. Once you'd heard someone die in a nest you could never forget. A sudden yelp of pain broke the silence. Then another yelp, but no prolonged screams. Sinoia was being tasted. The nest was upset and nervous, allowing some soldiers to wield their stings here and there but not sending the order for her death.

The silence returned, and the tension began to drop among the observers. Parties of worker chitin emerged from the main nest hole and explored the area around it. Sinoia worked inside the nest, projecting reassurance, love, and calm goodwill. Eventually the southern exits of the nest clogged with workers and soldiers, and shortly thereafter a somewhat dazed-looking Sinoia appeared from the central vent, which had been widened once again to let her out. Through her binoculars, Rowntree could see that Sinoia had some red swellings on her shoulders and neck where she'd been stung, but she seemed able to continue.

Now she waited patiently, surrounded by an eight-foot-deep patch of warriors and workers. At last, having kept everyone waiting for many minutes, the queens, a group of fifty, each three inches long with the green stripe of its breed on its abdomen, emerged and joined the throng.

Behind the queens came a squadron of drones, bodies the size of warriors, but with tiny heads and miniature mandibles. They fell in right behind the queens.

And finally, from the depths of the nest, came the masters of the show, the vizier chitin, a dense mass of green-banded insects with characteristically large abdomens and long feelers. In them was stored the material that would form the embryo mind of the young nest, the "vizier mass." Here also was the chitin workers' target, the prize they sought.

Sinoia stepped forward. The mass parted slightly, then surged in the direction she took. Soon a mass equal to about a third of the entire colony was spread out around and behind her in the shape of a comet as it moved away from the old nest.

Thinner and thinner drew the lines of workers connecting the cometary "head" with the old nest. As the mass of insects entered the territory of the next nest along the ridgeline the warriors bristled, ready to repel attacks, but none materialized. Another talker was offering gifts to the nest on whose territory they trespassed, in a successful attempt to divert its attention from the vulnerable colony group. Sinoia accelerated her pace slightly and began to lead the way downhill.

Eventually they passed out of the nesting region altogether and entered a steeper slope. The insects crowded around Sinoia, the excitement quite palpable. They were on the brink of a great adventure, discovering a new territory beyond anything known to the old nest. Everything depended on the warm-love female who led them. The colony went on, and Sinoia led them past the lower nest ranges and onto the rocks around the streambed that lay in the bottom of the little valley.

Now the colony was stretched out along the limestone slabs by the river, and here the most dreadful treachery occurred. With a sudden leap, Sinoia darted out of the cometary carpet of insects and flung herself across the stream. Before the startled vizier mass could begin to react, other talkers emerged from cover. They wore protective suits and deployed black nozzles that spewed a gas that stunned and slew among the colony.

The gas was laid over all of them, and when they had succumbed, their bodies were vacuumed up, packed tightly in cloth sacks, and taken up the ridgeline to the camp. Thus ended the great day of the White Tree nest and its plans for a colony.

That night they sat around the campfire, sorting chitin by hand and drinking beer and singing songs. Sinoia was happily drunk, relieved that she had survived her ordeal.

"Boy, wait until Devan comes back, eh?" she said over and over, relishing the moment.

"A good haul," Rowntree commented as she cracked viziers and tossed the abdomens into the bag. A warrior popped in the fire, then Lesli threw in a handful and they popped, too, and gave off their characteristic toasty aroma.

The next day was mild and sunny, perfect weather to take the dirigible down to Ghotaw Station. Once there, Rowntree visited Spreak Labs and had the harvested chitin weighed and logged in. She left it there to be separated out. Abdominal chitin chaff would be removed from the invaluable communication protein that caked thickly on the surface of those abdomens in thousands of layers, each one molecule thick, patterned with the complex hole and socket "language" of the vizier chitin.

Across the muddy street that had grown up down the middle of the incipient settlement of Ghotaw Station, she strode into the Ghotaw Saloon. It was a two-room enterprise built of local materials and run by Proudfoot Fundan, a grandson of old Agatha Fundan and therefore one of the so-called ruling Fundans.

Proudfoot's saloon was controversial. According to the agreements with the local Fein villages, the humans were to build no towns, nor create farm fields of more than a hundred paces in any direction. They were to live in the manner of the Fein, at low densities, scattered widely.

The collection of domes, inflatables, big tents, and puffcrete structures at Ghotaw Station was technically outside the agreement. But, with the addition of puffcrete walls for places like the saloon, the place was becoming a permanent town.

There were similar places in other high valleys. Humans just could not get completely away from their urge to socialize and to live in communities. And, of course, these little towns grew up around the laboratories. Wherever there was a chitin laboratory there was bound to be an airstrip and a cluster of dwellings, even an inn.

Inside Proudfoot's, Rowntree fortuitously discovered Garth Fundan taking a glass or two of Proudfoot's lager beer. Garth was a big man, with his grandfather's frame and lots of firm flesh. He had the deep tan of all chitin folk and the blue eyes of Fundan-dom.

"Welcome back, cuz," he said with a characteristic purr.

"Thank you, Garth." She had a cup of instacaf and sat at the table Garth had occupied for brunch.

"I've been thinking about what you told me from the old man." Garth had an old microcomputer on the table. She could tell he'd been working out shares. Garth's team on Ramal Meadow was seventeen strong.

"Set in his ways." She shrugged. "He won't change."

"Yes, you're right. No, I wasn't worrying about that. He intends to die and there's nothing I can do to stop him. No, he can go right ahead with that. I was thinking about the new people coming."

She sipped coffee. For some reason, she could not imagine these new people very well. People talked about it and there were ships on the way, some of them quite enormous, much bigger than the *Founder*. There would be new people on Fenrille any year now.

"They'll fit in," she said.

"No way," he replied quickly. "They're going to turn this whole world over unless we're real careful."

She didn't want to talk about this. For some reason the whole subject made her nervous.

"Well, we'll see. Anyway, did I tell you about the funeral?"

He nodded, then shrugged. "Hell, yes. No, someone else did. So Miflin was buried with all honors. Good. But you didn't tell me what else you did down there. How come you stayed so long?"

No getting around that. Garth and Martha would want the gossip, probably had it already. This was a small community, even if it was spread out over a continent-sized area of mountains.

Garth would think she was crazy. Still.

"Actually, I went out and visited some distant cousins.

Gainer and his family—they're still farming, clearing the forest."

"Waste! What a dumb thing to do." He caught her expression and checked himself. "No, I don't mean going out to visit, I mean trying to farm down there. It's about as hostile an environment as you can get. How many tried that and ended up in a monster's guts?"

"A lot of people," she said, and sipped more coffee. She wondered what Helen's real coffee beans would taste like. Probably a lot better than this.

"So, what was it like?"

"What? The farm? Oh, it was, ah, interesting. They've got more than two hundred hectares cleared and planted with different crops. And they've got a way of dealing with the monsters by identifying the trees that are doing it and dynamiting the monsters inside the trunk."

"Sounds like a good idea. When those things get out you're generally in a hell of a lot of trouble."

"And they're growing a lot of really great stuff. You should taste their tomatoes and salad greens. I watched the market in action on the Island. They sold everything they had: every vegetable, every fruit, completely cleaned out their stall. So it's very popular."

Garth grunted. "Sure, but helluva dangerous. Still amazes me that anyone's trying to do that anymore. You've got synthetics, sea fruit, fish, and kelp, what more do they need?" He had a wolfish smile sometimes. "Poor bastards. If you ask me, it's a case of where they made their beds now they gotta lie in them."

"Well, everything we eat we still have to treat with detox. Unless we eat synthetics, too."

"Most do, easier to digest, fewer allergies. But, still, I think we're adapting. Those new enzyme treatments Spreak put out, I think they really make it possible to take the native meats without stomach upset."

"Well, down at Elbow Creek they're growing things that really taste, well, better, I guess, than any synthetics I've ever had."

"More power to them. As long as it keeps them off my range, eh?"

"I guess."

"And when all the new people come, maybe they'll finally

have a technique that will kill monsters for good, clear all that forest. They can all have farms then."

"Yes, of course."

Someone was calling her name from the bar. "Excuse me, Garth." She stepped away to take the call on the bar phone.

It was Helen. Her voice sounded thick, muffled, as if she'd been crying for a long time.

"What is it?"

"Can you come down? I know you were just here but it's just that something's happened and I think we really need you. It's Gainer, he's falling apart."

"Why?" Rowntree was confused. This was sudden.

"Well, Randolf was killed yesterday. We found his crab smashed up on the perimeter. He wasn't there. We don't have his body. We're still hunting for the damn thing, it's out there somewhere."

"Oh, my . . ." Her words trailed off. Things became disjointed, her vision blurred, and she sat down heavily on a barstool.

"Yes," she heard herself say. "I don't know when the next plane is coming in, but I'll be on it. I'll call you when I get to the Island."

"Gainer's been locked in his room all day and night. He has a gun in there. I'm so afraid."

"Helen, hold on, you've got to hold on. Where's Elgin?"

"I don't know, he and Ish and Ladbrook are out on patrol, they're trying to find that fucking thing."

It ended at last. Helen could not speak any longer.

Rowntree did not try to explain to Garth. She checked the next known plane flying coastward and found that a Spreak-owned cargo flight was due in that same evening. She would be down at the Coast by the next morning.

She booked a seat and then called up to the ridgeline. Her people up there had good hearts. They bade her take her time and told her to be careful. She promised to make it up to them.

She left again with the sun's dying rays caroming off the wing of the plane.

11

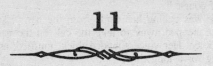

Rowntree came back to Elbow Creek under an intense tropical rain. The *Firefly* tied up at the dock and Ishmael produced a huge umbrella, under which they scampered up the path through veritable torrents of warm ocean-smelling water to the house.

Inside she shed her shoes and pants, which were soaked up to the knees. The rain was still drumming on the tin roof of the shelter outside the front door. Occasional stabs of lightning lit the scene while thunder rolled thickly across the forest and swamp.

There was a heavy atmosphere in the house, too. Helen was sitting on the mezzanine deck by the bookcase, looking out the window at the downpour. Ishmael put the umbrella away and disappeared into the kitchen. He had hardly said a word.

"How is he?" Rowntree inquired.

Helen's face was blank, her eyes red and puffy. "In his room with a gun. He asked me to call you; that's the only thing we've heard from him all day."

"And Elgin?"

"He's out with the defense on the north side, thinks he has a trail on the monster. Ladbrook's with him."

Rowntree sucked in a breath. Her heart was hammering. "Isn't that dangerous?"

"With the defense around you it's not so bad. We'll all go up and join them later. Ish has fixed one of the back tanks, which shed a tread, and he has to take that up to them. We can go inside, it's got room for four people."

Rowntree didn't like the thought of that. The forest was bad enough when you were sure there weren't any of *them* out there. She doubted she could make it through such a trip without breaking down shamefully.

And Elgin was way out there, chasing it. Risking his life. And his elder brother was in the thing's guts, devoured . . .

64

swallowed whole . . . Her blood seemed to freeze in her veins when this thought crossed her mind. Randolf had been killed close to the perimeter, while on a routine fencing check. Somehow the thing had gotten through the barrier and onto Randolf before he knew anything about it. What if Elgin was killed, eaten? She felt nauseated for a moment.

Helen was staring at her, measuring her, finding her wanting.

"I guess I'd better go up," she said after catching a breath. Helen nodded silently.

At the door she identified herself and it ópened electronically. Gainer was inside, sitting on the bed with the gun in his hand, an old Fundan-made automatic. She noted that the clip was lying on the bedside table.

She went to him quickly, put her arms around him, and sat beside him on the bed. He felt as hard as bone to the touch, his muscles stressed tight.

"You can't blame yourself," she said quietly.

Her words produced no effect. Gainer sat there, locked rigid, the unloaded gun in his hand, staring at nothing. Lost.

Rowntree whispered reassurances and stroked his neck and shoulders, but only once, when she mentioned Elgin, did she feel anything in response, and then it was just a flicker in his eyes, a desperate look like that of a hunted animal. Then he retreated again and could not speak, could not respond. After a while she realized that Gainer needed medical help. This had gone beyond back rubs and soothing words. He was burning himself up from the inside. They had to relax him.

She left him and went to Helen. Together they returned, and Helen gave her father a shot with an injection gun. He showed no reaction to their presence.

"Forty milligrams of Equilibe, that's what the med program recommends," Helen explained.

Rowntree watched Gainer relax slowly; his muscles lost their rigidity and his spine finally unlocked and his shoulders sagged. Suddenly he gave a groan, put the gun down on the bedside table, brought his feet up onto the bed, and curled up and went to sleep.

Rowntree stayed with him for a while, trying to make sense of the whirl of emotions churning inside her. She'd thought she'd gotten away from all this, but she was back and the tangle was worse than ever. Randolf had been Gainer's alter ego, as close to his father as a man can be. Gainer had taken him for granted but had relied on him enormously, far more than he did on Elgin, the son on whom he was fixated. Gainer would not be able to manage Elbow Creek without his oldest son. And she knew he would not be able to hold his second-oldest son on the farm any longer.

While Gainer slept, Helen and she stayed at Elbow Creek and Ish took the repaired defense tank up to join Elgin and the pack of other machines.

The two women waited through the long hours of a dreary gray afternoon while the rain slowly ceased and the land steamed. At dusk more storm clouds blew in, a thunderstorm erupted, and rain twice as torrential as the earlier downpour came down through a chorus of thunderclaps. Jagged flashes of green lightning slammed into trees and high points all around. Rowntree was so on edge that she jumped every time a particularly loud clap of thunder went off. It felt as if every nerve in her body were being wound up around her bones like thread on a spool.

Hours later the men came tramping up the farm road, amid a sudden blaze of lights, a gang of eight walking machines, anthropoid giants thirty feet high, with driver compartments in small square cabins that looked like the heads of metal gorillas.

Ish was the first inside; he was pale, exhausted. They had lost the trail in the brackish swamps thirty klicks west. They were sure it was the same monster; its tracks showed signs of a pronounced limp. Randolf must have got in at least one shot before it took down his crab.

Helen made Ish some coffee and dug out a casserole from the microwave. Ish was eating ravenously in moments. Ladbrook came in silently a minute or so later, took coffee and food, nodded to Rowntree, and went to his room. Elgin came in last. He was obviously weary, but his expression lightened when he saw Rowntree.

"You came," he said, then paused awkwardly. "Thank you for that."

He turned quickly to Helen to cover his embarrassment. "How is he?"

"Asleep, like you'd be if you had forty mil of Equilibe in your system. He's taking it very badly. Basically, he's in shock. Maybe we should call the Psychs at the hospital."

"Always knew this would happen," he muttered. "Always knew." Elgin ate a little, then pulled a bottle of whisky out of the liquor cabinet. Helen had gone to check on Gainer; Ish had gone to bed. Rowntree watched Elgin.

"I think I want to leave here tomorrow," he said quite suddenly after the first belt of whisky.

She stared at him, quite unable to say a word.

He flashed her a bitter smile. "It probably won't kill him. I mean, with this great a shock to his system already he'll be prepared. You'll see."

Be prepared? she thought. The man would be under deep sedation. His mind had gone. And this would only seal his fate.

Elgin had another hit on the whisky. "And it's the only way I can do it. I have to make a clean break. Only way."

He scratched his scalp and rubbed his eyes.

"Of course, I might be wrong about that, might be wrong about a lot of things. But one thing I'm not wrong about is the future of this place."

He looked at her and she sensed dangerous emotions running through him.

"No future," he said.

She nodded vaguely. As long as they were together somehow nothing else would matter. Maybe Elgin would come to the Highlands. He would like it there; he'd said he wanted to come.

"There *is* a secondary reaction," he said. "I warned them, I told them." He waved a hand upstairs bitterly. "He wouldn't listen. Oh, no, couldn't be possible, not for him. Well, he doesn't have to listen, he can stay right here if he wants until they come out of the trees by the hundred and smash the whole place flat. They will, you know—it's going to happen just like that."

He snapped his fingers loudly. Lightning flashed outside. The rain intensified.

He was trembling, his mouth twisted with misery. She reached over and took the whisky bottle out of his hands, led him to the couch, and made him sit down. She sat beside him.

He turned to her suddenly, his face animated. "I want you to come with me. Will you?" he asked.

She nodded.

He leaned forward and kissed her on the lips.

She didn't pull back but she didn't respond wholeheartedly, even though she wanted to. It still wasn't right, somehow. Different parts of her being were wrenching apart on different courses. The ship of her heart seemed fatally wrecked on the rocks.

He put up his hands, "All right, I know, I mean I understand, but I had to. Ask, you see."

For a moment there was nothing except the strong attraction between them, a field that seemed to crackle with electricity.

"The rain's stopping." He went to look out the window at the wet fields and the heavy mists. "Do you want to go for a walk? You must have been cooped up in here all day."

She joined him. Outside, it was astonishingly hot and humid, but there was a fresh wind coming in from the ocean, a stuttering breeze that promised to eventually clear out the damp and the heat. They strolled away from the house, down to the inlet where the dock had been built long ago by Randolf Flecker when he started Elbow Creek Farm with his bride, Melissa Fundan. The breeze was stronger still on the dock which stuck out into the wide, flat waters of the creek.

"Did you really mean it when you said 'let's go tomorrow'?"

"Yes."

"That soon?"

"Yes. I can't stay here any longer, it's doomed. Not after this."

The breeze blew her hair about as they strode along the dock path through the dark. The few lights that were kept lit were haloed by dancing insects. "Do you hate him? Is that it?" she asked.

"No. Yes." He picked up a stone. "Probably." He hurled the stone out into the inlet with all the strength in his body. It flew a long way and they barely heard it strike the water.

"If he'd listened to me then maybe Randolf would still be alive, you know? But that might not be true, because even if they had listened Randolf would have been out there anyway taking that patrol and Randolf still would have cut corners on defense and taken risks."

"What about the farm? How are Helen and Ish going to make out without you?"

"Have to make their own choices. I'll put the evidence out for them, that's the best I can do. Then it's up to them. If I'm right and I make the difference between them staying out here or leaving, then I'm probably saving their lives."

She nodded to herself before replying. "He couldn't listen to you, Elgin, he's too invested in this place. How could he leave?"

Elgin looked at her with rage in his eyes. "You know something," he said, "this place is a monument to my mother. You know about that story, I'm sure."

She nodded slowly.

"And you know what killed her?"

"Yes. And they almost killed him, too."

He fell silent for a moment. "This whole damned farm has been nothing but a folly. Those things are seventy feet tall, strong enough to tear a steel plate in two—they weigh thirty tons or more. They were fucking crazy to ever come out here and have a family! It's not worth risking lives for the sake of fresh tomatoes and lettuce!" There were tears in his eyes.

"I think I'm in love with you, Elgin."

"Yes," he said. "I think I love you, too, Rowntree. Strange world, isn't it, where you have to hurt someone to the heart just to love someone else?"

She agreed. What she was going to do to Gainer was so cruel that she could scarcely believe herself capable of it, but it was the only way that her heart could go. She sighed inwardly. She foresaw a lot of emotional pain ahead. And beyond that, well, there would be Elgin and she would survive. She would hate herself, but she would survive.

The mists were dissipating across the inlet. The far fields became visible, with straight-cut lines showing through the murk. To the right the bank grew sandy and eventually merged into the distant beach, where the ocean combers pounded home.

The stars were out, misted slightly by the thick air of sea level, not at all like the hard, bright glories that she was used to. Still she picked out a handful that she knew well: Canopus, Rigel, Deneb—great super-giants that blazed in the heavens. "You'll like the stars when you see them in the Highlands at night . . ."

"Yes, I'm looking forward to that. Must be very sharp, very bright."

It was a moment of exquisite irony. She yearned to fly on the emotional updraft of the knowledge that she had finally found the man she would love for all her life, but the thought of Gainer's misery anchored her to the riverbank like clogs of concrete. She mused on how strange the world could be at times.

Suddenly Elgin stiffened. She heard a sharp intake of breath.
"What is it?"

He pointed down to the inlet and, with the weirdest sensation of terror, she noticed something darker than the waters moving upstream, wading stealthily. It was enormous and it was not a machine. Her bowels turned to ice and her breath seemed to stick in her throat.

Elgin was pulling her down. "Lie flat on the dock," he whispered.

She pressed her face to the wood. Had it seen them? Was she going to die here?

Elgin was whispering into his communicator, trying to raise the home station in the dome. "We have an intruder, wading up the creek. Must have come 'round the headland under the surface. Never happened before. They've learned a new trick."

Still no one had picked up at the dome. "Come on, damn it, pick up . . ."

Long seconds went by with nothing but the hiss of static. At last Rowntree dared to look up. The thing had gone past the dock; it had missed them. Now it turned in toward the shore and soon waded out of the shallows. It was less than two hundred meters away and she could see it clearly as it started up the path toward the dome. It had a noticeable limp, lurching from side to side.

"It's limping."

"It's the same one, all right. They never give up, never!" At last someone picked up at the dome. Elgin whispered urgently. "The one that got Randolph is back. It's inside the perimeter, traveling up the path to the dome now. It came up the inlet."

There was a shriek from the phone, a sound that pierced the night like a knife before Elgin cut it off.

Three hundred meters away, framed by the lights of the farm complex beyond, the monster stopped while the turretlike head rotated. Rowntree knew that a battery of black eyes, like glossy buttons, were now focused on the source of the shriek. The thing gave a sharp little hoot, turned about on its heel, and started toward them.

"Run!" Elgin said, scrambling to his feet. "Don't look back, go to the left."

They ran from the dock up onto a road that led to a sub-depot serving the three big fields established out along the headland. A field of ultrafalfa stretched away on the left, a flat openness that went all the way to the scrub marking the edge of the beach. On the other side, the ground had been prepared for foodbeet and was bare of vegetation.

The woodwose lurched after them. For Rowntree, everything had become dreamlike, unreal, although her lungs felt like they were going to burst and her head spun dizzily. Her legs continued to extend, driving for every fraction of distance. Her arms clawed the air as she ran as she hadn't since she'd been on the track team for the Ghotaw school.

She'd left Elgin ten meters back by the time they reached the depot, a huddle of agric shacks, sheds, and bubbles. Then she looked back. The thing was close now, gaining remorselessly on those enormous, forty-foot-long legs. The cylindrical torso, the turretlike head and the huge pelicanlike bill that jutted out in front—all were clearly visible.

Elgin caught her hand as he raced up and pulled her into a long, low shed. "Down!" he shouted. "Under the trestles, there's a drain to our recycler sump. It's the only way."

She ducked beneath the tables that filled the shed. There was a drain laid in ceramic, angled down toward a hole in the puffcrete slab. Elgin was shoving her from behind.

"Hurry! It's here."

There was a ripping, smashing sound behind and above. Sections of the shed roof were being pulled up and tossed away. Things were crashing onto the foodbeet tables, upending them.

The drain vanished down a wide vent, and Rowntree dropped into the hole feet first with no idea how far down it went. She caromed off the wall of the tube, then hit the bottom. Her head struck the opposite wall. She went down on her knees in six inches of muck. Elgin landed virtually on top of her and pushed her body to the floor. The muck provided a cushion, but the air was still knocked out of her lungs. Gagging and choking, she clawed humus from her face and sucked air back into her chest.

Directly above them, the center of the shed was demolished and a hoot of rage bellowed down the vent. She looked up the tube and saw something vast block out the starlight. For a second she fancied she could see one of the glossy black eyes of the woodwose peering down into the hole. She lurched forward with desperate haste on hands and knees and fell into a tank filled with slime and agricultural runoff from the foodbeet fields.

"Swim, it's only a few strokes across," Elgin said.

There was a loud thump behind them. The monster had thrust its huge hand down into the space they'd so recently occupied. Now it groped around for them.

On the far side of the tank there was a recessed space, only two feet high but ten feet wide. They crawled down this spillway into deeper and deeper muck and finally exited the processor system into a settling basin that extended like a narrow swimpool behind the sub-depot complex.

There they lurked for the moment, hidden in the dark water by the side of the pool. Elgin called in on the commo again and got Helen once more, now under control of herself. "Defense is activating," she said. "Ish is going out with them. Be with you in a few minutes."

The monster was still struggling to enlarge the drainage hole leading to the recycler system. It grunted with the effort as it broke the ceramic pipes and shoved its arm farther into the ground. The whole area shuddered as if some huge digging machine had run amok.

Elgin clambered out of the tank. He was covered from head to foot in brown slime. Rowntree followed, her ribs aching where he'd landed on her. He was limping with a bad ankle. They were no longer capable of much more than a shambling stagger.

They tottered down an alley between two more sheds and emerged onto a narrow court laid out on puffcrete slabs. More violence shook the ground behind them. The monster had virtually excavated the recycling system and was now tipping over the runoff tank.

Elgin found a small tractor. She clambered up behind him and clung as he started the thing and sent it rolling down the forecourt. After a momentary hiccup the hydro-engine purred into life, and the tractor picked up speed until it reached its maximum twenty miles an hour. Elgin sent it directly across the fields, heading back toward the dome. They had to find the defense, and quick.

The violence behind them came to a stop. The monster had heard their engine. It rose up against the night and peered after them. Again came the hoot, this time with overtones of exasperation, and it started after them.

The monster was limping, definitely damaged in one leg. That slowed it enough that, though it gained on them, it gained only gradually. They had a chance.

Rowntree looked ahead. They had crossed the first field and

were heading for a rickety little frame bridge that crossed the drainage channel. Ahead was a field of tomatoes. In the field was the huge robot, Picker One.

The woodwose followed, striding over the drainage channel in a single bound. Its huge hands twitched in anticipation as they reached out toward the fleeing figures. It gave another hoot, the rage now modulated with a note of triumph.

Just then the tractor gave a sudden jerk and shivered to a halt. With a loud curse Elgin jumped down and kicked the machine. It remained stubbornly inert.

"Engine's blown up, probably why it was there."

"Run," she said.

The woodwose had entered the field of tomatoes. It had them in its sights, there was no escape now. They ran, shambling, spent. The ground trembled under the monster's huge feet. It would have them in a few moments and then they would be devoured.

Abruptly Rowntree became aware of another sound, another source of heavy vibration. She whirled in time to see Picker One drive past on heavy treads. Openmouthed, she watched as the truck-sized picker thrust itself forward to confront the woodwose.

"You okay?" an anxious voice asked over the commo. It was Ish.

"Yeah, we're still alive. Picker One has it puzzled, but I don't know for how long."

The woodwose monster had slowed. It paced slowly back and forth in front of the picker, examining it closely.

Picker One extended all its arms to the maximum five meters. Each arm ended in an opposing pair of picker hands—five-digit metal manipulators designed for picking tomatoes at high speed without breaking the skins. These delicate hands were all it had to offer. It carried no offensive weapons, nothing but its bulk and its big engine.

The woodwose suddenly emitted a long hoot filled with undiluted rage. Then, without more ado, it stalked forward, reached down, seized the side of the picker, and tried to lift it. Picker One lurched and began to turn over. Elgin gave a small groan of despair, but then the picker's eight-hundred-horsepower engine gave a big roar. The right side tread dug dirt and the robot broke free from the woodwose and bounced away over the tomatoes. There it turned and charged back with a blast from its paired smokestacks.

The woodwose attempted to tackle the machine, ducking down and wrapping its arms around the front, but was bowled over in the next moment and fell with a tremendous crash among the tomatoes, destroying a dozen rows at once. Elgin and Rowntree gazed back with amazed eyes. The picker had stopped once more; now it reversed itself and returned to the fray.

The woodwose was getting back to its feet when it was again rammed by Picker One. This time it tumbled onto its back and rolled on its side.

Before the picker could stop, turn, and charge again, the woodwose was back on its feet and able to skip out of the way. This time it tried to clamber onto the back of the picker. One huge foot sank into a pair of fruit bins laden with half a ton of tomatoes, making ketchup of their contents. Then it slid off the picker amid a fountain of crushed tomatoes. Once more the woodwose crashed to the ground, which shuddered at the impact. For a long second it lay there; then, with an energetic hoot, it climbed swiftly back onto its feet.

The two titans confronted each other once more, the bipedal predator and the high-tech herbivore. Then the woodwose charged with huge arms swinging. Picker One grabbed the shaggy mat of "fur" that cloaked the huge biped and tried to lift it off the ground, but the woodwose could not be held. With a ripping sound, several sets of picker hands snapped off. A few of the remainder clung to wisps of woodwose shag. The woodwose thrust an arm down into the rent in the picker's back where two fruit bins had been destroyed. The diamond-hard claws cut into metal sheeting but slipped off ceramic plate. Still, the monster was able to break into the interior of the picker's thorax. It seized power cables and tore them loose.

The picker lost control of its rear treads. Ineffectually, it tried to grasp the woodwose and pull it off its back. A few tatters of shag came free but the woodwose remained, crouching over the picker as it dragged itself slowly along on the small front treads. Sparks arced into the night air as more internal damage was done.

Rowntree and Elgin were running again, staggering down into a drainage ditch, where they flattened themselves against the rough puffcrete surface.

Something broke inside the picker with a sharp, loud bang, followed by the sound of metal and ceramic parting and being smashed and shattered. Elgin peered over the edge. The defeated Picker One was being dismembered by the monster. The control box, with the optional seat for the occasional driver, was hanging by a thread of spylo wiring. The back was broken wide open, and the right rear tread had come off.

Wordlessly, Elgin pointed down the channel to the dark mouth of a drain. There seemed no other way out. In moments they were inside, lost in a perfect blackness, with a gentle flow of water running along their legs and hands.

12

FROM THE DEPTHS OF THE DRAINAGE TUNNEL THEY COULD RAISE neither Ish nor the dome on the commo. They crawled as swiftly as possible down the passage. At one point the ground nearby shook and they crouched, expecting that the tunnel would be flattened at any moment and their bodies crushed within it. Then the heavy vibrations ceased. After a moment they crawled on.

It was a long journey through the dark toward no visible light, but at last they emerged from the narrow tube at the top of a water slide that led down to the inlet. To their left the dome lights cut the velvet night.

"Helen!" Elgin had the communicator out at once. "Answer me."

There was no response. Elgin repeated his urgent whisper. Finally Helen replied.

"Elgin? You're alive?" She sounded close to hysteria.

"Yeah, we're okay. What's happening?"

"I can't stop him. He's gone out in a pursuer."

"Who has?" But as Elgin said this, Rowntree's heart sank.

"Dad. He just came down suddenly and went out and took the blue pursuer and drove out. He didn't seem to see me, like he was in a trance."

"Where's the monster?"

"They lost it, down by the beach. I don't know how, but Ish

says he's got its trail again, it's coming back up the inlet. They're shooting at it. Where are you?"

"Top of the outflow channel from the midsection."

"Hide, it must be coming your way."

And to confirm their own proximity to the monster they heard the sharp rattle of automatic weapons from behind them. A moment later the woodwose appeared at the top of the slope behind them. With a lurch it struck down toward the inlet. Tracers whisked past it for a moment, and then it was out of sight of its pursuers.

Elgin and Rowntree were crouched in a thicket of blue knuckoo that grew on the bankside, just above the narrow paved road. The woodwose came directly toward them, limping still, its breath making a heavy susurration. The head spun to look back and spun again to the front. The huge hands moved back and forth.

From her hiding place, her heart in her mouth, Rowntree watched the huge, ungainly feet slap down into the roadway right in front of her. The ground trembled and then it was gone.

"Gone past our position now, heading for the dome. Better get out some defense."

"Everything's out there with Ish. Where is he?"

"Ish? Come in, where the hell are you?"

Ish's voice broke in immediately.

"I had to switch over, my pursuer broke down. But we're gaining now and we'll be in range shortly."

"Better hurry, it's heading straight for the dome. Helen, you better get out of there. Go!"

"But where's Dad?" she asked, sobbing. "I don't know where he is."

Elgin looked up at that moment and gave a soft groan.

"We've got him. He's coming down the road from the dome."

"The monster . . ."

Elgin watched, frozen for a second as the woodwose noticed the approaching slim, ten-foot-tall pursuit walker. Then, with a loud hoot of rage, the woodwose picked up speed.

"Ish, hurry it up. No time . . ."

Gainer had seen the monster long before. He opened up with his twin twenty-millimeter cannon. Bits and pieces of the woodwose blew out and away behind it, but it came on, staggering slightly but still charging.

"Oh, no," Rowntree said.

There was no time—Elgin was correct. Gainer kept firing, in radio silence all the while. The wose did not stop. In a few more seconds the two were conjoined in one image. The pursuit machine was plucked up as if it were a toy and hurled overhead, to carom off a puffcrete support wall at the top of the embankment, tumble down the bank, and explode at the bottom. The flash blinded them and the detonation reduced the pursuer to small componentry.

When she could see once more, Rowntree saw Ish's team of defense machines come speeding down the road. The big walkers were firing with everything they had. The woodwose staggered, wobbled, and tried to evade by climbing the embankment beside the inlet. But its strength was ebbing at last. It was struck by a hail of missiles and collapsed with a final hoot of dismay.

A few moments later the defense robots were standing over the dead creature, inspecting the smoking remains. Ish was there, scrambling down from his pursuer.

"Are you two all right?" he asked as they crawled out from cover and approached.

"Fine," Rowntree mumbled, still stunned by these events.

Behind them smoked the remains of the pursuer scattered around a crater in the road. Ish turned away with tears in his eyes. Rowntree sobbed and sank down upon her knees. It was over for Gainer forever.

13

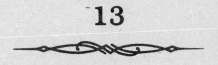

THEY BURIED GAINER IN THE LITTLE CEMETERY ON BIG ISLAND, behind Hospital Square. It was a hot, humid day with gray skies and a sullen ocean. There had been a long soaking rain in the early hours of the morning, and everything smoked with vapor.

Helen was there, pale and drawn, her face partially hidden by a scarf in the black of mourning. She avoided exchanging the slightest of glances with Rowntree or Elgin. Ladbrook was there, and he acknowledged them with a curt nod. This was the burial of more than a man; this was the burial of a dream.

Ishmael had come to them, shyly, outside the small cemetery and embraced both of them and wept on their shoulders.

Helen read from the Fundan Archive, the Instructions from Talbot Fundan. "Go forth into the systems and multiply, and always remember that you are Fundan."

When the small blue casket had disappeared down the narrow shaft, the crowd gave a murmur and began to move apart. As they walked away Rowntree noticed old Compton Shanur, being wheeled along by the implacable Wong. Compton waved to her, seeming cheerful enough despite the occasion.

"A sad day, my dear. We've buried the dream here, the dream of my father and his grandfather."

Rowntree looked off across the leaden ocean into the heat haze. "It wasn't a dream, it was a nightmare. They made the mistake of assuming that this world would be something like Earth. They were wrong."

Old Compton bobbed his head and grinned.

"Home, Wong, home."

Compton was wheeled away, and Rowntree turned to find Elgin waiting for her. Together they headed for the airstrip.

Part Two

SWEET FIFTEEN

THE CHILD OF EDENA FAXEEN AND COMPTON SHANUR FUNDAN was named Fair Fundan as her mother had wished. However, she lived with her mother for just the first two years of her life, at which point Edena's problems with alcohol and instability became overwhelming and the little girl was removed from her care.

The rest of her childhood was a relatively lively and happy one. She grew up in the sunshine, living the outdoor life of the chitin talkers, under the vast vault of the mountain sky. Something of the solemnity of her Grandsire Dane surfaced within her during this time. She read more deeply than was usual among her peers, and her inquiries into history and philosophy grew both numerous and involved. All who taught her agreed that she was precocious.

It was not until her fifteenth birthday that she discovered something of the hurt that existed in the world. Until that day, she realized later, she'd been sheltered.

It began as a normal enough morning in the camp of the Cinnabar Mountain chitin group. It was a sunny day in the midst of the dry season. Temperatures were predicted to rise into the upper twenties centigrade. Humidity was low. A cool breeze descended from the upper slopes, wafting scents of snow and frost meadow. The Cinnabar Mountain chitin group was Fair's extended family. She had grown up among them, camping up and down the long ridge named for the red rock that underlay it. They moved with the seasons, tending the chitin nests they had established on the softer ground. There were twelve adults and eight children at that time, and they were led by Elgin and Rowntree Fundan, who had founded the group twelve years before.

Fair looked to Elgin and Rowntree as her father and mother, and indeed they had formally adopted her in her infancy after her mother, Edena, had been shot dead in a fight in a bar down at Ghotaw Central. By that time she had already lived with Rowntree and Elgin for a year. Her father, of course, she had never known at all.

Cinnabar Mountain had thus been Fair's home, where she lived under the skies as an apprentice chitin talker. She had shown promise in the art since she was seven. She had never known repugnance at the thought of going naked into a chitin nest—to her this contact with the hive insect was quite acceptable. That was a rare ability; most humans retained a horror of insects, even after being divorced from terrestrial insectdom for five hundred years. It was something that operated on a visceral level, perhaps even a cellular one. But to Fair the chitin was a dangerous yet beautiful monster, a monster to be beguiled and befriended.

It was understood that she had a good future ahead of her with the Cinnabar Mountain group, and all looked forward to seeing her skills deployed to the common good. Already, of course, she was an extraordinarily wealthy young person. This despite the paucity of her wardrobe and the fact that she lived in a high-tech tent. In the Fundan vault at Ghotaw North she had a slate of entries to three accounts. In addition she had a cache of longevity protein hidden in a hollow rock on a frost meadow on the flanks of the mountain. Elgin and Rowntree had cut her in for a share of Cinnabar Mountain's output since she had first showed promise with the chitin. Now she had a century's worth of extended life in the vault at Ghotaw North.

Outside of her wealth in longevity drugs she owned hardly anything. She shared in the basics of life on Cinnabar Mountain, she wore Fundan work pants and boots, usually with a camo shirt in Fundan green. Her most prized possession was a collection of rare video clips, mostly of family figures, that fit into a box small enough to go in her shirt pocket.

This collection was a thing of love; she'd worked at it for several years now and had stuff spanning the centuries of the spacer clan descended from Talbot and Emily. She had copies of bloopers that were famous and antique, such as one shot of Prince Edward Fundan slipping on wet grass and tumbling down a sloping bank at some long-ago outdoor festival. He came up looking most disgruntled, with a cigar mashed flat on his face and his top hat destroyed. It was a hoot.

All in all, it was an active life she led, with many interests. She had discovered the "Genshuku" or "Serio-Mode" school of music, which had developed on Earth, largely in Japan and

Europe, during the preceding century and a half. Consequently the long, drawn-out tone poems of Yokashi and Kurusutufa were heard most days issuing from her tent, along with the odd aural imagery of Stevanus Glorev, the musical genius of Connecticut. Her companions heard these strange, wispy musics and chuckled together. They themselves preferred the cheerful talker songs and chanties which all sang in group fests around the fire, but they understood that the dark-haired girl was given to more serious pursuits.

Fair's own efforts at composition in the mode of Glorev and Yokashi, however, proved clumsy and even dull. Despite her appreciation for the music she was not herself gifted as a musician.

Sometimes she wondered what she was meant to be, if not just a well-off chitin talker with a projected lifetime of several centuries. Rowntree and Elgin treated her questions on these themes with care, but in the end their answers were limited. Who but Fair could ever know?

She maintained good grades on her compulsory schooling over clan-net. She spent four hours every day linked in, and afterward there was always homework. When asked why she liked to listen to Wassenski's mournful orchestral works for computer-synth while working on mathematics homework, Fair would only laugh. Most people just didn't understand how closely related they were and most people were not patient enough to listen to Wassenski or any of the so-called Sensory Drama school of modern music.

On the morning of her fifteenth birthday, the group was camped on the midpoint of what they called "Fatback Ridge," an area of particular scenic beauty about halfway along the length of the Cinnabar range. There was considerable excitement in the group that morning, since there were two young nests on the flanks of the Cinnabar that were very close to bearing. Red Trail Nest and Fatback-XP, which was an experimental nest with the Slade Mountain chitin hybrid, were both very close to making their first attempt at founding a new nest. Soon they would give up the precious vizier mass.

Fair had breakfast, her usual nutty-tasting "wheat cakes" griddled on the group's portable galley irons and washed down with "juice" created in the group's drinks machine. She was the first one up, but that was nothing unusual. She sat outside the gallery tent, where they had four camp tables set up. This was the natural center of the camp throughout the dry season.

She wondered what this fifteenth birthday would bring her. In the last year, she had become so much more aware of the world and her special place in it that she could scarcely believe how ignorant she had previously been. She had finally realized how unique her Cinnabar Ridge family was and how precious was their freedom. Somehow she had never really been aware of it before, it had never come home to her.

When she looked in the mirror she was sure she'd grown up a lot in the past year. And it was true that the other kids had started to exclude her, now aware of her near-adult status. That had hurt. It was sad to be cut off from the secrets and the games with the others.

On the other hand, she was already joining the older Highland teenagers who frolicked in their mobility, gathering down at Ghotaw outside the settlement limits. There was a little strip there now that catered to them exclusively and was a source of much editorial fury in the censorious media net. Down there Fair was close to being accepted by the rulers of the pack, like Genuine Dortman, Sibby Volksprung, and Buksman Delore. Being accepted by the older kids was great, but there was a lot more that came with the acceptance. She wasn't sure she wanted to date anybody just yet. Her experiments with the opposite sex had been confined to the person of Hermi Chaze-Fundan, who was a month younger than she and lived along the east bank of the Ghotaw River, thirty miles away. Hermi was all right, but the whole business of taking off one's clothes and rolling around on an airmat in a small tent had never really seemed like a lot of fun. Going out with the older boys down at Ghotaw would certainly involve sexual pressures. Fair knew she was attractive. Her pre-pubescent panic about her breasts had subsided, and she had developed into a curvaceous teenager.

Still, she wasn't entirely ready for sex, either. Sometimes she was afraid that maybe she wasn't even heterosexual, except that she'd never felt the slightest sexual interest in any other girl.

Gracilda, her analyst on the net, tried to help, but would freely admit that, at this age of fifteen, a lot of things would seem to make very little sense. Fair was left to wonder at it. Fifteen seemed like a remarkably big number sometimes. And yet she knew that everyone in her world expected to live for hundreds of years. This was only the beginning of an enormous life, a time that would number decades the way people once numbered years. It was hard to comprehend, even though they studied longevity science at least once a week on the network.

Rowntree was the next person to appear in the galley, and after a special birthday hug and kiss, she presented Fair with her birthday present: an old Fundan vidreader, hand-held size, and with it a vidset of clips on Compton Fundan, Fair's long-dead father. The handreader was the real thing, with the blue triangle on the upper surface, "Fundan Made." It was hundreds of years old and came from the home system. The little readers were very scarce now, but they were also the only ones that could read certain kinds of Fundan imaging clips.

Fair hugged Rowntree, "Oh! This is great, it's just what I need. And what are all these?" She held up the pile of imaging clips.

"Well, I found some old stuff in Fundan Archives. There's a lot of video stuff from the early days, but you have to know where to find it. Your grandfather was responsible, I think. When he was an old man he was obsessed with recording the history of his time. But he was paranoid, always unstable, and very secretive. There are encrypted things hidden all over the Archives, in fact."

Fair pushed the "on" button and watched while she ate. Rowntree's voice narrated introductions to each piece. First there was one of a little boy running across a sandy patch of ground. There was a close-up on the little boy's face as he shifted from interest in the camera to fear of it and then broke out in a wail. The clip ended. The next was of a young man, playing hoop with other young men in a courtyard between domes. The young man was quite tall for his age; he played well and dominated the game. Someone slipped a pass inside to him and he posted up and stuffed the basket.

Onward it went. Rowntree gathered her own breakfast from the grill and moved off to the side, leaving Fair to watch her natural father age gradually into an old man through short clip after short clip.

Breakfast over, Fair stayed put, reviewing a clip that started with Compton, posed in a swimsuit, sitting astride the sleek bow of a blue sailboat. The boat shifted suddenly and the clip ended with Compton falling off into the water and bobbing up in its wake with a great grin all over his face. She knew that grin—she had seen it before in other video memories of

Compton Shanur Fundan. Of course, he had died when she was only three and she remembered nothing of him.

Rowntree had explained it all to her when she was eleven. Her mother, Edena, had obtained Compton's sperm from the family gene bank. They had lived together before that; Edena was sixty years younger than the old man, but she came from a violent and poverty-stricken background. Compton provided her with an escape route.

Fair had been bitten with the urge to know all about Compton Shanur Fundan. She'd learned how important he was, and who his father was, her grandfather, Dane—the Founder. In her free time on the net she'd downloaded all sorts of stuff about Compton. There had been a number of video clips from the period when Compton was a young boat builder, a cocky young man with a good physique, tall and tanned. Some of the videos also had shots of young women—quite a lot of young women. Compton had had many girlfriends.

There were later periods with very few videos. Compton had a family through his relationship with a dark-haired beauty named Claire Montoya. Fair had seen clips of two babies who had grown into little boys.

Then had come a disaster at sea, a boat that sank in a great storm, and all but Compton had drowned. Someone had subsequently edited out most references to this family of Compton Fundan's youth. Fair suspected that Compton himself had done this. There were only a handful of still frames, a portrait, and some video taken by relatives.

And after that point the number of clips of Compton declined dramatically. He became camera shy. Only when he was much older, already looking like an old man, did someone else get him under a lens.

But Rowntree had made a copy of a very rare clip from that long empty period and inserted it into the collection. Fair bit her lower lip with pleasure at the sight of it. Because it came from the Compton Fundan Inner Files it could not be copied freely, so Rowntree had obviously gone to considerable trouble to obtain it.

On the viewscreen Compton Shanur Fundan was now in his middle years, probably around fifty. He was a heavyset man with a beard and a balding head. He wore a white suit and sat in a swing chair on a porch overlooking a body of water crowded with sailing boats. Other people were in animated conversation, something to do with an election. The voices had been edited down to a background rumble, however, and the shot concentrated simply on following Compton Fundan as he sat there, accepted a drink of wine, then stood up and walked about among the other people, exchanging polite conversation. It was apparent that he was much less excited about the election or whatever it was than anybody else present. Occasionally he leaned against the rail and watched a boat move in or out of the harbor.

That was it, ten minutes or so, but Fair watched it all avidly. This was rare stuff and a great addition to her collection. She was already wondering how she could make a copy from the hand-held into the group Datcon.

For just a moment she thought about her mother, the mother of whom she had no conscious memories. For some reason, Fair had never been much interested in her mother's life history. It was almost as if she had deliberately shut out what memories there might be of Edena. The psych-testing had showed that her two years of life with her mother had been highly "stressful." Edena had not lived a settled life.

Fair had taken therapy with Gracilda Weers-Bancroft since she was seven, and they agreed that she was getting along very well. There was still a lot of trauma there, and sometimes Fair experienced sudden rages that made her want to scream and hurt someone. Nor was she able to penetrate that painful period of infancy in memory trials. Gracilda did not believe in mindprobe or anything that might change a patient's personality by physical means, so she was limited to the free-run memory trial. Fair could not or would not go into that area of infancy. Perhaps Fair never wanted to see her real mother's face again, and that was why she shrank so completely from that side of her life.

On the other hand, Edena had been a complete nobody, while Compton had been one of the members of the ruling family, a direct descendant of Edward the Prince. Fair had to admit to herself that Compton was by far the more glamorous. Edena's life seemed squalid by comparison.

After the "white suit" clip she sat there, absorbed in the clips of the older man. These had been made by the succession of mistresses he took when he was in his sixties and seventies. The women were all beautiful, all very young. They passed through the old man's life at the rate of one every two or three years.

There was a long clip of a fishing expedition, Compton reeling in a big permiad, a thing of glittering blue scales. Fair wondered what it was like to do that, to reel in a fish. She had very little experience of the sea. She'd only been to the coast twice in her life, and on the first occasion she'd been too young to absorb much more than the impression of vast flat water, spread out in immensity. There was something about the water that seemed magical to her. What must it be like to sit in a boat and go places, blown by the wind, with hardly any effort!

The only comparison she could make was to hang gliding through the mountains, something she'd done a few times now despite Rowntree and Elgin's disapproval. Elgin had been most impassioned with her on the subject after the last disaster, when two youngsters in the Butte family had been killed in a midair glider collision.

After breakfast, Elgin appeared, signaling to Fair as he came. He had a rifle strapped over his shoulder and he was carrying another for her, a small sporting .25 semi-auto. Elgin knew that it was her favorite of the rifles in the small Cinnabar armory because it was light and easy to aim.

"I know you have a class later this morning," he said after she'd hugged him, "but I thought you might like to come out now for an hour or so. We need some meat—everyone's getting sick of synthetics."

Fair jumped at it. Elgin usually hunted alone; he didn't even take Rowntree, normally. And her main class that day was a two-hour mathematics and geometry special that would take up the whole afternoon by the time she finished the homework. If she was going to have fun on this birthday, it would be now.

They went eastward down the flank of the ridge into the denser jik forest around the headwaters of the River Ghotaw. There they prowled quietly through the thickets, watching for the telltale traces of gzan, the top herbivore in the mountain valleys.

It was a great morning. The air was still cool under the eaves of the jik, and there was a profound hush. They slipped along from tree to tree, keeping a wary eye open for signs. There was little underbrush here, mostly just young jik fighting to survive in the shade of their elders.

They reached the cliffs that overlooked the broader valley farther down. The vegetation petered out as the bare rock emerged, and they ended up on the edge of the cliff gazing out at a view of the Ghotaw bowl. Far away, but clearly visible in the mountain air, was the dark cone of Ghotaw Mountain.

They had seen no sign of the mout mook that they sought, the dwarf gzan of the high slopes. They had had one shot at a scarlet skrin but had not taken it. Skrin were getting too rare to shoot for food now. Nobody in the group would want to see a scarlet skrin cooked for dinner.

"No mout mook," Fair said wearily, thinking of the synthetic they'd be eating at dinner.

"No mout mook," Elgin agreed.

They started back. The cliffs were an hour out of camp, and Fair needed to get back and take a look at the upfront on the material she would be going over in her math-geometry class.

Elgin was somber now, preoccupied. Things were getting just as bad as he'd always feared they would. Cinnabar Ridge had been just about shot out. There were simply too many people in the central part of the Ghotaw Valley for the wildlife to be able to sustain itself. Nobody was actually living off wild animal meat, but with everyone just taking an occasional skrin or gzan they had annihilated the stocks anyway.

As they wound back up the trail onto the Fatback Ridge, Fair commented on the fact that there were no Fein on the ridge anymore either. The Uk-ho kin group hadn't been around in months.

"Too many people," Elgin said. "The game's been shot out and the Fein won't come back."

"Aren't the Fein angry? It's not meant to be like this."

Elgin shrugged. "Who can say. The Fein don't talk to humans much anymore. Not since the killings."

Fair knew this, of course. The precious concordat between Fein and human had broken down. A couple of drunk Fein had been shot and killed in Ghotaw Central, giving the place an evil reputation among them. But that had been superseded in horror by the killing of an entire kin group, machine-gunned by unknown humans from the air and then skinned. The skins had been sold in the big domes on the coast, in the new cities. There had even been television coverage of the auctions. As a result, the Fein had slipped out of contact with humans wherever possible. Other Fein had threatened people and forbidden them to enter certain valleys.

And yet the Cinnabar group had always had good relations with the Uk-ho. For twelve years they'd exchanged gifts at season's end. It was another saddening sign of the changing times. Too many people were living in the central valley. Ghotaw Central was becoming a town. They were polluting Ghotaw Lake. And people down there were inexcusably breaking the game-hunting laws and shooting everything that moved.

Elgin and Fair finally moved up to the top of the ridge, just a few minutes away from camp. Despite the absence of game, Fair's thoughts were devoted to happy concerns. When her homework was finished she would catalog all the new family clips Rowntree had given her.

Abruptly, the peace of the day was shattered. First they registered a droning sound, unmistakably an engine. It grew much louder and then, with a sullen roar, it passed close overhead, although they saw nothing because of the jik cover. A few seconds later they heard and felt heavy thuds of explosives. Sharper noises followed almost immediately, and Fair recognized the percussive crack of rifle fire.

"Shooting!" she exclaimed with a startled look at Elgin.

The rifle fire was punctuated by sudden rips of a deeper, more menacing sound.

"Raid!" Elgin snarled, starting forward. There were thumps and thuds from ahead, more explosive detonations that shook the ground under their feet. Elgin stopped for a moment and directed her off the trail. "Go to ground—don't show yourself for anything."

"But I want to help."

"I know, but this is the best way to do that. You might be the only one of us left to tell the tale afterward, so stay here and make sure you survive."

He was gone a moment later.

She watched him go and was torn briefly with indecision. She couldn't stay here, safe and out of the way; she had to go and fight the raiders. She'd never felt anything so strongly in her entire life.

She ran on, toward the tumult.

A white flash broke across the sky and was followed immediately by a heavy detonation. The drone-roar moved away. The rifle fire died down.

When she was slightly less than two hundred meters away, she came into sight of the camp. There were flames licking up from the tents and from the storage dome.

The engine drone came again and a moment later she saw the attacker, a squat thing with the appearance of a giant insect covered in black stealthmat. Everything about it spoke of death, from the glitter of the viewports on the front to the weapon pods dangling from the sides. It came in low over the campsite, and the white streaks of rockets leapt from its belly. Fireballs burst in the jik woods around the camp.

Rifle fire cracked back. The thing swept overhead. Another rifle cracked close by, and she glimpsed Elgin standing behind a tree, his rifle raised.

She dove for cover, a crevice between slabs of rock, slamming into it before she heard the *spraaaap* of the gunship's antipersonnel weapons. Pieces of the jik trees showered down, whole limbs blasted from the little trunks. Fair rolled over, pulled her rifle free, and looked up. The gunship was out of sight, but she heard it turn to come back.

Again the high-speed guns sprayed the woods with thousands of projectiles. The drone grew louder and the monster thudded past right overhead. She glimpsed the gunners in the side bays, looking for targets for the ugly snouted weapons.

Something snapped out of the trees beyond the campsite, leaving a bright yellow trail. With a tremendous clap of thunder a white flash went off, seemingly right against the side of the gunship.

Fair's vision was blurred green and red after that and she lost track of the gunship, but she knew it was still flying because she could hear the engines droning on.

The *spraaaap* sound came again, accompanied by heavier detonations of more air-to-ground rockets. The dirt under her back shuddered.

Elgin went past her position, not seeing her, running crouched over. He disappeared in the jik to her right. After a second or two she pushed her head out cautiously and clambered from the space between the rock slabs. Trees had been slashed down wholesale here, and in a moment she could see the war machine through a break in the foliage.

Now it looked like a dragonfly roasted on one side. The stealthmat had scorched away to leave bare metal in places and the guns on that side were gone, but it was still flying. She could see a half-dozen bulky figures dropping on lines from the rear as it hovered over their camp.

Elgin's rifle cracked from her right. One of the figures spun 'round, but continued sliding down the line. More rifle fire came up from the woods, but the ground party was down now, hunting in the camp ruins for cache. The sound of small-arms fire grew louder. The ground party was encountering resistance from just outside the camp area.

More rockets struck down, fireballs blossoming in the jik. Fair knelt and slipped her sights up onto the gunship. Carefully she aimed for the intake on the left-side steering cone. A bullet in there could damage the rotors.

The rifle's gentle recoil against her shoulder thudded three times in a second; then she ducked down and lay flat. There was no visible effect. The gunship turned, laying down covering fire for the men on the ground. The *spraaap* sound became continuous.

She got to her knees again, raised her rifle, and found the left-side cone once more. She squeezed off five quick shots. The gunship turned and the cone slid out of her sights. Her heart sank. But a moment later she was aware of a change. The timbre of the rotor noise was different, and soon there came a harsh whine moving up the scale to a metal killing screech.

More rifle fire broke out. Another rocket burst out of the thickets and detonated with a loud blast right beneath the gunship. The gunship suddenly slewed over, no longer hovering on an even keel. The drone was revving—they'd lost one rotor cone, no doubt of it. The thing was drifting away to the right.

Fair found she'd emptied the clip on her rifle. She needed to reload, and the only source of ammo would be in the camp—in Elgin's tent most likely. She scrambled to her feet and ran up the path through the trees to the clearing. The tents were all shot up. The generator was on its side smoking, and the cooking grills were overturned.

She darted forward and came up with a grunt as the breath was knocked out of her. She went down on her backside and saw an armored giant standing over her.

Weakly she tried to sit up, to move a muscle. The man thrust a boot up on her chest and pinned her to the ground. He leaned down with a foot-long bowie knife in his hand. She saw his face frame the words, "Say good-bye to life, little bitch!" She realized that she was going to die, here, so shockingly early, at the weirdly youthful age of just fifteen. It was impossible, it couldn't be happening to her. She closed her eyes.

Then the man was knocked aside and she glimpsed a figure in Fundan greens swinging a rifle like a club. There was a crunch and the man in black combat armor fell over with a crash.

Fair was back on her feet. Elgin looked at her with a look

that she knew meant she was in big trouble. "You aren't supposed to be here!" he said. His eyes did not meet hers.

"I just couldn't . . ." She broke off. There was another figure, gun raised.

Elgin was already dropping to ground and cover, and she threw herself down in the other direction. Projectiles whipped overhead. Some exploded just behind her, impacting on the jik saplings. Something rattled hard off the metal case of the commpack on her hip, and she landed on her side, spun halfway 'round by the impact. She was going to have a hell of a bruise on that hip later.

If she lived, that was. She was out of ammunition, completely helpless. It was a peculiarly enraging sensation.

Elgin was firing back. The man in black armor dropped out of sight among the rocks on the far side of the camp. He seemed safe from them in there.

A moment later there was an explosion right where he'd vanished as a grenade went off. She watched as his body was tossed up and out by the force of the blast.

Someone unseen yelled a triumphant epithet from the trees.

"Come on, then," Elgin said, barreling past her and running on into the camp.

Fair noticed, without much emotion, that her own little tent, green and gray camo, was burning along with the others. Then Elgin was shoving some ammo clips into her hands. "Here, now get to cover, that gunship's coming back."

She turned and ran, leaping high over a bush and hurling herself down behind a clump of dwarf hobi gobi. She sprawled under a tangle of short jik. There was someone lying not far away to her left.

The gunship was back, its weapons flaying the ground. Fair crouched in a fetal ball, praying that she would not be hit. Explosive bullets shocked the ground nearby but did not touch her.

She looked up. The hobi gobi was gone, mashed to pulp, and the gunship had roared past. She rolled and got to her feet in one smooth motion. She brought up the little rifle, but too late; the target had gone.

That was when she saw Rowntree, sprawled on the ground not five feet away. There was something very wrong—her head was at an unnatural angle, her arms splayed out.

A sick feeling jumped inside Fair like a live thing. She stumbled over and looked down. With a horrible numbing sensation she saw that Rowntree was dead. A huge hole had been blown through her midriff, and blood stained the ground all around her.

Nausea overwhelmed her. She retched uncontrollably until the sobs overwhelmed the nausea with a throat-buckling effect that made it hard to breathe. She felt a sudden, crushing sense of loss and then only anger, a red-hot rage that dissipated the rest like lava cutting through a forest. With a primal shriek she whirled and charged ahead, rifle at the ready.

The gunship was back overhead. Pickups were let down from the rear access hatch. A man in the black armor broke from cover. Fair was the first to fire at him, her bullets striking his legs, knocking him off his feet and sending him rolling in the dust. A grenade slammed into the gunship and exploded and it wobbled away. The man on the ground got to his feet once again and tried for the nearest pickup, but a crescendo of rifle fire struck him. He fell and did not move again.

It suddenly occurred to Fair Fundan that she had perhaps killed her first human being. She had never thought that it would come to this, but it had happened and she felt almost nothing. Yet she was ready to kill again—every one of these raiders if possible.

The gunship returned once more and again she took cover. But the machine had taken a lot of punishment now. Both engines were stuttering and the stealthmat was stripped and scorched. Only one set of guns still worked, so the ship had to turn constantly to cover all the ground.

The raiders had overreached. They had caught a bear and he would not let go. As the next man in the ground party broke cover he was hammered by rifle fire from the hidden defenders. Eventually one man, wounded for certain, made it back up to the gunship. After that it left, abandoning the rest. One surrendered; the rest were shot.

The interrogation went on all night. The man was resolute. He would give up nothing unless they used mindprobe. He bargained for his life and liberty. Finally Elgin took him out to the old Winter nest, which had gone feral and would soon have to be destroyed. Somebody threw one of the raider corpses onto the ground. The surface soil broke into sudden movement, a swarm of swift-moving brown-and-green insects, their carapaces throwing back the light with winks and gleams. In a minute there were thousands of them, and an odd roar of mandibles filled the air with a sound that was almost mechanical. The corpse began to melt away right before their eyes.

They brought the raider back to the devastated camp, weeping with terror. Elgin shoved him down by the ruin of their galley equipment.

"Talk, or you'll feed a nest in the morning."

At last the man talked. He gave them everything he had.

In the morning they gave him a quick trial and found him guilty of premeditated raiding and murder.

"Let me kill him," Fair said.

Elgin would not allow it. "It cannot be personal, Fair, it cannot be that, or we descend to their level. We must uphold our clan laws."

In the end they chose Barnes Demitro to do the job: one round in the back of the head. Then they threw the body to the Winter nest, which devoured it with relish.

Part Three

DRUMS AND RIFLES

1

THE BIG MAN WAS IN A THUNDEROUS RAGE. HIS GROWLS ECHOED through the big dome. Subordinates took notice of the fact and did their utmost not to attract his attention.

The medic gave the other man present, the one cuffed to the bed, an injection of hypastine, a powerful all-system stimulant. The man's heartbeat soared, his breathing quickened, sweat broke out on his brow. He was unable to say anything because of the gag forced tightly into his mouth, but onlookers could be sure he would have liked to say many things, beginning with a plea for mercy. The medic checked for an allergic reaction to the hypastine and then packed his things and left.

The Big Man strode up and down the small room ranting in an angry voice, as if he were addressing a crowd. Gunter, the bodyguard, stood stolidly by the door, quite used to such behavior.

"This is our new home!" the Big Man roared. "But our position is not as strong as it might be. We have a problem with personal weakness. Weakness that saps our position. Weakness that gnaws on our strength like insects in the wood. We know what weakness means and what it can lead to. To be strong we must be unified under our leader. We cannot afford to let the weaker ones among us cheat and get away with it!"

He swiveled easily on his thick, stumpy legs and reached deep for a bellow. "Our leader is strong! In this truth we shall find our salvation."

He paused a moment as if listening to a wave of applause, then raised a hand as if to calm the excited masses. "So we have a new home, a new world for our own! But our position is still not as strong as it should be. We face dangers! This is unacceptable to the people of the EASU."

He beamed and nodded in fierce benevolence. "What is to be done? With the cheats? What steps have to be taken?"

He stretched out a hand, and with his arm rigid, jabbed a

finger down toward the ground in rhythm with the rising cadences of his voice. "We know we must unite under our leader. Our leader is strong—I have proven that enough times. On the old world we faced many a crisis. When our policy leaders began to weaken I was forced to take strong measures. Some decried those measures, some said I was too harsh. But someone had to act, and act decisively, to save the situation and it fell to me to carry out those acts. Our policy leaders had become a cancerous growth, it was my job to cut out that cancer and cleanse our body. Any weakness in such a situation would have meant oblivion, destruction, the annihilation of our hopes. I showed no weakness, that is why I am leader. That is why we are all here. That is why we escaped together, that is why we are the masters of our own fate!"

Once again the Big Man paused and looked up, as if seeing off to the horizon, rather than to the ocher wallpaper, now ruined by spats of blood and spittle. On the sofa, staining the sulon cover, were the instruments. The man on the steel bed had received a thorough interrogation.

"We have learned through bitter experience that only complete unity of purpose under a strong leader can keep our position intact. We cannot tolerate weakness. We cannot tolerate disunity. We cannot tolerate cheating!"

The Big Man leaned over the figure bound to the frame, his face contorting suddenly into a rage of jowls and pudge.

"Nasty little cheat!" The Big Man prodded down with a thick forefinger.

The man on the bed, naked, cuffed to the steel at wrist and ankle, could make no reply, but he tried—oh, how he tried. The Big Man pulled the brown silk robe around his monstrous gut and looked up again to the imaginary hordes.

"To maintain our unity requires more strength of purpose on my part. I will keep our discipline up to the mark. I will purge our ranks of the disloyal and I will kill all the cheats!"

There was a knock on the door behind him. Gunter investigated and opened it to Lawler and the short little man they called "Pedro." Pedro was the operator of the bed. Pedro knew how to make the unlikeliest of pupils sing while on the bed. Lawler was a tall, lean man with silver gray hair and the look of arrested age that was typical of the leadership of the East Anglian Social Union, or EASU. He came and stood beside the Big Man.

Pedro squatted down beside the frame, connected the power

hookup, then stood up with the little control unit in his hand. He looked up to the Big Man.

"You want him to suffer?" he asked.

The Big Man frowned. Lawler frowned, too.

Pedro saw the frowns and looked down at once. He was just the operator. He could just keep his mouth shut.

"He is to die," the Big Man said. "Cook the fucker right through!"

Shit, thought Pedro, that was going to make the bed really a bitch to clean up afterward.

Lawler leaned over the bed and looked down with the cold eyes of a member of the Enforcement Section.

"You stupid little bugger," he snarled. "You had everything on a plate, Garrenger, what the hell did you go and cheat for?"

Garrenger's eyes bugged out of his head. He made noises in his throat. He wanted to tell Lawler that it was all a mistake. The stash they'd found had been a piece that he just hadn't gotten around to distributing yet. It was for the West Londons, that was all. He wanted to beg Lawler to tell the Big Man the truth. It wasn't true that Garrenger was a disloyal cheat. It wasn't true, the Big Man had been misinformed.

"He is a cheat!" the Big Man growled.

"Very stupid thing to do, cheating on our leader," Lawler said coldly.

The cords in the doomed man's neck stood out, and his noises rose to an impassioned groan. The Big Man snapped his fingers and Pedro pressed the switch. Electric current surged into the steel frame and the grid of wires beneath the man quickly grew red hot, then orange, then white.

The man expelled the gag with the force of his reaction. His body leaped from contact with the wire, shaking the whole bed, muscles taut like springs. Then he fell back and his shriek went up an octave while foul smoke rushed up. Again and again the body spasmed on the hot grid, bouncing straight up with each renewed contact. The shrieks lost volume quite quickly, though, for which Pedro was glad, since they were very loud to begin with and the room was small and Pedro was very close to the bed.

As the screams ebbed down into gurgles so did the strength begin to go out of the wretch. The flesh of his back was cooking now, the skin charred, thick smoke rising. Lawler had stepped across to widen the expellers, and the air system whooshed as it sucked the smoke out and blew it into the sky.

The Big Man simply sat there, watching the last moments of his victim.

The man's final noises were gone. The room was quiet except for the whoosh of the air system and the hissing of fat spluttering on the hotbed. The smell of roasted flesh was horribly pervasive. Pedro began to get hungry without noticing because he was really pissed off about the mess this was making of the bed. He'd be cleaning the damned thing for hours.

"He's dead, I think," Lawler said.

The Big Man didn't blink. Another long second passed. Smoke rushed up in volumes.

"Enough!" He made a chopping motion with his right hand.

Pedro flicked the switch and gradually the metal cooled and the hissing died out.

The Big Man was in motion, rolling out of his chair with Lawler at his shoulder, heading out the door.

Outside the room Lawler snapped his fingers to a couple of henchmen. "Get in there and help clean up the mess. The body to the recycler."

The Big Man was still muttering to himself. Lawler caught up. They went into the Big Man's EASU office three floors down.

"I've got a job for you, Lawler."

Lawler nodded, knowing already what it was.

"You, Lawler, are going to go out there and you will purge the ranks for me. There's too many of these little fuckin' wideboys who think they can cheat on Arvin Erst. All thinkin' they can run some little scams on the side. All compromising their loyalty to the EASU."

The Big Man smacked a big fist into a meaty palm.

"I won't stand for it. We're going to tighten things up around here and we're going to catch all these little cheats and show them the error of their ways."

"You want them alive?" Did the Big Man intend to cook all of the little bastards? Lawler hoped not. The scene in that room had been upsetting; he didn't want to have to repeat it. Certainly not ten or twenty times.

The Big Man seemed to think about it for a long moment before coming to some internal decision.

"No, just kill them. Run them down and kill them, Lawler, and then come back to me."

"You want prior notice for each name?"

The Big Man hesitated for a second. "Yes."

2

THE MONSOON WAS LATE, AND THE CHITIN NESTS IN THE HIGH mountain valleys were suffering from dehydration. The bright light of a cloudless midday coruscated off the snow on the mountains while a dry wind soughed through the jik trees and whistled across the camouflage covering the tents. It sucked moisture out of the air, out of the chitin, and out of the people, too. It made everyone, insect and human, irritable and prone to bite.

Everyone was out on the range, except for the two of them. He because he was a visitor to the camp with no chitin to mind, she because she was expecting to harvest a nest very shortly and thus could not afford contamination with the smell of another nest. Nests were insanely jealous of each other, and during a nest founding they were exceedingly ill-tempered and likely to bite for the slightest reason.

"You know what will happen and you know that we have to avoid it somehow." He was a man of indeterminate age with gray hair and soft blue eyes, a tall man, slightly stooped, wearing dark green camo and a bush hat. He had the distinctive soft accent of his birthplace on Earth, Los Angeles, California. He hunched over to peer out of the tent. There was nothing to see but the little jik trees, all twenty feet high, supporting crowns of dark little leaves.

She didn't agree. "Hof, we can't change them. We just have to look after ourselves." As if to emphasize her meaning, the young woman sitting in the camp chair picked up an assault rifle, checked its magazine, and worked the action. It was smooth, precise, light but deadly in her hands. It was also an antique, a family heirloom. She started to clean it. On the upper surface of the gun barrel was a small blue triangle and tiny letters that read "Fundan Made."

"No, Fair, it's gone beyond that sort of response now. We can't escape the problems anymore. Hell, we already share the problems. How many killings have there been this year alone?"

She shrugged, still unmoved. "Hof, I love you, but you groan on far too much."

"It's because I'm old and wise, my dear. More than just the usual ambulatory penis, you know."

She smiled. He turned back to look at her, saw the gun in her arms, and for a moment he trembled. She was so sure, so confident, and so beautiful. He loved her very much and he was terribly afraid for her, and for everyone else.

"Just being old doesn't give you the right to be so obnoxious," she said while shaking her dark hair back from her face in a way that she knew affected men most strangely.

"Obnoxious? Come on, Fair. The settlement is riddled with spies."

She was wiping the gun down with a twist of rag that she'd pulled from inside her belt. "We don't live there, and they don't even know where we are most of the time."

"I think they know a lot more than you like to give them credit for. Men like Erst, they're well-equipped now. You think they don't know about this camp?"

She seemed absorbed in the weapon. When she spoke it was with the same dogged imperturbability that had already upset him. "They don't know where we are: if they did we'd have already had a raid. You think we're fresh out of the nest or something, don't you?"

"Not at all, but then neither are they."

For a moment she stopped as if she was actually reconsidering his point; then she shrugged. "Look, Hof, either way there's not a hell of a lot we can do about them. We have our work to do, and if they try anything we'll kill them if we have to."

She said this so matter-of-factly that he wanted to laugh and scream at the same time. This child of the mountains, schooled in the outdoors, at home with guns and ambushes and sudden death—she was totally possessed by the false confidence he dreaded the most about her people.

"There are too many of them for us to kill; we have to work out a peace with them. There have to be negotiations and a legal framework. We need laws and mechanisms to uphold them."

She shook her head as she had hundreds of times before.

"You want to put the family back under outside rule, don't you, Hof? You have to understand that that will never happen. We are Fundan, we are free, we rule ourselves and we have done so for centuries. You are not Fundan, you do not understand."

Well, it was true. He was from a civilized city of forty million people. None of his forebears had ever trod outside of California, as far as he knew, let alone traveled to an alien world more than forty light-years away. He was not one of them, these wild ex-spacers. But, still, he was hurt. Since so much had happened between himself and Fair, he'd thought he'd become at least an honorary member.

He sighed, remembering what Happy Samson had told him when all this started. "They'll never accept you, Hof, you'll always be an Earther to them, a dirtball, if you know what I mean." Happy was always the vindictive type. Maybe Happy was right. He'd been here all his life—he knew the old families a lot better than Hof, who'd only arrived on an EASU ship.

"Well, my dear, you're right. I'm no Fundan, no spacer spawn. But I'm old and wise anyway and I do know this: either there will be laws or there will be war. And in a war they have most of the advantages."

She held out the gun, glistening with oil, a deadly look on her face. "This says to hell with their numbers."

"Fair—" He was almost pleading with her, which he knew she hated. "—Fair, will you just take some time to think it through? Remember your history tapes, think about it. The situation we enjoy today cannot hold unless we unite. There's a huge wave of colonization coming, they want land."

Fair looked out past him, across the ocher slopes. "Reyanne's coming. Must be almost time."

"Fair?"

She looked up to him. It was time to make a concession. The poor, dear man had come all this way to see her; the least she could do was to try and calm his fears a little.

"Of course, Hof, I will think about it. We'll talk more, in the wet season."

He straightened up. "Good, I'll see you at the lab." He was ready to leave, seemingly satisfied with her response. She knew he was priming her, setting her up for the decision he knew she must make.

"We'll be there. In about ten days, I'd say." She was smiling. He was such a dear man, and so determined. "And I'm glad you came. I was lonely, I missed you."

That was true. The sex was always good, something that still surprised her, since so many men were so disappointing in bed, and Hof was so much older than she. She'd never imagined an older man could be such a vigorous lover.

"Thank you, my dear." He'd grown mock formal. "As always, I'm sad to have to leave you."

Reyanne came in a few moments later, moving carefully from cover to cover, using the step rocks they'd laid down to avoid creating any trails centered on the tents. It was an instinct now with all of them: while they were out on the nesting area they moved as if snipers were looking down on them from the higher ground.

Once inside she pulled off her hat and camouflage poncho. The space suddenly seemed crowded; Reyanne's blond exuberant body always seemed to fill a tent. Normally Fair had no objection—her friend had always been this way and Fair, dark, quiet, and controlling, had always been content to sit back and manage the stage that Reyanne strutted on. But today she wanted her quiet moment with Hof back. She wanted to feel him beside her in the sack, his lean but muscled body on hers, his hands holding her, his mouth pressed against hers.

Suddenly she broke the spell, chiding herself. Space, but sex could make you stupid! There was work to do, dangerous work, and she was sitting there thinking about making love for the umpteenth time in three days!

Reyanne was dumping some notes from her wrist comp into the camp's main unit while gulping down cold water from the cooler. "It's ready," she announced. "They've broken the ground for an exit."

"Then it'll be this afternoon."

"I think it'll be as soon as you can get back there."

"Have you told the others?"

Reyanne nodded. She was as experienced as Fair in this mining of the insect. "Wally's coming down with the sprayer and Stook and Ronaldo are already there with the sweepers."

"Well, in that case it's time I went to work."

Fair slipped the cloth cover over the gun barrel and put the gun over her shoulder. She stooped to pick out some spray vials from a chest in one corner and slipped them into her pocket. Hof Witlin watched her with sadness and love. He shared her with those nests, and he knew their sweet salt smell on her body, though, of course, he could not differentiate between them; no human could. They could smell him on her—in fact, they could taste him. What did they make of that? She said they were very jealous, even of him. Sometimes they bit her out of spite if they detected Hof's smell on her.

"You know there's a new ship in-system," he said suddenly.

Fair looked back to him, eyebrows raised. "Another one?"

"It's a Hakkoid ship—twenty thousand more colonists in deep freeze."

"More of them? Where the hell are they going to live?" Reyanne complained as she ducked back out and slipped her poncho over her shoulders.

Fair met his soft blues with her cannon black gaze.

"I promised to think about what you said. I will do that. Are you coming?"

He shrugged, then shook his head. "No, I'm no good around live chitin. I've got to pack, since I'm heading back this evening."

She came over to him and kissed him then, lightly on the lips. He hugged her to himself, squeezed his eyes shut, and kissed her much harder. Then she grabbed her hat and ran out in pursuit of Reyanne, and he followed her movements with a lover's trained eye.

She caught up with Reyanne under the nearby jik.

"Hof's nervous about all the newcomers," Reyanne said.

"No change there," Fair said, "but I love him."

"He thinks we're going to have to fight EASU and the rest."

"No, well, really he thinks we have to weld them all into a nation, like it is on Earth."

Reyanne wrinkled her nose in disgust. "No way. The families will never go for it. Nor will the Spreaks or anybody else. Fundans have ruled themselves for three hundred years, no way we're going to let somebody else have a say in our affairs."

Fair felt uncomfortable for a moment. Put like that, it suddenly sounded selfish. Was that how Hof saw it? The Fundans as arrogant and aloof? "Right," she said.

"We didn't leave the home system just to submerge in some kind of colony government."

"Well, actually, I think that was the original plan."

"Yeah, well, I think that part of the plan got left behind when we moved up here. This isn't the kind of life the old Fundans had in mind when they started the *Founder*."

"No, but that doesn't mean we couldn't be stronger, if we were united, all the families together."

"With the Spreaks? No way, Fair."

They entered an area of bare rock with little cover for a hundred meters or more. They went fast, feet shuffling across the dry, white limestone. On the far side the trees began again, covering the ridge above the section of exposed limestone. Here were several of their working nests.

Once they were under the trees they soon ran into Davi Butte, who was keeping guard with automatic rifle in hand. Up ahead were Wally Gregoran and Stook Dewok. Stook was leaning on his sweeper, a powerful vacuum cleaner designed to suck up struggling insects from the forest floor.

"Nest is ready," said Wally, an open-faced youth of twenty, with a splay nose and soft brown eyes that always made her think of the dogs she saw in the ancient learnware. Carefully she went forward, past them toward the meter-high ventilation fins that projected above the nest like the fins of a school of land-bound sharks. Wally smelled strongly of the spray, so she motioned to him to stay well downwind. The limestone strip would be the horizon marker for this harvest. The parent nest was young and had no understanding of the world beyond the limestone, which its scouts had never crossed.

Now was the time for her to risk her life again, as she did every season she worked the chitin. Carefully she pulled off her clothes, oiled herself with a sweet-tasting concoction called Miflin grease, and dabbed spots of pheromones R12 and M13 on her body, in the navel, the crotch, and the armpits. When she was naked and greased she took up some ripe glob glob fruits and went forward.

As she approached the nest the ground began breaking up around her. Soldiers and workers in great numbers were moving about in a dense mass. All had the green stripe of the Ghotaw strain, a relatively gentle breed of chitin. Her arrival over the central nest core produced more activity, soldiers bristling and scurrying onto her legs. In moments, if so ordered, they could begin stinging and biting, and their stings packed more venom than any of Earth's hornet species.

But she was not bitten, merely inspected. Then she scattered the ripe fruits she carried. Dirt boiled around the offerings and they were taken below into the maw of the hive.

She sang softly to the nest and crouched low in front of the main accessway, a set of five fist-sized holes in the ground.

"You're ready to come now, I know it. You're ready to follow me," she sang in the soft, cooing voice that always worked best with the chitin.

She crouched down and put her hand into the largest nest aperture she could see. Chitin swarmed on her hand, their mandibles making a tickling sensation as they carefully tasted the sweat on her skin, confirming her identity. The activity around her feet increased. More soldiers appeared, a solid phalanx of one- and two-inch-long insects with big heads and strong mandibles. There were ten thousand of them or more on the ground now, and she knew that if so commanded they would rush upon her and quite probably kill her in a matter of seconds.

But they did not. She was no intruder; she was the friend of the nest, the beloved, the helper, the slave.

The five entrance holes were being rapidly enlarged. She moved across and placed one leg into the nearest. Within a minute she could get the other in. Her entire lower body was covered in workers. The hole got larger as she watched, and she was able to crouch down while the soil was replaced above her head by a carpet of more workers, each carrying a speck of soil.

The chitin swarmed over her body, taking her pulse, tasting her essence, licking the Miflin grease. She could feel the excitement pulsing in the ground around her. She took long, slow deep breaths and willed herself to be calm and relaxed. To the nest, she projected confidence and readiness. Everything had been taken care of, everything was planned for.

More chitin surrounded her; she felt the heavier bodies of warriors and vizier. Thousands of vizier, representing a fortune in longevity proteins, pressed around her, exchanging the tastes and flavors of her and the Miflin grease. A veritable storm of complex chemicals was in play among the chitin themselves, with lactones and ketodecenoic acids prominent.

It was time!

The curtain of workers above her head broke open. The excitement in the nest rose to a near hysterical frenzy. Daylight broke in. Hexadecalactone levels were rising, and the smell of complex organic acids was strong. This was a dangerous moment for the talker. Any minor event now, from a fallen tree branch to the flight of a skrin overhead, could set off the panic attack reaction. Slowly she stood up. Around her feet was a thick mat of soldiers and workers. Above her was the blue sky.

More ground broke open and a group of queens appeared,

long slender insects with inch-long abdomens and gauzy wings. Once they had been mated she knew they would swell into monstrous, gourd-sized egg machines and would spend the rest of their lives in the dark, pumping out eggs.

Workers, less than half an inch in length, seemed to boil out of the ground as if spontaneously generated there. In moments there was a solid mass of them spread out for ten feet in every direction. Hundreds of soldiers had clambered onto her body in the meantime. The lactone smell was strong but not one soldier used its sting, and only a very few workers bit hard enough to cause any discomfort.

The insect excitement was still rising. A solid mass of workers was on the ventilation fins, gathered to bid good-bye to the exiles.

At last they came. A vent opened almost directly between her feet as workers moved dirt aside, and from the vent came a tumbling mass of chitin with large, heavy abdomens, almost as large as the largest soldiers: the vizier mass, the evolutionary trick of the chitin that had boosted it far beyond any other known social insect.

With the same soft, cooing voice she murmured sweet nothings to the chitin. They could not understand the words, of course, but they felt the warmth in the tone of her voice and that was what was vital. So Augustine had taught, and Augustine had always been right about nest etiquette.

Whatever happened, they must not get a hint of the betrayal ahead of them. In her the young nest had placed its trust, its hopes for successful reproduction.

And with that gentle tone she started to walk slowly, leading the vizier behind her down to the edge of the trees. They called this the "Pied Piper" walk, after the ancient myth of the piper in a small town of Europe who bewitched the town's rats and led them out to their destruction. The insects tumbled behind her, with warriors massed in dense divisions on the flanks and bringing up the rear, and workers mobbing around the queens and the vizier.

As she went she worked to dislodge the warriors on her skin, the so-called skin-guards. She flicked them off or brushed them away, one at a time, dropping them back into the dark mass that covered the ground about her feet. She missed a flick with one. The soldier got on her hand and bit and she winced and shook it away. There were still a few of them on her, especially on her hair; she would have to work fast when the moment came.

Now they reached the limestone and here they paused, milling about, uncertain and anxious. This was the horizon of the known world and their fate was to go beyond it, beyond anything the old nest had ever known. And what lay there?

Unknown.

Fair's practiced eye estimated there were upward of five thousand vizier in the small mass she had led out of the old nesting grounds. If they were captured with skill, there would be thirty or forty grains of pharamol here.

Eventually the chitin were ready to go on. She led the way across the wide, desertlike strip of limestone. Now was the time when they were most vulnerable to predators and to spying eyes far above, but this was an essential part of the process. The parent nest would not allow a new nest on its territory, and it was vital that it never know what happened to its colonization effort. This wide belt of empty limestone provided a perfect knowledge break.

The chitin followed her through the rocks and crannies and finally into the trees on the far side.

Here was the killing ground.

Wally could be seen just ahead, clad in the protective suit with the sprayer in his hands. Stook and Ronaldo and Reyanne were off to the left, sweepers at the ready.

The chitin filled up the space beneath the jik trees. Onward she led them, farther onto the strange territory. Questions bubbled among the insect mass. Here? Was this the new home promised by the helper? The soil tasted much the same as the soil of home, the trees were the same as the trees of home. This would be a good place, then.

Still the chitin were confused. This was new territory, unknown. The mass moved slowly, tentatively, but soon it was far beyond the limestone strip, beyond any contact with the old nest, lost in the world outside the known.

And now came the awful moment of betrayal, of the cruelest treachery. Fair signaled Wally to close in. When he moved, the others moved in, too. When they were just on the perimeter of the insect horde's perception zone, Fair picked her moment and hurled herself forward, leaping with long strides to get clear of the chitin massed beneath her feet.

As she went she batted away the soldiers that jumped onto her legs. She was stung, twice on the right leg and once on the left buttock, but despite a howl or two she was clear in a few moments, and basically unharmed.

The young nest that she'd abandoned was in turmoil, its line of march completely disturbed. A million or more insects swarmed this way and that.

Instead of Fair, Wally moved on them and a cloud of yellow gas gushed from the sprayer. In seconds the ground was littered with chitin in the death throes.

Horror, panic, frantic attempts at flight convulsed the chitin. Soldiers scattered outward, seeking to attack the enemy. A few reached Wally, clambered onto him, and bit furiously into the thick fabric of his clothing, but they were too few to produce any effect, and the yellow gas was death to them in moments. When Wally had slain the chitin on the ground he used puffs of gas to clean the last few soldiers off his suit.

The yellow gas was an oily vapor that subsided quite quickly and slowly blew away. All was still beneath it, but for an occasional wriggle among the dead soldiery.

Reyanne and the others were already at work, their sweepers humming as they sucked up the vizier chitin. In a few minutes the harvest was complete. They pulled the sweeper cans off and handed them to Fair, who set off back to the camp to begin the process of claiming the communication proteins.

Finally, they swept up the corpses of workers, soldiers, and queens and pushed them into a tidy pile. Wally sprinkled them with some distillate. In a few moments they were ablaze on their funeral pyre.

3

NIGHTS IN THE MOUNTAINS WERE SPECTACULAR. THE SKIES GLITtered beneath the sprawling vault of the heavens. The air was cool and very dry, and the stars barely flickered at all. Everything was harsh and sharp and crystal clear.

Fair and Reyanne sat out late, drinking the last of the good whisky. Stook, Wally, and the rest were in the tents, asleep. In the morning they would be at work on their own nests; everyone had nest duty.

Out in the jik forest a biskoon uttered its occasional sobbing wail. Somewhere farther away a bull gzan announced that he was in rut with the characteristic booming call that echoed off the crags.

"Well, here's to a good season, Rey. I want you to know that I was very thankful you came up this time. We really need you here. I really need you here."

Reyanne was faintly surprised. Fair was not one to say things like this. Admittedly the whisky was good—it came from Trader Erst's and was called "Scotch" because of the peat overtones that someone got out of his fabrimek. Still, she hadn't seen Fair unwind this far in a long time. Fair had always been tightly wrapped.

"Well, it's good to be needed," she said after a moment. "Besides, if I stay down there too long I get tangled up with all these men."

They laughed. Hell of a problem, men.

"Sometimes I think men are an addiction or something," Reyanne said.

"In your case, sweet, I would agree."

Reyanne pouted. "Well, you've picked some stinkers, too, you know."

Fair shrugged. "Yeah, but nothing like Bernarde."

Reyanne giggled and almost fell out of her seat.

"Bernarde was wonderful, he was really sweet."

"Bernarde was the weirdest person I have ever met, Reyanne. You know he came on to me the very first night I met him, that time you made the dinner with the tilapia steaks? When you lived in the building by the lab."

Reyanne gave a little squeal of glee. "Oh, my. He was awful, wasn't he? But he was so enthusiastic in bed."

"Yeah, I know, you were young and all that."

"And horny as hell. I drank too much—that was my trouble. I'd meet these men when I was drunk and wake up involved with them."

"You just never learned to say 'no' on that second day."

"I am perfectly capable of asserting myself," Reyanne said in mock bluster.

Fair disagreed. "No you're not. I've seen you simpering over them weeks after you should have kicked them out."

Reyanne sighed. Fair gestured with the bottle in her hand.

"You have to move fast when it comes to men or else they stick to you. They're covered in emotional adhesive, it's quite disgusting."

Reyanne rolled her eyes. "Space! How many times have I had this lecture from you, Fair?"

"Well—" Fair stared up at the distant stars. "—I suppose I am a little hard on them."

"And then there's Hof," Reyanne said with a a light tone of malice.

Fair flashed her a look. "Hof's great, I've learned so much from him."

"Look, I know Hof is great, he's the sweetest man I'll ever meet, but Hof doesn't need a computer, he *is* a computer."

Fair smiled. "Not all the time, Rey."

"Well, I knew there had to be something more than talking about chitin chemistry between you."

They both giggled again and shifted off the subject. Fair wouldn't admit it but Hof had become very special to her. She didn't like to be vulnerable in that way.

"So how long will you stay down there?" Fair asked.

"Until after the wet. I'll come back then, run old Nest One for you if you like."

"And you'll stay with your sister?"

"At the Barricades, yeah, you know the place. I'm sure you came to a party there once."

Fair had a confused memory of a young person's apartment and lots of other young people with drinks in their hands and voices raised loud. "I think so, it was a long time ago."

"Well, I'll be there most of the time."

"I'll call you when I get in, in the wet."

"You should leave now; it'll be raining in less than a week. Why wait? You don't have any nests left that will give this season."

"Rey, you know I can't leave yet. Wally and Stook are still finding their way. Wally might have a giving nest next season with that Lower Redrock nest. It's close. Dodacatrienol levels are way up high for a nest that young. Already signs of advanced heptatones—maybe Wally's going to be a natural."

"His prime test scores were high, right?"

"Not that great, Wally's no genius. But he can empathize, even with bugs."

"Natural bugman." They both smiled.

"Could be, in which case we'll have a replacement for Tyler at last."

"Tyler still working for the Spreaks?"

"He was the last I heard. I don't expect to hear much from that direction anymore."

Another man who had passed through Fair Fundan's emotional life in a brief, burning month-long passion, before fleeing.

"If Wally's that good, then with you and me we could run ten nests on this site."

"Two seasons and retire."

"Retire?"

"Yeah, it's getting too dangerous in this line of work."

Reyanne was surprised to hear this. "No raider's ever come up here. We're eight hundred kilometers from the settlement."

"Hof told me some alarming things, Rey. We don't want to die out here."

Reyanne finished the whisky in her glass.

"No, we don't. You're damned right about that. So what are you afraid of that I don't know about?"

"Arvin Erst, who else?"

"But EASU needs us. They're all using pharamol. Why would they fund raids? If anything could curtail supplies it would be raiding."

"Who knows what Erst is involved in? Face it, Reyanne, we don't know much about what goes on down on the coast these days. But I hear the worst things about EASU. They kill without regard to any laws, even their own."

"But Erst is our friend. I mean, surely he would be killing the golden goose if he was behind any raids."

"Maybe, but Hof was certain. He's seen things, I don't know what, exactly, but he says the evidence is in. Erst has been backing raiders for more than a year."

Reyanne sank into herself. A fear that she would rather not have admitted to was making her tremble.

"Erst is a powerful enemy to have. If EASU were to back the raiders overtly then we'd really have our backs to the rock. But at the same time, when this becomes generally known, then EASU will be finished up here. I mean, nobody will deal with them—they'll be cut off."

"Except for what they can get by raiding."

"And the Spreaks will try to kill him."

Fair nodded in agreement. "They've got their scores to settle. Old Ervil will want blood."

"It makes it seem so crazy. Erst would be destroying his own access to pharamol."

"Hof says that it's all part of a grand plan. Erst has enough of a power base down in EASU to take control, maybe set himself up as a dictator. He works hard to project that folksy, friendly image up here. We never see the other side, except for all those bodyguards he always has around him."

"Not always, Fair. You know it's just for when he's in public. He's got a lot of enemies."

"And he's the meanest, toughest bastard of them all, which should make you naturally suspicious."

"Perhaps it should. Perhaps I've gotten a little too close to it in this one."

"Erst backs the raids and he gets half the take. You know when they hit Axel's group they got enough for a half gram of pharamol. Think how it could add up for Erst. A raid like that happens every month now."

Reyanne felt sick. How could she find out for sure? She had to know. She had friends down there, EASU people. She dealt with them regularly. "Well, you're right then, we all have to retire. I'm not doing this so I can die young, that's for sure."

"Anyone who thinks standing up to their neck in bugs is work just doesn't understand, eh?"

They laughed together.

"Whisky's gone."

"Shit."

"Yeah, well, time to sleep, I guess. You need to make an early start. Get over the scree slope before it gets really light."

"Yeah, you're right." Reyanne looked around her, soaking up the feel of the high country. The cold stars blazed down.

"It's so beautiful up here, still so wild."

Fair hugged herself against the night wind. "We have to try and keep it that way. That's our task now, and for the future."

Reyanne broke away and went to her tent. Fair turned in and slept uneasily, plagued by dreams of raiders, dreams she'd had far too many times already.

4

Evening on the Coast in this season was usually a slow-motion pointillist display. The sun, lost in the red haze, eventually sank below the horizon and the temperature dropped a few degrees from tropical hell to tropical purgatory. Fortunately, the season was about to change—the monsoon rains would begin any day now. As a result, the heavy air was filled with an extra charge, almost a physical longing for the rain and the release of the tension.

That morning Martin Overed had woken with a vague feeling of impending doom. A sixth sense was at work, just a vague unformulated feeling, a distant rain cloud, invisible in the murk of the day's beginning, but heading toward him nonetheless.

This feeling had been there when he'd woken up, and it didn't go away, even when he'd chased off the hangover from the night before with a little hit of a stim inhaler. There'd been one too many cold lager beers, it seemed. There often were.

Something bad was coming down. Something really bad.

Of course, he was guilty as hell, he knew he had it coming. He'd taken advantage too many times. But it was the "temptations," he just wasn't that good at resisting them.

Like the lovely Nadali, now that was a temptation with a capital T. When he watched her undress for him in the darkened room he tended to forget the stuff about temptations and trouble. When he slid into her and closed his hands about her incredibly attractive glutei maximi, he forgot about everything except pure sensation.

Nadali was a weakness. So were funkshun and booze. Martin had too many weaknesses. He also had a lot of enemies. Inevitably he was going to have a date with major trouble. If he had been in any other line of work, it would not have been so important. But keeping the peace for the Big Man was demanding; you couldn't afford slipups over the little temptations life set before you.

Still, for all this apprehension in his gut, the day passed uneventfully. The surfboat races in the afternoon brought him a couple of winners and a placer. He played squash, had lunch at Thurcy's, and at three he attended the customary daily meeting at the EASU Social Hall. All the enforcers were there. The reports showed an uncommonly peaceful day in the Quarters, and it looked like it might even be a quiet evening.

But later, the little cloud of worry hoved up on the horizon again, sat there, and wouldn't go away. Martin had a good sixth sense; he was a wary hoodlum. He listened to that sense. He took precautions, avoided front doors, walked the lower tunnels, and kept his eyes open for tails.

Finally the trouble came up and whispered in his ear down in the Blue Zero, a drinking spot run by the Arab.

The evening was still early, the red glow still visible in the west. Far away in the swamp, animals were shrieking in their customary fashion. An alley rat named Xipmin moved close to him at the bar.

"Messire Overed, hello. Word is out that Hidoko is really pissed off with you."

Martin's brow furrowed. He was tempted to tell the gook to piss off, but he restrained himself.

"I know that—what's it to you?"

"What're you drinking?" Xipmin asked next.

Martin stared at him. Who did Xipmin think he was, trying to buy drinks for an enforcer for the Big Man?

"Look, I don't take drinks from . . ."

"Gooks? Hey, I know that, but you're gonna need one when you hear what I'm gonna tell you. So what'll it be?"

Martin's distaste cut into his voice.

"I got plenty of chink friends, don't give me that 'gook' shit. I don't think like that."

"Sorry, Overed, I thought you were like all the EASUs."

"Look, Xipmin, those days are over, you know that. EASU is making an effort to include everybody."

Xipmin gave him a look that implied that Xipmin knew he was just saying that because he had to.

"Of course, EASU loves everyone. But you will want a drink. Do yourself a favor. What'll it be?"

Martin stared at the smaller man for a long ten seconds and

then relented. "All right, Arab's best brandy. Small one, it's still early."

"They said you were a drinking man, ne?"

"What does that mean?" Martin wasn't going to listen to any crap from this little street hustler.

"You need heavy fuel, eh? Burn up a lot of energy in your work."

"So what? I work hard and I play hard."

Xipmin grinned, though it was hard to say whether there was any humor behind the grin. "Yeah, I know how hard you work, Overed. I saw the way you trashed up that refridge man on the Soak. That place was done in with a touch of genius."

"So what's it to you?"

The Arab slid another glass of his finest super XO, one with a distinctive scent of oak and caramel, across the bartop. Martin took a sip. It was early in the evening, people didn't normally buy him drinks, and he normally wouldn't have accepted it. Nobody had anything on Martin Overed except the Big Man. But everything was telling him that this wasn't normal.

"The word I got, Overed, is that the Big Man is gonna lift his hand on you."

Martin felt a chill run down his back. The taut face of Xipmin leaned closer. Martin could smell the little rat, all sweat and cheap perfume.

"I heard that you really pissed him off at last."

"Get out of here," Martin snarled and pushed back from the bar. "Go tell Hidoko to fuck himself."

Martin walked away. In the back room, under a senso field, he called the usual number.

The pick-up was too quick. A cool robot voice told him to leave a message. Disaster crashed into place. He babbled the time and place, delivered a short report on the meeting that afternoon, and hung up, devastated.

The Big Man didn't pick up his call.

It was true. The Big Man had lifted his hand. No protection existed now for a certain slightly-too-prominent enforcer working the dusty puffcrete alleys of the Hospital Quarter.

The Big Man had found out? But how? Who knew of his little maneuver involving a hundred grains of pharamol?

Nadali? How could she have found out? Unless she'd put a bug on him somewhere along the line. Hell, he always showered with the care of a fanatic after a session with any female. They could always put something on you and then you'd be broadcasting in living color for someone else's amusement and profit. He always scrubbed. He ran his clothes through a checker, he took every precaution.

But someone had gotten to him. How else could the Big Man know? He would've sworn he hadn't told Nadali, unless she'd gotten it out of him while he was asleep.

He had only been drunk around her that one time. He knew that that was one thing you didn't do in his position. That was how Eddy Dinbok bought it. Martin remembered it well.

Drinking made you say stuff that got you killed, and on the New Essex Coast, women just about inevitably carried bad news to those who would kill you on account of it. Martin thought it had to be some kind of biological law, this routine of treachery between the sexes.

None of which helped him with the problem. And he had a hell of a problem. He needed the Big Man. In the EASU-dominated city of New Essex Coast there was no such thing as an ex-enforcer.

And, hell, the Big Man needed him, too. Surely he could be persuaded of that? A rift over a few grains? It was too small a loss, too inconsequential a thing to waste a good man for. Still, Martin wanted that drink now. He wanted to hide somewhere and drink himself into oblivion.

He licked his lips. He couldn't do that, that would be suicidal. He had to straighten out and he had to hide and he had to work out what the hell he was going to do.

Nadali was out. If she was the source, then the Big Man knew all about her. Hell, he probably had video of them in the act.

He tried to think clearly. Panic at this point could be deadly. But a sense of panic kept rising in his chest nonetheless. First, get safe, then work out a way to get to the Big Man. That was what he had to do, he had to get to the Big Man somehow, then pitch his case. He had to get this turned around. Otherwise he was dead meat. He went back to the bar.

The Arab was solicitous. Xipmin was gone.

"You have a big trouble, my friend."

"I don't understand this."

"The Big Man, he lift his hand from you. Sometimes this happens in a young man's career and he survives. The hand is replaced upon his shoulder. He goes on and the Big Man is re-warded for his patience and his insight. But that does not happen often, so I advise you to put your affairs in order. Do you have a will?"

Martin got on the move. He pushed out of the Blue Zero and headed away from Hospital Plaza and onto Soak Alley. It was hot and muggy outside, and the old tenements on the alley threw occasional beams of yellow light onto the pavement. The thrum of tenement air conditioners labored in the darkness.

He needed to hole up somewhere nobody knew about. It was time to use his hidden ace.

Martin looked around carefully as he moved. An insect zapped itself on an attractor up above and he jumped at the sound. Fragments fell into the street. His hand was already on his gun. He expelled a breath. Space, but he was tense! He had too many enemies, and without the Big Man's protection, he was naked to them now.

He paused at the junction to Boat Slip. Ahead was a jumbled mass of old buildings in considerable disrepair. Rotten puffcrete, gone soft with alien fungus, was flaking off the frames. At street level the outdoor market in Spreak Street was a blaze of lights, with neon strip and senso amid hard white. A mass of shoppers moved around the stalls and stores.

On the other side of the slip the slum alleys were dim mouths in the tropical darkness. He fled on. He thought he was doing well at this point. He thought he might get to Mari's place without any trouble. He was starting to think positive thoughts. Maybe he could stay low for a while then negotiate his way back into favor. Thankfully, he had plenty of credit and at least two accounts that the Big Man couldn't know about. He could stay out of sight for a long time.

He climbed a fence by the old sewage canal and ran down the concrete strip that marked where the canal was buried. Looming above and behind him were new tenement towers built on stilts over the canal and the warehouses that lined it. Ahead lay a channel that carried wastewater away from the kelp-processing plant that bulked ahead like some gigantic beetle, lit up here and there by brights on the three refract-towers.

The concrete broadened here into a wide wharftop streaked with oil and rust stains. The only light came from the security overheads at the warehouses.

Beyond the kelp plant was his destination, a slum of old temporary domes that had been rendered permanent by overcrowding. Here lived the Roiders, the people of the Ceres ships, refugees from centuries before who'd arrived packed solid in suspended animation in front of a plasma drive. They'd arrived with nothing in the way of useful goods and little in common with the Earthers and Saturns who made up the majority of the colony then. So they'd ended up here, stuck in dome slums on the edge of the swamp.

Of course, this was dangerous territory for an EASU man, especially one with a rep like Martin Overed. But his enemies would never think to look for him in here, in the slum domes.

He started across the paving beside the channel. There was a footbridge about a hundred meters farther on inland. His shoes scuffed some broken puffcrete. The sound seemed loud all of a sudden. Figures stepped out of the shadows beneath the footbridge.

"Well, if it isn't my frien' Overed," someone said.

He recognized the voice. It was Vinh Toc, a small-time chump killer with a pocket gang that ran errands for Hidoko.

There were three of them, including a huge man named Thurlow, a renegade EASU who ran with Toc's gang. The third was a knifeboy; Martin didn't know his name but he'd seen him around. How good he was with his blade was also unknown.

But it was Thurlow who had Martin worried. Thurlow was huge and unusually mean.

"What do you want, Toc?"

"What do I want? I don't want nothing from you, but someone who's paying me does."

"Hidoko?"

"Now, I'm not playing any guessing games with you, EASU boy. We just gonna set you down now and cut off the part the man wants."

"Oh, yeah? And what part is that?"

Toc giggled. "Your head, stupid, what else?" Toc had a gun out, a little silvery thing.

No room to maneuver. Martin shifted into gear. There was a reason he'd lasted six years as one of the Big Man's top enforcers. He knew how to fight. Unfortunately, his gun was inside his shirt. No time to reach it.

He concentrated that extra degree that always seemed to freeze time and space for him. Then he uncoiled, striking with terrific speed. His jab took Toc on the mouth and he fired wide, the bullet whining off the concrete and heading out into the swamp.

Martin wasn't going to get any further breaks like that, but he was already in motion the other way, spinning on his right foot and connecting with his left, kicking the gun out of Toc's hand long before he could recover.

Toc let out a howl of woe and cupped his bleeding mouth. Thurlow thrust forward and hit Martin in the ribs with a crunching right hand. Martin backpedaled frantically; still no time to draw. He picked off the next punch with his forearm and deflected a heavy kick aimed for his crotch. Thurlow was ponderous but he had power. Every time he touched you he hurt you.

Meanwhile, the knifeboy was circling, vibrablade in his hand. Martin could almost feel that damn thing slicing into his back. Cutting through the spine to leave him paralyzed.

Thurlow was coming. A big right hand forced Martin to duck. The knifeboy cut at him then and he dodged, but Thurlow got him with a solid left to the chest that felt like it was breaking ribs and lifted him off his feet. Martin went down, rolled, and came up in a crouch. He wasn't breathing, and he wasn't sure how he was managing to stand up.

Vinh Toc was crawling toward his gun. There was no time for any of this. He had to have his own gun. He went for it, reaching behind himself, but his arm felt as heavy as a piece of lead.

Knifeboy came in, blade singing. Martin had his hand on the gun butt, but it was not in time. The blade sang into his left arm, grating on bone with a most peculiar sensation as he grabbed the gun. Then the knifeboy was falling backward, his guts blown out, and Martin whipped the gun barrel over to land on Thurlow's meaty Anglo-Saxon nose. He pulled the trigger and Thurlow ceased to be.

The gun cracked twice more and Vinh Toc stopped crawling toward his gun. It was over, for now. He took stock.

Blood was running out of his arm and onto the concrete. He noticed with a curious sense of calm that there was little pain, just the numbing shock of seeing right into his own exposed flesh. He was lucky—knifeboy had taken the blade with him when he flew backward. Another nanosecond and his whole arm would have been on the concrete.

A wave of nausea shivered through him. He fought it down. Blackout here meant death. Feverishly, he slipped out a stimtube and took the whole thing, neckshot. His eyeballs bugged in his head and he shook hard for a few seconds as it took effect and the blood pounded through his system.

Then he took the vibrablade and cut a length out of the brown spylo jacket on the blade boy. With this he tied off the wound as tight as he was able. He would die of blood loss unless he got somewhere where he could find erythrogrowth real fast. Mari didn't have that, of course—Martians didn't have anything. She'd have to go out and get it for him. Salkander would have it, no questions asked, at the back door of the hospital.

But first he had to move; the shots would draw attention. The EASU enforcement arm would be on the scene in a few moments. He turned and staggered away.

To get to the other side of the kelp plant suddenly seemed impossible. There were fences to climb and his arm was useless. In addition, he ached wherever Thurlow had landed a blow.

At the edge of the concrete platform he looked back. A few heads were visible in windows up above, and he heard someone yelling about the gunfire. Another voice answered the first. He slipped off the platform and fell into the water with a heavy splash. Surfacing, he kicked off his shoes and swam, sidestroke, slowly, down the channel and out into the tepid delta waters. He kept his wounded arm above the surface for the most part. Still, he knew he was leaving blood in the water.

This was not a good place to swim—he knew that, too. The creatures of the swamp gathered here to feast on whatever came down the channel. Heavy-bellied permiads would be cruising here. If they caught up with him they'd rip him to pieces.

Back on the concrete dock there were lights and people. An ambulance was coming, its sirens wailing down Spreak Street.

His hand struck mud. Soft and clinging, deep and stinking. His arm went into it; then he was kneeling on it, sinking in an inch or two. Something big and wormy slithered out beneath him. He crawled up the slope of muck and out of the water. It stank. The tide was out. Tidal worms moved around on the mud. If he lay here too long they'd gather to eat him. He had to get back into motion.

Suddenly he noticed a flash on the water as a fin crested and disappeared. He shivered. The permiads were out there—they'd picked up his trail. If he hadn't come ashore they'd be eating him right now.

Behind him the concrete seawall stood six meters high and beyond his strength to climb. He had to walk along beside it, aiming into a dark, unknown distance. His arm felt as if it were made of lead, while his head felt light and airy. It was almost as if someone else were piloting his legs.

His luck lay with the tide. That it was out meant he was able to walk past the kelp plant and around the curve of the landfill on which the builders had flung up these cheap domes. Eventually he came to a sloping mound of rocks laid up against the concrete seawall. Here they were building a new dike to wall off another polder, which they would fill with garbage and detritus to create more land, an incredibly scarce commodity in the colony.

It was a struggle, but he managed to haul himself up the rocks to the top. He sat down and, with his back to the outer wall of a shabby dome, briefly lost consciousness.

He awoke again. Nothing had changed. He was covered in mud and blood and he stank and he was dying. Mari was his only hope. He hoped he could find her address in the dome park.

He took another stim shot and got to his feet. He swayed there for a moment, and then stumbled forward.

Kids playing in a back alley ran away from him with shrieks of horrified amusement. Then they threw rocks after him until he vanished around the curve of the dome. Luckily they were into their game at that point and they did not pursue him. He avoided the lights, and was fortunate not to meet any further groups of youths. A gang of teenagers would have been lethal at this point. He was easy prey.

At the top of the next walk he saw it: the big yellow number 17 stenciled on a dome's exterior wall.

Somehow he got there and slipped inside. The light was dim as he remembered. The elevators were out; they never worked anyway. In the stairwells he disturbed a couple of kids having sex. They cursed him for the disgusting smell he brought with him. He apologized and left them to their devices.

Mari's door, number 402, floated before him at last. The stim was wearing off fast and he was wobbling around, very close to the end.

Mari opened the door, her face creased in astonishment. "Martin! What have they done to you?"

He was falling. It was time to fall. He slipped into oblivion.

5

When he awoke it was with a vague feeling of the miraculous. He was still alive. Mari, bless her dumb little Roider ass, must have worked out what to do.

His arm was still attached! He breathed a huge sigh of relief. Having to go through a regrowth in the tank would have been impossible—he'd have ended up with a prosthetic of some kind, attached to a stump.

No amputation, so he'd beaten the gangrene. He calmed himself, and took stock of the situation. He was naked and he was clean. There was a huge erythropad taped to his chest. Tubes ran into his arm alongside a drip feed from an overhead plasma bottle. Mari's tiny apartment had become an intensive-care ward with a single patient.

Over the wound on his arm was a medipac, regulating the red-filled tubes from the erythropad as they passed into his arm. Blue seals on the top pockets had drug tabs attached. He scanned the tabs and learned that he was being given a pair of antibiotics and a cocktail of cell-growth boosters. Since he felt virtually no discomfort from the thing, he assumed he was also getting some pretty wonderful painkillers on top of it all.

Mari's apartment had never seemed smaller. He was lying on her bed, surrounded by her scant possessions and a ton of medical clutter: bags and tubes and small winking instruments. The erythropad made a slow sucking sound every so often as a valve popped open inside. The med pad on his arm was warm and emitted a high whine most of the time.

He'd made it, so far.

Mari came in a few moments later. Short, dignified in her slight, slim body, with that Roider way of becoming completely still while holding the head lowered.

"I'm so glad you're alive," she said, and reached down to touch and kiss him.

"I bet. Tough to get rid of a body these days."

"Not so hard. We could tip you into the canal and the fish would eat you in no time."

He grunted and coughed, and that hurt. He had bandages on his ribs. That big bastard Thurlow had possessed genuine hands of stone.

"You got the job done, Mari. I thank you."

Mari knew she'd just received a compliment from Martin Overed's limited canon of such. "It was expensive, but I knew what you needed."

"Where'd you go, Salkander?"

"At the hospital, yes, he sell me the blood thing and told me to get plasma in Spreak Street."

No medics, then. He sighed in relief. They'd question every medic on the islands. They'd turn the whole Coast over looking for him.

"You did well, kid. You saved ol' Martin's life."

She blushed and looked down. "You were filthy, covered in mud."

This was her way of asking a question. He knew he didn't have to answer, but he owed her. "Look, Mari, Martin got big trouble. I won't lie to you, you figured it out already."

"They cut you bad, Martin."

Without a medic to sew up the wound she'd been forced to seal it herself and pack it with skin-gro. Martin would have a huge, ugly scar as a result.

So what? He was alive, wasn't he?

"I had to come to you. Smart girl, you knew what to do."

"I remember, Martin, you came here one time before and I help you."

"Yeah, you were good to me. I pay your rent for two years for that."

She smiled. For someone at the bottom of the economy, having a rent-paid place was tantamount to riches.

"You've earned a good reward, girl."

"Thank you, Martin. Is there anything more I can do for you?"

He struggled to sit up and immediately felt a little queasy. He settled for raising his head and fixing her with as intense a glare as he could manage. "Keep this tight. No talking to anyone, not even your mama. You know that already but I have to repeat it. If word gets out then they'll know where to come to kill me."

She nodded. She knew that this was his bolt-hole, his secret safe place. "They will have to tear apart the whole city before they find you here. Nobody in the dome knows who you are and I clean up the hallway as soon as I could, after you came here. I don't think anyone on the corridor noticed. No one has said anything to me and I think they would have. Everyone here is very sensitive, you know how it is, Martin."

Proud people, suddenly very poor, struggling to survive on the economic margins of the tightly packed colony. In the Asteroid days, they'd been the elite. But as the Earth's economy began to collapse under the effects of overpopulation and environmental breakdown, the social synthesis movement had arisen from the ashes of old-line communist dreams. The Roiders had skipped out of the home system ahead of the social synthesis and undergone a voyage of centuries in deep freeze, only to wind up as the underclass on the New Essex Coast.

He could trust her; Mari knew that, if they found him, they'd kill her, too. Space, but Hidoko would kill her entire family! All the neighbors, blow the dome. Hidoko had a famous old-style Japanese temper. Losing three men and his prey was going to send him into a pure volcanic rage.

And Hidoko wasn't the only higher-up who'd be hunting for Martin Overed. Lawler and even the Big Man himself would want to know what had happened.

Of course, it was always possible that he'd gone into the canal and been devoured by permiads and crabs. They'd have searched the canal right away, maybe even dynamited it to kill the permiads so they could be gathered and their stomach contents checked. Hidoko was always very thorough. In EASU it was expected.

He sighed. He was safe for now, though. He relaxed a little more. He was hungry, and more than hungry. Nutriboost and the erythropad could only take a person so far.

"You know what I need?" he said, giving her the look.

She smiled demurely, with a little glint in her eyes. "You always need that. Martin, you need more sex than any man I have ever known."

"You only knew Martians, girl. I'm EASU, you know. Come here and get some of the real, bloody thing."

She giggled, and obeyed.

Later she brought him food. Synthetics, the usual mix of protein cake and pita bread, with savories and pickle. It didn't matter that it was bland; he ate as if he hadn't eaten in ten days.

Thereafter he made plans.

The communicator was out. Sure, he could call the Big Man and try to plead his case, but that would tip them off that he was still alive, and if the Big Man wanted him dead there would be a tremendous search. They might even rip apart the Roider quarter.

He thanked his lucky star that he had kept Mari in the background. She'd been worth every credit. Disappearing was not only good for the defense, it also gave him the opening he needed for offense. If they thought he was dead and gone then they would loosen up a little. The Big Man and his intimates were always on guard, that was how they stayed alive. Nobody outside of that innermost circle even knew where the Big Man was at any moment in time.

Martin Overed certainly didn't know such secrets. His access to the Big Man had been limited to the phone line, his loyalty obtained by the promise that the Big Man would always pick up when he called his coded number. Now he was cut off from everything.

But Martin did have one ace in the hole. He knew the secret of Slovo Milsuduk, one of the Big Man's innermost circle.

Milsuduk was known to have a lot of influence with the Big Man. He was also a man who had succumbed a little too much to the temptations of life. He had a male lover in a condo tower on Beachfront Terrace. Martin had discovered it almost by accident, a lucky break that had delivered a choice, and now perhaps quite vital, piece of information.

So first he would get well. He would rest up here and plan this thing out with meticulous care. By staying low for a long time perhaps he would find things even more relaxed. Even Hidoko would have to be comforted by the thought that Overed had fallen to the fish.

And then later, when he was perfectly ready, he would strike.

6

N'KA OF EMOKI WAS THE MALE FEIN CUB OF SHTINGI AND HER lover Bakut. Shtingi came from a famous line of artistic females. Her grandmother, Gumida, had made a dramatic series of ceremonial aprons that began the Gumida school of such work.

N'ka himself grew up in Shtingi's yard, for her relationship with Bakut did not last long. Bakut eventually died in a quarrel over another female, and N'ka knew little of him as a result. During his lifetime B'kobi, known as "Graytop," served as his father in residence, for he and Shtingi were bonded for many years.

N'ka was tall and strong for his age and, most remarkably, he was quiet and purposeful, quite unlike the boisterous majority of cubs. His strength was legendary. He was the first and the last eight-year-old to throw an adult's kifket clear across the village fish pond. He was respected for his strength and skill in all their games and sports. His mother knew that he was a remarkable one from an early age.

"So unlike the father!" she would say. "Bakut was beautiful, but he was no strongfein. He was no hunter either, he was just very good at sex. You now how it is, eh?"

Most of her friends agreed with her about Bakut. The general opinion of that ne'er-do-well was "sexy but worthless."

But N'ka was something else. Strong as stone, durable as well-cured hide, stubborn as a gzan in season, Shtingi said of him. N'ka might have gone on to become that rarity in Fein village life, a genuine male village leader. Destiny, however, intervened. In the tenth year of his life, he discovered that which changed him forever and turned him away from the narrowpath life.

In Emoki Village the Fein were tradition-bound. The pace of life was slow and moved with the gentle rhythm of the seasons in the equatorial mountains, monsoon followed by dry season followed by monsoon followed by dry season. So it had been since the beginning of the remade world and the birth of the Ay Fein themselves.

Ten-year-old Fein were at a difficult stage in life. No longer cubs, they were not yet adults, either. Having youths aged nine through eleven around the village guaranteed trouble. Thus, they were normally given the task of following the local herds of gzan, keeping an eye on these ultimate sources of food and raw materials.

Gzan were not domesticable, but they did not stray far from their home territories, and thus the Fein could harvest them as they saw fit while maintaining the village in one location for years at a time.

This duty kept the nine-, ten-, and eleven-year-olds out of the village and out of the sorts of trouble they would inevitably get into if they were there. They spent long days trailing the gzan up and down their routes through the valley. Only during the monsoon were they allowed home.

Thus N'ka was with his normal cronies, Ny'pupe Hubugeni, who was also ten, and Uban and Ky'pupe, the twins of Kosmet Duka. They were a long way up the deep little valley of Zenaboni, following the Sansa Pool herd. The herd had a young bull close to prime who had so far resisted the efforts of the patriarch, the premier bull, to drive him away. The young bull sensed that the old bull might be weakening. The presence of the young bull made the rest of the herd edgy and overactive. The females were torn this way and that by their own hormones. The presence of the young bull with his shining nose crowns made them noisy and skittish on the one hand, and maternally anxious on the other. Most had calves and were concerned for their safety.

The pod leader had chosen to lead the herd on a long trek up the Zenaboni with its shanked course and steep rocky sides. The only feed up here was rotifex and spine tuber, and the young shoots on the jik trees. But the premier bull was less intent on the forage than on the young bull.

Above the Zenaboni in a cleft between the hills was the old bull's favorite battleground, a flat pan where a shallow lake formed during the monsoons and evaporated soon afterward. It was a good, wide space where he could employ all the tricks and tactics he had learned in his life, and really give the young bull a drubbing that would send him away once and for all.

The young Fein knew better than to try and follow the

Sansa herd along the rocky streambed. In the tunnel formed by the branches of the jik and liskal trees, they would be sensed by the bulls and ambushed. To the ill-tempered bulls a successful ambush of the maddening ghosts they always sensed nearby would be irresistible.

This meant the Fein had to keep to the higher ground, above the steep slopes of the Zenaboni gorge, where the vegetation was thick and progress was difficult. It was tiresome work and N'ka and the others were hoping that, when the pod reached the Emoki pan, the old bull would finally decide that enough was enough and that the young bull had to go. Then the Sansa pod would turn back to the lake and the good grazing in the meadows above it. The gzan would stay there for several days and the young Fein would be able to hunt for subbits and ding jackal in the higher jik. There would be campfires and fresh meat and the chance to lay up during the day, because the gzan would not move.

"I know this old bull," said Uban, the confident one. "He is taking them all this way to tire the young bull. The old one knows that he has the greater stamina. When they get to the dried lake then he will beat the shit out of him."

"Lot of shit in that young bull," Ny'pupe Hubugeni said.

They were in agreement on this. All had been chased at some point by the young bull.

"Will be long fight."

The day wore on. They started to perspire under a relentless sun.

The first intimation of trouble came very suddenly from the front of the herd. There was a gzan scream from an older female; N'ka could not tell which one precisely, but it was one of the leaders, either Bucha or Sweets. The old bull let out a heavy snort-grunt and the young Fein knew at once that something was really up. The source of the commotion was on the other side of the stream and a quarter mile in front.

N'ka was the natural leader of the group, so he crossed the stream and climbed the other side to join Uban, who was posted there. He found Uban overlooking a steep-walled tributary gulley in which sprawled tumbled rock masses covered with weeping moss. Glob glob bushes grew along the sides.

The big gray shapes of gzan were just visible from this position, down the gulley, standing amid the rocks of the Zenaboni.

"What is it?" N'ka asked.

"I do not know. Listen to the bull."

There was the sound of a violent huffing and chuffing.

"He snorts in rage."

"Yes, but it does not sound like the rage of a bull with fear."

"What would a bull fear on the banks of the Zenaboni stream? There are no longlegs here, there are no nachri. And why would a bull fear anything but longlegs?"

"Bull fear Fein, everything fear Fein."

"*Muachad*, of course. But there are no Fein here except us."

"So the bull snorts at something other than Fein."

"Maybe it is an old trail."

"Maybe he sense a spirit."

"Up here? I have never heard of such a thing up here. The Zenaboni is not spirit stream."

"We must move closer, I think."

They signaled to Ny'pupe Hugubeni that they were moving down to investigate, then pushed forward, crossing the boulder-strewn canyon and climbing back up the other side, forcing their strong young bodies through the brush above. It was hard to move quickly and be silent, but they felt that, with the bull and his leading females making so much noise of their own, they would most likely go undetected.

The two Fein advanced out onto a spine of rock and soil that lay between the main stream and the sharp, V-cut valley of the tributary. Soon they drew level with the commotion.

Down below them, on one side, the old bull was raking through some undergrowth close to the stream. His huge nose horns were muddy from the work. Several females were standing behind him, urging him on with their own snorts and moans. Still there was no sign of what might have disturbed the gzan. N'ka and Uban kept their bodies bent down low, hidden in the tangle of jik and satursine scrub that crowned the narrow ridge between the tributary gulley and the wider valley.

Then N'ka noticed a movement in the gulley. Something was slowly, painfully crawling through the rocks. It was hidden from view by a patch of purple glob glob. N'ka felt the fur rise on the backs of his arms and neck. It was not Fein; it was not anything he was familiar with.

"Look there." He nudged Uban.

Uban's eyes widened.

"What the hell is it?" he asked.

"I've never seen anything like it."

"It must be a human!" Uban exclaimed with a gasp.

N'ka felt his pulse pound. Trust Uban to know. Of course that was what it was. One of the naked-skin things, the aliens from the outer space.

N'ka was stunned by the thought. An alien, right here in Emoki Valley. He knew they were to be found occasionally in the big valley, Ghotaw, but never had he heard of one way up here in the Emoki.

"It is hurt," he said. "It drags itself."

"The bull knows where it is. It is coming to crush the alien."

N'ka caught sight of its face for a moment. It was streaked with mud and blood, and the eyes were wide and staring. It was in desperate need of help.

N'ka moved. The bull was starting to follow the trail of the alien blood. It would soon catch up with this human and there would be a short, unpleasant scene.

N'ka was moved purely and simply by mercy, although his curiosity was strong. As his mother was wont to say, N'ka got himself into trouble more often by wishing to do good than by trying to wreak mischief.

He slipped down the rocks and fairly crashed into the glob glob right beside the human. His reward was a sharp shriek of fright as she whirled around to face him. N'ka sucked in a breath. The alien was a female. Her garments were torn to tatters and she was on the verge of collapse. Still, she held a small, glittering blade toward him, a kifket no bigger than a toothpick. Her face was contorted with fright, her teeth bared.

"Back off, *s'dramash, s'dramash!*" she shouted, holding up the tiny sliver of steel.

"You speak?" he said, completely stunned for a moment by this idea. Who would ever have thought that aliens from space could communicate like the Ay Fein?

N'ka stood there for but a moment. He realized he had acted impulsively without thinking all this through, just as Shtingi was always telling him.

"What do you want?" the woman asked, still keeping the knife pointed at him. He saw that her left side, above the hip, was the source of a heavy blood stain. N'ka waved a hand downstream to where the bull was making a lot of noise.

She was afraid, that much he sensed for certain. N'ka pointed up the gulley. *"Yavash!"* he said. It was time to hurry.

She shook her head sadly. "Not possible, I'm afraid."

She pulled aside the green denim shirt to show him the large wound in her side. There was a crude bandage over it, but a lot of blood had leaked around the edges. "No good, you see. Too weak."

The bull was coming. N'ka could hear its massive tread at the other end of the glob glob patch. There was no time to hesitate. He moved forward, knocked the little sliver of metal out of the way, grabbed the wounded human in both arms, lifted her off the ground to sling her over his shoulder.

She emitted another shriek, this time of pain.

The bull had decided to charge. It emitted the characteristic roar of ill-tempered triumph and began crashing toward them. N'ka went up the side of the gulley, holding the woman under one arm, grabbing small trees and pulling himself up the rocks. Stones slipped beneath his feet. He scrabbled at one point and almost lost his balance before he recovered, grabbed a branch, and steadied himself.

The bull arrived at the base of the cliff, posted itself up on its hind legs, and tried to reach him with those big nose crowns. But it was too late for that—N'ka was already beyond his reach. The bull was left to vent his rage on the rocks, and this he did, with prodigious noise.

The woman was unconscious when N'ka laid her down in front of Uban and the others.

"What shall we do with her?" Ky'pupe inquired, eyes very wide at the sight of this alieness.

"We had better take her back to the village," N'ka said.

"Will we get in trouble?" Ky'pupe asked, who was usually as lacking in confidence as his brother was brimming with it.

"I do not care," N'ka said quietly.

The others accepted this. N'ka would take the blame if blame there was to be.

"Kosmet Duka will know if it is right to keep this creature," Ky'pupe said.

"First it will have to survive. It has lost a lot of blood, I think." Uban sounded unusually pessimistic.

"Help me carry it, but be careful," N'ka said.

It was a slow journey because of their burden, and even N'ka was weary by the time they reached Emoki. It was dusk, and the brilliant mountain skies were dimming to purple-black, although the white caps on the mountains were still glittering in the setting sun.

7

HOF WITLIN STOOD BACK FROM THE FABRICATOR WITH TEARS IN his eyes. The machine was old but it was a beauty, Fundan-made, with the little blue logo on one corner of the front panel. It stood on four adjustable legs, a solid gray rectangle four feet tall, three feet wide, and a foot deep. With it you could make just about anything, as long as you could get the raw material reduced into slurry form for the assembler tech.

The machine was old, though, a lot older than Hof himself, and he already felt ungodly old at the age of fifty-nine. Carefully, with a feeling of genuine affection for the thing, he ran his fingers across the raised numbers on the front panel, 4416246668, and beneath them the small letters, "Assembler-Tek." Access ports broke up the top surface, and on the side was a slim little panel that could be raised to reach the unit's controls.

Unfortunately, they were no longer working.

Inside the simple exterior, the fabricator contained a set of Keidako assembler tanks and the complex chemical processes associated with each. On the other side was the output port. The small door that covered the output port had been taken off eighty years before by old Randolf Flecker himself, who was using the machine at the time to make spare parts for boat engines.

Hof Witlin knew nothing of this, although he was aware, in a vague way, that the machine had a long history. But now it was junk. Even with the Fundan software manuals to go by, Hof doubted he could fix the thing. Moisture had gotten inside that control unit a long time before, perhaps when the machine was still in use down on the Coast. The microcircuitry was damaged and it had finally given up the ghost. What was needed was an entirely new control module. Unhappily, the Fundans didn't make that sort of thing anymore.

But that was just the way it was now; the Fundans had lost

their technological roots. The older generation had been pretty useless. Only old Dane and his immediate entourage had kept the flame of technology alight and, with his passing, the old ways had disappeared for good.

Hof stared at it helplessly. The machine was broken, beyond his skill to repair. He was a protein man—proteins and chitin were all that he knew. Everything else was old tech and, even with guidance from the Fundan computer catalogues, he knew the repair was beyond his powers.

Hof Witlin wondered what the hell he was going to do now. He needed some small chem retorts but the machine was only producing a sludge of granulated glass from the sand inputs. With a soft groan, he turned away. It was crazy to get so emotional about an old machine, except that it was one of the last links to the old life, to the home system, to civilization itself.

Outside the window, the green meadows paved the foreground and beyond them the massive mountains soared to their sparkling white crowns. Hof shook his head and went down the hall to Delilah Spreak's office.

"Hmm?" she responded when he knocked.

"The fabricator's gone," he announced. "The assembler architecture is dead."

"Oh, dear, that does give us a problem."

"Don't see what we're going to do now. This has been coming for a long time; now we finally have to face the music."

"EASU?" she asked.

"We can't buy from them."

Delilah, who was generaly known as Dali, sighed. "We probably don't have a choice."

"They won't help us with something like this, I know it."

"Then what are we going to use for labwork? Can't do it all by computer. We need things, and we've relied on that fabrimek for decades."

"The entire lab will come grinding to a halt," Hof murmured to himself.

"We either get a new fabrimek or we buy everything from EASU."

"Nobody has new tech now, except the EASU and their ilk."

"Well, we need it. Everything up here depends on it in one way or another. We recycle all our medical equipment through it—how are we going to make system boost without that machine? We've got problems that will force us to talk to EASU."

Hof saw that these unpleasant options were just about all that were open to them.

"Damn," he said bitterly. "Looks like we're fucked." He headed for the door.

"Where are you going?" asked Dali.

"Down the Trader's. I want a drink."

Delilah went with him. With all the tragic events of the last few months, she knew that Hof could get maudlin pretty quickly, and then he'd drink way too much. She didn't know if her being there with him would deter him or not, but it was almost lunchtime anyway, and it was certainly worth a try.

The Trader's loomed ahead, a dirty white dome surrounded by rough-hewn, single-story wooden buildings, with heat transformers jutting out of the walls like giant tennis rackets. Inside, Dali got him to pass up the barstools and take a small table by a window. If she got him to eat then she might succeed in keeping him at least halfway sober.

Trader's was an outgrowth of the original Trade Post, set up thirty years before on the flat expanse of bare ground near the laboratory complex. The Trader then had been Saki, a sharp-eyed woman from the Neptune ships. She'd sold out eventually, under pressure from an EASU gang.

Like the rest of the settlement, Trader's had changed a lot under the EASU people. It was much bigger; they'd added two large rooms, one on either side of the original dome. It was always crowded, too, like the lawless streets outside.

And like those streets it never closed. There was constant activity that would have been forbidden just a few years before. But, now, all the old restrictions had been thrown out, along with tons of trash. The place was already an eyesore: hundreds of buildings, domes, flattops, inflatables, tents sprawled across the southern slopes of the old volcano. The airstrip thundered with transports day and night.

The settlement was a lawless place, filled with desperate people, fueled by an explosive greed that drove people to do the damnedest things, anything at all that might help get them some of the precious longevity drugs. Extortion and murder were commonplace. Pollution and poor sewage disposal were already causing an unpleasant stench to waft from the stream that cut through the site. Indigestible trash, scrap metal, junk plastic, and ceramics were scattered around the margins. It was a real boom town, all right.

With the boom had come a terrible security problem for the

laboratory. They had had to hire a team of guards to patrol the place and keep out infiltrators and thieves. People would steal just about anything that could be carried away.

When the waiter came, Hof ordered whisky. They made it at the bar in faithful reproduction of the great style that had evolved on Earth in a place now known as Euro Nord-Twelve.

Things were getting downright awful, he thought, but at least there was always the Trader's "Scotch." The bar's blender was another piece of ancient hardware, something that had come out of a workshop on Mars centuries ago. If it ever broke down then Trader's customers would be reduced to his vodka, or the evil beer made in the yeast tank from an unholy slop of garbage slurry and water.

Dali ordered sesame burgs for both of them and a drink made from the native glob glob fruit. It was a favorite with the old colonists.

"You're letting it get to you," she said after a while.

"What the hell does it matter?" he growled.

"It matters a lot. It matters to me, Hof. We work together, have done for a while now. We work together well and we're making real progress. We've assembled the protein exterior."

"The inside is more complex than a lot of cells. I don't think we're ever going to replicate it."

That was close to blasphemous. Dali put her fingers to the middle of her forehead and squeezed her eyes shut. Hof saw it and burst out, "I can't help it, Dali. Hell, what right have you got to expect anything different? We're down to having to beg for labware, and we don't even have the fabricator anymore. The moment you leave the lab unguarded for five seconds some damned settler is in there stealing. In the settlement, there's gunfire and killings every day. Garbage all over, pollution going into the river . . . I mean, what's the point of carrying on?"

Hovering behind this, she knew, was grief for young Fair, missing now for months, since raiders hit the Blue Cliffs camp. Hers was the only body not recovered, although most had been attacked by chitin and reduced to bones. She was assumed to have died with the rest.

Hof and Fair had been lovers for a year or more, at least as far as Dali knew. Between herself and Fair there had always been that line between Fundans and Spreaks. It went back to the Khalifi war; the Spreaks had sided with the Khalifi against the Fundans, and that had never been forgotten. But Hof had loved Fair, and, as far as Delilah knew, Fair had seemed to love the old chemist back.

"The mission hasn't changed, Hof. We've still got to do it, otherwise there'll be a complete devastation of this planet. You know what's going to happen."

"I know already. It's going to be destroyed."

"Look, Hof, there are a hundred ships on their way here. There'll be a million people in twenty years. They'll destroy this environment to get the drugs."

"It's the curse on the colony, the longevity poison."

"Not if we can find the replicator! If we do that, we can give long life to all humanity at reasonable prices."

In recent months, Witlin had become less sanguine about their chances of success. Even before the Blue Cliffs camp disaster, he had wondered if it really was possible to create an artificial analogue of the chitin insect's communication proteins.

The proteins were fantastically complex. The vizier chitin used them to physically encode thoughts in a chemical matrix that incorporated both virtual memory and real memory at the same time. Analysis was exhausting. There were so many flexible loops, so many inbuilt enzymatic regions that changed and fluctuated constantly, that mapping them was still incomplete after decades of work. Assembling them from amino bases required such an array of enzymes that it seemed to exhaust bacteria, and some of the enzymes were so fierce that they consumed the bacteria as fast as they were made by them. The difficulties were enormous.

Hof knocked back the whisky and called for another. Before it arrived the burgs came and, to Delilah's relief, Hof tucked into his immediately.

"We need a fabrimek, can't get by without one."

"Then we'll have to deal with EASU. We'll start the negotiations right away."

"They'll want pharamol."

"So we give them pharamol. We'll tell everyone that this is the situation and if they want us to carry on they have to chip in and contribute."

"It'll split the talkers. A lot of them won't want to deal."

"Then they'll have to get their conversion done somewhere else. They'll have to go to EASU."

Hof nodded. She was right. The chitin folk would be extremely loath to do that. Hatred of EASU-inspired raiders was at an electric level in the high valleys.

"You've got to stop blaming yourself, Hof."

"I can't help it, Dali; what would you expect?"

"You have to put it behind you, Hof. Otherwise you can't work. You know that, and the work is too important."

"I don't think the work is going anywhere, Dali. Not now, not without a fabrimek."

"I don't mean the fabrimek."

Hof sucked in a breath. By the ancient gods, he felt the pain in his chest again.

"They killed her, Dali, those bastards killed her. How do I forget that? How do I deal with them, knowing that?"

Dali sighed. This was a problem for which she had no real answer.

8

FAIR FUNDAN RETURNED TO CONSCIOUSNESS TWO DAYS AFTER SHE was brought to Emoki Village, near death from loss of blood. At first she remembered nothing. She just stared up at a dark ceiling with unfocused eyes. She had no idea where she might be or how she had got there. Then, slowly at first, hazy outlines returned, with more and more details as things fell into place.

The first real memory was of running on the loop trail that wound around the crag on which the Blue Cliffs group was camped. She'd felt strong that morning, reveling in fitness and happy with the solid production from their chitin nests over the season. Her running shoes slapped against the hard ground under the jik trees, and sunlight dappled the trail up ahead.

Then there was Wally, face distorted in fear, holding a hand to her mouth, begging her to be quiet.

Another memory, a sinister gray balloon, a phallic dirigible that drifted over the blue cliffs. She could hear the guns ripping and a long sobbing scream.

And then the nightmarish flight, running with Wally, heading north, up into the higher valleys. The dirigible pursued them. Wally was gunned down, killed, his head shattered. But she got away—almost.

They would not give up. Tracking her under the jik forest with infrared and olfactory sensors. They had to find her because she was the one who knew where the Blue Cliffs cache was kept.

But Fair knew the locality like the back of her hand. In a maze of little canyons on the limestone belt she gave them the slip by using a pothole and going straight through the ridge instead of over it.

Eventually she reached the crags on the cliffline. Even the stubborn little jik trees gave out up there, but the ground was so riven and broken that she was able to find cover. Still the dirigible hung in the sky above and behind her, tracking her with mobile olfactors the size of sparrows, which dipped and ducked across the ground far behind her.

Occasionally long bursts of automatic fire scoured the rocks, seeking to flush her out. But by dint of enormous effort she'd kept far ahead of them until, at the very last, as she lay shivering just below the snowline, a stray round had caught her in the side.

She'd spun out of control, tumbled through a patch of mossbush, and slid down a long slope into a rocky canyon. Somehow she managed to land on her feet, without any broken bones. Still, the force of the landing sent her sprawling into the shallow stream.

Then came an agonizing crawl into the shadow of the perpendicular walls of the gorge, where she lay bleeding. The balloon had passed overhead soon afterward, but she was lost to them now, buried in the darkness.

Later she'd examined the damage. There was a hole clean through the flesh of her side, just above the hip. There was a hellish amount of blood, but it eventually stopped flowing and she concluded that no major organ had been hit. Maybe she would live for a while longer.

Gritting her teeth, she set to work to try to seal the wound. For a bandage of sorts, she ripped strips off her running shirt, which she wound around her waist. At one point she fainted, and when she woke up she was stiff as a board and very weak.

Then had begun the nightmarish trek down the gorge and into a wider valley. She was miles from anywhere, not even in the Ghotaw Valley anymore, and she had to get help fast, there was a good likelihood that she would die up there and no one would ever know. That journey had taken far too long, and she'd grown certain of death. Everything had seemed pretty hopeless at the end, except that it was now clear that she was alive. Someone had saved her and brought her here—wherever this was.

She tried to sit up and instantly gave out a little shriek as a spasm of pain flashed from her wound. She had never felt pain as intense before in her life. With a gasping sob she lifted her head and looked around. Even that hurt too much and she had to lie down again. The pain throbbed evilly. She moved her head from side to side to suppress it. Her mouth felt like it was full of leather; she was drier than dust.

'And yet there was new hope. Clearly she had fetched up in the hut of a Fein, the mysterious native people of planet Fenrille.

Moreover, she could tell that this was a special Fein, a Fein with a strong sense of decor when it came to baskets and wall weaves. Everything around her bore the alternating black and white lines that were the dominant craft theme of the Ghotaw-region natives.

Fair now realized she was lying on a pallet raised up on bed pegs, under a ceiling of woven knuckoo. The floor was thickly covered in gzan-skin rugs. Whoever owned the hut was a Fein with many possessions, which implied a certain degree of age and prosperity. From the absence of kifket sheaths and kifket sharpeners Fair was also close to certain that this was the hut of a female.

Then she remembered the Fein in the gulley. She'd been trying to get away from the damned gzan that had come up on her out of nowhere. For such bulky animals, they were very quiet when in motion. They came up the main stream channel so she had struck off into a side gulley filled with rocks. She'd been so weak, though, that she'd been barely able to negotiate the waist-high boulders that filled the streambed. To make things worse, they were mossy and slippery and treacherous to walk on. The gzan bull was making a lot of noise somewhere close by. The situation was extremely critical.

And then? The young Fein had burst out of the brush behind her and told her she had to hurry and get out of there. She'd tried to explain but her Feiner was little-used.

And there her memory ended.

She shook her head and immediately gasped again in pain. What the hell was she going to do? She was out of system boost and stimulants and she was miles from help of any kind. So there was nothing much she could do about the pain.

She tried raising her head again, moving more carefully this time. It still hurt like hell, but she persisted. She wanted a good look at her surroundings. With the elevation of her eyes, she promptly made further discoveries.

Her homemade bandage was gone—indeed, all her clothes were gone, and there was a large poultice slapped over the wound area around her hip. The poultice had the consistency of papier-mâché and was held in place with a sash fashioned from a large narrow leaf pinned around her waist with long thorns.

There beside her hand was a bright red gourd set on a stand of some dark wood. A ladle handle projected from the gourd and she could smell the water inside. Trying to ignore the pain, she got up on one elbow and reached for the water. The pain was horrible, but she had to drink. After a ladleful, though, she could stand it no more and sank back. The pain burned and fluttered and slowly died down. After a while she could think again.

Unfortunately, somber questions immediately sprang into her mind. First and foremost was the question of what the hell might be in that poultice. Fair had known a number of Fein and she could even speak their language to a degree, but she knew little about their art of medicine. She craned her head to examine the thing. It looked as if much of the material consisted of mashed leaves. She prayed it didn't include Fein spittle or a lot of mud. She had no boost and no medical kit; if she took an infection she was likely to die.

On the other hand, she recalled one of Augustine Miflin's stories about living with the Fein. He'd always maintained that they had a medicine based on some natural antibiotic they got from a mushroom. In his years in Ghotaw Valley, he never saw a Fein die from wound septicemia, except once when someone was crushed in a rockslide and the infection developed from internal injuries.

Her second realization was that she was probably the only survivor from Blue Cliffs. It was up to her to avenge the others.

Quite abruptly she blacked out once more. When she came around again she was still on the pallet, in darkness, underneath a warm fur blanket. She sensed that it was night. There was a dim light to her right side and, by turning her head, she was able to see that the light was coming from another room in the hut, which was round and sectored into different rooms like an orange.

From that direction she heard the sound of Fein voices, talking in their thick-toned language, so rich in sibilants and glottal stops. They were far enough away that she could not distinguish individual words from the general mutter. She remembered the pain and this time moved more carefully in raising her head.

There was nothing to see, it was all too dark.

Despite the agony involved in moving, she took two full ladles of the water, then forced herself to stop. Any more and she knew she'd be sick, and the thought of how that would hurt was too much to even contemplate.

She lay there for a while, running the recent events back through her mind. The face of the young Fein kept cropping up. He was jumping toward her out of the brush. She was frightened of him. And then there was a blank space with no memories.

Her thoughts flew onward to other questions. Who had sent the killers? How did they locate the camp? Anger surged in her heart until she shook with it and her wound flared in a sudden nova of agony. Biting her lips, she forced herself to stay still while she vowed to avenge the deaths of her people. They who had organized the raid would pay—blood for blood, pain for pain.

Eventually she dozed. The next time she awoke she found an enormous shape sitting close by, intent on some handwork. She saw at once that it was a female Fein, and not a young one at that. The Fein had heavy arms and considerable girth. Clearly she lived a comfortable life, without undue exertion. Her fur was a gray and black tabby, what was often termed "brindle" by the colonists. Her features betrayed an age of two decades or more. There was enough sunlight in the room to see white hairs on the muzzle and around the nose.

She was working on an apron, gzan hide from the underbelly of the animal, softened and treated with oil, sewn and embroidered with the heavy brown thread the Fein made from russet knuckoo fronds.

The Fein looked up, suddenly aware of Fair's eyes upon her. "Aha, alien is awake again," she said quietly to herself.

Fair tried to speak but her mouth was too dry to form words. She gasped and reached for the water ladle.

The Fein leaned close; she seemed enormous, blocking out the light. Her big hand lifted up the water ladle and Fair drank it dry, hardly spilling a drop. After another ladle she was able to work her tongue and lips.

"I thank you. Life, save," she croaked.

The Fein reacted with a startled move backward. Her handwork fell to the floor.

"You talk like Fein?"

Fair swallowed and whispered the word for "yes."

The big yellow eyes were wide and staring. The Fein was on the edge of the state called *shirrithee*, in which mental confusion produced temporary paralysis.

Fair coughed, a fit that racked her hard with each convulsion, sending waves of agony through her. Eventually she stopped, gasping, with tears streaming from the corners of her eyes.

The Fein proffered the water ladle again. The water was sweet and cooling to her throat.

"Thank you," Fair managed to say. "So glad you can understand me."

The Fein waved a hand in delight. "You very good with Fein tongue. Impressed, is old Shtingi."

"You are Shtingi?"

"Yas, I Shtingi, daughter of Gumida. She was great artist, you know."

"I'm—I'm honored to meet you."

The Fein batted the lids on those immense yellow eyes. The alien knew something of courtesy! Incredible! Who had ever heard of such a thing? Not in Emoki village, that was for certain.

"My name is Fair."

The Fein repeated this, very carefully, then gave a snort of amusement. "Old Shtingi learn something new, eh? Alien can speak like Fein!"

Fair smiled, too much in pain for anything more. Shtingi leaned forward a little.

"But you have bad wound. You are lucky to be alive. I do not understand what could have caused this wound."

Fair tried to explain, but she lacked some of the words, and others, like "gun," had no Fein equivalents. Shtingi was virtually in *shirrithee* again before Fair stumbled to a stop.

"Well, it is good that my cub N'ka find you when he did," Shtingi said after a moment's reflection.

"N'ka?"

"N'ka, he young and foolish, but not as foolish as they usually are. He is my last, you see; I will not have any more."

Fair nodded. Shtingi was an old female now.

"I hope to meet him sometime," she said.

"Well, you will. Soon be monsoon and then cubs come home for a time. We need to keep an eye on them every so often, you know."

Fair had no idea. Shtingi continued, speaking of this final cub of hers.

"N'ka troubled me when he was younger. I did not understand such a cub. N'ka maybe has wisdom; this mother of his, me, is beginning to think N'ka is very unusual for male cub. When he find you he could have done many damn silly things but he restrain himself. This is unusual in male cub. Instead, he bring you back here, quick as he can. We clean your wound with the boiled water and then pack on Fein poultice. I try to mix herbs for alien but I know not what best for alien flesh, so I just use musku as much as possible. Musku kill the corruption before it can start."

Fair was startled to hear of the use of boiled water.

"Boiled water is good. Poultice, I don't know, did it have mud in it?"

Shtingi laughed and slapped her big hands on her thighs.

"Mud? No, little alien who talks like Fein, no mud. Fein poultice is mirimbi leaves and strips of satursine bark. We mash it up good in wood, churn with musku and other strong herbs, and then we wet it with the boiled water. Always this work must be done with the boiled water. You see, all things are touched with corruption. A wound opens the body to this corruption which comes from any source that is not cleaned with the boiled water, or heated red-hot in the fire. A wound that is not cleaned with the boiled water and packed with musku will often rot and that can kill a Fein in three days, sometimes less."

Fair gulped. Old Augustine had been right, then; the wild Fein in the mountains had an instinctive understanding of medical cleanliness. It was part of their extraordinarily graceful, vaguely matriarchal culture, carefully restricted to be in harmony with their environment. Their numbers were constant—births balanced deaths, and both were few in number.

Fair relaxed. It was just as old Augustine had said: the Fein were not like any of the models of human primitivism. It looked like she had a good chance of surviving the wound now that she'd made it this far.

After discussing with Shtingi what she might eat safely from the native flora and fauna, Fair was given a porridge of boiled mudu, a good source of carbohydrates and B vitamins with a mild, almost nutty flavor. For vitamin C she turned to unripe satursine pods, which were very acidic but quite safe. She was utterly ravenous and, as with the water, had to struggle to keep from overdoing it and becoming sick. The food made her drowsy, too, and soon afterward she slept once more.

Thus it continued, with small victories along the way, such as the day she was able to sit up on the pallet, and the day she was able to walk out to the latrine unaided. It was almost too much for her to attempt at that point, and she was shaking badly by the time she managed to crawl back to the pallet.

But through trial and error they had found that teosind, the plant the Fein smoked for its mild narcotic effect, produced a painkilling effect in humans. Fair had never smoked anything in her life, however, and she found the experience very strange. Besides, it made her cough, and that hurt worse than anything.

A better day was the one when Shtingi gave her a piece of gzan skin that had been made into a short robe with sleeves, and a belt to tie around the waist. The workmanship was like most Fein-made things, simple, elegant, unfussy. The robe was instantly comfortable and warm.

Slowly she grew stronger. Shtingi's poultices prevented infection, and Fair decided that Augustine Miflin's writings were an invaluable source of Fein lore. If she ever got back to Ghotaw Central, she promised herself she'd get a printout of the Miflin files.

Her conversations with Shtingi also progressed. Thus, when the monsoon began and the young Fein males returned from their duties with the herds, she knew at once which one was N'ka. She also could converse reasonably well in the Fein tongue.

The rain was pounding down. She was sitting on a stool, wrapped in the robe, with her battered running shorts, socks, and shoes on as well. Under the clouds and rain it was distinctly chilly in the high mountain valleys.

The young Fein came into view in a boisterous group and

gathered under the awning in front of Shtingi's hut with the rain dripping off their fur. It was like suddenly having a convention of bears in the room. Fair saw shining teeth and the sharp eyes of intelligent predators. Shtingi welcomed them with maternal wit, scorn, and affection in equal measure.

There was one that stood there, staring at her. He was the tallest of them, a brindle as big as most men and considerably heavier. She knew at once that this was N'ka.

Shtingi greeted her cub with an affectionate hug that would have broken Fair's ribs, then acknowledged the others with slaps and ear rubs. They shuffled and looked uneasy, so much like human teenagers for a moment that Fair almost laughed out loud.

Later N'ka came to sit beside her. He was big, but not yet full-grown. Still, he seemed enormous. She sensed a strong intelligence in him at once. What was more, he was full of questions and not shy at all.

"My mother says you can understand much Fein speech," he began.

"Yes," she said quietly.

He brought up a seat, a tree stump partially hollowed out.

"You remember when we met?" he asked.

She nodded. "I do, although not well. The gzan was too close."

"Gzan was going to kill you. I had to act."

"I thank you, N'ka. You saved my life."

N'ka looked at her for a moment.

"When you leave, N'ka will come with you."

She gaped.

"You are healing, yes? You will leave before next rains."

She nodded. "Yes, I suppose so."

"You will get Shtingi to send for me and I will go with you. I am widepath Fein, you see. I know it now. It awoke in me when I pick up dying alien in Zenaboni stream. I tell Shtingi. She is my mother, she understand, she know N'ka very well. She probably know N'ka better than N'ka know N'ka."

He convulsed momentarily in a Feinish chuckle.

"I cannot stay narrowpath; I have to leave Emoki. I come with you. It seems that the spirits want this."

She smiled back—"So it seems, N'ka."—and held out a hand to him. Her hand vanished for a moment into a vast paw.

"N'ka must see the world outside Emoki."

9

Slovo Milsuduk was an unusual sort for a success in the EASU, especially with a name of such slavic overtones. But, in fact, Slovomir's ancestors had lived in London since the mid-twentieth century, so he was as much a real EASU man as anyone.

Slovo was a gangster, but his weapons were the telephone, the predictor software, and insider information, rather than teams of thugs with their guns, clubs, and knives.

He was in his late sixties and had been taking longevity drugs since he first arrived on the New World. The Big Man had brought Slovo with him from the Dikezones of Havering and Dagenham as part of his entourage. In fact, Slovo was the Big Man's unofficial business "geez." What he did was overseen by the Big Man himself and nobody else.

Thus, he belonged to the innermost group, along with Soko, Lawler, Wilson, Congo—all of them men of violence. But, in day-to-day fact, he was a cut above them, closer to the ear of the Big Man. The others were good at killing and maintaining discipline, but the Big Man didn't trust them to cut a good business deal.

The truth of it was that the EASU had to cut a great many deals. EASU was on top in the New World, but the organization itself was riven by factions. There were the West Londons, the Dikezones, the Hamburgs, the Hollands, the Norfolks and Suffolks; they all worked different angles within the machine. And beyond EASU itself were the other colonists—the Hakka and the Saturns, the various Neptune ship groups, even the old original colonists from the Uranian habitats. All of these controlled sections of the pie and all had to be accommodated to some degree or other to keep things moving along smoothly.

Slovo was essential to the process. He was also homosexual and, although he maintained an iron sexlessness around the Big Man, who was known for his dislike of samesexers, Slovo kept a handsome young man for his personal use in a discreet luxury condo in a beachfront tower.

Hal was Slovo's young prince, a slim, athletic youth, with pretty features and a lot of skill in bed. To Slovo, thick-waisted and stuck with the looks of a man in later middle age, the boy was irresistible folly. Unfortunately, no amount of longevity drugs could restore the looks of youth, and only careful diet and plenty of exercise could keep the torso from spreading into flab. And Slovo disliked exercise enormously. Hal was everything Slovo wished he could be, and Hal worked hard at flattering his master. Hal knew that for such as he the world outside the beachfront condominium was a lot tougher than that inside.

And so, whenever it was possible, Slovo would make his way, with all the secrecy he could summon up, across the small city to the beachfront condominium.

So it was on the night that the Big Man gave a party for Lawler, who had completed a purge through the ranks of enforcers in the organization. The bosses drank freely at such events; it was expected of them. The Big Man himself liked to drink on these occasions. He drank sake, and sometimes chased it with white spirit. The Big Man was a lion drunk, prone to roars of rage and roars of laughter, fond of brawls and practical jokes.

Slovo was the only one who was not expected to get stinking drunk at such affairs. The Big Man knew Slovo hated to get drunk, and Slovo was bad at remembering jokes or telling them. As a result, his presence was scarcely missed as things got raucous. He always slipped away before the hookers were let in to start working on the bosses. The Big Man understood and forgave Slovo his weakness. And so Slovo slipped his minders, gave his bodyguard the night off, and headed for the beachfront tower.

It was a typically warm, muggy night. Clouds hung over the sullen waters of the southern ocean. In the beachfront condominium Slovo rocked gently on the bed under the massaging fingers of young Hal, while the pleasurable aftereffects of a grain of ultra-costly pharamol washed through his system.

The interior doorchime tinkled. Slovo frowned in annoyance and snapped his fingers. A small screen set in the sidewall came on like a chromatic jewel in the darkness and offered up the view of the security camera at the door. A man in the gray uniform of the Beachside Terrace House stood there with a silver tray in his hands. On the tray was a small black data module.

"Message from a Mr. Erst, sir."

What? The Big Man? Slovo felt a chill run down his spine. The Big Man knew about this little hideaway? Slovo had fooled himself into believing that nobody knew. It was disconcerting to find that his little attempt at deception had been pierced.

Alive with sudden anxiety, Slovo sent Hal to the door to get the data module. "Tip the man nicely," he said to Hal's mincing backside.

Slovo hoped fervently that the Big Man wasn't too angry about Hal. Surely the Big Man would be merciful. The Big Man indulged his own needs quite willfully, after all. He had a dozen women at any one time.

The screen snapped off at his command and he rolled over and reached for his glass. He didn't drink much alcohol, but he had a fondness for champagne, and this latest batch from the wine lab was pretty damn good.

Hal did not come back at once. A minute dragged by, and Slovo started to get annoyed. He got to his feet and lurched off in search of the youth. Hal was probably in the kitchen, pigging on something sweet in the refrigerator.

Slovo would put a stop to that! Slovo was going to do some pigging out himself, and Hal was the something sweet in the refrigerator. Slovo giggled to himself.

There in the hallway was the man in the Terrace House uniform, down to the silly little red hat with gold braid. Hal was kneeling beside him, sniveling, with his arms bent behind his back. The man had a choke chain around poor Hal's neck and, at the sight of Slovo, he tugged hard on it. Poor Hal gave a squeak of agony and started to turn blue.

"No, please, don't hurt him," Slovo said.

The man had a dull, solid face. Slovo did not know if he had seen it before, although a faint memory tugged at him— nothing strong enough to even suggest a name.

"All right." The chain relaxed a trifle, and Hal gasped for air. "You have a big reputation as a good man for negotiations. We're going to put your rep to the test."

The man was EASU all right—the unmistakable flat, nasal tones of a Dikezone accent spoke of his origins. Slovo spread his hands gently. "I'm sure we can come to an agreement."

The man had a wolfish grin. "Oh, yes, I'm sure about that, all right."

Dragging Hal behind him, the man pushed into the living room, where he tied Hal over an exercycle. He shoved a rubber bung into Hal's mouth and then stood back. Slovo made no move. He sensed that the man was truly dangerous and most certainly armed. Slovo was determined not to lose his life in the situation if he could at all prevent it.

"Do I know you?" he asked quietly.

"No."

"Please don't hurt the boy, he knows nothing."

"I won't hurt your piece if you give me what I need."

Slovo licked his lips. "If it's credit you need, I can be generous."

"Don't need credit, I need something much more precious than that. See, I'm what you might call a cornered rat."

And the man in the silly bellhop hat proceeded to ask the questions that would put a sentence of death on Slovo's head if he answered them correctly. But the man was good. He had worked it all out carefully. If Slovo cooperated, then Slovo and Hal would live. If he lied, then they would die together. There was no way out of the noose. Everything now depended on the success or failure of the man's mission.

10

BY THE HEIGHT OF THE DRY SEASON, WHEN THE BULL GZAN RODE the zenith of the night sky and the Pale Moon was full, Fair Fundan and N'ka, Shtingi's cub, left the village of Emoki.

Shtingi was sad to see her cub leave. She was concerned that he was too young to leave Emoki. She was even more concerned by his choice of destination. Like most Fein of the Ghotaw region, she regarded the main valley as infested with aliens and no longer a good place for Fein to wander. The Emoki villagers were cut off from most others, however—it was a five-day trek to the next Fein valley—and so they had not heard of the Fein killings by raiders from the Coast. Fair had warned N'ka repeatedly that it was dangerous, but he was imbued with the sense of immortality common to adolescents of most advanced species.

Finally he had agreed to a compromise. He would return to Emoki within the next dry season. He would spare his old mother the pain of eternal separation.

Shtingi still feared she might not see him again. He was of the widepath, a completely different mentality from a normal narrowpath Fein who would happily stay in his or her home range for a lifetime. There was no way to know what would happen to him once he had visited the great valley. He might roam forever, all the way around the world. It was said that this was the common fate of the Fein who were bewitched by the widepath.

Furthermore, Shtingi was sorry to see Fair leave. She had grown to love this one, this human who spoke good Feiner—now with an Emoki accent, of course. Fair had told Shtingi many things of the outside world, especially things concerning humans. Shtingi had rarely felt fear in her long life, but these things she heard about the humans brought terror to her heart. The humans were not the sky demons of the legends. The humans made the sky demons seem virtually harmless. Sky demons were said to land and take one or two Fein aboard their sky ships. After examining them, they returned the chosen Fein to their homes. It was weird and unsettling to be so selected, but it was not fatal. Humans had come to the Knuckle of Delight to settle. They attacked the great trees and fought with the longlegs. They went into chitin nests in pursuit of drugs that would make them live forever. And, most bizarre and horrible of all, some humans would kill Fein and take their skins to make ornamental rugs!

Shtingi shuddered. It was enough to make her want to recall the Arizel tki Fenrille. The gods should come down in person and help the humans to change. The society of humans was filled with a passion for "things," for ownership of property, and this passion drove the humans to cheat and oppress one another, even to kill.

Shtingi feared for Fair because she was returning to that human world. But there was no holding her back. Shtingi had never seen such determination as the little alien female summoned up. And so, after the monsoon, the old Fein accepted that she could hold neither of them back any longer. She faced a future stripped of N'ka's sparkle, which had so amused her through these last seasons. Whenever she thought of it, she would heave a sigh. Eventually, she decided to weave a great bark tapestry, a *bakwa dwam*, like her own mother used to make.

For her part, Fair was also sad at the thought of leaving Emoki. Her life had been saved there and she felt the course of that life had been irrevocably changed there. She had thought out her mission, defined what she knew her role had to be. When she returned to the human world, she would change it. She had seen the future that Hof had warned her about and knew it had to be avoided.

Fair was sorry to leave Emoki, but she vowed to return. She was back to nearly normal strength, although her fitness was still below peak level. The wound was now a series of huge, ugly scars. The bullet's exit area was the worst, but she was able to walk without pain and was quite capable of keeping up with N'ka as long as he went slowly. Every so often he'd forget, however, and lapse into the normal predatory lope of the Fein on the move. She would have to call his name and he would halt and look back at her while she marveled at the grace and strength of the Fein physique and hurried to catch up.

N'ka bade farewell to his fellows, who returned to the herds of gzan with the coming of dry weather. He alone had no regrets, for now. He was eager to see beyond the High Pass, and to go where his eye had only been able to peer before, past the huge mountain they called *Blissa*, "The Anvil," and into the great valley.

N'ka was also eager to see the places of the humans. Listening to Fair had kindled his burning interest in the aliens. They did such fascinating, crazy things, like living in underground structures and flying in huge machines. N'ka tried to visualize the flying things of the humans, but he found it very difficult: something like an enormous kifket, cast by a giant's strength into the air far, far beyond the horizon, to the legendary land of water, the ocean. There were so many things he had to see. N'ka knew now that he was of the widepath, and he did not look back to Emoki. In his heart of hearts he was not sure he would ever come back. But this he did not tell Shtingi. Indeed, he barely told it to himself.

Through the days they marched up the slopes of the mountain to the high pass. At night they slept inside heavy wraps of gzan hide and huddled together for warmth. Fair felt she undoubtedly got more out of this than N'ka, but the big Fein was used to sleeping in the cold and the outdoors.

The upper slopes of the mountains were home to patches of rainmoss and small groups of tangi, rat-sized herbivores who fed on the sparse tufts. The air was thin and cold, and towering above them were great ridges of bare stone that mounded on top of each other toward the snowline of the mighty mountain the settlers called "The Yellowman" and the Fein called "The Anvil."

On the second day they reached the place where Fair had been shot. In the rocks farther down she saw evidence, in the form of star-shaped pockmarks and shattered stone, of the gunfire that had stalked her. The sight prompted her to explain again the dangers that N'ka faced. There were threats everywhere. Fair herself faced danger from those who had already tried to kill her. If they found out she was alive they would exert themselves to extinguish her voice.

N'ka found some aspects of human society difficult to grasp. Fein-to-Fein evil such as theft and killing occurred, but always Fein were obsessed with a life of honor. Their conception of honor was quite close to the human. To kill someone outside of fair fight was a terrible crime, but if the fight was adjudged fair, in that the age and size of the opponents were matched, then it was another matter.

Of course, there were always those who were especially skilled with a kifket. For these, in normal times, there were handicap rules. But Fein with such skills were even more restrained by honor from killing and in fact were rarely challenged to combat. To kill in the ways Fair described was utterly without honor. N'ka knew that no Fein in Emoki would ever stain the names of their lineages with such crimes.

Fair understood N'ka's difficulty; her time with Shtingi had given her a glimpse into the way of the Fein. Fair knew that N'ka would find it hard to accept the kinds of evil of which civilized humanity was capable. When she listed them she had a hard time believing it herself. There didn't seem to be much that people wouldn't stoop to, often simply for the pleasure of it.

That thought steeled her resolve. She faced a momentous task, but she knew that it had to be tackled. Fortunately, she would not have to start alone. Hof would help, and he had many friends in the older generations. She would need their support.

As they descended through boulder fields, they began to see more vigorous signs of life. The rainmoss became abundant. Other vegetation sprang up, gray forbs and black bush. Farther down, scarlet bloodmenots dappled the green of lush meadows of arble.

N'ka sustained himself with jerky from his pack and Fair ate dried porridge. As they entered the range of the dwarf gzan, N'ka began to hunt, roving away from the path in different directions to follow the spoor of the elusive creatures. On their fourth night under the stars, they roasted the flesh of a young gzan that N'ka had taken with the kifket during the late afternoon. They drank crystal clear water, very cold, from a mountain glacier. They talked animatedly about what lay ahead of them.

Fair tried to explain what had driven humans from their home system all the way to Fenrille. She described the massive populations of the home system: millions of hab dwellers orbiting the outer planets and billions of the poor crushed under the permanent gray skies of greenhouse Earth. N'ka found it dizzying to comprehend these numbers and even harder to understand what it had all meant to the planet Earth: atmospheric pollution, radiation, fire, and the spread of vast, endless cities, burning untold energy to maintain the grip of industrial civilization in a shattered ecosphere. Fire N'ka understood, and he could grasp the idea of gases. Fair had found that the Fein possessed a surprisingly sophisticated understanding of the atom and the molecule. Radiation was much more difficult; N'ka was lost when it came to the subatomic world. But the urbanization of whole continents caused him to go into the *shirrithee* state, the fur on his shoulders rising on end, a state frozen on the fine line between fight and flight.

Fair described what she could of the old struggle between her ancestors, out on the planetary frontiers, and the vast masses of the Earth. N'ka lay awake long afterward, his mind whirling with these images of huge populations and deadly warfare in the outer dark of space.

Two days later they reached the first chitin-talker territory, that of the Swallowtail Skrin group. Fair was welcomed as if she had returned from the dead, which, in a sense, she had. She introduced N'ka to the Swallowtails, who regarded him with awe. There had been no Fein in their area for decades now. That evening they dined with the chitin talkers and N'ka entertained the children, who found him irresistible.

The following morning they hitched a ride down to Ghotaw Central on a passing ATV and spent the day whirring steadily east and south across the great valley. N'ka marveled at the speed and ease of such transportation. Fair slept.

11

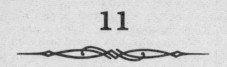

HOF WITLIN CALLED THE MEETING TO ORDER. THE BACK ROOM OF Trader's bar was packed. Everyone was there, or at least, everyone who was still alive was there. The recent wave of terror had left a number of empty seats in the council of the old families.

For example, Colorado Butte was no longer leading his big family. In his place was his half brother, Arvad. And Jaime Matoya was gone, gunned down by raiders just a week before. They were still talking about his death; he was shot right in front of his wife and children. And, of course, Fair Fundan was not there, lost along with the entire Blue Cliffs group six months previously in a bloody massacre. Hof's heart was still heavy from that loss.

Still, there were lots of Fundans present. There were the members of the family council, led by Proud Fundan, including the Toronto-Fundans. There were also the outsiders like Elgin Fundan, who skulked in the back row while his eyes never left Hof. There were Chungs and Hoechsts, Pang To Kosho, Ruby Butte, and Kobuto. And then there were the Spreaks, a solid group of the old enemy clan, lead by old Ervil. Ryder and Malan Spreak sat beside Ervil, and behind them were Vroot and Wynt.

When he had their attention, Hof listed the most recent raids. "So, that's four more raids this past seven days, almost twenty for the month," he finished.

"If they keep this up, they'll kill all of us within two years," Ervil Spreak growled.

"How are they getting their information?" Butte asked. "How do they always manage to strike at the right time?"

"How do you think?" Ervil said. "This place is crawling with spies."

Proud Fundan broke in. "Everything in this valley is being monitored now. They have satellites, these unmanned balloons, and plenty of willing helpers in Ghotaw Central."

"We cannot trust anyone outside our own circles."

"Only those with the courage to risk the insect," Malan Spreak said.

"There is less risk in attacking us."

"Then we have to make it riskier for them," Elgin said.

"We must kill them." Spreak was definite.

Hof raised his hands. "We can't hope to fight them and win. They have the numbers. They will kill all of us through attrition in a short time."

"Damn fools will kill us and then there'll be no chitin drugs at all."

"It won't be the first time human beings have killed the golden goose they depend on," Hof replied. "Look at our homeworld."

"You look at it, Witlin. You came from there," someone sneered, and others snickered.

"Wait!" Ervil Spreak growled. "You are correct, Messire Witlin. Long-term, we face severe disadvantages. What are you suggesting?"

"Negotiations. We have to talk with them."

Ervil's frown became thunderous. "Waste of time," he snapped.

"But . . ."

"Already tried it. You can't talk to them. Lawler, Congo, all that bunch, they don't accept any positions other than their own. They want everything. They want to get rid of the families and turn the chitin talkers into peasants."

Hof's jaw dropped. He'd never imagined that Ervil Spreak would talk with the EASU.

"But," he began feebly, "there must be a way."

"Forget it, Witlin. They don't want talks."

Elgin Fundan strode up to the front and stood beside Hof.

"There is a way, but it requires that we give up on our mutual feuds. We have to cooperate, form a joint command, and raise a mobile defense force. If we all work together, we can hammer the raiders and make it too damn dangerous for them."

The heads of the clans shifted uneasily in their seats. Suspi-

cion was in the air, the legacy of the bad old days in the first
decade of chitin drug production. There were dark deeds
aplenty done in those years. As a result, the idea of cooperat-
ing with one another went against the grain.

In particular, it was hard to stomach dealing with the
Spreaks.

Elgin saw them struggling. "Look," he said, fighting to regain their attention, "EASU has it all worked out. First they allow the raids and the killings, until we're close to panic.
Meanwhile, they work steadily to replace our laboratory system with their own. Then they offer protection to those who
will join them. In the end, the chitin talkers will be helpless
peasants, tied to overlords who will own them body and soul.
Eventually, Ghotaw Central will be theirs. Our depositories at
Ghotaw North are simply hostages in the making."

Concern mounted with that idea. The depositories held vast
fortunes in pharamol and optimol. But still, the hatreds were
too strong. Arvad Butte spoke first. "I do not think I can ask
my people to cooperate with Spreaks or anyone tainted by the
Khalifi evil. They did great harm to my family; we have not
forgotten."

Elgin shrugged. "Will you cooperate with the Fundans?"

"Hof Witlin knows we have no love for Fundans, but we
can work with them."

"Then the Fundans will work in the middle. That is, if the
family council will agree."

Proud Fundan sniffed. "Can the Fundans trust the Spreaks?
Have Spreak knives and guns not taken enough Fundan lives?"

"That is the past. We have to leave it behind."

Adalbert shook her head angrily. "Easy for you to say that,
Elgin Fundan! Your family was still out in the forest, playing
suicidal games with the woodwose, when we were producing
the first supplies of optimol. Spreaks cut some evil deals in
those days. We have not forgotten."

"It's true that my family never left the coast. My father believed in an old idea, and he went to his death still believing
it. But I did come to the Highlands and I can see that we must
form a Highland nation. And no one here will deny that I have
suffered loss since I made my life in the Ghotaw and began to
work Cinnabar Ridge."

They held their tongues.

Hof was marveling at the thought. Was it possible? A Highland nation welded out of these disparate, feuding clans? Some

of them were wavering, struck by the novelty of Elgin's idea. Hof began to wonder if they really might not do it.

And then a message was brought to Hof on a scrap of print-out paper by a teenage Butte who'd been posted at the front door of Trader's. Hof read it and felt the color drain from his face. He thought his heart had stopped. He got to his feet and turned to the door just as it opened and admitted Fair Fundan, followed by the towering form of a young Fein.

Fair looked lean, almost gaunt. There were lines on her face that had not been there three months before. She wore Fein-made clothing worked from gzan hide. And behind her loomed a giant with bright orange eyes and a large satchel over his immense shoulder.

Hof stared at her, unable to speak. Meanwhile, Elgin had pushed by him with a wild shout of joy and was lifting her off her feet. They whirled together for a moment and then Fair set herself down and came over to Hof.

"Hof?" She was beside him.

"Fair, I thought . . ."

"I know, and I almost was. But the Fein found me. I want you to meet my friend. This is N'ka, cub of Shtingi, of the village of Emoki."

Hof reached out to grip the huge paw of the Fein. He shivered when it said his name.

12

THE BIG MAN WAS A VORACIOUS BASTARD, HE SAID SO HIMSELF. Of course, nobody else was allowed to say so—that was well understood. Anybody who thought he could disrespect Arvin Erst would soon find out what was what.

But the truth of it was that he was a real voracious bastard, all right, hungry for all the pleasures of life, and particularly for women. He'd always had a thing for women. He consumed them by the dozen. With women his manners took on their purest form. He was a big predator; what he wanted, he took.

He had risen far in the world on the strength of his ability to take things.

After the party for Lawler, the Big Man had gone up to apartment 26 on the upper deck of the Essex dome. The girl there currently was called Teena and she was soft and plush, amazingly plush for such a slender little witch. Just thinking about her round little buttocks got the Big Man excited as he headed for the elevator. The damn girl had the haunches of a goddess! Erst belched, and laughed at himself, something he'd always been able to do, and which he credited as an important part of staying alive. When you stopped being able to laugh at yourself, you were on your way out.

Teena's sexy giggle was another thing he found irresistible. How he enjoyed it when they said they liked it, too. She was a rare one, was this little blond bit. He chuckled to himself. By the womb of the whore that was his mother, he was a horny bastard and he made the most of it. He laughed again. He was virtually drooling over what he planned to do with the girl!

If only his mother could see him now! Shit, but she'd have had a fit! His mother had always hated him. Hah! But he'd got her in the end, fixed her wagon all right. Had her buried alive in the new dike they put up on the Chelmsford front. What a life! What other men desired but never had, he consumed every day of his life. If only mother could see him now! He roared happily in the elevator.

The guard with him knew better than to react. He was simply part of the furniture as far as the Big Man was concerned. Guards were not expected to offer opinions, advice, or even the slightest of comments. Guards just kept their mouths shut.

Out of the elevator and onto the purple rug. It had been a good roast, old Lawler had been touched. Good, the bastard had done well even if he was a slimy old wanker! Someday the Big Man would have to cut Lawler's nuts off and stuff them in his mouth, but that day had not yet come. Lawler still trod the straight and narrow.

The door was open. Teena was waiting, dressed in a red silk gown. Her hair was pale gold and trailed down to her buttocks. She wiggled provocatively inside the red silk.

The Big Man let the door slam behind him. The guard stood there with his back to it and tried not to listen as the Big Man caught up with Teena, grabbed her around the waist, and began planting huge, wet kisses all over her neck and shoulders.

Teena was unzipping the Big Man's trousers and drawing him into the bedroom. The door closed.

The guard reported in by his wrist radio. The Rover took his report and then told the back men to stand down. Their replacements would be on line within ten minutes. The front men, the man at the door of the apartment and the man on the balcony, were on until the next shift.

The Big Man was devouring little Teena in the bedroom, a thing of which he made a great performance. There was giggling and a horrible hoglike snorting. The guard closed his eyes and shook his head. Everyone hated these night shifts! He tried to tune out the sounds bubbling from the bedroom, though it was hard, since the only other noises were those of the dome air conditioning system and the elevators softly whirring up and down.

The Big Man came for the third time with a long, triumphant groan of pleasure and lay back on the bed with a heavy sigh. Teena, her body slick with sweat, slid off him. He lay there like a fat whale, his belly beading with perspiration. She knew she'd done him good. It should be worth something good, too—maybe a few grains of Spreak Skycrystal.

She looked over at him. He was breathing deeply, lost in the pleasant post-coital contemplative state. Her delicate little nostrils wrinkled. Faugh! Didn't he stink! Of booze and sweat and God knows what else! It was incredible that she was able to even do this with such a creature. But then, she reminded herself, she didn't have that much of a choice, and he was the Big Man.

Her mother hadn't exactly left her with much of a position in life, let alone in the EASU. A cheap whore, that's what her mother had been. And a stupid one, too, because she'd missed her opportunities every bleeding time.

Teena suddenly noticed that the balcony window was open and that a tall man, wearing black, was standing by the side of the bed. There was something bulky on his back. He saw her eyes widen and shook his head decisively. In his hand he held a gun, a small black plastic thing with an evil glitter.

Teena felt the sweat on her body congeal. For a horrible moment she thought she was going to wet herself. But not a sound escaped her.

The man kicked the bed. The Big Man pushed up like a startled bear, blinking with rage. "Who the fuck are you?" he snarled.

"A cornered rat," the man in black replied in a calm voice.

"A fuckin' dead rat, that's what!" the Big Man snapped. He began to get to his feet.

"I wouldn't do that. If you force me to, I'll have to use this." The man gestured with the gun.

The Big Man stopped. The man's voice was calm, professional, serious.

"If this is a robbery, you picked the wrong person to rob. You know who I am?"

The man snorted. "Course I know who you are. You're my boss. Don't tell me you don't remember. You lifted your hand from me. I worked for you all my life and then, poof, just like that, you took away your hand and let that bastard Lawler have me killed."

Comprehension sank in on the Big Man's slab of a face.

"You're this Overed, then. Overed, Martin, been with the Union since you was in the Youth Group. Yeah, I know you. You're a little cheat! Just another little disgusting cheat! I'm wise to your little tricks. You thought you could cheat on the Big Man! You thought that nobody would notice! You thought you were the clever one, didn't you?"

The Big Man was sitting up, stabbing the air in front of him with a thick forefinger. Martin took a step back. He didn't want to fight the Big Man; he wanted the Big Man to restore him to his former position.

"Look, I admit it, I slipped up a bit. But never enough to rank a killing."

"You took from me. That means you took from EASU. You think I can let that go on? No chance, son—we had to have a crackdown. Put some of you little buggers on the grill and cook you!"

Inexplicably the Big Man burst into harsh barks of laughter at this. Martin felt the situation starting to spin out of control. The guard from the front door would be outside the room by now. Too far away to do much good, though. The gun was pointed unerringly at the Big Man's head.

"Go away or I'll blow his head off!" Martin yelled. "Right out the front door, got it!"

The bedroom door stayed shut, the guard retreated.

Suddenly it struck Teena with a peculiar clarity that the Big Man wasn't afraid. He was acting like he was on top of the whole thing. This amazed her, since she was shaking like a leaf.

"I always gave you my best," Martin Overed said.

"You cheated! Negates all the rest."

Overed licked his lips. "Well, that's in the past. Look what I've done for you here. I'm in on you and not even your security system could stop me."

The Big Man had been curious about that point. Where the fuck was the front man who should have been on the balcony to screen this freak Overed out?

"How the hell did you do it?" Had he been that obvious about this apartment lately? Sure, Teena had had him mesmerized at night, but that didn't mean he came here more than a couple of times a week. There were too many other women for that.

"I'll tell you that, but first I want to be reinstated. I want you to put your hand back on me."

The Big Man pursed his lips. So that was it, was it? "Not many other choices for you, are there?" he said with a wolfish smile.

"I'm good. I've learned my lesson. I'll never cheat again."

The Big Man chortled. It was not enough—it could never be enough. Fool Overed!

The Big Man thought for a moment. How should he play this poor fool? The fool was coming on straight. He was desperate and he was trying to cut a deal down the middle. He could be gulled or he could be humiliated, ground into the rug like an insect. The Big Man smiled to himself and nodded. There was no need to lie to him. And the Big Man could impress this little cunt Teena, as well. The Big Man would take this fool down with just his words.

"No," he said quietly. "Sorry, son, but the die was cast when you first nicked in and helped yourself to goods that were never yours. I'd like to help you but I can't. Now you can go ahead and kill me, or do your best anyway. After the first shot the boys are going to come in and take you down. You better hope you don't live through that, because if you do, you know Lawler and Congo are going to make you regret you were ever born. Of course, I'd go easier on you. Know what I mean? A pill here, a little pharamol, go out nice and easy, on the tide, like."

Martin stared at the monstrous man. No mercy! That's what he was hearing. No way back, no way to rebuild his position. His worst nightmare was coming true.

The Big Man was grinning now. "So why don't you put the

gun away, son? Let's cut a deal my way. You surrender now, and I'll see you go out nice and easy. You won't feel a thing."

Martin stared. The trap was shut around him.

"Come on, son, give it up. Then go and get down on the floor while I get the guards in here. It'll be best that way. You have to understand this—you couldn't be left in place. You were a fuckup in the system, a cheat."

Teena watched with bulging eyes. The gunman was wilting. The Big Man was talking the poor bastard down to his knees. It was amazing—it was no wonder that the Big Man was who he was. And then something snapped in Martin's face and the spell was broken.

"Nooooooo!" he screamed. He rose and fired twice, once into the Big Man's chest and the second time into the bedroom door, which disintegrated in a hail of explosive slugs from outside. Men tumbled in. Teena hurled herself off the bed and curled up in a fetal ball.

Martin was already out on the balcony, where he stepped off the top of the rail and floated out into the darkness with a line behind him reeling out of his backpack. He hit the outer skin of the dome and slid down to the balcony on the floor below. The line broke his fall and he barely paused to cut the first line and hook on the second before he went over the rail and continued his high-speed descent, floor by floor. A few shots whined off the dome skin around him but by the time they zeroed him he was over the edge of the dome's curve.

He knew they'd also be too busy looking after the Big Man to move quite as fast as they should. He dropped the last eighty feet in one go on the third, heaviest line.

On the ground he dumped the pack, ran straight down the beach, and dove into the sea, forcing his way through the big breakers that crashed endlessly on the sands. He pushed himself out with strong strokes. His escape was predicated on his prowess as a swimmer.

This next part was a calculated risk. The tide was on the ebb and the big permiads had drawn offshore for the night, seeking to feed on pentarchs rising from the deeper waters. He reached the offshore nets that kept the permiads from picking people off in the surf. He was about two hundred meters offshore now. There was a steady deep ocean swell, but that didn't concern him as much as what might lurk beneath the waves.

He crossed the nets and swam. There was no choice, no going back. The water was warm, the surf fizzled in the wind. He kept up a quiet breaststroke, trying not to cut up the water too much. The permiads would soon pick up those sort of signals.

Time passed; he started to tire. The swell on the ocean lifted him to the crest of a wave every so often, but all he saw around himself were more waves. Even though he was a strong swimmer, he knew he was reaching his limit. He decided to float on his back for a while. It was restful, and after a while he felt some of his strength return. He wasn't far enough out yet.

He swam some more and when he looked back the isles were just a string of lights in the dark. It was a big place to be all alone in. He unclipped the rescue light, put it on his wrist, and turned it on. It sent out a bright green flash, blinking every few seconds. It seemed tiny in this vastness of water.

He swam, alone in the vast darkness of wave and night. His thoughts circled back endlessly to the Big Man's face.

"You surrender now, son, and I'll see you go out nice an' easy. You won't feel a thing."

There was no way back to his old position; there had never been a way back.

He swam and occasionally he rested.

And then, quite suddenly, there was a boat bearing down on him under a single sail. He waved and shouted, and someone waved back. Within a minute the boat was on top of him and Mari's uncle Ho was helping him out of the water and into the cockpit. Ho led him forward into the waist of the boat, past the fishing equipment, to the front cabin. Mari was waiting there with a heatpack and some hot soup in a deep cup.

Uncle Ho went back to the cockpit and turned the boat into the west, slicing across the wind with the computerized sailset working to gain every fraction of lift possible. The boat was a beauty, an old Fundan-made Westwind-class that was quite capable of sailing all the way around the world, if necessary.

The hot, sour soup was good, and it set off a glow in his stomach. As he felt the warmth return to his body, he reflected that his choice of allies in this unequal struggle had been a damned good one. The Roiders were too poor and too late to get much of a slice of the economic pie, but their exclusion from the colony's society had kept them intact as a people, and they had kept their pride and their honor.

Of course, the boat had been bought with Martin's money and given to Ho as a gift. It automatically lifted Ho out of the ranks of the impoverished who worked in the danger and the muck of the kelp beds, freecutting the huge strands of algae that formed the base for much of the colony's synthetic foods. Suddenly Ho was a fisherman, working the inshore waters for blacksnap and various large but tasty crustaceans that were much prized in the restaurants that catered to the EASU elites. So Ho had a big debt to pay, and Mari, well, Mari had become important in many ways to Martin Overed.

He just hoped he lived long enough to repay her. He tried to thank her, later, tucked in a sleeping bag in the forward compartment, with her body folded against him nice and warm. She told him to go to sleep and save his strength.

13

THE CRUISE TO COAST CITY TOOK THREE WEEKS, AND WOULD have taken longer except that they caught the leading edge of a typhoon off Cape Terror. The Westwind's computerized sailset rode the storm winds at speeds of twenty and twenty-five knots. As they went, they monitored the media coming out of the Essex Coast. The attempted assassination of Arvin Erst had been the big news story for all that time. Of course, they knew they had failed. Within a day or two that was definite. Looking through the statements from the EASU leadership, Martin gradually had to accept it. They weren't lying. The Big Man had survived and was being nursed back to health.

The search for the assassin continued. The tenements and domes of the Essex Coast were being raked over in the search.

Martin knew he was done for. The Big Man would never give up now. He would search for Martin forever until he was found and brought, quivering, into his presence. The pain would be horrible and it would last a long time.

And so he was in no hurry to get to Coast City. The hue and cry was at its hottest during the first few weeks. It would die down after a while. Martin and Mari already had a plan. In fact, it was mostly Mari's plan. Martin had been astonished at the thoroughness with which she'd worked it all out, but he'd found no obvious flaws. It was just another example of how useful to him Mari had become.

Fortunately, he had some good credit reserves in Coast City at the CC Chitin Bank, a locally owned operation free of EASU influence—which was pretty much true of all of CC. The rocks and cliffs that made up Coast City were populated by refugees from the old colony capital on what had been Hospital Island. They'd left rather than slip under EASU control.

Unfortunately, this dislike of EASU extended to troublesome types like Martin Overed. The local setup wasn't going to allow him to hang around very long once they identified him. Meanwhile, the credit would let Mari get things moving smoothly enough. Credit could make up for a lot of things. He had a few good contacts, but on Mari's strong advice he agreed not to get in touch with anyone.

The escape had been good and clean. Lawler and Congo had never been particularly imaginative, and the thought that Overed had sailed off into the blue never occurred to them; they kept raking over the Essex Coast. There was a twenty-five-thousand bounty out on him now but, of course, they'd found nothing.

Mari would handle everything. Martin was uncomfortably aware that he was putting everything on the line behind Mari's shapely little figure. If she flipped on him, he was meat for the Big Man's grill. Occasionally when he said something coarse, unable to help himself—it was just his way—he caught her looking at him with that flat, Roider stare, and it frightened him. He'd given her plenty, he knew, but he'd made her pay a price. He woke up at night sometimes, jerked awake by some stray creak of the boat, and every time he expected to find Uncle Ho at his throat with Mari behind him, both with that same flat stare.

At last they sailed into the artificial harbor built around the offshore crags that were home to forty thousand humans clinging to the margins of the New World's single, enormous continent. Uncle Ho brought them in with a bunch of local pleasure craft. There were a couple of other Westwinds in the pack. At the marina, they rented a slot without occasioning more than mild interest. They explained that the storm off Cape Terror had pushed them so far west that they had decided to come on the rest of the way.

Martin stayed below, out of view. There was no formal search of the boat. Coast City government didn't hold with the idea of taxation. The mind-set was old-time Colony; nobody cared what you brought into CC or took out. Just check in and pay your marina bills, that was all that was required.

They soon learned that the Big Man had already recovered enough to be able to go before the EASU Policy Committee and deliver a set speech. He had publicly promised an awesome retribution for the crime.

Mari went ashore and established credit identity, drawing on Martin's prepared accounts. No names were attached to these accounts, only numbers and code words, and there was nothing to hint at Overed's ownership. Mari bought tickets for the two of them on a plane leaving for the Highlands base, Ghotaw Central. Uncle Ho would take his boat back to New Essex when he was ready, after their signal from Ghotaw that they were staying there.

To survive and prosper, Martin had to move upstream on the chitin drug line. He had to get to the Highlands and blend in. Just surviving, becoming a deep-sea fisherman, for example, did not appeal to him. He wanted more than that and was determined to fight for it. And besides, he knew perfectly well that in the end his only chance of avoiding the retribution promised by the EASU was to build some other power base, or join another organization. It would be difficult and it would be dangerous, but it would be better than waiting for the day when the EASU men finally tracked him down.

Martin went ashore at night and moved quickly through the narrow streets of Coast City, which clung to a strip of woodwose-proof cliffs and crags. The airstrip was an inflatable that floated out between two of the largest crags. Airy, collapsible bridges and walkways connected the various fragments of the place, which was crowded and claustrophobic, even to dome dwellers like Martin Overed.

Once on the plane, he and Mari relaxed slightly. Despite the outcry over on the Essex Coast, no one at the airport had seemed to notice him, while on the plane the other passengers were all too absorbed in their own affairs to pay much attention to anyone else. Like many other people, he wore a light senso rig, which shielded his features behind a veil of shadow.

The jets were still the Fundan-built models, the old Talbot 440s. They were wide-bodied, comfortable subsonics that were stingy on fuel and flew at an altitude of forty thousand feet. The trip took more than twelve hours, and Martin was desperately tired of the confinement by the end. It reminded him of the nightmarish stories the old-timers told of the trip out from Earth—years in confinement in the bellies of the great ships, years of "living in a seat." Martin was sure it would have driven him crazy. He always felt that it was what had made his mother so paranoid and suspicious. The hours seemed to drag on forever, but at last the old plane thudded down on the strip and they stepped out into a vast natural basin ringed with colossal mountains.

The great Ghotaw Valley was a tremendous experience for those who had spent most of their lives confined to the coastline. The vast, distant peaks soaring in precipice after precipice above the equatorial snowline, the chill, the deep blue sky, and the harshness of the light, made it virtually another world.

After that initial impression the squalor of Ghotaw Central was a shock. On his previous visit, several years before, it had been a small town, a collection of domes, shacks, and a few larger structures housing laboratories, vaults, and stores. Now it was a much bigger place, and the population had increased tenfold. There were hundreds of domes sprawling over the whole south slope of the volcano. Plumes of dust arose above big trucks busy around construction sites.

Smoke and the smells of poorly planned human habitation rose from the town in a choking cloud, to mingle with the dust thrown up by the traffic on the raw ash roads. There was garbage strewn thickly in the gullies lower down. Beyond that was a vast pile of debris, a moraine of human junk that had built up at the bottom of the mountain. In the center of this exhibition of the frailties of human settlement there was a shopping strip, flanked by another street filled with bars and whorehouses. Electric generators whined constantly to keep a forest of tall signs illuminated, blinking through the night on either side of a straight street of stabilized ash that even boasted traffic lights.

They checked into a place that called itself a hotel and wound up with a tube space, nine feet long and five across. Martin could have had better but he didn't want to attract attention. Already he had a feeling there was a pervasive EASU presence in Ghotaw.

When they moved around on the strip of restaurants, shops, and bars he soon recognized faces. He wore the shrouding senso, something that was pretty common here, but still there were plenty of people who didn't mind showing off their faces and among these he noticed EASU gangsters. Once they stepped into the Blue Mountain restaurant, a large, expensive eatery that had only recently opened. At a nearby table he observed a thug he'd known on the coast, one Camilo Ganymede.

Camilo was actually a Saturn, but somehow he'd wangled his way into the EASU at the entry level. His strength and ferocity had taken him far. Now he was munching wild-animal steak and being courted by a group of traders. Camilo was too busy listening to the pitchmen to pay attention to the rest of the restaurant, so he never noticed Martin. Still, Overed's uneasiness did not go away. EASU was all around him here.

The next day, the vital senso unit began malfunctioning. It would blink on and off at odd moments. He went into a shop that advertised the repair of consumer electronics. While he was there a narrow-faced woman came in with an order for a piece of lab equipment. He knew her at once; she had been on the EASU Science Board. He'd been given the job of shaking up her boss on one occasion.

Fortunately, she had plenty of EASU arrogance and though she interrupted his own business with her demands, she never looked at him. When she had the equipment, a deformer unit with a flux generation controller, she stalked out, oblivious of his presence.

Martin swapped his senso rig for another, more expensive model and ducked outside. There was a cold feeling in his gut. There was just so much EASU up here, they had the place covered. How was he going to stay ahead of them long enough to get into a strong position?

He and Mari kept moving around. They stayed a night at the Old Ghotaw Hotel, a place with real rooms and troublesome native vermin. Some feral chitin had gotten loose in the town and become almost impossible to root out. The chitin was a nasty pest, quite capable of attacking and even killing people if it mustered sufficient numbers. A roving worker bit Mari during the night and they left the next morning. They went on to the Duluxi, where they stayed two nights, then went to the Blue Sky House, a cheaper place up above the town. They soon discovered why it was cheaper despite the lovely views. At night, the town lit wood stoves to keep warm, and the smoke rose over the Blue Sky House in a thick cloud that made everyone inside cough and gasp.

Martin found that the dominant local banks, the Spreak Bank and the Chitin Bank, were reluctant to handle credit drawn on accounts in Coast City. A wave of bankruptcies down there some years before had soured their reputation. Things had improved recently, but the Highland banks were still very cautious. It would take time to establish a credit position that drew on his real reserves. Meanwhile, he had some credit at the Spreak Bank, a separate thing he'd set up years before, and he had some pharamol. That was the local currency, but it was not going to last more than a month or two. He had to get started on something. And yet there was so much EASU around, and they were bound to have seen his picture recently with the big manhunt. It was inevitable that he would be reported.

And then?

He stayed inside a lot while Mari went out and did their business. Once, he stepped outside and some children took his photograph. He ran after them but they bicycled away into a maze of alleys and slum shacks. It was mysterious and threatening. They were probably only playing a game but still it shook him. It made everyone seem a potential threat, so he was afraid to go out. But, after a while, he began to feel like a caged animal.

One morning, after Mari had gone down to the Spreak Labs building to see if she could get work there, Martin felt he couldn't stand the cabin fever any longer, so he went out and made his way to a greasy diner called Neet's. It was built of ceram packing crates and sailcloth awnings set up on a puffcrete slab on a street just above the big strip. He ordered synth fries and caf. While he waited for them, he watched the traffic go by on what they called the New Street outside.

He was working his way through his synthetics when a slim young woman with piercing dark eyes slid into a seat opposite him. He started thinking that the prostitutes in this town were the most aggressive he'd ever run into, but she turned these thoughts upside down as soon as she opened her mouth.

"You're lost."

He looked about himself carefully. If he had to kill her, he needed to know if there were going to be a lot of witnesses.

"I don't know you," he growled.

"No, but I know who you are. We've been looking for you." She reached out and patted his arm. He almost drew on her. "Relax. We're not EASU."

He'd gone as white as a sheet and his heart was pounding in his chest.

"We're not trying to kill you."

The breath was stuck in his throat, there was a roaring in his ears. He blinked and struggled for breath.

"Relax. We can help you."

He stopped struggling. Who was she? Carefully, he slid his hand away from the small handgun taped to his left side.

"What do you want?" he asked.

"We're going to rescue you. When you've had your breakfast, all you have to do is walk to the rear of the diner. Someone will meet you there."

"Who are you? How do I know if I can trust you?"

She put a small hand-vid unit on the table.

"Plug into the central net, just key in five."

Suspicious, sweating, he pushed the five.

"Now type Q. Now 'Seek Fundan.' "

He typed. Finally she said, "My name is Fair Fundan. Ask it for a graphic."

The picture came up in a second and it was her, perhaps a little younger, but undoubtedly the same.

"A Fundan, eh? One of the old power players, eh?"

"Right. We need you." She paused for a moment. "And you most decidedly need us."

14

It was a small meeting in a small tent between Martin, Fair Fundan, the older-looking geezer called Hof Witlin, and the mystery man of indeterminate age who looked in for a half hour or so, then ducked out without a word. The mystery man had never been introduced, but Martin knew that he was important. Fair deferred to him and he knew now that Fair didn't defer to very many people.

They sat in a circle, wrapped in sleeping bags with a faint light set up in the center. It was very cold, for the tent was perched high on a mountain slope in the back of beyond. In the background was the steady rumble of a glacier-fed torrent that thundered through a nearby gorge. It was wild country, and Martin had never seen anything like it. Hell, you had to wear an oxygen tank most of the time, and at night it got cold enough to give you frostbite.

And it was lonely. Martin hadn't seen more than five people in the entire two weeks since he'd left Ghotaw Central, smuggled out in the trunk of an ancient ATV driven by some pretty young assistant of Witlin's from the chitin labs.

He'd been scared shitless back then, but now, well, now things were different. He was tanned and felt pretty damn healthy, but he was wondering how much of this outdoor life he could stand. He'd be barking mad from loneliness if he had to stay out here year after year.

Of course he recognized that this was debriefing time. Things would get better eventually, as long as he played it clever enough this time 'round. Accordingly, he'd carefully parceled out the intelligence he fed them, and in the process he had learned something about his captors. They were deadly serious and they were few in number.

The people he did see a lot were the amazing Fair Fundan, old Hof Witlin, and the slender figure of the mystery man. It had become apparent that the mystery man had been using longevity drugs for a long time, and he had a hell of an attitude. There was real hostility in him just about all the time.

There was also a strong something between this man and Fair. It seemed like an old love affair. Martin didn't know how to read it, especially as this man would never say more than two words at a time. Martin eventually sussed it; the mystery man had probably lost someone to a raid. He hated all EASU people as a result—quite natural, really.

Problem, that, he mused. Funny how unimportant the raiding had seemed to him down on the Coast. People knew it went on, they knew the younger guys usually volunteered for it since it won them points with EASU. It brought in a lot of longevity drugs but unless people were in the receiving line they didn't care too much. They were more interested in the prices on the street for chitin drugs and making enough credit to keep on stream.

Of course, none of these people had to worry about staying on line for pharamol. They could probably roll in the stuff. He tried to imagine such wealth, handfuls of eternal life. It was too fucking much. And this group of people, they were tight. He could tell from the looks that strayed his way that old Hof

Witlin was dangerously jealous of the good relationship Martin already had with Fair. So he knew that Witlin and Fair had had a thing. And there was also something with the mystery man. Yeah, they were tight. He whistled to himself again. She put herself about a bit, didn't she?

The amazing Fair, a beauty with brains and a sort of ferocity he was unused to in women. She was either more than a woman or the first real woman he'd ever met, one who was free to shape her own destiny in complete freedom, and with the command of immense resources. She had power. In fact, he felt the same kind of aura around her that he'd noticed around the Big Man and around old Congo. Automatic respect was what it was. He'd lived in the hierarchy of EASU all his life—he knew respect when he saw it. Mind you, it was a rare day that a woman made it far up the EASU ladder. Cor, they saw one coming on like this and they'd whack her at an early age. Just termination, no questions asked.

She was clearly the leader here, though. And the things she dropped into conversation! Martin didn't know where even half of it came from. Of course, his education had been limited, even minimal. He couldn't have told tennis apart from polo nor named a single state in the ancient United States of America. Hell, he didn't even know all the countries of North Europe, where he'd been born. So when she took off into "syntacticism" and started into the "dialectics" and "imperative-normatives," he was left behind.

Instead he'd just look at her, drinking her in, enjoying the view. She was tanned like all the Highlanders, and wore her black hair tied back. There was something about her that was very different from the washed-out blondes that Martin thought of when he thought of spacer norams. And when you thought of old-time spacers you had to think first of the clan Fundan, who were a legendarily pale, cold-looking lot, with those wide faces and long limbs associated with centuries of low gravity.

Fair had none of that. She was more tightly constructed, more a tigress than a spacer. She had this vitality that went with the aura of power; together they were a frightening mixture. It was scary, but it really turned him on.

And it did something to her, too. Martin could tell now that she was also interested in him. At some point, pretty soon, they would be getting better acquainted, and he had a pretty good idea that neither of the other two was going to be happy about that. In the meantime, he had something good to give them; in fact, it was by far the best piece of EASU intelligence that he possessed and he knew he'd been wise to hold on to it. The bargaining power was maximized. He knew what they needed most.

Hof Witlin laid it out for him. "Look, we can find out when a raid is coming, but we have to know more than that. We have to know where. We need exact locations to be able to strike and stop them cold. With the huge area we have to protect, there's no way to do it otherwise with the resources we have."

Half the cards were on the table. He had to be just as bold; no point in holding back now.

"Right. Well, I think I can help."

Fair stared at him, measuring him. "There's other things we need, too," she said, "to fill in the picture. I think we need friends among the Roiders, so we need to get through to them. You have friends there."

"Yeah, well, I knew they needed friends, y'know. But, well—" Martin shrugged. Judging by Mari's reactions, it might be that the Roiders weren't too ready to make friends with the first families. "I don't know, chief. I mean, like, the Roiders aren't too fond of anyone else. No one's ever given them a break. You know, I sometimes think they hate everyone. They certainly got no reason to want to deal with you people."

She understood this. "Of course, but we have pharamol to spare. Plenty of it, and we'll pay very well for what we want. We don't have to oppress the Roiders."

"Right." Naturally, they would buy the information they needed. Martin felt better and better. Well-paid spies were the most loyal kind. Still there were problems.

"The Roiders don't have the info you really need. That's all EASU stuff and tightly held, too."

Hof leaned forward, eyebrows knotted in a frown.

"How high up would this be restricted to? The Executive Group, for instance, would they know?"

Martin shook his head. "Nah, PolCom only, probably not even the whole committee. On something like that it wouldn't go much outside of Lawler and Congo, and Slovo, of course, and Wilson and Soko. Wilson and Soko basically represent the interest of the Londons. See, in EASU, it's the joining of the Londons and the Essex Coasts that forms the power base, so they have to be included in PolCom decisions."

"And Lawler, why Lawler?"

"Lawler's Enforcement Section. He's been the ES boy since arrival. He took over from Givver Flax. Actually, he killed Flax when Flax started to make a move on the Big Man. Flax thought he could be the Big Man on the New World. The Big Man beat him to the punch."

"I see, and Erst always consults with the Enforcement chief."

"Yeah, well, now he does. Lawler's his man. But when Flax was head of Enforcement it was a different matter. The Big Man had to negotiate all the time with Flax. It was almost like they were joint rulers. Of course, I was just a junior in Enforcement then so I didn't get the clearest picture of what went on, but I know there were some pretty heavy struggles on board the ship. Some geezers got put out the airlock quietly once we were in this system and down to safe speeds."

"Did that happen to Flax?"

Martin grinned. "Nah. Flax was a hard one to get—they had to kill him in his own bathtub. He wasn't about to surrender. He killed one of the guys sent to get him. I knew about it because that geezer what got killed, I knew him. We were sorta friends in training group, see."

Hof flicked a glance to Fair. "Okay, how about Congo?"

"Congo heads up the Inside Group, counterintelligence, counterpenetration, all that. Congo knows too much to ever be left out. I tell you, if the Big Man ever slips, I wouldn't be surprised if it was Congo what took his place instead of Lawler. I mean, everyone goes around saying it'll be Lawler but I dunno, Congo's the one with the best moves if you ask me."

"And Slovo Milsuduk?"

"Yeah—" Martin grinned wolfishly. "—Slovo. Now, Slovo will know everything. The Big Man trusts him more than anyone else. Of course, Slovo totally depends on the Big Man, much more than the others, 'cause they got power bases of their own. But Slovo's got nothing except his skills. He's the Big Man's extra human brain, see, like he doesn't have an ego or anything. And, without the Big Man, he'd be dead in a flash since neither Lawler nor Congo can stand him; everyone knows that. But Slovo's good at what he does and the Big Man keeps him close."

Fair could sense it; he could tell from the way her nostrils flared. Martin was holding something back.

Good. She was making a decision.

It was time to give Mr. Overed the offer and see how he

came down. Fair looked over to Hof, who nodded. Poor Hof hated Overed, and he was already jealous. Poor Hof, he was going to have a hard time of it for a while. Obviously he was going to hate her having anything to do with this hard, brutal thug from the inside world of EASU. But something was going to happen. She could tell. There was something very attractive about him to her. Those qualities of hardness and cold-eyed cruelty perhaps. Poor Hof.

"I think it's time we made clear to you, Mr. Overed, that we want you on our side. We've decided to recruit you."

"Recruit?" His mouth had dropped open momentarily. He hadn't expected this, or at least not so soon.

"Well—" He regained control quickly. "—Nice."

"Maybe, but it will also be dangerous. However, you'll be well compensated."

Fair held out a hand and opened it to reveal a small metal tube, similar to a bullet casing. "Take it," she said. "Squeeze on the thicker end, that's the bottom."

The pressure caused the top half to split open, revealing a glass vial inside. The vial had a tiny screw top. It was about a third filled with sparkling blue grains.

Pharamol! High quality, probably Fundan Blue, maybe Spreak Skycrystal, top-of-the-market stuff.

"I'm impressed," he said.

They wanted him bad, that was clear.

Fair held his gaze with a stare. "There'll be more, later, when you've earned it. One thing though, you need to remember that all the pharamol you'll ever take will have had to be earned. It has to be won out of the ground. The nests don't give it willingly—they're not bees that can be easily duped into giving up their honey. They kill sometimes, quite unpredictably, too."

"Yeah, sure. Thanks." He smiled at them, doing his best to ignore the dislike in Hof's eyes.

"Do you feel safer now, Mr. Overed?"

Safer? Stuck up here on this bloody mountain? Sure, they wanted him, and when they had what they wanted they could kill him and retrieve this small fortune in pharamol and go their way and leave his body to mummify in this cold alien desert.

"Well, I suppose so. I mean, I'd like to join up. I accept the offer, but I dunno if it's for real. I mean, what's to stop you just killing me and taking this back whenever you want?"

She nodded. "Oh, sure, we could. But we won't. We need you just as you need us."

Hof Witlin couldn't hide his contempt at that, but he kept silent.

"Yeah, well, great."

"So you accept?"

"Yeah. Count me in."

"Good. So tell us what's important about Slovo Milsuduk."

He whistled inwardly again. Sussed him out, hadn't she? Blimey!

"Slovo's a samesexer, what do you call 'em, homosexual."

"So?"

"Well, the Big Man is irrational about samesexers. He hates them. Me, I could care less, I mean, that's their business, innit? But the Big Man, he's psycho about it. So Slovo keeps it secret. He's clever, is our Slovo. He don't go with women very much, but he does once in a while, at the big EASU things. I bet he makes sure that the Big Man sees him do it. But several times a week he fades out of the picture and slips away to this little love nest he has in an expensive beachside condo. He's got this pretty boy set up there in luxury. Once a week Slovo shows up. I know about this, see, because I happened to spot Slovo sneaking through the back of the domes on Green Street. I got curious about this 'cause there was no security out and here was one of the top men in the political committee. So I followed him and I found out where he went and I investigated."

"And then you blackmailed him, I suppose," Hof Witlin said.

"Nah, I used him to get in on the Big Man. So old Slovo, he's fucked. I mean, if I told the Big Man that Slovo gave him away then you know what's going to happen to Slovo." Martin winced.

"Yes, I can imagine," Hof murmured.

"So Slovo Milsuduk is very vulnerable to blackmail, isn't he?" Fair said.

"Right, exactly."

"Excellent. We thank you, Mr. Overed. This is a precious resource and one that we must not waste. He must be protected. We need a pure courier method to get his reports. He must not resort to any telcom."

"Easy—use the boy. Get him to drop the stuff to someone outside. Slovo already covers his tracks when he goes off on his little visits and I really don't think Lawler knows. Use the boy to drop you the data when he goes to the shops or something. You can set up that kind of trail easy on the Essex Coast."

"How can we be so sure that Erst and Lawler don't know about Slovo Milsuduk's amorous affairs?"

"Come on, if they knew that they'd do him right away. They hate him. They just think he's a wanker. If they had the chance to get rid of him they'd take it in a flash. Slovo keeps EASU accounts. Lawler and Congo can't take as much as a grain that don't belong to them."

"Good. We seem to have just what we need, a source placed right in the innermost councils of EASU."

"I suppose you'll need some help from me in getting in touch with him. I could guide you in, sort of."

Fair stared at him again, testing him.

"We thought we'd send you, with some company to keep you safe, if you want it."

Martin paled. "Shit! I can't go back there. Essex Coast? You're crazy, they're looking for me everywhere."

She shook her head very precisely. "Actually, not so much now." She noted his surprise. "You won't be our only agent down there, you know. We have our sources of information. I could show you copies of the X-rays of the Big Man's chest. You came close to killing him all right—missed his heart by an inch."

Martin's breath hissed out of him.

"He'll never let up, he'll never let go. You don't know him, he's fucking implacable."

"Well, you'll be staying out of sight pretty much, won't you."

"Why don't you go in on Slovo yourselves. You gotta see that it would be wasting a great asset if you lost me down there."

"We all have to take risks now; it's the only way we're going to stop Arvin Erst."

"Yeah, well, that's nice, but he's going to kill me real slow and nasty."

"You won't be on your own. You'll be safe enough if you do as you're told. We need you there, though. If he knows that you're our agent he'll know he can't sell us misinformation, that we'll have your input on it."

"Right." Martin grinned nervously. Send him back to the

Coast. Shit, but that could be a death sentence. If the Big Man ever got his hands on him . . .

"Look at it this way," Hof said as the meeting broke up and they stood outside the tent, stretching in the cold night air. "If you don't turn Slovo and make him useful to us, then we're probably going to fail to stop Erst. And that means he'll have you in the end."

There was a real unfriendliness in the old man's eyes, as if he'd like nothing better than to give Martin Overed to the Big Man right then.

15

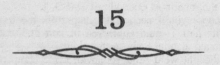

THE BIG MAN WAS BACK, WITH TWO MEDICS IN CONSTANT ATTENtion and backups all the way down the line to the emergency ward at the EASU clinic. He moved around the Essex Coast in a whirl of sudden appointments and audiences, with Slovo at his side. Lawler and Congo hovered anxiously on the edges. Everyone fawned, awed by his strength and the speed of his recovery. He was the Big Man and they knew it. He liked the light of that knowledge shining in their eyes. They were all his spaniels and they'd better not forget it!

But the Big Man felt a hollowness at his center, right there beside the considerable pain from his wound. That damned cheat Overed. Got in a lucky shot. Got away, clean away. Still hadn't picked up a trace of the little cheating bastard.

Damn! But he, Arvin Erst, PolCom of EASU, was lucky to be alive. That was the real hollowness. The Big Man couldn't afford to live by luck.

The hollowness had only become worse with the failure to track down this elusive Martin Overed. At the beginning, there'd been a suspicion that he might have gotten away to the mountains. There was a report of him staying in a hotel up there with a Roider woman, but a search of Ghotaw Central had failed to locate the wretch, and the Big Man was still frustrated.

There had been a break of sorts, a weird thing that was also troubling to the Big Man. Congo had hauled in a doctor, the very surgeon who had repaired the bullet damage in his chest, a Dr. James Esro. Except that Congo's boys had found that he was really one Esro Fundan, a distant cousin of the ruling Fundans.

They put the doctor to it on the hotbed and, in time, he broke and they learned that he routinely fed information to a network of agents who reported to a mysterious committee that operated up in the Ghotaw Valley. He babbled about a "Highland nation" that they were building and how they were going to keep EASU out of the big mountains.

The Big Man was filled with questions. What was this committee? What did they think they were playing at, planting a Fundan in his surgery, running agent networks on EASU turf? With the questions came fear and rage. However, the Big Man did not kill the surgeon; they put the fellow on ice and started working on finding the rest of this network of agents. The Big Man felt a profound unease at the thought of the old Fundans being at work in this way. They were supposed to be out of it these days, a pack of chitin talkers and little more.

But that name, *Fundan*, worried him nonetheless. That was a name out of legend: Asteroid Princes, builders of spacehabs in the outer planetaries. The best tech gear was still usually Fundan-made.

The Big Man pressed hard. He wanted more and he wanted it fast. Congo and Lawler put their people to work but, despite everything, it was slow going. They hauled in every old Fundan they could find on the Coast. A couple of them committed suicide when the lads came knocking on the door; the rest knew nothing. There were about twenty of them, mostly elderly women in retreat from the world. They had no connection to the ruling Fundans and no useful intelligence. The network of agents that the doctor boasted of was still out there.

Erst was very unsatisfied. He pressed other organs of the EASU to obtain a complete picture of the ruling Fundans. Who were they now? What were their activities? Where were they and how might they be reached?

This information was easy to come by. The control of the central family funds had shifted away from the descendants of Edward the Great. His great-grandson had been the end of the acknowledged lineage, except for a maverick great-great-granddaughter whose claims to legitimacy were contested. But she was reported dead, killed during a raid in the early part of the year.

Now it was the line of Luther Fundan that held the governing reins of control, Luther and his grandson, Proud Fundan. The Big Man ordered an intensive investigation of these two and all their associates. If these were his enemies he wanted to know everything about them.

The information came back in short order. Luther was semiretired, lived with a couple of younger women on a range near Mt. Fundan. He had benefited from early speculation on the price of chitin drugs and, though he had never worked the chitin directly, he was very wealthy.

Proud Fundan was more active. He ran an extensive chitin-farming operation on the eastern flanks of Mt. Fundan. His group had fought off an attempted raid some years before and no one had tried for his caches recently. Proud was said to be an arrogant example of old Fundan "quality" who had little contact with outsiders, keeping to his circle of kin and old friends. Proud occasionally visited Ghotaw Central, however, usually on his way to one or another of the chitin vaults on the North Slope.

The Big Man was puzzled. These figures seemed too withdrawn, too distant to be involved in spy rings down on the New Essex Coast. He didn't like to be puzzled. He ground his teeth and slammed his fist on table and desk. "Find me Martin Overed!" he roared.

Thousands of miles away, in the western foothills of Mt. Fundan, Martin Overed was in the process of thawing out from his weeks-long sojourn in the high pass. Out in the sunshine of the middle morning, he enjoyed the warmth of the sun in the dry, clear air. Outside the caves, the vast bowl of the mountains surrounding Ghotaw stood out clear and sharp, and Ghotaw Mountain itself could be seen in the center, a dark volcanic cone quite diminutive in comparison with its mighty neighbors.

Martin was feeling a little better every day. He liked this warmth. He liked the dry air, so different from the tropical heat of the Essex Coast. He stretched carefully, working the kinks out of his back muscles and his legs. Then he started down the line of exposed rocks that, in the right light, resembled a row of gigantic molars and provided cover for the trail that led away from the Fundan base in the caves. At the end of the line of big rocks, the jik forest grew thickly across a little stream valley that ran down to the chitin-raising areas below. The entire route was almost completely hidden from overhead surveillance.

Martin liked to take a walk when it was offered. He'd been exposed to all this wide-open beauty but had had little chance to do much more than stare at it. Up in the high pass, he'd had to stay inside the tent most of the time, safe from accidental satellite pickup. Down here they hid in an extensive cave system. But he hungered for the light, the brilliance, and vistas of wide-open spaces.

While out on the line of rocks, he moved quickly from shadow to shadow along a route marked out with rosettes of gray radar baffle that to the uninitiated eye looked like circular clumps of lichen. Then, when he reached the stream, he could afford to move out of deep concealment, for by then he was far enough from the caves. But even then there were orders to be very discreet and to move quickly away from the molar rocks.

The tempo in the caves had picked up recently. The ever-mysterious Elgin Fundan had come and gone and come back, or so Martin had heard. And Fair herself had shown up for a brief visit two nights back. Martin had been consulted again on the ways things were set up in EASU. They'd had dinner together, the usual synthetics, sitting on a narrow bed in Martin's pop-up. She'd let slip that things were fine with Mari, who had responded very well to the offer of pharamol payments, and who had returned to the Coast to build a network of agents for the Highland families.

At this thought Martin let out a sigh. This idyll up here in these colossal mountains was soon to end. He would be going down to the New Essex Coast himself to tackle the job of getting in on Slovo Milsuduk again and conducting the required blackmail. Uncle Ho would be waiting for him in Coast City, and he would go back to the Essex Coast in a reverse of the way he had come out.

From then on he would be hidden by the Roiders. The big difference this time was that they would be wielding a powerful weapon, in the shape of enormous wealth in chitin drugs. They would be able to buy security. They would be careful, of course; there would be no flamboyant display. They would live in anonymous mid-level apartment domes, and Martin would not appear in public except to visit Slovo Milsuduk. It would be a life of boredom, completely shut in, and yet there would be constant tension, even terror. The EASU well deserved its reputation for vigilance.

Moving on, he rounded a corner and came to the place where the trail left the rocks and went down a zigzag canyon beneath the little jik trees. A large shape moved in the shadows. Someone was coming the other way, someone big. He tensed and then realized it was the Fein called N'ka. He had been introduced to this Fein, and still found it amazing. Here was an alien life-form that could think and speak interlingua! The fact that it looked like a bear crossed with a cat and had been given a heroic physique just intensified the strangeness of the experience. The only Fein he'd seen before had been on video or as rugs on the floors in the homes of elite EASU operatives.

As the Fein came close, Martin nodded and smiled. N'ka nodded and smiled in return, exposing big canine teeth in a fearsome grin. Martin would have gone on, but the Fein held his eye and spoke directly to him. "Greetings to the one called Mar-tin, who come from the other world in the far away. You fear the other ones that come from the other world in the far away. It is good for you to have rocks over your head, eh? Mar-tin Over-your-head, eh?"

Martin gulped. Alien jokes about his name? The Fein chuckled at his astonishment. "N'ka learning human tongue, yes? Good, yes? Hah! N'ka use the machine, it help."

"Machine?" Did this mean the Fundans were wiring this alien up to an old language machine? The idea was bizarre and menacing to him. Here was this alien monster, looking as if it might like to eat people for lunch, and it was speaking interlingua to him in a quiet, albeit growly voice.

"You speak lingua very well, Unka."

"No, Mar-tin, no Un-ka, N'ka."

"Yeah, well, N'ka, then." Martin did his best to master the odd modified glottal in the name and was rewarded with another ferocious grin.

Sheez, but these critters were big. This one was supposedly only a kid but already it was taller than most men and a whole lot heavier. Back on Earth, it would have a place in any football or rugby team that it chose to join.

"I speak human tongue good and I drink beer good! What you do?"

What? Drink beer good? How was he to explain himself? Martin groped. "I guess you could say I'm on the run."

Drink beer good? Yeah, he bet the Fein could drink beer good. He tried to imagine what a drunken Fein might be like. Probably destroyed entire bars.

The Fein laughed, a loud and fearsomely cheerful thing. "You run? No, you walk. What means guess-you-could?"

Now Martin was seriously stumped. He groped again. "Well, lingua is a little loose sometimes. Colloquial-like, don't you see?"

"Don't see? Don't see what? N'ka see very well."

"Yeah, right." Martin was getting confused himself. He was struggling to form a comprehensible answer for the big alien when he noticed that Elgin Fundan had appeared beside him, wearing his usual faint smile of contempt.

Elgin greeted the Fein in some of the alien's tongue and received a reply in the same. They conversed together briefly in that tongue, which sounded thick and heavy with sibilance to Martin. N'ka addressed some questions to Elgin and received replies, after which he shook hands with Martin, slapped Elgin's palm with a huge paw, and went on up the hidden path to the molar rocks.

Martin was left face-to-face with Elgin Fundan. It was an uncomfortable moment, and Martin said nothing, used to receiving little but a chilly contempt from Elgin Fundan.

"You like walks, do you?" Elgin inquired suddenly.

Martin started with surprise. "Well, yeah, sure, you get cooped up in those caves." What was this all about? In the weeks since Martin had left Ghotaw Central, Elgin had barely exchanged ten words with him. Now they were going to have a polite chat out here on the trail?

Martin eased back a step. This might mean anything. Elgin hated him and all of his kind, it was easy to tell. Perhaps Elgin thought his usefulness was over. Who the hell could tell what Elgin wanted? The geezer had a face of stone.

"Cooped up for your own good. Sure you agree."

Martin grinned. Of course, you bastard Fundan, I love being confined to a cave because I'm on the run from the Big Man.

"Well, sure," he said. "I don't want EASU to find out where I am, oh, no, thank you."

"Funny, that. You're going down there again. You're going to be risking your life."

"Yeah." Why did everyone keep harping on it? Couldn't they see he was in pain over this? What was wrong with them?

"Risking it for us, too," Elgin said.

"Yeah, well, you lot have stuck your necks out for me and it looks like we have to have this info you need to stop them."

Elgin's eyes seemed to bore into him like twin pillars of blue ice. "So you've changed sides, haven't you?"

So? What was the guy's problem? Martin was tired of the attitude. "Yeah! And I don't have any fucking choice, do I!"

"No, I suppose you don't."

"Look, you can trust me—I got nowhere else to go. I can't go back! You know what they'd do to me."

Elgin gave him a thin smile. "Yes, your friends seem to have miscalculated on that part of their reputation."

"EASU has been on top too long; they've gone soft in the head. The Big Man, though, he'll never give up. He's old-line EASU."

"We have to stop them."

"Yeah, right. I know that. We lose, they get me—among other things."

Elgin gestured down the trail. "I want to show you something, to help you understand."

Martin hesitated, still astonished at this approach from Elgin and still not entirely trusting him, either.

Elgin smiled again and held up his hands, palms out.

"Hey, stop worrying, I'm not going to kill you. We need you, Overed. That need overrides everything else."

Martin swallowed. Fuck you, Mister High and Mighty Fundan! "Yeah."

With Elgin leading, they went on down the trail. They crossed the stream and entered a sector with woods of jik, mindal, and laloop trees punctuated by clearings and areas packed with dwarf hobi gobi. In some of these clearings they began to observe pale "fins" of mud that were raised anywhere from two to ten feet above the level of the ground. These fins were usually aligned so as to present the wide faces to the sun, the chitin seeking to store heat during the day to keep the nests superwarmed during the night.

So what were they going to see? What was this mysterious "something" that would help him understand these lordly Fundans? Slowly he began to notice a buzzing sound. It grew in volume as they went on, and took on an angry tone.

A pair of lanky figures clad in green camo emerged from the trees, carrying binocs and small packs. They also had automatic rifles on their shoulders. Elgin greeted them with a salute and a quiet word or two. They looked up and raked Martin with their eyes, then ignored him.

Elgin turned back to him.

"I wanted you to see this. Come along."

They went forward and climbed a small rock outcrop. Below their position the ground was stained black with the bodies of millions of chitin insects. From them came the angry buzzing sound, here so loud it was more like a roar. At the base of the outcrop stood a pair of eight-foot-high fins. Around them was arrayed a dense mass of chitin. Streamers of insects stretched out to the trees on the far side.

"This is a nest war. Look closely." Elgin handed him a pair of binocs.

He looked. The black mass differentiated into thousands of warring individual insects, some of them warriors with immense mandibles, others simply workers. One kind had a dark brown abdomen with no markings, another had a green stripe on a lighter brown.

The slaughter was intense.

"Two nests at war. You see? The green bands mark a young nest: Slade Mountain variety, good to work with. That's the nest under attack. The others are from a nest that's gone feral. It's old and mean and no one can work with it anymore. We probably have to destroy it."

Martin stared down at the battle. Accompanying the angry sound was an odd chemical stink, a reek of powerful acids.

"If you fell into that now you'd be dead in no time at all, since they'd all sting you."

"Yeah." It was easy to believe.

"But when a nest kills a chitin talker it usually doesn't sting them completely to death. It prefers to eat them alive."

Martin said nothing. The nest armies continued their grim struggle below.

"Just so you know what it is we deal with to get you your longevity drugs."

"Yeah, right." Martin turned away with a shudder. He caught Elgin's sleeve.

"Enough of this shit, I'll do the job."

16

HOF AND FAIR HAD FLOWN EAST TO THE MEETING POINT, A CLEAR-ing on the northern slopes of Mt. Fundan. They'd set down in an ultralite flying on tiny battery motors and stowed it away beneath the trees. These little aircraft, part hang glider, part air-plane, had become their preferred method for getting around. They were as fast as any ground transport and used a lot less energy. The radar signature was tiny, too.

They were there at Elgin's request. He had something to show them. All he would say when Fair asked him to explain further was, "It goes right to the heart of what we have to do if we're to survive."

She'd been a little surprised by that. "You think we *can* survive, then?"

"Yes."

"Sometimes I wonder if you do. You seem so downcast, so bitter."

"Life hasn't turned out the way I'd hoped."

There'd been nothing she could say to that.

Someone in green camo signaled to them from the edge of the clearing. They followed and eventually entered a narrow mountain gorge, misted from the river thundering down below, choked with vegetation. Eventually they came to the cave, a narrow opening that led inside to a wider space. There were sound baffles stretched across the cave here, and when they'd passed through them they realized how good the baffles were. Outside they'd heard nothing; inside they were assaulted by the sounds of an excavator at work, way down the length of the cave. Metal crunched rock and a heavy IC engine growled.

As they went farther in the cave became square, enlarged, with structural columns holding up the ceiling. Groups of peo-ple, most of them young and vaguely recognizable to Fair, were at work around a set of big white cabinets. A sharp chemical tang hung in the air. Something stirred strange half flavors on the tongue.

Elgin was waiting for them there. He wore a set of stained overalls and had a rag tied around his head. His face had visible smudges over a heavy tan that spoke of a life spent on these mountain slopes. Behind him a machine was crushing chunks of dark rock as fast as a robot loader could shovel it into the hopper.

Hof's eyebrows rose inquisitively at the sight of the oil stains on Elgin's face and hands.

"Some of the old machines are really balky. The engine on one of our excavators has been down all day."

Fair chewed her lower lip and looked over to the workers and the tall white cabinets.

"Yes," Elgin said, "it's time you saw what we've been up to."

Hof already understood. He was slightly awed. His group down at Ghotaw Central had been talking about building assembler tanks and reviving the old Fundan technology for manufacturing with metals and ceramics. And here it was. Elgin Fundan had seen the need and, with characteristic energy and secrecy, had simply gone ahead and done it. Hof wanted to applaud, but something held his tongue. He was increasingly at odds with Elgin and he didn't know why. He suspected it was just his own natural dislike for the high-handed ways of the old family. They almost wanted war, he thought sometimes.

"Hope you haven't left a heat signature," Hof said.

Elgin shrugged. "Small. We're on the site of a major deposit of iron ore with a purity around sixty per cent. It's all through the rocks below us. Surveillance is skewed to account for it. We're right on top. Wouldn't show up unless they analyzed intensively. I doubt that they think we're still capable of doing this."

Hof grunted. Elgin knew the older man was impressed. He also knew that Hof liked only a single Fundan—Fair—and that his feelings for Elgin were largely dislike. To Elgin, this was all irrelevant. All he needed was Hof's cooperation.

He saw Fair's eyes light up at last when a cabinet was opened at the far end of the line and a rack of newly created gun barrels was pulled out, each snugged in the matrix cradle that had gone into the tank. Young men and women in green overalls broke the cradles apart with their hands and laid the gleaming steel tubes on a bench behind them.

"It's a triple-level process," Elgin said. "The ore gets separated by an iron-seeking bacterial clone. From an iron-rich slurry we have a lattice assembler, and a molecule cleaner in the final tank works up the sludge for the macroassembler."

"Steel barrels. For what?" Fair looked around.

"These are for nine-millimeter automatic rifles, number four-oh-two in the Fundan Arms Catalog. We found a lot of useful things in the old computer files."

Hof was studying one of the finished weapons, a black matte thing of deadly appearance, a ghost of ancient wars fought on Earth five hundred years before—a terrible two-edged tool of civilization that had become a memory to the spacers and their descendants in the outer planetary systems. "I think this is based on the classic M33, U.S. Army in the twenty-first century."

Elgin's eyes sparked with a momentary respect.

"You're right. M33-A, in fact, issued to combat units in 2025. Very hard to improve on. We have six types of ammunition for it so far, and with plain steel jacketed we have effective range of two miles."

They passed an assembly line where more young people were putting together the pieces of grenade-launcher attachments for the new assault rifles. Hof was smiling. "I know what this is—this is a Fundan Assembler Plant, straight out of the old catalog."

Elgin nodded. "Low power needs throughout, chemical reactions, no heat, no signature."

"So we have the weapons, we have intelligence."

"And we have fifty trained fighters."

"And three Darters from the Spreaks."

"We can do it—we can stop them."

The drinking room in Bekunni's shebeen was a rough-and-ready place. Bekunni sold terrible beer, which he brewed from a carbohydrate slurry he bought in concentrate from the EASU supply store. He also sold vodka that he distilled himself out back on a piece of stolen laboratory apparatus. It was nearly pure spirit and got men drunk so fast they barely noticed. Bekunni rationed the stuff; that way he kept the idiots drinking the terrible beer a little longer. He made his money on the beer, which cost almost nothing to make and for which he charged a crank and a half per liter.

The sort of people who came to Bekunni's shebeen were those who were not welcomed any place classier. The freelance chitin robbers and grifters that hung out there were difficult customers, and Bekunni only just managed to eke out a profit from them.

One rule that Bekunni did insist on, however, was a ban on violence inside the shebeen. Outside, there was a gravel-topped parking lot where men regularly beat each other senseless and no one took any notice.

On this night there was something unusual in the drinking room. There was a big Fein in there and he'd gotten drunk on the white-lightning vodka. He'd come in looking for a beer and, when he'd had one, he'd turned to leave, since the beer was terrible. However, some fool had pitched into him and offered him a glass of the vodka. Bekunni had protested and cursed the fool, but it was too late.

The stuff seared N'ka's throat and seemed to explode in his stomach. He felt a sudden nausea and in a matter of moments he was drunk—wobbling drunk, unable-to-think-straight drunk, hard-to-even-walk-without-staggering drunk. N'ka had never felt like this before. He found it impossible to think clearly. It was not particularly pleasant and quite unlike the milder feeling he got from drinking two or three liters of beer. He sat down heavily on one of the crude chairs made of unseasoned jik wood. It groaned under him and almost broke. N'ka clutched his head.

Among the drinkers was a crew of muggers headed up by an EASU reject named Vlad. Vlad had a mean-eyed spirit, and the sight of the big Fein reeling about from the effects of Bekunni's vodka brought the evil to the surface pretty quickly. "What say we have a little fun with the fur rug," he grunted to his comrades.

With a few quick looks among them and some nasty grins, they nodded assent. All felt irrational fear and loathing of the big alien critters. They weren't seen around Ghotaw much anymore, for which they were all glad. This one needed a kicking—that would teach him to come into Bekunni's and drink like he was people or something.

Vlad sidled over to the seated Fein and squatted down by his side. Speaking very slowly and clearly, he told him that he wanted to show him something out on the street. N'ka struggled to focus on what the man was saying. He was disoriented. He did not know this man, and yet this stranger wanted to show him something. Outside, where the air would be cleaner. N'ka decided that going out to look at whatever it was was not a bad idea. He wanted to breathe clear air.

He went outside with Vlad. The others followed and, once they were in the gravel-topped parking lot, they jumped the big Fein. With nunchakus, a club, and a pair of steel knuckles, they set about beating him senseless.

The first blows were a shock, a complete surprise. N'ka reeled from a rice flail in his face. A club struck him across the arm, and someone kicked him in the stomach. He doubled up and the club thudded against his head. He fell to his knees, and boots slammed into his sides.

He could not breathe, and it was hard to move. He caught the club with one hand and twisted it away from its owner, but more boots thudded into him and he lost consciousness before he even hit the gravel.

It was incredibly humid and the temperature was hovering in the high nineties. Martin Overed looked out the apartment window at the row of pale blue domes opposite. All the domes in this sector were pale blue or pale green. Blue ones had names from old China, green ones had names from the Pacific Ocean. The one in which Martin was hidden, on the fourth floor, was the "Bora Bora" dome.

Past the blue domes, across the way, bulked larger buildings, including the towering kelp plant. Over that way, he knew, lay the old town and EASU headquarters, and that thought made him shiver. It was damned frightening just being here, knowing that Erst was over there somewhere.

But, as they'd made clear to him, the only chance they had of stopping Erst from eventually ruling the whole world was to turn Slovo and use his information to check the raiders from EASU. In a way, it was all up to Martin Overed.

He prayed he'd be able to get in on Slovo and do the job. Failure was unthinkable now.

The door activated. The computer told him that Kerri and Woag, the young Martians who were tracking Slovo, were outside. He signaled for them to be let in. He could tell from their happy faces that they'd tracked down their quarry at last.

"All right then, where?"

"Solarstrasse, the new Hamburg dome. All Germans. And Slovo."

17

IT WAS WARM IN HOF'S BED. HOF'S PLACE, A PUFFCRETE DOME bermed into the ash of Ghotaw's north slope, was warm, too, even on the coolest, clearest nights. It was typical Witlin, well-planned and carefully built. He had four small rooms, each functional, each decorated with Californian designs.

Fair lay quietly beside Hof and ran her fingers along the lines of his back and shoulders. His body betrayed the signs of late middle age, since he'd been that old when he reached the New World and traveled up to the Highlands.

"That old gray head is worrying. I can tell."

He wasn't asleep. "Plenty to worry about right now."

"You worry too much, old man. We're making progress. We're in the best position we've ever been in."

"Fair, I love you, and I have to say this. You've done wonders, but they have all the advantages still: they have the numbers, the technical capacity, and the access to higher technologies. We have to be incredibly lucky to win."

"Hof, I love you, too, but you're overlooking human nature. These people we're fighting, they're capable of making mistakes. If we hit them hard enough we can frighten them out of raiding, maybe forever."

He tensed momentarily and then relaxed.

"I don't know—yes, maybe. But we haven't pinned down this Slovo Milsuduk yet, have we?"

"We're close now, very close."

"And what about the Spreaks? Proud Fundan is threatening to call Ervil Spreak out in a duel in this matter of Naomi Fundan."

Fair shrugged and smiled. "Naomi has a right to complain. Volker Spreak tried to rape her. Anyway I think justice will be done eventually. Ervil is rallying his family against Volker over this. I think you can take it for granted that Ervil Spreak isn't about to fight any duels. He wants to live forever."

Hof was silent. Fair went further. "Look, we can deal with the Spreaks. They need us to survive and we need them."

"Correct."

"The Spreaks are the only ones who can make a good fighter plane. But even for them it's pretty damn difficult. You know how many parts there are in one of their Darters?"

"Easy, a hell of a lot."

"Thousands, most of them different. Even with an advanced assembler, it's a difficult job. Even getting all the rare metals we need has been pretty hard. This planet is low on titanium and that's a pity since titanium apparently is really useful for little fighter aircraft."

Hof rubbed his beard thoughtfully. "Yes, I know, the Spreaks kept up the old tech. But I also know that the Spreak Darter is a Fundan design."

"Well, of course it is. This is a Fundan-designed colony, or at least it was."

"It's not the Spreaks I'm worried about, really. I agree with you, they need us as much as we need them. I just don't understand what's to be gained by having you go down there to the Coast."

That again, of course—the underlying argument between them had surfaced again. In her heart, she'd expected this since she'd first broached the subject.

"I want to show the new people that we're really in this with them. We can't have them think that we're just the paymasters, sitting up here in safety while they risk their lives for us under the noses of EASU. We have to show them we're not afraid."

But Hof was afraid. "You don't know what you're risking, Fair, but I do. I know the EASU. And you are more important to us than I think you realize, my love." Hof lifted himself up and turned around to face her. "You're the glue holding us all together." He kissed her lightly on the forehead. "Who else do we have who can work with the Spreaks? Not Elgin, not myself."

"What nonsense! You work with Dali Spreak all the time."

"Dali isn't like the rest of them. No, Fair, you're the one we look to, everyone does, ever since you came back from the dead with that big Fein at your side."

And Fair knew that he was right. It was something that had

been coming for a long time, a looming consciousness that she was becoming the unofficial leader of the Highland forces. Was she going to be the "queen" of their Highland nation?

She still didn't know if she was really ready for this, but there didn't seem to be any way out. Hof was right: she was the glue holding together the factions headed by Ervil Spreak and Elgin Fundan, who ordinarily didn't get on too well. The other families, too, disliked the name Spreak. It all harked back to the terrible first days of the colony.

And now it was happening just as she'd foreseen it—the nightmare future she'd glimpsed while she was lying on her cot in Shtingi's house in Emoki Village, an endless war with the Coastal peoples, each side slowly escalating its response as the struggle to control the chitin production went on.

"And besides—" Hof spoke again with a different bitterness. "—I have information now that Ervil Spreak has found some plans for nuclear weapons. He intends to equip cruise missiles with them and destroy the Coastal cities."

Fair shivered. Of all the disastrous things that might happen, holocaust weapons would be the worst.

"Not atomics!" She sat up. "We absolutely cannot do that. We would become the enemies of all humanity, an abomination, a name to go down with Timur and Hitler and Khalifi, eternal infamy."

He grinned. "We agree on that. I'm glad. I was starting to worry about you."

His thrust was ignored. She turned to him with a strange look. "There's more than that, though, there are other reasons. The Fein say that atomics are expressly forbidden by their gods."

Hof looked at her, "Yes, well, I'm sure human gods would have forbidden them, too, if anyone had paid them any attention."

Fair shivered. Hof knew none of the secret knowledge. He could not speak Feiner and indeed he felt uncomfortable around the big aboriginals. Fair had come to understand something of the nature of the New World of the Fundans, the world called "Fenrille" by the Fein. Their word meant "eternal home," and the Fein described themselves as those who had been left behind by the high ones, the Arizel.

"Atomics are forbidden here. Spreak must stop this."

"Spreak has other plans, too. I happen to know he's building a shuttle, a small one he plans to float up to the stratosphere on balloons, in an attempt to regain the hulk of the *Founder*. There's still technology up there we need to secure."

"A shuttle is a great idea, but atomics are absolutely out. If what I think is correct about this place, the use of atomic weapons would bring on something that might end the human race."

Hof stared. "What?"

"You know Miflin's theories. The chitin insect appears to be unrelated to anything else in the biosphere here."

"Oh, that again. I thought that had been abandoned. Not enough evidence either way."

"Not true. More and more evidence indicates the chitin did not evolve here. The Fein say the chitin came from the skies, that they came in vessels of the outer dark, that they cleared the forest and began to build the great hive."

"Right, the great hive. Sounds like the Australian Aboriginals and their 'dreamings'. You ever study those, Fair?"

"Yes, Hof. This is different. The Fein say the Arizel destroyed the threat of the chitin—changed the insect and 'humbled' it and placed it in the forest as an efficient scavenger and predator species."

"Doesn't sound that different to me. The gods came down and rescued the world from the satanic insects. Sounds like the gods knew what they were doing. Sometimes I think it would be a lot better if there was no chitin insect. We'd only live normal life spans, but our colony would have been left to us. What we're fighting to control here is the rationing of life for all human beings. Those who can afford optimol and pharamol can live forever. You know what that will mean in a century or so."

Fair knew. "Production must be high enough to provide for the elites of the home system. As long as those groups are given adequate supplies, they will hold the rest in thrall and provide us with a frozen situation, one that might last for a very long time."

Yegods! he thought. "You've done all the computations for this."

"Of course. It sounds cold-blooded, but it's the only way that our people can hold their position. Otherwise we'll be destroyed and swept away on a tide of settlers that will invade these Highlands and probably slaughter off the Fein and all the wildlife."

Hof nodded somberly. "Maybe so, but maybe even that

would be better than turning yourselves into the ultimate drug lords."

"Not so, Hof, because such a society would eventually grow strong enough to destroy the great forest and overwhelm even the woodwose monsters. And if they did that then they would eventually provoke the Arizel to return."

"So the Fein say."

"So the planet says, Hof." She became animated now with a fierce energy. "We have to prevent that at all costs, Hof. Look, I know this kind of thing is difficult for you. You're one of us, but you're not a chitin talker; you live here in Ghotaw, not out in the bush like we do."

Her face grew pensive. She bit her lower lip. "There's a place we should visit. I was told of it by N'kobi, an old Fein who they call an *'eener,'* which seems to translate as 'wizard.' He explained some things to me that I had not truly understood before. There's a place where we can get the answers to all these questions."

Hof was impatient. He didn't believe in any of this Fein nonsense, and he didn't care for the borrowings from Fein culture that permeated the Highland families. He became a little condescending in response. "We can't make decisions on the basis of what the Fein myths say, Fair. We can't tell people that that's what we're basing our actions on. They're beautiful stories, I'll agree, but it's like the Greeks or the Australians. All human tribes had primal myths and legends. You can't turn back that tide of settlement with myths."

She set her jaw. "Hof, doesn't it strike you as weird that a primitive people like the Fein, basically Stone Age in culture, should understand the concept of atomic weapons, or spaceships for that matter? These 'myths' are damned specific."

"Specific to you, Fair, and those who want to believe in this kind of thing."

"Hof, we must go and see this place that N'kobi tells me of."

"If you've got the time, I guess I can make time, too. When and how long?"

"I worked it all out with N'kobi. We can get there using one of the old expeditionary dirigibles. They were designed to carry as many as seven people. It'll manage two people and two Fein without any trouble."

"We're going to fly there with a couple of Fein? But Fein hate flying, everyone knows that."

"They'll fly for me—I persuaded them. We already did it once, a test, when Elgin inflated the dirigible."

Hof resigned himself. Fair had this thing about the Fein and their culture. She'd been saved by Fein, nursed back to health, and had lived among them for half a year. She spoke fluent Feiner, the best Hof had ever heard. He knew that he would have to indulge her in this. Once they'd visited the shrine, he would resume the argument. He was convinced that in the end she would recognize the inevitable path of human settlement and colonization. The Fein, alas, were doomed to life in a reserve of some kind. These beautiful Highland valleys would be swallowed in a tidal wave of buildings, cities, suburbs. A solution to the problems of chitin chemistry would be found eventually, and even the chitin talkers would fade into the mists of history, a colorful people to fit into the pantheon of human heroes, to set beside the early spacers, or the cowboys of North America in the nineteenth century. Hof saw it as inevitable.

"Fine." So they would go, and afterward perhaps he would be able to bring her around. Fair was prone to these wild enthusiasms. He had to expect these things. What he'd said about her was true: she was the one person holding the Highland alliance together.

Slovo Milsuduk admired himself in the mirror. He was wearing a new pair of gray silk trousers he'd designed himself. With them he had on a cream-colored shirt and brown taffsandals that Hal had picked up for him from the Hakka market where poor people sold all kinds of well-made handwrought products.

Slovo whirled about, moved a little. Yes, they were a good fit and made him seem much slimmer than he really was. He hoped they would have a good effect on Hal. Just lately Slovo had gotten a little worried about Hal. Was there someone else? Someone more like Hal's age? Shit, but it would really be upsetting to discover that Hal was shifting his affections elsewhere. Slovo might even have Hal killed if that happened. Getting another Hal might be difficult, too. Hal was just picture perfect for Slovo.

He turned and went into the kitchen, passing the tall security robot in the hall. The Secbot was on, little red indicator lights winking under the gleaming black translucence of its surface. The thing looked like a predatory giant fish, but it spoke with the tones of a brassy female whore, a roguish effect created by Hal when he was playing around with the thing's programming soon after it was bought and activated.

And yet, joke monster that it was, Slovo felt so much safer with it around. If anybody ever tried to get in on him again, like that bastard Overed had, this machine would protect him. In fact, this machine would rip the bastard apart.

He pulled a soft drink from the fridge and opened it.

Where was Hal? He was late as always, and when time hung heavy on him, Slovo tended to fret. His betrayal of the Big Man had left him with ulcers and nightmares. He was still above suspicion, he was sure of that, but he lived in terror of some fragment of information reaching Erst's ears. And the incident with Overed had done more than put Slovo under a constant death sentence. It had spoiled the good times with Hal. Hal didn't like to be scared, and when Hal thought about his position these days he tended to whimper in fright. If the Big Man ever came down on them, he, Hal, was doomed. And who knew what other thugs of the night there were out there who might break in and hurt and humiliate Hal? Hal was looking for a new berth, and who could blame him? Slovo sipped the drink and looked out the window. The dank mists were extraordinarily heavy. The humidity outside the air-conditioned domes was ninety-nine percent, and the temperature was up in the mid-nineties, too. Everything out there looked green and insubstantial in the warm mists.

How long could he go on like this? Some nights the nightmares were so bad he couldn't sleep. Not that Hal would stay up with him and comfort him. Oh, no, that would be asking too much of the sensitive Adonis. Hal was good for about a half a minute's muttering of "go back to sleep" and then he rolled over and resumed snoring. Slovo grimaced. He hated the snoring.

The door chimed at last and let Hal in. He was wearing his "whore suit," as he described it. It was a little tight, a cream-colored silk, and went nicely with the pale blue shoes. Slovo went to greet him but instead of hugs and reassurance Hal fobbed him off with a flurry of light kisses and vanished into the bathroom. Slovo was left with a bag of ice cold treats for consuming in front of a video screen. Disgruntled, he headed back into the kitchen. As he passed the Secbot it woke up and asked permission to interface with the building. It was a scheduled contact, part of the security company's system. Slovo told it go ahead.

In the kitchen he put the tubs of fudge-frost black cherry and eclair nut delite in the freezer.

The Secbot extended a probe into the socket on the wall computer station, a rectangle that controlled phones and doors and all the other comforts of civilized living. The lights built into the Secbot's head suddenly flashed bright and then dimmed. The Secbot withdrew after a few moments. What followed was forever etched into Slovo Milsuduk's memories.

The Secbot rolled smoothly toward him with arms extended.

"What are you doing?" he shouted, and then it grabbed him, lifted him into the air, and carried him kicking and screaming into the bedroom, where it held him down, tied him up, and gagged him with a pillow case.

It left him on the bed and went out of the bedroom. A few moments later it returned with Hal, naked and wet from the shower, and proceeded to bind and gag him. Eventually they were both left there, barely able to grunt, secured with plastic restraints of which the Secbot seemed to have a limitless supply.

The Secbot opened the front door. Shortly afterward, Martin Overed came in, accompanied by a young woman with dark hair, a healthy tan, and a manner that suggested authority. Slovo could barely believe his eyes. The fiend Overed had somehow subverted the Secbot. He couldn't believe this was happening to him. Twice this bastard had gotten in on him. In the parlance of the EASU, he'd been fore-and-aftered and deserved to die.

"Hello, Slovo. Back again, I'm afraid." Martin reached to relax some of the bonds and to remove the gag. "These are very tight. I must say your security machine could be a little more relaxed. Who programmed the damned thing?"

Hal had programmed it, of course. Hal knew something about bondage, all right.

"What do you want?" Slovo managed to grind out the question through a throat that ached from suppressed fury.

"Quite a lot, actually, Slovo old chum, quite a lot. Look, here's someone I work with, her name's Fair Fundan."

Slovo stared up at the dark-haired young woman. So this was the one he'd heard so much about. It was a stunning thought: Fair Fundan was in the heart of enemy territory. By the blood, she was a fearless one! If the Big Man got wind of this. . . .

N'ka awoke after a long period of unconsciousness. He found himself in a small, white-painted room. A big Fein was sitting on a bench nearby. N'ka had seen the Fein before, an elder with gray in his whiskers and down his back. He was a Fein of the widepath who had wandered for decades, the one they called *"eener,"* an old adept of the Great Spirits.

The old Fein leaned toward him. "I am N'kobi, of the widepath."

N'ka's head throbbed painfully. "I am N'ka, of Emoki Village and now of the widepath." N'ka tried to move and felt stabs of pain from several places in his body.

N'kobi chuckled very softly. "In your case, the wise Fein would move as little as possible. They almost killed you."

N'ka struggled to recall what had happened. He had gone to try the beer at Bekunni's shebeen. Now he was here with a throbbing headache and what seemed like broken bones in his arm and chest and leg.

"What happened? I feel as if the bull caught and trampled me."

"Worse. You went into Bekunni's drinking place. He gave you the fire spirit. It is too strong, it overwhelms the senses of Fein and men. Some men attacked you and were beating you to death outside. I was told of it, I was nearby, and I reached the spot in time to drive them away and recover your body."

Now N'ka recalled a face and a man saying there was something to see outside the bar.

"He said, 'Come see, outside,' and I went, and they hit me with clubs and boots."

"There are evil men among the humans here. There are things to beware of. You, my young friend, fell victim to the alien poison of strong drink. You should leave this place—it pollutes all Fein who stay here. It kills some of them, like it almost killed you, N'ka of Emoki."

N'ka digested this for a moment.

"But then, why do you stay here, N'kobi of the widepath?"

N'kobi flashed a fanged smile. "Good question, I ask myself this every day. I think it is because I am very curious and also I like the beer."

N'ka smiled despite his throbbing head. "Ah, yes, the beer. That is why I am here."

N'kobi's eyebrows rose.

"That is what the humans say, anyway," N'ka said.

"Ah, yes, human joke. They have a peculiar sense of humor. It is something I have learned about them from watching them."

"They are not like Fein."

"They are not like Fein. There is great danger for them in that. They do not understand this world." N'kobi gave a big sigh. "A pity. Headstrong young people from another planet. They are locked out of the natural life, encased in their technology. I fear their spirit is deadened. Only in a few of them do I find it still alive."

"It is alive in Fair Fundan."

N'kobi gave him a look of increased respect.

"You know Fair Fundan, young N'ka of Emoki Village?"

"Yes. She lived in Emoki Village for many months. She was wounded by the humans from the Coast."

N'kobi sighed again. "Yes, that is source of much concern to this old Fein."

"Humans bring much trouble to our world."

"They do, but they also bring beer. And snack food. Have you ever tried these 'salted chips'?"

N'ka laughed, despite the pains in his chest and legs. "The salt make Fein thirsty so he drink more beer. The man who sell the beer is happy. He gives more of the salted chips."

"Damned happy, N'ka. But you have to be more selective about where you drink the beer. You should know that there is good beer and there is bad beer and the beer at Bekunni's is not worth drinking."

N'ka seemed to consider this for a moment.

"Yes, you are right about that. It was terrible beer."

18

THE RAIDERS SWUNG IN LOW OVER THE VALLEY, THE DAWN LIGHT glinting here and there from window and gun barrel, the gunships moving quietly on fan-jets.

It was an impressive force. "Congo's Own," they called themselves, since the forty men aboard were all personally handpicked by Congo. And Congo had even come along himself, for the thrill, and to show everyone in the EASU, the Big Man included, that Congo was no wanker.

The two gunships were out of an ancient Chinese military catalog. They were called Hei Feng, "Black Wasp," and they were stealthmatted and equipped with six gun positions, two in the bow, two in the waist, and two in the rear. In addition, they carried four pods of missiles and two pods of miscellaneous terror weapons—incendiaries, poison gas, and the like. They had served the Chinese armies of the twenty-first century.

The target was the Cinnabar Ridge, a fat target, a place that hadn't been hit in ten years or more. It hadn't been hit because it was very tough, famously so. They still talked about the raid that had never made it back, fifteen years or more before. But now, well, ol' Congo was gonna show them. These Black Wasps were the real killers of the skies now. Anything they saw they would destroy.

Passing over a small lake, they startled a herd of large four-legged animals, which burst out of the vegetation ringing the lake and ran away ahead of the Black Wasps. Congo laughed and flashed his famous smile of teeth inlaid with platinum. He signaled the gunners.

The gunships swooped down on the panicked gzan and the fore and waist guns opened up. The animals disintegrated or blew up under the impact of a rain of explosive ammunition. The carnage was brief. The waist gunner on the left side was too busy whooping it up to notice the humanoid figure that he cut down at the end of a long burst through the doomed herd.

A few seconds later the herd of gzan was left behind, a feast for the chitin, a crumpled mess of flesh and bone. And among the carnage, a small group of Fein knelt around a fallen comrade and talked angrily among themselves.

Aboard the lead gunship, Congo laughed and slapped palms with his men, Rosko and Barker. The Black Wasps were fantastic, better by far than anything they'd put in the air before. Cinnabar Ridge was going to be smashed.

"Gentlemen," Congo pronounced over the commo, "we are going to make ourselves very rich this afternoon. You got that?"

Cinnabar Ridge would have plenty of stash out there in the woods. Congo knew the rule: for every grain that a chitin talker laid away in one of the heavily-defended Ghotaw Mountain vaults, there'd be another grain hidden in the terrain around the camp areas. Of course, the only people who knew where the stashes were were the talkers, so you needed to keep as many of them alive as possible so you could roast them over the fires and extract the locations. But, with these Black Wasps, they could overwhelm the opposition from the air, then go in on the ground and incapacitate the chitin people with gas and dart ammo. After that would come the fun and the digging up of little half-gram caches of pharamol all over the bloody landscape. The haul could be tremendous—a hundred grams, maybe more.

They roared over the dark little rivers, keeping down low, beneath the tree line sometimes. The gunners tensed; they were three minutes from the target. The Cinnabar radars still hadn't picked them up. It was going to be a quick slaughter. The gunners grinned to one another and flashed the thumbs-up signal.

Onboard radars suddenly flashed a yellow alarm. Two swift-moving blips were approaching quickly from the rear.

"What's that?" Congo demanded.

The pilot checked the radar. No doubt of it—two aircraft, moving very quickly, were coming in behind them.

Everyone whirled to look back. Two tiny gray blips flashed in, becoming small single-seater jet aircraft, matte gray, that stooped on the gunships like hawks on geese.

"Evasive action!" Congo yelled, thoroughly alarmed now.

From the planes came missiles, white streaks racing ahead, bursting on the gunship armor with heavy thudding detonations. The lead gunship was thrown up and over in the air, then rattled from side to side by successive impacts.

"What the fuck is this?" Congo bellowed.

More missiles lanced out while twenty-millimeter cannon fire ripped up and down the length of the gunships. On the lead ship the left-side waist gunner gave a scream and was blown out of his position. At the same time, the rear left fanjet gave a screech, burst into flame, and had to be jettisoned.

Then the small jets were past, streaking away and breaking left and right. The gunships were battered but still in the air. They fired missiles of their own but missed; the Spreak Darters were too quick and too filled with electronic countermeasure systems. These missiles were really designed as terror weapons, for use against outgunned ground targets.

"Cinnabar Ridge in sight," the pilot shouted.

Congo tore his attention away from the radar screen, which showed those deadly little jets circling to come in again. There was the ridge, a long sinuous mass, the jik forest somber and dark along the lower slopes, reddish rock showing at the crest. From the crest came a sparkling of ignitions, then a hail of ground-to-air missiles.

This time the raiders were tossed completely upside down, and everyone was hurled out of their seats and into the webbing with enough force to take the air out of their lungs.

Congo was beside himself with rage and fear.

The lead ship lost another fan-jet and had to switch to rotors. The second ship was hit inboard at the front; the pilot was killed and control was lost. The crew pumped out emergency buoyancies and the ship sank slowly down into the forest below, at least a mile distant from the targeted drop points.

Congo cursed. Those men would be useless now, too far from the target to help at all. Then a second delivery of missiles hammered his own ship and they were flung sideways. The rear right rotor was blown away, and the rear gunners were killed by a shrap burst. Worse, a hole was opened up in the front right armor and occasional rounds started coming in and ricocheting around in the interior.

"Down!" Congo screamed. He ducked as a fragment of hot metal hurtled past his face.

The pilot obeyed and the ship made a more or less crash landing about a hundred meters shy of the target zone.

"Out! Everyone out! We're gonna show these fuckers!" Congo roared, and the doors crashed open and the raiders lurched out onto the Highland soil.

Congo led them in a mad charge across a clearing toward the trees that fringed the base of the ridge. Defensive fire broke out ahead of them. Bullets went whipping past over their heads, and they were forced to take cover. Mortar fire began dropping on them within half a minute. First there was just a single weapon, searching for them through the forest, burst by burst. Then it was joined by two or three more and the position became untenable. Congo split the command and sent them off to either side to get around the flanks of the defensive forces. And then the small aircraft whistled by overhead and laid a trail of cluster bombs right over them.

Men somersaulted through the smoke and fire; helmets, weapons, human limbs went whipping away through the small jik-tree forest. Congo found himself on his belly, unmarked, clutching some wet roots at the side of a patch of bog. He'd fouled himself. He was weeping.

Then a gray drone was floating by, a male voice repeating a message. "You are cut off and outnumbered. Surrender and save your lives."

"Fuck you!" someone screamed in pain, and a burst of fire clipped the gray, sharklike drone. A storm of fire blazed out from the ridge and several more men died.

"Repeat, surrender now and save your lives. You will be taken into custody according to the laws of the Highland nation. Surrender and save your lives."

With trembling hand Congo reached for his communicator. "Who the fuck are you?" he whispered as he surrendered.

19

THE FIGHTING HAD BEEN OVER FOR ONLY A MONTH, BUT THERE were already vast changes around Ghotaw Mountain. Hof could see that as soon as his ATV turned off the town loop road and moved upslope on the road to North Ghotaw and the chitin vaults.

The sprawl of Ghotaw Central had been curtailed and dozens of domes and other buildings had been removed. The mound of trash, a virtual moraine of debris from unplanned civilization, was being shoveled up and burned by the prisoners in the new correctional system installed by the provisional town government.

The number of ATVs on the roads was way down. And out here in the forest all the outlying shacks had been destroyed, and the single-track paths leading to them were already becoming overgrown with arble and plugvine.

Thousands of people had already left, forced out by the new government, which was backed up by the Highland Response Force, the HRF—or, as the irreverent were already calling it, the Fundan Police.

Air traffic was way down, too. The new government was only allowing a couple of aircraft in or out per day. The airstrip had a deserted feel, especially when contrasted with the bustle of the old days.

Hof was happy with all of this. He was also surprised. He hadn't expected it, somehow. Despite everything he knew about Fair and suspected about Elgin, he still hadn't quite expected them to put into effect their plan for the controlled destruction and removal of the human colony in Ghotaw. Yet, there it was, shrinking week by week, and when they were finished it would be gone, except for the laboratories and the domes of the chitin talkers.

Fair was different now, too. She'd grown in stature during the fighting, when they were hitting a raiding group once a week or more. And she'd grown even more since the fighting had ended. She had become more prominent, while Elgin had retired into the shadows he preferred.

The two names that mattered now were Fair Fundan and Ervil Spreak. It had been their war and their victory. And with the growth in Fair had come other changes. There was a weight to her now, a tendency to command and to assume that her orders would be obeyed.

Hof sighed.

She was still seeing Martin Overed. They worked together in secret, on the spying operation down in the Coastal cities. They shut everybody else out on the basis of "need to know" rules. Hof was unhappy about that, but most of all he was jealous and he didn't like being jealous. It was demeaning and petty and something he felt he should be able to control. But, alas, he couldn't. Worse, Overed was everything that Hof hated: an ignorant thug, a dark residue from EASU, a link to that world of PolCom and Subord, Org and Buro, regulation and mass obedience that Hof had fled long ago. Whenever he heard that characteristic EASU accent, that whining tone that they all had, the hair on his neck rose.

Fair was adamant, as one would have expected, that she was her own person, and she would see whomever she wished to see. Hof could not expect to "own" her, nor was she planning on a monogamous marriage to him or any other man.

Hof had considered ending it and then had flinched. He wanted her too much. There was nothing to be done but to act his age, which was considerable, and hope that she would tire of Overed before she tired of him.

The ATV rolled smoothly around the flank of the volcano and entered the avenue of the vaults. Military-type vehicles were parked along the roadside. To the right, on the upper slopes that frowned down on the road, were set the various vault entries, each covered with oval blast shields, with gun batteries sunk into the mountain above and in front. Hof was well aware that he had quickly been targeted by a lot of high-grade weaponry, just in case he proved to be something other than the usual happy customer he seemed.

The vaults announced their names with signs bermed into the mountain flank beneath their doors, close to the individual car parks they maintained along the four-lane road. The Eternity Vault always brought a smile to Hof's lips. This was a volcano, albeit an extinct one. Still, the entire mountain chain was highly active, still growing as the continental plates ground against each other around the equator. To think of anything up here as "eternal" was surely asking too much.

Hof's ATV rolled to a stop in the parking lot outside the Destiny Vault, an established company with which Hof had been dealing for some years now. He split his vault savings between the Destiny and the New Fundan, an ambitious new venture started up by some of Fair's friends.

The Destiny was guarded by both robot and human warriors, dug into defensive systems of awesome strength. Behind the ferroconcrete blast shields and the steel outer doors lay a charmingly designed interior with the plush feel of a twenty-first-century Tokyo bank.

The interior hush was aided by the inch-deep carpets and the flocked wallpaper. Hof was guided quickly through corridors designed to suggest a castle in ancient Osaka and thence to a private room, where he was joined by a young woman by the name of Lin who activated a small input device in the table and processed the details of Hof's business that day.

Hof already had a reserve in this vault, and on this occasion he was adding to it. At the appropriate moment the young lady bowed and proffered a small black silk cushion on which he placed the vial containing another quarter gram of pharamol, a tiny clump of glittering blue specks.

After carefully weighing the vial on an analog balance and checking the weight with Hof's own measurement, Lin placed the small cushion inside a two-way cabinet and closed the door on it.

"Following preliminary analysis, your account has been credited with point-two-four-nine-nine-nine-eight gram. Your account total stands at eleven-point-four-oh-six grams."

"Thank you," Hof said with a smile after he'd signed and thumbed the receipts. There it was, enough pharamol to let him live for decades, even a century past his normal allotted span. With his immune system boosted by the subtle hormonal effects triggered by the pharamol, he would be safe from cancers of all kinds, not to mention the degenerative diseases and most of the other effects of aging.

Only his hair and his nails would fall out. At least, that's all that had happened to the oldest users of the drugs so far, just as it had happened to the experimental rats that still lived on, through life spans expanded to seeming infinity. If rats could live for fifty years, humans could live to five hundred or more.

Hof had as much pharamol as this secreted in another stash, a ceramic cylinder disguised to look like a stone, buried beneath the roots of a certain tree in a valley some ten kilometers away from Ghotaw. And, in his accounts at the New Fundan Vault, a little further along the row of vaults, he had another small fortune in the drugs. Hof was like everyone else, intent on covering all the angles. The vaults might be attacked and destroyed one day, despite their heavy defenses and their crucial role in stabilizing the prices of longevity drugs, but Hof would still have a supply to last him for centuries. Conversely, his outside stash might somehow be stumbled on and lost, but he would have enough in the vaults to cover his loss.

Sometimes Hof thought he might simply live forever, and sometimes he thought the whole business was crazy. Could he really just go on forever? Was he that curious about this world? Did he really want to spend centuries here on this alien planet at the farthest edge of humanity? Wouldn't he just get bored to tears and finally choose suicide?

It used to be that he had no doubts. But since Fair had begun to downplay their relationship, they had come on aplenty. Was it that he just couldn't face living without love? Was that it? Wily old Hof Witlin was no more sensible than any foolish, callow teenager in love? So it seemed. It was a galling thought.

He remained absorbed in these mournful musings while Lin gave him a hot towel for his hands at the conclusion of their business. He strolled out into the corridor and almost bumped into a slim figure, clad in a suit of black spylo.

He pulled back. "I beg your pardon," he began, and halted.

A face dominated by dark eyes swept a look of hate over him for a fraction of a second. Then the hate disappeared, like a stiletto into a hidden sheath.

"And so you should, as a servant of the usurper."

Hof was startled. He had only met Proud Fundan once since the fighting began, on a matter of obtaining a signature to change the Fundan family testament. Proud had been cold and aloof enough then, but the tone of sheer hate in his voice now was completely open.

"You act surprised, Witlin. You think I should have accepted her and the usurpation of my ancestral position, don't you? You accept her as a 'Fundan.' What do you know of the family Fundan? You are from Earth, an outsider. You can never understand. That woman for whom you work is not a true Fundan. Her mother was a whore, a bitch who used her sex to keep a poor befuddled old man under her control and then conceived this bastard via the sperm bank! All we have to prove the girl's parentage is her mother's word and a worthless scrap of paper from a defunct sperm bank!"

Hof was stunned. He'd known Proud was angry at being outshone by Fair, but he hadn't imagined that it had soured into this. For a moment he merely stared at the man; then he spluttered into speech.

"Bizarre, just completely bizarre, if I may say so—all this frantic concern about genetic inheritance. What the hell does it matter? She's a terrific leader, she's doing a great job, better than you people have any right to expect."

Proud made growling noises in his throat. "So they all say, but it is my right to control the family funds and it is wrong for the bank board to vote her into my position. She has no seniority, she does not even belong on the board!"

Hof stared at him. How petty could the man be? "I don't know how you could have avoided noticing, but we just fought a small war around here. She was the driving force from the beginning. She's proved herself, what more do you want? I mean, keep your stupid bank board. I'm sure she'll withdraw from all that pretty soon anyway. She doesn't want your position, Proud, she's making her own."

"How dare you," Proud spluttered. "You're nothing but a mercenary scientist, a mere Earther! And you dare to lecture me about the rights of the usurper?"

There was something insane here, something old and mad and warty, a monster from the family cupboard. Hof shook his head in sorrow.

"I get it. This usurpation shit is the cover. What you're really crazed about is that the family returned the control to Edward's line. That's it, isn't it? You're from Agatha's side, through Luther. You folks have just never forgiven Edward for being right. You know she's truly Compton's daughter and you hate the idea that Edward and Dane have produced another worthy ruler for your monstrously old, obscenely wealthy family."

Proud sniffed loudly. "You should try working the chitin directly sometime, Hof. All you parasites who live in that town and feed off the chitin people, you should all try your luck down a nest once in a while, don't you think?"

"Stop this, Proud. We can't afford feuds, we have to get over petty jealousies."

"She will be proved a bastard. The family court will convene to consider her genetics and she will be disowned. She will automatically lose control of any forces considered to be Fundan."

Hof balled his hands into fists. "Good day to you, Proud Fundan." Hof walked on, leaving the slim figure in black to mutter at his back.

In the top-floor suite of the Lustre Hotel, inside the new Saukhausen dome, the Big Man met with Slovo Milsuduk. On the table screen were projected the plans for the "big show," as Erst liked to call it.

A dozen big transport planes were chartered; four gunships had been retrofitted with air-to-air missiles; two thousand men and all the supplies they would need for fighting a small war would be shipped into the Ghotaw area in the matter of an hour or so. They would take control of Ghotaw and cut off access to the row of vaults on Ghotaw North.

The chitin people would have to come out and fight for the vaults and, when they did, they would be crushed by the superior strength of the EASU forces.

"When this is over, my friend," the Big Man said, putting an arm around Slovo and pinching his cheek, "we will have all those chitin groups affiliated with the good ol' EASU. Then we'll set things up really tight."

Slovo felt the familiar terror turning into something else, a straightforward sense of doom. If the Big Man were to succeed with this plan, then Slovo's days of spying on the EASU would be over. But how could he hope for his secret to stay a secret? Someone on the other side would spill it, when they were strapped to the hotbed or had their feet on the bastinado. And then? Slovo felt certainty building up. He was doomed. There was no way to avoid the horror that loomed. The Big Man had an arm around his shoulders now. Everything was fine—in perfect working order, as the Big Man would say—but when that day dawned that the Big Man learned of Slovo's treachery, then he, Slovo Milsuduk, would be strapped down to that metal bed under the merciless eyes of the Big Man.

"No way they gonna get away with this shit," the Big Man murmured. "They hanged old Congo—old randy rooster—an' I am gonna finish them for it. They think they can pull this off, throw us out of the mountains and say 'keep out'?"

The Big Man stood up. The meeting was over. "No way, not while Arvin Erst is the boss."

"Right," Slovo said, smiling sheepishly.

"Right!" the Big Man said, stabbing a forefinger into Slovo's chest. "And those fucks are gonna find out the hard way, eh?"

Slovo laughed with him, then turned and left the suite. He had to move the credit around to pay for the two thousand mercenaries and the planes and the equipment. This was the biggest effort EASU had made in the raiding game in a long time. They'd been content to sit in as a partner for most of the raiding in recent years. Now they were going to take over physical control of the Highlands and the chitin groups. That was a much more expensive operation.

Slovo wished that life were simple again, like it used to be before that bastard Martin Overed had gotten in on him.

Almost as soon as Slovo had left, the door opened for Lawler and the Big Man welcomed the security chief. Congo's death had strengthened Lawler's position considerably. Truth to tell, Lawler hadn't even been that sad to see old Congo go. Now Lawler was running Security and Enforcement, the two premier divisions.

Of course, there was a lot of work that went with that much power, and the Big Man was pushing him hard. Lawler knew that Erst had a younger man, Darby Matlok, primed to step into his shoes should he slip. He was having to really keep busy to stay on top of it all.

"So, what you got for me, Lawler?"

Lawler smiled a slow smile. Well, this was one of those occasions when he really had something good.

"You know we had a contact within the Fundan family?"

"Yeah, but with no power, no intelligence, nothing we could use, I thought."

"Yeah, it was a disappointment, but it's just come good. We've known for a long time that a certain Hof Witlin was one of their prime advisers. He's a bit of an unknown quantity, this Witlin. He's from Earth, originally, came out here on the first EASU ship. He was down here when we arrived, moved up to the mountains soon afterward. Then nothing but a quiet life as a lab tech working for the Spreaks, until a few months ago when he becomes one of Fair Fundan's constant companions."

"So, what about this creep?"

"So, we know where he may be found. Where he might be collected and brought to us here."

The Big Man's face split into an ugly smile.

"Sounds good. Do it."

20

THEY WERE ARGUING AGAIN AND HE DIDN'T KNOW HOW IT HAD happened. Nor could he choke back the words even though he regretted them the moment they were out.

"I think it's stupid and wrong and irresponsible and I wish you would wake up and quit doing this."

She shook her head. "Sorry, old man, negative on all counts. I need to know what's going on there. This entire operation is a 'need to know' thing. You know that."

He felt a vein throb in his forehead. It infuriated him that his enforced ignorance was on a continuum with her need to meet with Martin Overed in person. Hof felt his temper slip.

" 'Need to know'? Need to know what? Martin Overed's sex techniques?"

Her eyes glinted with anger, but she said nothing. With a shrug, she slammed her fist into her palm.

"All right, perhaps I deserved that. I know it's been hard for you. Perhaps we should be formal and proper and stop sleeping together. Perhaps it's over."

"Over?" Hof thought his heart would break, but he was angrier than ever. "So, just like that, you walk out on me and take up with an EASU enforcer and, for your personal pleasure, you risk everything by going by there to see him in person. I don't know, Fair, I guess you're not the person I thought you were. I thought we were trying to build a nation here."

She laughed, but bitterly. "That's funny coming from the man who always says we don't have a chance."

He tossed his head in annoyance. "What I say and what I do are two different things, you know that, Fair. I love you. I thought you were the woman I'd always dreamed of."

"The women in men's dreams don't exist, any more than the men in women's."

Space, but she could sound cold, he thought.

"Anyway, I'm sorry to disappoint you, darling, but I am my own person, I don't belong to anybody else. You don't possess me—nobody possesses me."

He snorted in disbelief. "Yeah, from where I'm standing it looks like Martin Overed possesses you, body and soul. You'll risk anything to be with him."

Her eyes got a little wider, and her nostrils flared. "Damn it, Hof!" She waved her hands. "Impossible, you're asking the impossible, Hof. I love you, but that isn't going to keep me from seeing other men if I choose to. I said that at the beginning and I've said it many times since then."

He stepped back, and fought down the raging emotions for a moment. He didn't want this, any of it.

"Look, I'm sorry, I just . . ."

She heaved a sigh. "Hof, it doesn't matter. Perhaps it isn't over. This means nothing. I understand your concerns, I know I'm not the easiest person to have a relationship with. If you want to forget what we just said then it's fine, I'll forget it. We can go on."

Pure manipulation. Over? Of course it was over, and she knew it, and she was just working to keep him calm through a difficult period.

The anger came back. His lips twisted with the bitterness.

"Yeah, well, maybe. Maybe you're right, maybe it is over." He turned to go, then looked back. "And forget the thing about going to see the Fein shrine in the deep forest. I've got plenty of things to be doing that are more immediately important than that."

She watched him leave and then said in a whisper, "I hope you're right about that, old man. For all our sakes, I hope you're right."

She surprised herself; there were some tears. She got up and went into the bathroom to wipe them away.

Witlin left the hidden bunker by the usual circuitous route, exiting through a door-sized air vent in the groundwall of a large dome. There were shops on the ground floor, places allowed to continue operating to offer consumer goods and services to chitin talkers in from the bush.

The vent deposited him in a dark alley between domes. The street side entrance was shut off with a security fence. In the other direction were a vapor stack and the rear aspects of more domes. On the left was the back door of a restaurant, the Pearl & Oyster. Hof sidled into the kitchen area where a half-dozen workers, mostly Roiders up from the Coast, were turning synthetics into haute cuisine. They barely looked up as he passed. Of course, had he been a stranger, then it would not have gone so easily.

From the kitchen he moved into a little hallway and then into the main dining room. He followed behind a waiter heading for a table by the door, then slipped on outside into the street. The evening air was cool and fresh, hinting of the night chill to come. The sun had set behind the vast mountains to the west and the stars were beginning to shine in the east. The purple velvet of the dying dusk lay over the great valley.

Hof felt his heart expand at the sight. It was a beautiful land, worth fighting for if anything was worth fighting for. Here they could build a nation that would be a model to the whole race. Here they could rediscover the idea of a morality that had been lost long ago. Here they would be citizens in a free state, gathered in a republic with honesty and respect for law.

Here they would have a nation that would respect the natural environment and live in harmony with it. They would not build the usual smog-haunted cities; they would keep the population deliberately small.

Space, but they would have to fight to keep it that way.

There would be more fighting, of that he was sure. And that caused Hof considerable uneasiness. He disliked the entire concept of fighting, of killing other human beings. He'd grown up on Earth in the ancient city of Los Angeles during a time when the social synthesis had been rigorously enforced and social corruption had grown to an overwhelming level. His teachers had taught him that violence was futile and that cooperation was the proper way for human beings to organize their lives. Unfortunately, in the collapsed social synthesis of his times, violence had become a plague darkening the world.

That had once been a beautiful land, too, a shining plain under stark mountains in a glorious climate. It had become a forest of giant domes, enclosing whole towns, laced with highways and fringed with dead zones where the socially excluded lived under choking pollution in a climate close to that of hell. No one had seen the mountains in centuries.

From that he'd come to this. Why shouldn't he fight to preserve this beauty? Why should he expect that human beings would be able to restrain themselves and keep from turning this vast mountain bowl into another polluted hell? Human beings weren't evil, they just wanted to get ahead, to gain a higher standard of living. They had ineluctable wants as natural as life itself. The tragedy of civilization was overpopulation and the environmental degradation that came with it.

And here, in this beautiful, fragile place, what would the race do if left to its own devices? No, he knew the answer to that question and he could not allow it to happen. In addition to all the normal strivings of the race, here there would be the pressure for the drugs. Here they would all seek to live forever, fortified against the power of death by the eternity drugs produced from the chitin insect.

No, it couldn't be stopped. Hof knew, in his gut, that they would never solve the task of building the chitin proteins from scratch. They were too complex, almost as if designed that way, and none of the old human biomachines, bacterial or artificial, could create all those whiplike curves, those complex shapes and folds, and the mass of enzymatic tentacles that sprang out of the complexes.

It couldn't be done, and so the land must be kept for the harvesting of the chitin insect. More people would inevitably move out onto the land, crowding the nest sites. There would be war, endless war, no matter what happened. In which case he might as well attempt to save things as they were at this precious point in time, when correct action might, just possibly, prevent the catastrophe he visualized a century or two down the road.

He pulled his jacket around him as a sudden chill wind blew in from the plains, and turned and went down the street past dome-floor shopfronts and a parking lot that was half-full of dirty ATVs. His own vehicle was parked in the back row, an old model called an "Explorer" when it was new, fifty years before. It ran on a hydrogen-cell engine for internal-combustion power and switched over to a battery engine for slower speeds. The exterior had once been green, then painted with black and brown for camouflage, and since then had been sandblasted by the winds of Ghotaw. It had half a million klicks on it and still ran well. Every time he contemplated the machine's history, his respect for the old Fundan designers went up a little more.

He thumbed the side-door lock and it popped open. The seats had lost a little something over the decades, but he still found them comfortable enough. Using the thumbprint sensor on the dashpad, he started it up and headed it for the south road. It drove in the streets of Ghotaw itself, and he only took over after leaving the south road and running through the scrub to his current hideout, an abandoned squatter's shack, in the rear of which he'd inflated a small sleeping tent.

It was Spartan accommodation but he was sure it was safe. He'd only been there for a couple of weeks now, and nobody except Fair and Elgin knew about it. Hof, like the others, now lived constantly on the run. His possessions were in storage at the Fundan Vault and once in a while he felt a pang or two for his old apartment and his balcony and backyard and all the rest. But survival came first, and there was too much to do for there to be any leisure time to spend in an apartment, even if he had one.

The ATV picked up his perimeter check, then vectored in on the security beacon. He parked it in a dugout he'd excavated under part of the old shack, then reset the perimeter alarm, went in to his lonely bed, and tried not to think about Fair and how it used to be until the war and Martin Overed had ended everything.

After a while he slept and dreamed about Southern California, the heat, the heavy smog, the occasional black rain that slicked down the walls of domes in waves of diffraction patterns, turning the sunlight into rainbows. There was a girl, her name had been Narsi—she and he had been lovers. She rose from a pool of dark water with a stone shining in her navel and a necklace of teeth that glowed green.

He woke to a shriek from his inside alarm. Blankly he stared around him in the dark of the little tent. An alarm flasher blinked red on the portascreen. He tabbed it and got a perimeter view from twenty seconds before. An ATV, a matte black shape with no lights, crashing through on a course for the shack.

They'd traced him somehow.

In another moment he was out of the tent, running for his ATV. It was very dark under the shack. He slid around the front of the Explorer to the side. He thumbed the doorlock, heard something move behind him, and was turning to see when something hard and heavy slammed into the side of his head.

He fell, landed hard, and felt someone bending over him to place a device on the side of his neck. They must have hidden in the goddamn ATV, he realized with a sick rage at his own stupidity. They knew how to get around Fundan alarm systems. There was a painful vibration at his neck for a second and he blacked out.

When he came back to consciousness it was with a raging headache and a dull nausea. He could barely move, especially since he was bound at wrists, knees, and ankles, and had something that tasted like a rubber ball jammed in his mouth to prevent him from doing more than grunting. It was dark; there was a plastic panel of some kind a few inches above his face. He felt a terrible feeling of claustrophobia and came close to a mindless panic. Someone had placed him in a coffin, it seemed.

Then he became aware of the steady thrumming vibration. Big engines somewhere nearby, then, which meant he was on a plane.

The claustrophobia was overwhelmed by worse terrors. He was on a plane, so they were taking him to EASU. They were taking him to the Big Man.

21

BY THE DAY OF THE BIG TRIP N'KA HAD ALREADY GONE UP TWICE in the dirigible balloon that Elgin's team of young technicians had produced from the old Fundan catalog. The balloon carried a six-meter-long gondola slung beneath it, a rickety-looking thing of wire and spylo paneling.

Each ride had been a weird mix of fright and exhilaration. Nothing in life had prepared him for the sensation of separating from the ground and floating away into the air. It was exciting and, at the same time, vaguely terrifying. N'ka had had to struggle hard to maintain his dignity, and with old N'kobi on hand to record any lapses, he was especially sensitive about that.

Of course, old N'kobi always made a point of showing no emotions at all during these intense moments, but N'ka had noticed a few signs of anxiety in the old Fein's demeanor, nonetheless.

N'kobi was proud of being of the widepath, "the widest path of all," he liked to say, so he was unable to object openly to the idea of riding in the dirigible with the humans. At the same time he was terrified of leaving the sacred ground of the homeworld. It went against all tradition.

N'ka had mocked him gently.

"We are not leaving for another world, N'kobi."

"Ha!" the old one said. "Wait until you see the *fidnemed*, young N'ka of Emoki. Then you will see some other worlds."

"So you say, old one, but no one in Emoki ever told me about this."

"That's because these are the deep secrets, young one. Only the widest path will bring you to them. I think Emoki is a very ingrown old place. No one there will tell the stories of the widepath. They prefer to stay where they are and live out the smaller life of the village and the valley." The "small life" was the complete opposite of the "widepath" where adventurers like N'kobi roamed.

"We will see other worlds, so you say. I look forward to it."

N'kobi's dislike of flying came to the fore. "Of course, we could reach the sacred *fidnemed* on foot. I went there before by making a raft and floating down the river. The glade is close by a group of rocky pinnacles. It is about a day's march from the river."

"But that would take many days, and the humans have always many things to do. They could not afford so many days for this trip."

Unlike N'ka, N'kobi was not impressed with the activities of the humans. "The things they do have no meaning. They should forgo some of these things and take the time to learn the deep secrets. They should visit with the old adepts, and they should go to the *fidnemed*. They should know the truth about this old world."

At last the day of the trip had come. Instead of floating up from the ground in the gondola under the dirigible and then floating down again after a few minutes, they thundered into the air with a throb of engines and moved off at an elevation of two hundred feet, across the jik forest of Ghotaw. There was no going back; this was the real thing.

N'ka was entranced almost at once. The wide world was spread out in front of him as if he had climbed a magical hill that could move across the land. They floated with scarcely a bump, like scapum flew on their silken webs. It was such an easy way to cover long distances, N'ka was amazed. No wonder the humans did this thing—it made travel so simple, so easy.

There was only one human passenger for the trip, Fair Fundan. For this, both the Fein were glad. The other expected passenger, the old one called Hof, had been unable to come. Since he was one of the many humans who were uneasy in the presence of Fein, they did not miss him. He spoke no Feiner and had difficulty in deciphering theirs.

Fair Fundan, on the other hand, spoke almost completely fluent Feiner and even told a good joke now and then. N'kobi relished having little debates with her about the ways of the humans that seemed to the old Fein quite mad.

Fair Fundan was distracted, however. While they sailed on, she remained oblivious, closeted in the back section of the gondola with a small portable computer, its screen a glowing jewel in the near darkness of the covered cabin. She saw nothing of the vast mountains and the high valleys that were cut into their flanks, ribbons of dark forest intersecting the snowfields and the glaciers.

So the Fein were left to ride up front alone. N'kobi was sunk in thought, his brow furrowed with concentration. N'ka was left to fly in silence, though he really wanted to whoop and yell and point out all the wondrous things he was seeing for the first time.

They flew for hours before they worked their way out of the mountains and left them behind, to venture across the endless rolling green mantle of the great forest. Away to the west glinted the enormous serpentine shape of the River Irurupup. Ahead lay nothing but endless jungle, rising and falling across the land, an entire world buried under a forest of three-hundred-meter-high giants.

All day they floated on, suspended between the blue sky and the gray-green forest, the only sound the muffled roar of the engines. And then ahead, far off, they saw the pinnacles, a clump of gray thrust up on the horizon. Soon they grew in size and differentiated into a cluster of volcanic remnants; then these resistant outcrops of ancient granite grew large and filled the view.

They turned there and skirted the pinnacles before flying on to the river. N'kobi was looking down with anxious eyes. Somewhere here, south and east of the pinnacles, was where the *fidnemed* lay.

At last N'kobi gave a shout and pointed down with excited motions. Ahead could be seen a long, narrow clearing where the trees thinned out and finally ceased to grow.

N'ka lifted the flap of the rear cabin door. Fair joined them in a moment and stared down at this odd sight, for there were few such clearings in the sweep of the great forest. What would she find down there? She hardly dared to imagine. Everything was coming to a climax in her life. She was torn between two men and entrusted with the responsibility for the future not only of clan Fundan but of the entire colony here on the Fundans' New World. And their enemy was now preparing a massive counterstrike. Could they be prepared in time? There was, of course, no easy answer for that question.

Soon, with the sun beginning to go down in the west, they clambered over the side and descended into the *fidnemed*. And there they discovered the inexplicable, the incredible, the terrifying truth.

When Fair Fundan returned up the spylo climbing rope to the gondola, she knew the deep secret of the planet Fenrille. Her mouth was dry; she was, in fact, shivering with fear.

It was all true, incredibly true! The Fein myths were not myths at all. No one had known, no one could have imagined. It seemed impossible, but it had to be true. Nothing else but the "myths" could account for the bizarre visions she had experienced down there. Other worlds, other stars, other galaxies even. Visions that slammed into your consciousness when you stepped upon a "node."

The ancient adepts who lived around the place, a handful of Fein so old and wizened they made N'kobi seem young by comparison, had spoken to her of the Arizel not as ghosts or spirits in the human understanding of the term. They spoke of them as living entities, being engaged in an enormous undertaking, reaching out through the immensity of the universe—or the universes, as the Fein insisted there were more than one—to make contact with the Creator.

Fair's human, scientific intellect was screaming. This was madness. It had long ago been determined that the odds against a god or a creative supreme being were utterly enormous. The universe was a grand accident, a warp in the textures of nothingness, a freak event that had begun on the micro scale and continued onto the macro scale through the "magic" of the procession of energy into matter. This accidental event had swollen from a pinhead to the vastness of the galaxies in the twentieth milliard of the universe's existence. All this had been accepted for centuries by everyone but the diehard religious.

And now this understanding was under attack.

Fair could not reconcile the two. Either human science had missed something, or this mad planet was almost as artificial as a space habitat. The Arizel were planetscapers and the Fein were a conservative remnant of the same race that had begotten the Arizel themselves. Nothing here was what it seemed.

It was too much. She could not allow herself to believe this. And yet, the myths about the chitin insect were corroborated fully. The chitin had come to Fenrille in spaceships, colonists with a mission to remake the planet into a hive city like that which they had left on their homeworld. They had attacked the forest, fought the woodwose monsters and finally employed atomics. They had provoked the return of the Arizel, which had sat in judgment upon them. The homeworld of the chitin insect was destroyed a short time later.

And now Ervil Spreak planned to use atomics against the Coast cities if they attacked again.

Fair went cold inside. What happened here could lead to the end of the human race. What would their future be? Perhaps they would become the marmosets of this artificial forest ecosystem. She shivered again. She had to prevent this!

A few moments later, the communicator beeped and she downloaded a message blurt with all the details concerning Hof Witlin's disappearance.

He had been out of contact for twenty-eight hours, not seen since he'd left the bunker after that stupid argument. His ATV was not equipped with a locator and his hideout was known only to Fair and Elgin. He had not called to check in in the morning, nor in the afternoon when the search began. It was now assumed that he had been abducted by EASU and was already on the Essex Coast.

Fair sank into a seat with a sick feeling in her stomach. Hof taken, to be tortured and then murdered by those blood-soaked swine. It made her want to vomit.

Then she leapt up in her seat. The network! *Her* network! What word had they received? Frantically she blipped a message back to the bunker in Ghotaw and sat there stewing, biting her nails, dreading the reply.

And all the while the thought circulated in her mind that the whole damned human race might pay for any mistakes that were made on this world, if the true masters of this planet should ever discover their presence.

22

MARTIN GOT THE NEWS WHILE HE WAS WORKING OUT IN THE ROOM they'd turned into a gym by adding a set of weights and a ski-trak. It was the sort of thing he'd expected for so long that he was barely surprised.

He rose from the bench slowly, a sick feeling in his stomach; Slovo! They would have Slovo. Their best asset was gone, and they would be searching for Martin again with redoubled fury. And, without Slovo, Martin was no longer the important figure in the Fundan military setup that he'd been. What sort of protection would the Highlanders offer him now?

His first thought was to make a panicky escape, at once. He would leave immediately and take only the essentials, including the compcom unit which he used to code and encode all his calls to the Highlands.

Then he visualized himself out there, beyond the safety of the front door, and he cringed. A runner, alone, on EASU territory? They'd have him in no time. There'd be guys on every corner in the Islands. They'd go house to house in the Roider neighborhoods. On the waterfront, every fucking boat would get a shakedown.

Even while these thoughts went through his brain he started moving. There was a lot to do. He made a point of blipping his first alert to the Roiders, to Ho Duc, and then to Mari. The alerts were prerecords logged in the compcom and he dumped them into the phone with a single keystroke. Uncle Ho would have his boat in motion within moments, and every second might count at this point.

Finally he started thinking straight. How could Witlin lead them to his door? What did Witlin know anyway? Sure, they would get Slovo, and probably Hal, but that wouldn't tell them anything more than that Martin Overed was on the Coast and working with the Highlanders. They would know that the Roiders were involved and they would be looking for the network among them, but that wouldn't necessarily turn up Mari. She and Ho were well-protected. Witlin knew nothing specific about that area; that was why Fair always said it had to be "need to know."

He took several deep breaths, trying to make the horrible fluttery feeling in his stomach go away. Shit but it was a bad thing to be this frightened.

Yeah, he would be all right where he was, he just had to sit tight. Hof Witlin couldn't give him up even if he wanted to, and Martin had a good idea that old Hof wouldn't have minded too much about losing Martin Overed's ass to the EASU.

No, he was cool just staying where he was. Leave the outside to the EASU. He was safe enough right where he was, in

disguise in a midclass dome with good security. No one knew
where he was. Slovo had no idea, nor did Hal.

Or did he? With a feeling of implosion he was abruptly
gripped with a new thought. What if Slovo did know? The
anxiety returned with sickening force. If Slovo Milsuduk
couldn't arrange for a tail to track Martin Overed when he left
their meetings, then who could? Slovo, after all, was one of the
highest-ranking members of the EASU. He could command
immense resources in men and time. There had been only a
handful of meetings; most of the time Slovo's information
came from a mail drop. Hal was usually the one sent to do it,
during his trips to the shops. But there had been meetings, and
Martin could have been tracked from any one of them.

But if he had, then why hadn't Slovo done something? Why
hadn't he jumped Martin and gotten rid of him? With Martin
Overed disappeared into the bellies of the permiads out in the
delta, Slovo would be safe.

Except that the Fundans had tapes of Slovo and Hal together, tapes that would go to the Big Man if Martin were to
vanish with no explanation. Slovo wouldn't dare. But if Slovo
was on the hotbed, under interrogation, he wouldn't hold anything back. He'd give them everything he had—there was no
way not to.

A few moments later, Martin made a panicky exit from the
apartment, clutching a single bag with the compcom and a few
clothes in it. He sped down the passage, avoiding the elevators,
and took the fire stairs down to the subbasement. Following
escape plan A, he left the basement through a maintenance
tunnel that connected all the domes on this side of the street.

He pictured the rest of the escape route ahead of him:
around the corner of the Hill Road, across the big east-west
road still called Hospital Road by some, and into a subterra-
nean parking structure under a shopping precinct. There he
would find a plain gray ground car, a two-seater that he would
drive the length of Hospital Road to the next hideout.

There would be EASU eyes out there by the hundreds. He
was going to need every atom of streetcraft he possessed. He
had a gun in his belt, one made of plastics that would never
show up on a street weapon scan. If they were closing in on
him, he promised himself he'd use it to kill himself. He
wouldn't let them strap him to that hotbed.

23

THE WAITING GAME DRAGGED ON FOR A MONTH FOLLOWING THE loss of Hof Witlin and Slovo Milsuduk. On the New Essex Coast, work redoubled on the EASU's coming offensive. In the Highlands, Fair and Elgin Fundan worked frantically to prepare for the blow.

But they were blind now, or almost. The network had held up; by dint of a desperate effort among the Roiders not a single cell had been caught. Even Martin Overed had escaped capture, but with the EASU pressure so strong it was as much as anyone could do to step outside on the streets. Active surveillance of military activities was almost impossible on the new base that Erst had built on the tip of the peninsula, where the first colony had foundered a century before.

By luck, they did get some video off one of EASU's own spy satellites, and this burst of intercepted data gave the Highlanders warning that Erst planned to move in force. They could see the outlines of a dozen big transport planes and stacks of munitions and equipment on the peninsula. They knew what was coming.

But the attack was still a surprise. Elgin and Fair were not prepared for the skill that Erst now displayed. Five separate raiding parties struck at chitin-talker groups scattered over the Ghotaw Valley. The Fundans dared not commit their relatively slender force. They expected an assault on Ghotaw Central at any moment, and then one on Ghotaw North. There was almost nothing they could do for the embattled chitin groups. The sense of frustration was terrible, and morale throughout the Response Force began to sink.

At the vaults, there had been continuous digging in of new fortifications for months. A lot of nervous depositors had withdrawn their caches, and others waited anxiously to see how the expected blow would fall.

Meanwhile, the outgunned chitin groups were dispersed,

captured, or annihilated. Secret caches were dug up. Chitin talkers were tortured, videoed, and the results broadcast. The message was: Surrender to EASU. There was to be a tax on the chitin talkers; they would surrender eighty percent of their production. The remainder, they would be allowed to keep. If they refused, they would be tortured into giving up everything. Some groups were fitted with explosive bands around their necks, primed to detonate should they fail to come in from the range with their quota for the EASU.

The helplessness and rage in the Highlands soon generated a wave of dissension that threatened to break up the fragile coalition formed by Witlin and the Fundans. Only the smaller clans still supported Fair and Elgin—groups like the Hendersons and the Campagnoli. Arrayed against them were the majority of the Fundans, led by Proud Fundan, the Weerses of Algae Canyon, and the Buttes, the large clan that ran all the scattered chitin territories over the Butte Uplift.

The official leadership of more distant clans, the Hoechsts and Kordwites, the Da Silvas and the Chungs, also aligned with Proud Fundan. They saw Fair as a fanatic, and some felt genuine doubt about her claim to be descended from the line of Edward Fundan. Her mother had been an unknown; the rest of the Fundans refused to accept her as a leader. Compton Fundan had been a very old man at the time of her birth.

Now Proud Fundan was demanding that control of the Highland Response Force be taken away from Elgin and given to Proud and the family council. Vicious attacks were made on Elgin in the council debate. Impassioned pleas for protection came from every chitin group in the valley. Proud demanded the right to help the talkers. The Response Force must be made to act, he insisted, to protect the people it was designed to protect—not to hide inside the barricades in Ghotaw Central.

A great unknown that clouded the whole matter was the attitude of Ervil Spreak. The Spreaks were outside the pale, but they were the most populous of the clans, and the best armed and prepared. Whatever Ervil said would hold great weight, regardless of his absence from the council.

Elgin argued that breaking up the Response Force was exactly what Erst wanted to do. Once they were dispersed, EASU would strike at Ghotaw Central.

In the atmosphere of crisis, clan leaders were eager to blame someone and to take some sort of action. It seemed they would ignore Elgin and force him out of his position.

Fear and panic were in the air. Ghotaw Central steadily
emptied out as people found shelter on the chitin ranges, or off
in the farther expanses of the great valley. Tensions rose steadily among those who had stayed. Meanwhile, the Response
Force militia trained every day and waited for the "big show."

As the pressure on Elgin mounted, Fair tried a desperate
move. She flew to see Spreak. Twenty-six-hundred kilometers
to the east of Ghotaw stood the fortress of Spreak Kop. Originally called Top Hat Mountain, the Kop was a steep-walled
volcanic remnant, thrust up through the floor of a rift valley.

When she arrived, Fair was impressed by the energy the
Spreaks had put into the Kop. It was riddled with tunnels and
bunkers. The exterior surface had been reinforced with plates
of ceramic smart armor capable of reflecting laser bolts and
ballistic weapons. Her guides were keen to impress on her that
this armor was a Spreak invention. They had reached the point
where they were going beyond the old Fundan Design Catalogs.

Out around the Kop were a great number of small antiair
batteries, dispersed and mobile, hidden in the jik forest and the
broken country of the foothills on either side of the Piet Valley.

Inside the fortress, the Spreaks had mustered nearly six hundred men and women. Fair was stunned. She and Elgin had
managed to raise a little more than two hundred combat people, all told, from all the other families.

It was galling. People were just so slow to awaken to the
dangers! They had put off joining the Response Force until it
was too late, and now they were dispersing all over the valley,
where they were useless to each other. As for her own family,
they were the worst, a gaggle of querulous and complaining
voices, all obsessed with not losing an iota of personal advantage through having to join together to face a common enemy.
As a result, the Fundans were no longer the true leaders of the
colony. For some reason, this deeply angered her.

Ervil finally showed himself in a dark bunker filled with the
hot lights of video screens. Voices murmured in the dark as
their owners monitored aircraft flying over Spreak territory and
exchanged data with other clans. They had a prominent place
given to a video feed from Ghotaw Central.

Ervil rose to meet her. Whatever doubts Ervil might have
concerning Fair's true parentage, he didn't doubt her abilities
to lead. He recognized a power in the young woman. He knew
that power; he wielded something like it himself.

"Welcome to Spreak Territory."

"Thanks. It's impressive, what you've done here."

Ervil grinned his agreement. "It is, isn't it? Who'd have thought that us old Spreaks would have had it in us? Why, we've been acting like Fundans of old. The cooperation! Hah, you should have seen some of the meetings we had."

"Yes, I can imagine," she said dryly.

"Old Kristins, he was beside himself. Having to be in the same room as his son Diergaard made his blood boil!" Ervil bobbed his head at the memory and a crazy grin flicked on and off. "But we prevailed on the pair of them and got things done anyway."

"Admirable. I only wish . . ."

He chuckled. "Yes, I hear that that booby Proud Fundan has stuck his dick in the wheels. Too bad, that."

Fair dropped any pretensions to family unity. "Look, if they prevail and bring down Elgin, they will lose to the EASU. EASU will then consolidate their position in the Ghotaw. Eventually they will come after you."

Spreak was nodding. The hot colors of the video monitors outlined his bald head in a halo of reflections. "So you came all this way just to get my vote?"

She pursed her lips. Ye gods, thought Spreak, she's a bold one, magnificent, but probably dangerous in the long run, like a young lioness. It would only be a matter of time before she turned on you. "Our families are blood enemies, aren't they?" he said.

"Yes."

"Some Spreaks did bad things in the old days."

"Yes."

"You probably think I was one of them, don't you?"

She shrugged. "It's hard to be sure. You might have personally shot Miriam Am-Bosett. You were there. The court decided that you didn't do it, though, but who's to say they were right? No one else was ever convicted."

Miriam Am-Bosett, a case that rang down the decades. Spreak's face split into a wintry smile. "Well, you have done your research, haven't you?"

"You did kill Maximum Pete. You killed Delor Fundan and you had a hand in the disappearance of Cortic Fundan."

Ervil's white wispy eyebrows rose. "They were right about you, weren't they! Dali and her friends told me you were a hard worker. A 'true Fundan,' they called you, the sort that only comes along every few generations, the ones that have kept the Fundans going all these years."

She plowed on. "Spreaks worked with the Khalifi, I know that, too."

"Yeah, we had a good deal with the Arabs." He sighed as if he really regretted the passing of the Khalifi tyranny. "And we were lucky to survive."

"You remember it all, don't you?"

A shadow seemed to fall over his face; he looked down. "You could never forget. Those things, what I saw—no, you could never forget. It was a miracle that any of us survived."

"Well, that's true for us, too. We can never forget the killings, the treachery." She took a deep breath. "But we have to put them behind us now and work together."

"All right, the new spirit of cooperation, I'm all for it. But let me remind you that we're allies already. Those are Spreak-built fighters you people are flying."

"Indeed they are, and I'm grateful for the good sense that prevails inside your family right now. In mine, as you seem so well aware, we have an excess of arrogant stupidity at the moment."

He nodded; it was true enough. Clan Fundan was surely doomed, if Proud Fundan had his way with it. "And so you need my vote to hold on to your power. You are young and not yet trusted by your family. I think they fear you, my young Lady Fundan. You're too energetic for them, you frighten all the useless ones."

"You exaggerate my importance in the scheme of things, I think."

"Hah, humbug, my dear, as my grandfather would say. I thought your family had finally played itself out until you suddenly emerged this past year. And, since your emergence, we have investigated you very thoroughly. You understand the 'widepath,' it is said. You are a legend among the Fein."

Investigated. Once warned, twice ready, she thought.

"You understood the menace from the Coastal scum, you moved to take command. Yes, I think we've seen your kind before."

He was smiling. She said nothing.

"So you need me," he chuckled softly. "You, Fundan, need old Spreak."

"Yes, I need you." Now came the price, she knew.

He grinned and held his silence. She was not about to waste time on this. "All right, what do you want?"

He grinned. "I am a reasonable man. I do not demand a ransom in pharamol. I do not demand a dozen virgin daughters of the Fundan line."

Ervil was enjoying himself. Fair scowled at him and he sobered. "I merely want unrestricted access to the Fundan Catalogs. There are some things I want to build."

She sucked in a sudden breath. By the freeze of deep space, she knew she was putting her head in a noose here. If her opponents in the family ever learned that she had done this, she would be finished. "All right, I think I can arrange that. I don't have all the codes you need, but I know where we might get it."

"Good." He was rubbing his hands together. Then he gestured around them at the farther reaches of the room. Hot screens glittered in the gloom, men and women whispered together over the net.

"As for my vote, you have it. I think Elgin did the only thing he could do defensively, if he wants to hold Ghotaw that badly. Personally I'd let it go."

"But the vaults—"

"Let them take the vaults. They'll be like a nest that's killed another nest and looted it—they'll be ripped to pieces by the infighting over the loot. You'll see them go crazy, and that's when we have to go over to the offensive."

"Let them take the vaults?" It sounded terrible. Then she reconsidered. "Of course. While they're absorbing all that loot and parceling it out, they won't be able to think straight."

"And we take it to them. We hit them down there on the Coast. When that's over, we won't have to worry about them ever again."

She felt a sudden pang of worry.

"You let them have Ghotaw," he said, continuing to propound his vision, "and you draw their strength into the heart of our strength. They'll have a force pinned there and we can hit it again and again with guerrilla tactics."

"Except that they have the equipment to build more aircraft than we can. It will be months before we have more Darters, even."

Ervil smiled enigmatically. "I disagree, my dear. We have forged a weapon that will obliterate the EASU."

Fair felt something turning to ice inside her. Had the Spreaks already committed themselves to that pathway? Was that what he wanted in the catalogs? She steadied herself with a hand on a nearby console. If she gave away Fundan nuclear technology, she would go down in history as a mad renegade. The family would never forgive.

There was a sudden bleep of activity on the commo from Ghotaw Central. A few moments later, they were getting incoming messages from everyone. The big show had begun.

The bunker came alive with screens and babble. The blow had fallen at last, upon Ghotaw Central, as expected, and Fair was out of it, completely unable to get back in time to take part. There was nothing to do but listen with a sinking heart as a litany of defeats began.

EASU had equipped a small fleet of gunships with air-to-air missiles. As a result, they were able to keep the little Spreak-built Darters from taking control of the sky. And thus the EASU ground forces were protected as they landed and seized the airstrip.

Then came the big aircraft, and within an hour there were two thousand EASU troops plus equipment on the ground.

The Response Force had been pinned down by remorseless weapons fire from the gunships that controlled the air. The Fundan missiles were not effective against the gunships at first, because of a sophisticated new EASU electronic defense that caused warheads to detonate long before they reached a target. Some batteries were destroyed on the ground after firing just one or two missiles, when their next missile exploded in the pod as it ignited.

EASU began to push into Ghotaw Central. The missile batteries on Ghotaw North were neutralized by patrolling rad-attack mother missiles. As soon as ground-based radar came on, these missiles dove to the attack. The batteries were forced to defend themselves rather than launch against the planes coming into the Ghotaw airstrip.

The two thousand EASU men split up into two groups, each about a thousand strong, and began to work their way into Ghotaw Central in a pincer movement, driving in the fragile defenses of the Response Force with air attacks whenever a strong point was held.

The Response Force fought hard. There was street fighting and many domes were destroyed. But the numbers were overwhelming and, in just a matter of two hours, the entire town area had been cleared of the defenders and the fires were being put out.

More transports began flying in from the Coast. Soon the barriers on the road to the vaults in Ghotaw North were under attack.

Finally the Darters were sent in, risking everything. They zipped in, naping the dirtline, dodging missiles, and streaked over the airstrip. A transport burst into a fireball in their wake and ground-cracking bombs struck the strip in several places.

But on their way out of the zone the Darters were zeroed by the gunships and the last plane out suddenly blew up and dove into the ground at twice the speed of sound.

A little later the fighting died down. Elgin and the Response Force had withdrawn, as they had feared they would have to, and moved back into the secondary positions. Everything had gone about as badly as their worst suppositions. The Highlanders had simply failed to do enough to protect themselves. Fair and Elgin had been unable to sell their own family on involving itself in its own defense. What good were a couple of hundred volunteers against thousands of mercenaries from the Coast? How was Fair going to defeat that remorseless logic, especially in the light of what Spreak was planning?

The Spreak bunker was noisy with all the urgent voices trading information across the Highland Commo Net. Ervil had gone outside to have a smoke. She followed and found him lighting a small cheroot made from the plant they called teosind, a crude rendering of the Feiner phrase *"tay augh sinji,"* which meant roughly, "head in the clouds." She waved it away when he offered it to her.

"Helps take the edge off these situations, I find."

"It's a narcotic."

"So? It's not opium. It affects the neurotransmitters in the brain for about fifteen minutes. Harmless and relaxing, much better for you than alcohol." He inhaled.

"What about smoke inhalation?" she asked. In her mind was a raging impatience.

"Certainly that is a consideration, but in moderation, it's not particularly harmful. This isn't nicotine, dear, I'm not about to kill myself with it."

"Ervil—" Her body was rigid. "—We cannot use atomics, Ervil. It is forbidden . . ."

He was silent, merely staring at her with those pale eyes.

"Ervil, there is a place in the forest, called the *fidnemed*." He nodded and rocked her with surprise. "Yes, I know." She gulped and stared at him. He knew? "You know?"

"I went there some years ago."

A vast surge of relief washed through her. He understood, he had to. She would not have to try and explain it all.

He gestured with the cheroot. "The use of atomic weapons against the super forest ecosystem is a suicidal move. I know. I went there with one of the old gray ones, the adepts of the Spirit. It changed my thinking forever. Indeed, I think I have not been the same man since. This was six years ago, now."

"The chitin insect . . ."

"Is not indigenous to this world. Yes, we understand that, too. Not an example we wish to emulate. What might they do to us, eh?"

"They sent the chitin home star into a nova flash."

"If you can believe what the Fein say, that's what they did."

"We must be very careful."

"Of course, the selective use of atomics against the Coastal places themselves would not necessarily send a strong enough signal to bring about a return of the Arizel."

She shook her head. "No, Ervil, no atomics at all. If we let that monster out of the box we'll never get it back in. If we use atomics, no one will ever trust us not to use them again, so they'll use them against us. That means bombardment from space, perhaps, and the use of enough weapons to certainly bring the ancient masters back."

He hesitated for a long moment and then he nodded. "Yes, exactly my thinking, my dear. We have not developed nuclear weapons, although we could and quite quickly if we had to. But I, too, realized that to use them would bring about an escalation and the strong likelihood of more nuclear conflicts. That would be disastrous."

She sighed with relief again. She would not have to try and change this old man's mind on this subject. When she opened her eyes again she saw that he was watching her closely.

"So, of course, you're wondering what our secret weapon is?"

"Well, of course."

"A rebellion against the EASU, right there in their own backyard, that's what."

He laughed at her wide-eyed response. "You aren't the only ones with a network on the Essex Coast, as they call it nowadays. We've been preparing for this for a long time, believe me."

24

THE GUNSHIP PATROLLED THE SOUTHERN MARGINS OF THE MOUN-
tain. From a distance it looked like some monstrous insect,
clad in the velvet of radar-stealth. It moved through the valleys
in sudden darting motions, interrupted by periods when it hovered as its sensors searched the forest and heath below.

It had been a good ride. They'd hit a chitin group the day
before and, after putting one old woman over a smoking fire
for half an hour, they had picked up five good micro caches of
high-quality pharamol. Every man aboard had scored fifty
grains.

Gask, who was leader, had then distributed his entire share,
giving every man another twenty grains. Gask followed the tra-
ditions. You gave liberally to the men and women in your
party. That was the only way to secure their loyalty.

They were flying with high morale and hopes of a record
haul from the trip. Everyone was veteran and, in fact, everyone
had been on three or more active raids. They were a tight
bunch. Gask had worked with most of them before and he had
recruited wisely. Things had gone smoothly as a result, and
they'd taken no casualties in four days' raiding.

They came over a section of harsh ocher rock, too bare for
anything but an occasional dwarf jik tree growing from cracks
in the stone. They spotted a herd of gzan, twenty big gray
shapes, moving in single file toward a swamp downhill from
the rocky outcrop. To one side of the gzan the sensors picked
up a team of Fein, five in all, who were tracking the animals.

With a harsh bark of laughter, Gask announced the fun. The
Fein hunted the gzan, but now the hunters would be the
hunted. The Fein were scattering but it was too late. The gunship thundered over them, and down dropped the raiders on
gossamer winged descent chutes, encircling the Fein as they
dropped.

"Red Leader down!"

"Blue Leader down!"

"Position is forty-one oh two three. Moving out now."

Gask lead them in on the hunt.

"Remember, everyone, one shot. Don't spoil that fur!"

Gask, Trenchet, Holmes, and Bosan moved cautiously down a rocky defile.

"Come in, Blue Leader," Gask whispered into his throat mike.

"Got you loud and clear," came the reply from Comoza. "We're dropping over the ridgeline and into an area of boulders and loose rock. They can't hide too easily in here."

"Okay, take them one at a time and don't spoil those hides."

"Blue Leader out."

The defile jigged to the left and then the right and they broke out into a thicket of the dark-leaved little trees. Two Fein were bounding along the rocky bed of a stream about one hundred meters distant.

"On the left is mine!" Trenchet snapped.

"I got the one on the right," Holmes said a moment later.

Gask smiled. Everyone was eager. He liked that. "All right, we take them as called. Second shots go to me on the left and Bosan on the right. Fire."

The assault rifles rose and emitted the dense crackling sounds of advanced ballistic weaponry. The Fein on the left tumbled, rolled, and fell. He did not move again. The Fein on the right was already in the air when the bullet struck him and he spun and fell awkwardly on his back. Still, he rolled into a crevice between two huge rocks and disappeared.

"Damn," snarled Holmes, who sprang out onto the rocks in the streambed and started down toward the kill. Trenchet followed, with Gask and Bosan bringing up the rear.

Holmes fired again as he ran, his bullets raising dust on the rocks around the spot where the Fein had gone to ground.

Trenchet was getting out his skinning knife. This was the second Fein he'd managed to take. The first one was now a rug in the bedroom of a woman he'd had a thing with for about six months. Some women really went for this alien fur; it turned them on. Trenchet giggled at the idea. Maybe that blond piece of ass that hung out at Morey's Bar would go for a nice fur rug.

Gask suddenly yelled "Shit!" and ducked. There was the sound of a gun going off wildly and the bullet ricocheting off the rocks, and something like a spinning football flew across the streambed and clipped Holmes at the neckline. Holmes's head separated from his shoulders and flew off, while his body toppled.

"Oh, shit!" shrieked Gask, who was firing now, short bursts into the rocks to their left from which the missile had been thrown.

Trenchet put the knife back in its sheath and crouched low while keeping his gun up, trained on the boulders on the left. Vegetation shook over there, and he manically fired ten rounds. Pieces of the jik trees flew up in the air.

"Hold your fire, dammit!" Gask was yelling at him.

"Freezing shit!" Bosan was standing over Holmes corpse. "Would you look at that?"

"Shuddup, there's another of them out there."

"Yeah," Trenchet said, "but they only have one of those weapons apiece. He can't get any more of us like that."

"Dive!" Bosan screamed. A piece of rock the size of a man's foot hurtled over Trenchet's shoulder and shattered on the rock behind him. Trenchet dropped into the stream, his head ringing from the impact of stone fragments on his helmet.

Another rock, larger this time, went wobbling up into the air like a fly ball in a baseball game. It was a howitzer shell from the Stone Age. Gask crouched, watching it anxiously. "Move," he snapped to Trenchet, who started moving left at just the wrong moment.

With the sound of a melon being hit with a hammer, the heavy rock caught Trenchet on the back. His dying scream rang off the rocks.

"Shit!" Gask said. Two men down, killed by the fucking ab-originals? It was incredible.

"Fuck this," Gask screamed into the throat mike. "Take them down, kill me all of these fucking hairballs."

The gunship pivoted in the air.

Another rock missile was on its way toward Gask and Trenchet. Gask moved, diving around the rock. A moment later a twenty-pound rock bounced off his former position and shot into the stream.

Shit, but the furball was accurate with those things.

They were all crouched over now. Gask waved them back, up the draw, away from the boulders.

The gunship was coming, swinging in from the west. It was time to go.

Another twenty-pound rock was lobbed up into the air. It

shattered there, hit by the first burst from the gunship, firing on autoseek. The twin Meganev twenty-millimeters let rip and the ground became covered in dust. The air filled with ricochets and flying splinters of rock.

The Fein were annihilated. They found hardly anything left of them.

Ricochets hit Gask and Bosan. Gask was spun around by the impact in his shoulder. Every bone in his upper body felt as if it had been broken. He was barely conscious of his own screams while the bright arterial blood pumped out of his neck and chest and stained the ground around him.

The gunship rode back to Ghotaw Central with the bodies of three men and the usable furs of two Fein. Before leaving the scene the gunship had slaughtered the herd of gzan and left their carcasses to bloat in the afternoon sun.

The mood among the survivors was somber. Despite the pharamol they'd looted, the bodies of Gask, Trenchet, and Holmes were a shock to the rest of them.

Thousands of miles away, on the steamy south coast of the great continent, the leadership of the EASU toasted itself at a celebratory bash following the smashing success of the big show. The Big Man was having a ball. He was on a roll, at the pinnacle of his success. Nobody would ever fuck with him now!

The big show had produced more than eight kilos of pharamol. It was an incredible fortune. At current prices in the home system it would have bought a planet.

They were all there, all the familiar faces, except for that squealer Slovo. Boy, had they done for him! There was Lawrence and Yoote, there was Fletcher and Tyler. Of course Congo was missing, and that was a pity—the Big Man had always liked Congo's black mug. Congo was good, too, the best security man ever.

But it was over now. The stuck-up Highlanders were scattered and defeated. Sure, there was a little guerrilla activity around Ghotaw, but it was slight and he was assured by his field commanders that it would soon be mopped up.

The Big Man raised his glass.

"To our success!" he roared. "To EASU and everlasting rule!"

The Big Man drank and the EASU men drank and they broke out into prolonged cheering and singing of "He's a Jolly Good Fellow."

Later they carried the Big Man shoulder-high around the suite. They soaked themselves in ersatz champagne. They roared and danced and drank until dawn. It was a wild night on the New Essex Coast, a precursor to an endless age of EASU domination.

25

THE FEIN OF EMOKI VILLAGE HAD TURNED OUT IN THEIR BEST RE-GALIA. Yellow skrin feathers decorated ear tufts and halters worn by the younger females. Kifket sheaths were polished and done up with fresh thongs. Marks of achievement covered the shoulder fur of the older males, red twists of neeble wool designating fatherhood of cubs, the dried white blossoms of darleea, looking like small stars on their chests, indicating marriages. The older females wore purple chaffa spines on their foreheads and wound braids of satursine vinelet around their heavy arms. Their aprons were decorated with embroideries in white and black, the traditional mode for Emoki Village.

Shtingi, daughter of the great artist Gumida, stood among the older females. She had her own claim to fame now among the Highland Fein, for she was the mother of N'ka of Emoki, who had saved Fair Fundan from death. She was the mother who had nursed Fair Fundan back to life.

Thus, in many minds, Shtingi, human-lover, was synonymous with Emoki. And elsewhere they called Emoki, "Shtingi's Village." This was a development that upset some of the traditional minds in the village, and so Shtingi had received some criticism. At the same time, her supporters and kin had closed ranks around her.

But then, nothing concerning the presence of the humans on their world had been benevolent. Shtingi had learned much from Fair and later from N'ka. She had spread this k___ widely in the village, for she understood that, de___ dency of the Fein to blame the messenger for the ___ important for them to understand what was happe___

The first ugly rumors had not been believed. Then, into Emoki had come Fair Fundan, falling like a comet from the early warfare right into their laps. They could not ignore her. The daily conversations at the firepit and the well had revolved about her presence and what it all meant. It had gone on for months, and then the stories had grown worse. A handful of refugees from Ko-Poko Village passed through and told of the raid from the sky and slaughter of their kin. The mood in Emoki Village had grown very grim since then.

And now Fair Fundan had come back to them. She was there with N'ka and Elgin Fundan. All the Fein knew well why Fair Fundan had come again; there was war between the humans down in Ghotaw Central and that war had expanded into an indiscriminate hunting of the Fein by the the Coastal raiders' gunships.

Fair and Elgin Fundan stood by the long boxes. N'kobi of the widepath stood with them. Beside N'kobi stood N'ka, who was now of the widepath, but was still of Emoki.

The humans brought war to the villagers of Emoki. The Fein understood war. Indeed they had a very long history of war, with combat Fein to Fein, with honor on all sides. War was a dark business, to be undertaken only in the most desperate of circumstances. War always had this particular feeling, and the Fein could sense that feeling in Fair Fundan.

She addressed them in the honor mode and blessed the village and the gzan that gave it life. She told them of N'ka's exploits in the outer world, the sights he had seen and the deeds he had witnessed. N'ka told them that she spoke the truth and that every Fein must pay attention to what she said. It was a terrible time for both the Fein and the humans who lived in the Highlands.

"I can only give you the things you must have to defend yourselves, modern-day weapons and training in their use. My power is limited beyond that," Fair explained.

Elgin bent down and broke open the long box. She took an assault rifle from it, a Fundan-designed nine-millimeter automatic rifle that fired a variety of ammunition types in both auto and semiauto mode. It was light yet sturdy and accurate up to two miles. She held it up to them.

"We have weapons here for every one of you. With them, you can defend your village and your gzan. But you must learn how to use the weapons properly and safely."

Elgin gave one of the rifles to N'ka, who worked the mechanism with practiced ease and took aim at a target nailed to a tree at the far end of the long walk that bisected the village. The gun spat five or six times before N'ka brought the weapon down.

"Go and examine the target," N'ka said.

They sent little Ook, son of Ganwana, running down the long walk to fetch the target. He gave a cry of wonder and came scampering back.

The elders clustered around. The target had been a storage box, woven from slats of young knuckoo, a typical household item for storing anything from tubers to tool sets. The box had five clean holes drilled through it.

"The weapon you give us throws small kifkets, but very fast."

"Just about," Fair said.

"This is what killed the Fein of Ko-Poko," said old Mombakus, one of the "old vinegars" in the village. He gestured in disgust at the rifle. "They told us of this thing. That and the thing in the sky that spat fire and noxious smokes."

Fair nodded somberly. "We will show you how to use this weapon. The enemy raiders are coming further and further afield from Ghotaw, so you must either prepare to defend yourselves or leave the country of your ancestors and move further west."

Mombakus shook a big fist in the air.

"You bring war to us. War! And we the ay Fein have had no saying in it."

Fair would not deny it.

"You humans bring us war."

Fair felt a flush of shame on her cheeks. "We can train you to fight so that you will survive."

Mombakus hadn't finished with her yet. "But still it is war you bring us. This is not a good thing. Truly are they correct who say that the coming of the humans was not a good day for the Knuckle of Delight."

Many of the others were obviously hesitant. They muttered together or went to talk with Shtingi. A few of the most recalcitrant even fingered their kifkets and made the point that, if there was to be war with the humans, then maybe it should be with *all* humans. They could start with these humans right here.

But the majority suppressed these hotheads. This was Fair Fundan. She had lived among them; Shtingi had cared for her when she was brought in close to death. Shtingi's cub N'ka had gone with Fair Fundan over the mountains to the great valley far away. This talk of taking heads here was foolish. Everyone had to open their ears, let in the understanding. This was a vital moment in the history of Emoki Village.

Still, the level of rage was high. The Fein were a conservative people. They were used to war—indeed, Emoki was currently in a state of war, Fein war, with two other villages: Boshi, one hundred kilometers to the north, and Kimopo, two hundred kilometers to the west. But these wars, while fierce, were of limited scope and the weaponry was that of the Stone Age: spears, kifkets, slings, and stones, not this alien weaponry with its gloss of oil on metal and the spitting sound of sudden death.

After an hour or so of debate there was a slight majority in favor of accepting the weapons. A small group wished to pick up and leave the village, to trek north into Kashu, where there were valleys with no Fein and no humans.

Fair spoke to them once more. "Truly, they are right who say that the coming of the humans to this world was not a good thing, and I say this as the granddaughter of the one who made it possible," Fair said, "but it is too late. We are here and more of us are coming. If the Fein are to survive, they will have to arm themselves. More than that, they will have to work with us, for our interests are identical in this."

They brought out the ancient drums, long drums made from stiffened green knuckoo, with gzan hide stretched tight at the ends. Eyes glaring, the Fein elders took up the drum clubs and began the rhythm. The drums thrubbed and the males of Emoki formed-up in two long lines, the young and the old.

Fair felt a painful watering of the eyes, and she blinked back the tears. This was wrong; she had no right to involve these ancient, peaceful people. But there was no alternative. Without guns they would be exterminated.

Mombakus was right. She brought them war, endless war.

The Fein came forward and took the guns. The drums throbbed steadily.

The meeting was delayed for two days after they brought him back from the Essex Coast. All he wanted to do was sleep, but they wouldn't let him relax for a moment. He was debriefed, and at times things grew harsh in the room. Of course, it was nothing like what EASU had done to him.

Finally, he got the call. A pair of young men in green camo came and unlocked the narrow room they'd been keeping him in. They marched him out of the dome into the raw cave and took him down a steep path to a deep section where there were hollowed-out cells. She was waiting for him in one of these cubicles. There was a narrow table, a dim lamp, and a bed along one wall.

"It's good to see you. I didn't expect to, ever again," he said.

"Yes." She reached out to him, but there was uncertainty in her eyes.

Their hands locked together. He squeezed tight. There were tears in his eyes.

She'd read the debrief; the EASU had used a mindprobe pretty savagely on him. They could have planted things in his mind, like time bombs. He could be dangerous. And she could never entirely trust him again.

He knew it, she could tell. He stood away and sat down in the narrow chair. The world had imploded on him and she was no more able than he to go back to the moment before that implosion.

"I understand," he said. She nodded.

"They destroyed me, Fair. But you know about that."

"It's what we expected from them. I'm sorry, old man, so sorry."

"Do you know?"

"Who gave you away? Yes. It was Proud, I'm sure of it. I have a source in his personal-affairs office. Proud has dealings with EASU now."

Just for spite, Proud had given him to the Big Man. Hof found it easy, just then, to hate Proud Fundan. He swallowed hard.

"Well, I just wanted to see you . . ."

"Hof, you can have a life. You can even help us—you know how much we needed your help before. You just cannot be part of the decision-making group. We can't be sure of you. *You* can't be sure of you . . ."

He smiled savagely. "I think you should make it easy on all of us. Why don't you just kill me? Save me from having to do it myself."

"No, old man, you have a life. We need your skills. They hope to terrify us with your release. You can show them they were wrong."

"And if they get me back again? What then? You know what then? They have a thing called the hotbed."

"We know about that."

"I have memories that I don't want to have. Things that will never leave me. What they did to me."

"This phase won't last forever—"

He grimaced. "You don't understand, Fair. They've got you. It's all EASU's game now. Erst had everything from me. You can't hold it back, you know. No matter what they say, you can't not talk once they get started in earnest. They know how weak we are and how much we depended on Slovo Milsuduk."

"Slovo is dead."

"Yeah, he's dead, they showed me the body. He died long and slow—they really excelled themselves with Slovo. He looked like a piece of dried meat, jerky."

"I'm sorry, Hof . . ."

"Kill me."

"Stop it."

"You don't have a chance. They're building nuclear weapons now."

She paled and trembled.

"That's what I've been doing for them for the past two months. Little fusion devices, hydrogen bombs, primitive really. Small ones, outputs in fractions of a kiloton."

He hugged himself and rocked back and forth.

"They're going to test them on the forest soon. They think they'll be able to defeat the forest now by nuking it. A nuclear cordon."

Fair was ashen-faced. "Then we have no choice, we must risk everything."

26

THE ROOM WAS DARK AND COOL, A NATURAL EFFECT OF ITS UN-derground location in the depths of Mt. Fundan. At one end was a wall screen, and arrayed in front of it were three rows of chairs, now partially filled.

Everyone present was Fundan and of the ruling lines. In the front row were Xavier Norel-Fundan, the legal signatory for all family financial instruments; Proud Fundan, grandson of Agatha; and Pamela Cleeves-Fundan, the sole survivor of the once flourishing Cleeves family line.

Behind them were the Toronto-Fundans, both branches, with Ruperth Toronto-Fundan on the right and Sykes Tarn-Toronto Fundan on the left. In the last row were several more junior members of the family elite, the next generation of torch bearers for an ancient spacer clan: Dakota Fundan-Shact, Merito Fundan, Ceres Fundan, Champeral Fundan, and Tuchor Toronto-Fundan.

This was the family council, an institution that was three hundred years old and had held the clan Fundan together during its rise to legendary prominence in the home system. So high had the Fundans flown, they'd leapt clear out of that system and across the vastness of deep space to this new world.

Of late, the power of this council had been lessened for a variety of reasons. First and foremost, the clan had atomized into the vast spaces of Ghotaw Valley and moved onto the chitin drug economy. Most were now enormously wealthy in longevity drugs, which meant they were enormously wealthy by any means and were independent of the old Fundan bank system. But still there was a resource, Fundan technology from the old days, that was controlled by this council, which gave it an immediate practical power. In addition, there was a symbolic power: as the only universally acknowledged voice for the Fundans, the council was the undisputed head of the clan and was looked to in all disputes with outsiders.

Unfortunately, the council had been a static presence for two decades, frozen by bitter internal disagreements. Partially as a result, the wonderful tech-set that had been bequeathed by Dane Fundan had been allowed to decay into ruin. The best minds had gone to work elsewhere, the old machines had broken down, and some were beyond their skills to repair.

On the political level, this inability to make any decisions had gradually rendered the council irrelevant to the problems the family faced, and the problems had intensified rapidly with the increases in raiding from the Coast. The council had floundered in trying to come up with any solution.

Then Fair Fundan and Elgin Fundan had come with their

Highland Response Force. The council had tried to ignore it but the other clans, especially the Buttes, were so enthusiastic that it got off the ground anyway. The Spreaks gave them three jet aircraft and they suddenly became a force to be reckoned with.

Somehow the Response Force had always known just where to ambush the incoming raiders. Within a month the raids had virtually ceased, at which point Fair and Elgin had become de facto members of the family council.

The horror among the old membership was universal. The "sperm bank" baby and the one they called "the Weirdo" had taken control. It was intolerable. Fair Fundan was considered "Fundan" only as a courtesy. Her claims were insolent and outrageous. Her mother had been a whore before taking up with Compton Fundan when he was in his eighties and unable to generate children. The sperm-bank claim was madness. There had been something of the kind once, but the council had squashed it and all the claimants back when Dane was still alive.

And as for the Weirdo, that creepy Elgin Fundan, he was only a Martian Fundan, anyway, and of no account.

The legitimacy issue simmered and bubbled in a cauldron of complaint among them and drove Proud Fundan, in particular, into passionate rages. With the loss of Ghotaw Central to EASU, the issue had grown once again. Proud was pushing for the council to take control of the Fundan family interest in the Response Force. Elgin and Fair were to be dumped and Proud was to take command.

The other families were ready to go along; even the Buttes had given reluctant assent.

Fair came in first, followed by Elgin a moment later. On his way in, Elgin held up his hands for their attention. "We are now going to watch a short film. It will show you how we are going to defeat our enemies." He nodded for the video to begin.

"Well," Pamela Cleeves-Fundan said, "I think we can call the meeting opened now."

Everyone except the Toronto-Fundans nodded to themselves. The Toronto-Fundans stared at one another momentarily and then looked back at the screen.

Fair took a seat in front of them. She was well aware of the hatred in the air. She shrugged, determined to ignore it, as always. There were too many things that were more important than their ritual hatred of her.

Proud got to his feet and called for the video to stop. "I move that we take a vote on the motion for a change in leadership in the Response Force. All those in favor please raise your hands."

There was a ripple of unease. Damn Proud! Why did he have to go and make such a public fuss? It could have been handled quietly, avoiding the embarrassment. After all, it wasn't as if anyone else on the council had even volunteered for the Response Force. What did they know about these things, about the sharp end of life where bullets and missiles fly? That was what Fair and the Weirdo did.

In truth they were also just a little frightened of these intense young interlopers, especially the Weirdo. They were scary, they had a fanaticism about them.

But Proud was hissing under his breath and glaring at them and calling in his markers for this vote. Unhappily, the hands began to go up.

Elgin stood up and laughed at them and signaled for the video to restart.

"I think perhaps you should watch our little film show before you vote on this motion," he said.

They stared at him.

"The reasons will become clear very soon. Watch."

Pamela Cleeves-Fundan liked this idea. She didn't want to publicly vote against them, even if she detested them. She respected them too much. They knew how to fight and she didn't. It was just that she felt such an enormous resentment at being left out of the loop on military affairs. As chief spokesperson for the council, the titular head of the entire clan, she felt she ought to be included in these things. It was a sheer disrespect for her position! And her position was very important to old Pamela, who had little else in her life.

So Pamela wanted to see this mysterious video. She was very eager to find out what they'd been up to. During the past months, while a reign of terror had devastated the Ghotaw, the Response Force had confined itself to a small campaign of guerrilla attacks on Ghotaw Central and the enlarged airstrip where EASU had a base. At the same time, a blanket of secrecy had descended on everything, and she and the council had been cut off, no contact allowed whatsoever. Pamela had not even heard from her granddaughter, Jessica, who was a volunteer in the Response Force Medical Section.

The lights dimmed despite Proud's urgent commands to halt the video.

"Shut up, Proud," Pamela demanded. "We want to see this."

Proud grumbled, but was greeted with further hisses from the others. He sat down again.

The image stabilized with a view of a cavernous space. Long rows of figures were engaged in regimental drilling.

A gasp went up, and Pamela felt her mouth drop open. It was a regiment of Fein, six hundred strong, drilling in disciplined formation. They wore a uniform of camouflage vest and baggy shorts, carried assault rifles, and wore webbing studded with further weaponry and equipment. They also wore their kifkets in their own individual sheaths.

"What you see here is the First Fein Regiment," the Weirdo said with a peculiarly happy tone. Pamela had never heard him sound so cheerful.

One of the Fein—they were all males as far as could be seen—stood out in front. He wore the same uniform but carried no rifle and had a square patch of dark blue on the shoulder of his vest. He bellowed commands in Feiner.

"This is First Regimental Neilk N'kobi. He agreed to take up the post only after a lot of persuasion. He is an old Fein of the 'widepath.' We don't know where his village was; he never mentions it. But he has a presence that the younger ones respect. N'kobi inspires discipline in them."

After a pause, the Weirdo continued with his lecture. "On the hunt, the Fein work as a disciplined team. They have adapted that sense of discipline directly into their military training. You have to understand, we have found a resource of incredible value. These Fein will make very good soldiers, perhaps the best soldiers there have ever been."

The images continued. Fein troopers worked through brush country, diving to the ground every so often to take cover. They exchanged fire with an unseen opponent, using blank ammunition.

In another series, they waited in ambush. They were utterly silent until the right moment and then they struck so fast it was terrifying.

Fein soldiers were shown making camp and then sitting around campfires with meat roasting on spits. They were shown drumming and dancing, a peculiarly modest dance, the big figures simply shuffling forward and backward, swaying slightly to the insistent, steady throb of the drums.

Finally, the lights came back on and the video ended.

"What have you done?" Toronto-Fundan asked from the second row. "What in all the hells have you done? You've given arms to the native alien life-form here. You must be out of your minds! You can't do this! Those are potentially dangerous enemies."

"They have to be able to defend themselves," Fair said. "We can't sit by and watch them massacred by the EASU, so we've been arming them for months. There isn't a known group of Fein within two thousand klicks of here that we haven't visited and given guns and ammunition to. You know what EASU was doing before."

"But didn't that mean that EASU left us alone? Why do we have to arm potentially hostile aliens?" Champeral Fundan demanded.

Fair grimaced. "I'll pretend I never heard that. Anyway, I don't really think EASU is diverting any of its energies from raiding to the extermination of the Fein. It's just that it's harder for them to raid since everyone's had to abandon their nest ranges and hide."

Proud was back on his feet, his finger jabbing the air. "Every day that goes by means we lose more nests to ferality. If we continue as we are for another thirty days, we'll lose them all. Long-term, we may be battling feral nests for years before we can root them out of the ranges."

"I know that, Proud," Fair said flatly. "Something will be done, don't worry about that. But we need your help, all of you! We need you to unite the family. We need more Fundans in the ranks. We have to have more men and women in the Force."

Proud purpled. "You want more? More victims for your bungling? You must be mad! You come in here, demanding this and that, and you're not even one of us! You're nothing but a sperm-bank baby! No legal claim to our name."

"Here we go . . ." Elgin said with a grin.

"And you are just a Martian. you have no right to be here, either!"

"Enough!" Fair slammed to her feet and stomped over to stand in front of Proud.

"My mother took great care over the DNA records. If you'd ever taken the trouble to look it up, you'd find my pedigree

listed in the Fundan Central Directory. My genetic father was
Compton Fundan, and my grandfather was Dane. If you want
a blood sample, I'll be glad to give it to any one of you. I have
as much right as any of you to be here and to raise a voice in
the family council. In fact, if it wasn't for my ancestors, none
of you would be here. You'd be in the home system dealing
with the Gung An Bu and the Social Union."

She whirled away from him and stalked along the front row.
"This is not a game. This is to the death, and you had better
all understand that. EASU has declared each and every one of
you a target for termination. EASU will not rest until all of us
are dead. The Fundans cannot be allowed to remain independent of EASU power. We have discovered that, among other
things, they have begun a nuclear weapons program."

There was a collective gasp. That had their attention!

"Oh, they have great plans, believe me." She shrugged and
spread her hands. "They're going to sow nuclear mines
throughout the inner system. They're preparing to keep out any
further colonists."

They gulped.

"And they intend to rule the chitin talkers. The clan leadership will be annihilated and the chitin talkers will become
peasants, working for EASU as sharecroppers."

The family council was reduced to staring at her with open
mouths. Finally, Pamela spoke up. "But, that will controvert
the Colony Covenant!"

Fair looked at her and Pamela felt the color rise in her
cheeks. The damn girl was amused!

"Well, since you say so, I must agree. Yes, the old Colony
Covenant will be completely done away with."

Fair looked to Elgin.

"Colony Covenant?" he whispered. These people did not de-
serve to run Clan Fundan. They'd made that amply clear. But
he knew that this breach of security was a good tactical move
and he had agreed with it.

"What are you going to do?" Pamela asked, suppressing her
fury.

"Well, we're going to retake Ghotaw and kick the EASU
out of our Highlands. Then we'll have to develop our own nuclear weapons. We'll be back to the old balance of terror."

27

WITHIN HOURS OF THE PASSING OF THE NUCLEAR WARNING TO EASU there came the first response. Flights of heavy transport jets rumbled into the airstrip at Ghotaw Central and disgorged more troopers. The EASU forces built up hour by hour.

Under duress, Proud Fundan continued to pass misinformation to his contact. Shortly thereafter, the EASU command in Ghotaw began a program of aggressive long-range patrols, as platoon-sized groups were sent out to investigate various places mentioned by Proud. In one of the first group of sites to be visited they found a hidden cache of Fundan industrial equipment and some weapons, rifles, and handguns. In another they discovered a small cache of pharamol and some chitin-talker equipment. In a third they found a cache of older-model rifles and some more industrial equipment. The excitement at Ghotaw grew and was passed on to the New Essex Coast. After these successes, however, little more was found, although Proud continued to give more site locations to be investigated for traces of the supposed Highland Nuclear Weapons Program.

Meanwhile, Fair Fundan and old N'kobi were in the forests outside Ghotaw Central preparing their own strike. With them for the purpose was the bulk of the Fein regiment, plus a force of three hundred men and women drawn from the Highland Response Force and the Spreak family militia. They had trained together for weeks for this operation. They moved into place as quietly as the Fein themselves, who, in the dark-leaved forests of jik and mindal, became as silent as wraiths. Morale was high—they were about to strike back, at long last.

For Fair and Elgin, there was the certain knowledge that this was a desperate throw of the dice. On it would depend the future of the planet. The odds against them were long; EASU had had months to fortify Ghotaw against an assault. Inside the perimeter were six thousand EASU personnel, and at least four thousand were troopers. Fair knew that this meant that she and N'kobi would have to rely on the power of surprise and the possession of the initiative. Whatever happened, the attack could not bog down.

Fair had some hopes that, in a real crisis such as a sudden surprise attack, the situation in the jam-packed town would explode into chaos. The place was overloaded with adventurers and hustlers, all seeking a short route to the pharamol connection.

There were the troopers and there were the two thousand support staff. Then there were thousands more hangers-on and free-lancers. The Ghotaw Command was extraordinarily popular on the New Essex Coast; thousands had signed up to be sent to the Highlands, and hundreds tried to talk their way onto the jet transports every day. The problems all these unwanted extras caused were immense. EASU command was constantly having to deal with robberies, robbery attempts, shootings, stabbings—the entire gamut of crime inspired by intense greed and an atmosphere of near chaos.

Thus, life was difficult for the administrators of the EASU force, but at least they didn't seem to have to worry much about being attacked. The guerrillas had just about disappeared from the neighborhood. In fact, it was remarkable how quickly everyone in the town had adjusted to the new relaxed pace. Sentry duty, for some, had become an extra sleep period, and a lot of troops no longer bothered to clean and check their weapons every day. Quite a few found ways to wangle a stay in the barracks or a visit to the Medical Section. A lot of these then disappeared into Bekunni's shebeen or the other hellholes that were still doing a roaring business in the town. And that meant more headaches for the administrators.

With this in mind, Fair let herself believe that they had a better chance than appearances would indicate. And so they split their meager forces and launched the dice, a final chance to turn back the EASU and bring the Highland nation into life.

Night fell over the valley. The Pale Moon rose in the east. At the signal, the Fein began to move.

The attack had three phases. First, a demonstration assault on the western end of the airstrip. The perimeter there was soft, the guards lax. The attack would be made by the Highland Response Force.

The second phase would begin once that attack had been solidly developed and had drawn the defensive forces. Then the Spreak force of two hundred men and women would attack the approach to the North Road, which connected Ghotaw Central with the vault district on the other side of the mountain. The Spreaks would press home as hard as possible and, when their attack had some momentum going, the Response Force on their right would abandon its own attack and shift left, falling in behind the Spreaks and assisting on the assault up toward the western approaches to Ghotaw Central.

Meanwhile, the third phase would be readied. The Fein regiment would be hidden in the garbage midden that coated the southeastern slopes beneath the town. When the two blows to the western side of the airstrip had drawn the attention of the EASU Command, the Fein would break out of concealment and make a dash for the southern edge of the town. The parapet there was only seven feet tall, with a pronounced slope that would make it simple to scramble across. The Fein would move fast and, with the darkness, they would be hard to see. If their luck held, they would make it. If not, they would be lost on the open ground directly in front of the parapet.

They had five Darters to provide air cover, three on loan from the Spreaks. With these Darters and the newest antiair missiles, they could disrupt attacks by any gunships that survived the first phase. It was vital that not many of the flying behemoths survive.

The signal was given. The men and women of the Response Force rose from prepared positions and rushed the perimeter of the airstrip at the western end, where the hangars and other buildings stood.

The few guards actually at their posts were taken by surprise. A few were shot, but most spooked and ran at once. Some put out a harassing small-arms fire from positions in the maintenance hangar. The attack went on and carried across the airstrip itself, through the parked aircraft, which blossomed into fireballs soon afterward, and into the buildings on the north side. Only two gunships managed to get aloft under automatic pilot. They moved off to the south and then circled back.

On the north side of the strip the defense finally stiffened and a firefight began, rising quickly to a crescendo as the frightened EASU troops let rip with everything they had.

The Response Force was held. The signal went out and on their left the Spreaks went in, moving quickly up the looping road that connected the airstrip directly to the North Road.

There was no one at the checkpoint and, after a cursory inspection, the Spreaks pushed on. At last, just a hundred meters from the North Road itself, they were met by an oncoming convoy of vehicles crammed with troopers.

The Spreaks stopped the column and blew up four large ATVs with smart-missile fire. The bright blasts of the explosions lit up the hillside and illuminated a wave of thousands of gunmen who were running in spontaneous movement from all over Ghotaw Central. The news was out across the town and all the adventurers and free-lance gunsels that had clogged the place were coming to join the fight. Inspired by the exhilarating sense of their numbers and their firepower, they were pouring out of the bars and restaurants.

From the Spreaks came the sparks of muzzle flashes and, with this visible sign of the enemy, the free-lance horde raised their weapons and began emptying clip after clip into the dark. Much of their fire was wildly inaccurate, but it was massive. The noise level increased quickly by several orders of magnitude, and millions of rounds mixed with red, yellow, and blue tracer went screaming out into the valley. The gunships flew right into the storm and were outlined in flashes as bullets fragmented on their armor.

The airstrip buildings, also directly in the line of fire, received a hammering. They were built of puffcrete and light struct, and under the impacts of millions of high-velocity rounds they began to disintegrate. The troopers who were defending them were dug in around their bases. In some cases they were buried under puffcrete falling from above; in others they were mown down by the fire from the rear. But nothing could be done to stop it—it was spontaneous, the outrage of thousands of undisciplined gunmen armed to the teeth.

The Response Force moved stealthily back and around the airstrip, then continued up the hillside toward the Spreaks' positions. A torrent of wasted ammunition howled above their heads. At length they made contact with the Spreaks and began filling out the line on the Spreaks' left.

So far, all had gone like clockwork. Fair absorbed the news and signaled N'kobi to start the Fein forward. Fair and the command group that traveled with her began to move, too, up through the tangled heaps of trash and busted equipment that cloaked the mountainside. Fair unslung her rifle; she always insisted on carrying her own weapon. Flashes of light from the battle off to the left and farther up the slope threw stark shadows on the garbage. Fair saw herself outlined, the gun in her hands, on a mound of containers and poly trash. Was this what her life would be? Fighting for survival, forever?

Directly in front of them, men were shouting excitedly to one another to come and look. There was a huge flash from the airstrip and a crackling thud. A cloud of white smoke was billowing up from the fuel station. A round had finally penetrated one of the big hydrogen tanks. The men on the parapet were all staring off into the southwest. Abruptly they ducked as five small jet aircraft, engines roaring, whipped past overhead and dove on the gunships that had swung in and begun to strafe the Spreak positions.

Sparkling bright flashes flared momentarily around the gunships and they wobbled in the air. These big air platforms were comparatively slow and ungainly, but they were heavily armored. One of them was able to ride out the multiple hits and speed a volley of missiles after the Darters. The other lost elevation and descended slowly into the woods beyond the airstrip.

The Darters took evasive action and disappeared around the western curve of the mountain. A few seconds later, two powerful explosions shook the north. The Highlander air force had been reduced by forty percent.

The remaining gunship wobbled back to strafe the Spreak positions once more.

Fair urged the Fein to move faster. If they were caught out in the open now they would be annihilated. They moved stealthily through the drifts of packaging, puffcrete fragments, and polyfoam containers.

Then they came on a small outlying strong point, thrust into the uppermost moraine of garbage from the EASU defensive perimeter. There were a handful of EASU troops inside, dug into a narrow trench with sandbags along the front. They were standing up, watching the fireworks over on their extreme right.

In front of them was an open stretch, at least fifty yards on either side—a potential killing ground. Fair hesitated. To open fire would alert those farther up the slope. To attempt to rush the position would run the risk of detection and heavy casualties. To go past it would leave a force behind their backs that could expose them to a merciless crossfire if they were pinned down above.

With a heavy heart, she told N'kobi to smother the place

without firearms. The old Fein had already decided on that option and the Neilks sent him volunteers, mostly older Fein with reputations for special stealth.

They went forward, moving across the killing ground with bodies close to the ground, on all fours like leopards stalking antelope. Fair felt a shiver run through her when she saw it.

One of the men on the parapet turned for a moment and looked right across the empty zone. Fair tensed, but the man saw nothing; he turned away and went down into the trench to vanish from view. The others, a half dozen or more, remained on the parapet.

A minute went past. The Fein seemed to have melted into the ground and Fair could no longer see them. Another volley of missiles burst around the gunship and the flashes threw stark shadows across the mountainside once again. Fair caught a sudden movement below the parapet. When her eyes had readjusted from the flashes, she saw a knot of struggling figures on the parapet. The knot collapsed and then there were just the shapes of Fein climbing over and rolling into the position.

Fair led the rest as they ran to catch up. Her feet seemed to make so much noise, and her heart was hammering in her chest. Then she was climbing the parapet, slipping over the top, and sliding down into the enemy works.

She went on into a trench that connected several bunkers built under the ruins of older domes and shacks cleared by the Fundans. There were a few bodies, all men, left where they'd fallen. Fair saw no Fein corpses.

Then she froze. A girl in EASU uniform emerged from a bunker doorway. In her hands she held an assault rifle. There were five Fein right in front of her; Fair stood fifteen feet behind her.

The girl was scared. She raised the gun. She hadn't seen Fair. Fair fired two shots, and the girl's body lifted and dropped, bouncing off the wall of the bunker.

Fair felt her gorge rise. She had never killed a woman before. She bit her lip. It was not a good feeling.

But the two shots had saved them. They crouched, listening, but there was no sound from above. No one seemed to have noticed the shots with all the uproar coming from the firefight at the North Road.

More flashes went off on the remaining gunship and now it, too, began to sink, losing altitude and slowly coming to rest in the jik forest a mile or so beyond the North Road.

The Fein went on. The town was deserted of gunmen. A couple of prostitutes saw the Fein go by and ran shrieking into a dome, but for the rest of the advance they saw nothing. In the alleys and walkways, the scattered drunks and skulkers hardly saw the dark shapes that shifted suddenly out of the shadows. They barely felt the big stone knives that took their heads.

At length they had traversed the town, and were close in on the rear of the mass of men blazing away at the Spreak positions on either side of the approach road down below. They paused and the Neilks checked their positions. The whistle blew and they raised their rifles and opened fire.

It was devastating. The Fein were good shots and their targets were facing away from them. Men were dropping right along the line when at last the mass realized it was being fired on from the rear.

There was a convulsion. Men whirled and returned fire, but the Fein were in a great position and their fire was continuous. After a few seconds, the men were either down or they were in flight, dropping down the steep slope into a canyon below the access road. Dozens broke legs and ankles in the process, and a few tumbled and broke their necks. Most survived and went tumbling on down the volcano's slopes in headlong flight.

The Spreaks and the Response Force raked them as they went. Those who made it to the bottom of the slope ran into the airstrip and took shelter there, among the remains of the trooper force that had been holding it. Some of the troopers, who had lost comrades to the destructive outburst, rose and gunned down the free-lancers as they came.

The battle was effectively over. The EASU commanders escaped in ATVs that drove to the far east and headed into the forest. A few other vehicles made it out close behind them, but the rest were trapped. The Fein and the Response Force moved through the town, pulling out EASU people and sending them back to the corral that had been built near the North Road.

The disorganized mass down at the airstrip was left to stew. Fein pickets were set out around them and a continual harassing fire was begun. Most of the gunmen were out of ammunition by now and almost bereft of the will to fight. By the time the Pale Moon set, the place was firmly under the control of the Highland Response Force.

That signal went out and was heard far across the continent.

28

THE BALLOONS HAD TAKEN A MONTH TO HARDEN PROPERLY ONCE they came out of the new assembler tank, and then it'd been a matter of another week to fly them to the Coast. On the way, the little armada was broken up in a storm. A few balloons went down, stranding men, women, and Fein in the vast forest interior, but the rest made it through.

They were scattered, however, and it took two more days for everyone to link up at the meeting point. Then, at last, they moved cautiously west toward the great delta of the Irurupup.

When they were still three days' march from their destination, they deflated their balloons and landed in the forest. Almost at once it began to rain, a steady, relentless downpour that soaked everything and everyone to the bone.

This was a nerve-racking time for all, particularly the humans. The woodwose monsters were not friendly to any intruding life-forms, but they would tolerate Fein. Humans they would immediately slaughter.

For Elgin, this march through the world of gigantic trees, vast root systems, and sloughs of mud was laden with memories both tragic and terrible. Even with Fein scouts out in front of them, Elgin could all too easily imagine the worst happening. The trees ruled this world, this was their domain. Elgin knew that power as few men could.

At moments through the day he would see his father's face, or his older brother Randolf's—heavyset men with red beards and strong hearts. At other times he recalled the time he had seen her. She had waved to him from the cab of the crawler. She never came back.

The nights were the worst. Although they climbed high into the great trees to camp on the enormous branches, any movement out there in the dark could cause the heart to freeze with apprehension. And these forests were busy at night, with animals of all sizes active on the forest floor and in the trees.

Elgin remembered how his sister, Helen, used to hate the noise of the forest at night. At times she wore earplugs, it got so bad, and she always slept with her room senso on white noise.

There was a difference now. In those days the noises had always been on the other side of the Fundan-designed security fences. Back then Elgin had liked to listen to the forest sometimes, sitting outside the dome sipping a beer and watching the stars come out. How far away it all seemed to him now! A vanished life.

He slept uneasily and was irritable as a result. He imagined the woodwose attack coming every hour of the day, but their luck held. In fact, the one monster that lay ahead was detected by the scouts well in advance. It was moving across their path, and they waited until it was well out of range before they filtered behind it and went on.

At last, on the third day, near dusk, they came in sight of the peninsula that had been the location of the first colony. A stout headland of chalk overlooked a long hook of sand that trailed off across the mouth of the enormous River Irurupup. On the peninsula there were several beige buildings. Bright lights winked from within cavernous openings and machines went about their business. Below the cliff face and extending out into the water on either side for a mile or more was a huge, powered fence. Behind it were two back-ups, and behind those were a pair of concrete bunkers with turrets bearing forty millimeter repeating cannon.

Behind the sentry cannon was a minefield with mines holding a yield of four tons of high explosive. They were set to be triggered only by weight equivalent to that of a woodwose, however.

Beyond the sentry turrets and motion detectors the ocean broke on the shoreline in rows of gleaming combers.

For Elgin, the shore brought up more old emotions, feelings that brought a hardness to his throat. The sea—he hadn't seen it in years. The air was warm and moist, and the smell of the great south ocean was very strong, sweet and salty. This was where he had grown up, in this world of trees and ocean.

He shrugged at last and made his way carefully down to the beach on the lagoon side. Projecting from the beach were some ruins from the early days, and four broken ceram struct legs jutted up from the sand. A thicket of blue knuckoo grew all around them. Under the knuckoo were heaps of eroded rubble.

Concealed in the knuckoo, he scanned the waters of the nearby swamp, then raised a light and gave two brief flashes. He waited. After a full minute there came an answering flash.

Fair had won! Old N'kobi and his Fein had done it! Elgin felt a knot of tension he'd been carrying for days dissolve. One of the dice had come up right, now it was time to see how the other would show.

From the boat went the coded signal and on the New Essex Coast the clock started running. A small group of men began their final preparations. They were lodged in an underground room in the basement of the Xanadu dome, a huge new addition to the skyline.

When Elgin returned to the rest of the party, the team of techs—four young Fundans who'd worked for Elgin since the beginning—inflated the small balloons. The party of twenty who were to make the crossing to the island took off and pushed out into the ocean breeze. Slowly the line of black minidirigibles disappeared as their near-silent fan-jets overcame the onshore breeze.

The rest of the force moved down to the water's edge a short distance past the end of the powered fence. They inflated boats and paddled out into the lagoon, heading toward the beach beneath the beige buildings.

29

ON THE TABLE SAT A POLISHED STEEL CUBE, ONE-SIXTH OF A ME-ter on a side. Inside the cube reposed one hundred grams of sparkling blue pharamol crystals, part of the loot from the vaults at Ghotaw, and a fortune of immense proportions.

Around the table sat the EASU elite, the Big Man at one end, Lawler at the other. Trockenbauer, the new numbers man, a pale Hamburger, was next to the Big Man on the left. On the right was Hammer Down, Congo's former lieutenant, who had replaced the fallen star of the security apparatus.

The rest were the chiefs of the Londons, the East Anglians,

the Bremens, the Schlesvigs, and the Dutch. They were all male except for Gestcha Samoresen of the South Londons, reflecting the ingrained bias of the EASU political structure. Women were equal in name and legal right, but were less adept at violence and intimidation. Consequently, they rarely rose to the highest ranks.

Arvin Erst was in full flight, roaring out his best bombastic oratory. The EASU elite banged on the table in agreement whenever he paused. Servant girls clad in scanties darted about refreshing drinks.

The faces were flushed with triumph. The operation in the Highlands had been a tremendous success. They had taken control of the heart of the chitin industry and ripped their way into the vaults to loot them of their hoards. Everyone at the table would have the chance of founding a dynasty, of ruling a personal kingdom, and of living for centuries, maybe forever. The gates to lives of legendary proportion were open to them; it was a moment of raw euphoria.

The door behind Lawler hissed open, and a man in security livery ran in and whispered in Lawler's ear. The burly figure of Hammer Down was half out of his seat. Lawler's eyes were wide as he shoved the security man toward the Big Man. "Tell him!" he said.

All eyes flashed from Lawler and Hammer Down to the Big Man. Trembling, the security man whispered in the Big Man's ear.

"What?" The Big Man stood up, his face suddenly white with shock. A second later it suffused with rage. "Damn them!" he growled. "I'll grind their bones, see if I don't!"

He stormed out of the room, followed by Lawler, Trockenbauer, and Hammer Down. In the screened-off control center, the Big Man exploded with rage. He ranted, he raved, he screamed orders.

On screen was Commander Durkheim, the former CO of the Ghotaw Command. He and three hundred of the most badly wounded troopers were on their way back to the Essex Coast aboard a heavy transport that had been repaired by Fundan techs in the aftermath of the battle at the airstrip.

"You imbecile!" the Big Man howled. "You dolt! How could you let a few hundred fur rugs toss you out of the best defensive positions you could possibly have had?"

Commander Durkheim had never seen the Big Man in a rage like this. It was terrifying. "Discipline broke down,

Burochief. The men panicked. I don't know what we could have done differently given the state of the men's training, but—"

"Shut the fuck up, you worm!" the Big Man roared, now almost purple with rage. Durkheim blanched and reconsidered the wisdom of going back to the Essex Coast. If only there were somewhere else to go.

The Big Man had turned to Lawler. "Shit a brick, Lawler, I dunno what it takes to keep these fuckers on their toes. I've done everything, we put in everything they could have needed. And look what they do! It's enough to make you want to take a hammer to their heads."

Lawler knew this was not the occasion for any words from him.

"This stupid fucker Durkheim, how could he let this happen?"

Lawler shrugged. He hoped he wasn't going to be blamed for Durkheim. Durkheim was looking terrified.

"Who else is aboard with you?" the Big Man asked Durkheim.

"Three hundred wounded and Lieutenant Kaltz."

"Where is Lieutenant Kaltz?"

Durkheim signaled offscreen and, a moment later, a young, dark-eyed man with thick black hair and a bandage over his eyebrow appeared.

"Lieutenant Kaltz, sir."

"Lieutenant. Are you armed at this moment?"

"Yes, sir."

"Good. Take out your weapon and show it to me."

Kaltz displayed a handgun, a .25-caliber rapid-fire auto.

"Good," the Big Man said. "Shoot Commander Durkheim just below his belt buckle."

Durkheim stared at the screen in horror. Kaltz turned. There was a shot. Durkheim crumpled and slid from view.

"Lieutenant Kaltz?"

"Yes, sir."

"You are now promoted to Subcommander. What have you got to say?"

"Thank you, sir."

"Good. Now keep Durkheim alive if at all possible. I want to interview him later. There is much he may be able to tell me."

"Yes, sir."

The Big Man cut the contact. "I want an immediate counter-attack. What have we got that we can use?"

Lawler had an uncomfortable look.

"Well?"

"Uh, well, actually, not too much. I mean, we have about three hundred trainees, plus two hundred or so standing guard over at the plant on the peninsula. Then there's the gunships. We got five ready to go."

"Shit, that's all?"

"Well, we put just about everything up there, you know, because of the info we were getting from our contacts there."

The Big Man nodded. Lawler was right—they'd had good stuff from Proud Fundan.

"Yeah," he growled, "we can't have them developing nukes. We're the only nuclear power we're gonna have in this system."

Lawler breathed a little more easily. "Yeah, so everything was up there. It's gonna take me some time to put together as much strength as we had before. I might have to take in some of those Hakka."

"Shit! I can't trust them. I only want EASU people carrying weapons."

"We got all the volunteers we're gonna get from that direction. I mean, that's all there is to say."

Erst was giving Lawler a look Lawler did not like to see. It made him nervous. Erst then looked over to Hammer Down. Something passed between them, a flicker of the eyes, and Lawler felt a cold sensation run down his spine.

"We'll come up with something," Hammer Down said calmly.

Lawler suppressed his fury. "Yeah," he said nonchalantly, "we'll manage. Have something for you in a week."

"Three days," Hammer Down said.

"Three days?"

"Yeah, we been getting ready, just in case man, you understan'?"

Lawler didn't understand for a moment, and then he did, with a flash of cold, chilling insight. Hammer Down had been building a secret armed force for the Big Man, something completely outside the Security Station—something way outside the regular military channel.

"Well, in that case, great," he said with a careful smile, "but we'd better get them ready fast. The gunships are a go, so when you're ready, they'll be ready."

Erst liked the sound of this. "Good. That's better. Now we will hammer them, eh? Eh?" He slapped hands with Hammer Down. "I want them destroyed. But remember, catch these two troublemakers and bring them to me alive."

"Sure t'ing, Burochief," Hammer Down said.

"At once, Burochief," Lawler muttered.

The Big Man signaled an end to the meeting and left with only Trockenbauer at his side. They took the elevator up to a secluded suite in the upper reaches of the dome. In the main room was a machine table, an incongruous sight among the furs on the floor and the leather couches and the reproductions of ancient art on the walls.

On the machine table was a dull metal cone four feet tall and three feet across at the base. There were a number of opened ports in its side, and to these were connected wires and jumpers of various grades. Also on the table were some monitors and some black boxes containing analysis equipment.

Inside the cone was a thermonuclear device with a yield of seven kilotons, the prototype of a series of warheads that would soon be placed on the missiles they were building over on the peninsula.

Erst looked up into Trockenbauer's pale face. The Hamburger licked his lips nervously.

"Makes you nervous, Trocky? Yeah, well, it makes me nervous, too. This goes off and there won't be a fucking thing left here, just a hot piece of sand glowing in the dark."

Erst strolled over to the table. The monitors lit up at his approach. All was stable inside the warhead. There was a button pad with four thick, black, rubberized buttons set into a white box, lit up by a green light on its top. Depressing those buttons in correct sequence would arm the thing.

"All ready to go, Trocky, all ready. Those bastards won't know what hit them. They're all celebrating now, but if we wanted to, we could turn them to dust tomorrow morning."

Erst was, of course, ignoring the fact that the missiles weren't working properly yet. The last two test firings had blown up a few seconds after takeoff. They were still trying to figure out why.

"It's scary, Burochief."

"Yeah, Trocky, that's right." The Big Man grinned and punched the numbers guy on the shoulder. "But think how much scarier it would be if they had it and we didn't!" The Big Man's face crumpled into laughter. "Am I right?" he roared.

"You're right," Trocky said.

The Big Man caressed the arming pad and roared some more.

30

THE INSTALLATION ON THE PENINSULA WAS AS WELL DEFENDED AS it could be from the giant enemies that occasionally came down from the headland and sought to penetrate to the big building. The fact that the woodwose did not swim, or even wade out as far as they might have, had influenced the design of those defenses. They covered the peninsula itself and the area in front of the fence. They were fearsome and effective defenses, forty-millimeter automatic cannon that could deliver eight hundred rounds a minute—enough to cut down any woodwose, even the oldest of the old ones, the giants with those legendarily tough hides.

In fact, only two monsters had ever got past the guns, and that pair had attacked in company with five others that had been destroyed.

That had been a bad one, an occasion that was still remembered at the EASU installation. The tech teams were split between the majority, who had come after that attack, and the distinct minority that had survived it.

The majority thought the minority were paranoid. The defenses had held up fine, except on that one occasion, and EASU had taken some further precautions since then. The newcomers assured themselves that they were secure. It was important to feel secure, and they could see the effects of the fear on the few survivors, who were a twitchy, anxiety-ridden lot. For example, the survivors always carried their sidearms, even in the lab, and they had all upgraded their weapons to the maximum allowed—monstrous, .50-caliber, semiautomatic models made for the crack commando squads of the new EASU military.

They said that the new people just didn't understand. Interestingly enough, the video records of the attack had been destroyed. There were just the stories told by the survivors, and EASU had made it plain that they were not to "blab" too much, since it would harm morale.

Increasingly, the techs in the minority, who had been out on the peninsula for a couple of years now, saw themselves as unwilling inductees into an army. EASU refused to allow anyone to leave, for the work load was enormous. EASU monitors were all over the place, insuring that nothing was sabotaged, and anyone suspected of "subversion" was likely to disappear. It had happened a few times already. No one had seen it, but such and such a person would simply vanish during the day or the night. Such people became nonpeople, their records vanished, and they were supposed to have never existed.

The survivors knew that these people had lived and worked among them, but the missing were not important to the newer, younger people, who had never known them and preferred to believe what they were told by EASU.

So it went among the tech force in the building where they were manufacturing missiles and the various components for the warheads. Their job was primarily to troubleshoot the complexities of manufacturing in the biochem mode, in which many ores had to be refined, many vats employed, and a great variety of finished products made. Final assemblies were mostly done by robot, but occasionally techs even had to get wax and solder on their work gloves.

Which was what had happened that very day when a primary assembly robot broke down on the missile first-stage line. Some had worked on the robot, others had filled in for it in piecing together the forty-foot-long missile. EASU was screaming for it—rush job, priority, no questions to be asked—even though it was a month early.

But it was done and wrapped and waiting for the tide, to be shipped over to the Big Island where it would be installed in a brand new missile base built over the crushed domes of the Roiders who had been displaced when their quarter was flattened.

With the super-rush job done, the workers were unwinding in the refectory. This was not a big drinking crowd; the norm was soft drinks and quiet conversation over meals from the refectory kitchen. But not on this day. EASU had really put the pressure on, and they'd responded and gotten the job done even without the main assembly machine. Almost all of them ordered beer for a change, and at first there was an atmosphere of tired jubilation. Soon the conversation grew animated and loud.

The TV had the all-world surfing championships on, but very few were paying attention to the aces cutting the wavetops on the other side of the planet. Everyone was too busy complaining about the current situation. The unaccustomed alcohol had loosened their tongues and tapped the wells of anger. A few were yelling as some arguments grew heated and the minority attacked the majority.

There was a loud crash somewhere in the building. A few looked up—old-timers, of course. Their eyes met across the room.

There was another very loud noise, as if a door somewhere had been broken open. One or two of them rose nervously to their feet.

Heavy feet were thundering across a floor above them. There was a scream and the sound of breaking glass. The nervous ones were already heading for the exit; the rest, including the newer people, were standing up and listening.

More screams came, and the sound of gunfire, a heavy-chugging automatic rifle. With looks of astonishment, people started for the doors. The minority folk were already jammed in the doorway, and a struggle began. People fought to get out of the refectory, clawing and punching each other, scrabbling for advantage.

Outside they saw the unbelievable: big Fein, wearing military gear and helmets, holding effective-looking assault rifles, charging down the corridor toward them. One or two of the older men pulled their guns out and started shooting. Those who were still sensible enough threw themselves to the floor.

The Fein returned fire. The men with the guns went down and so did a lot of others directly behind them.

The Fein came on, weapons at the ready. The surviving techs were pushed back into the refectory. Fein closed the doors, then opened them again. A young Fein with a proud bearing marched in and put up a big paw. On either side of him, other Fein trained their guns on the techs.

"You people surrender to us," the Fein said in bafflingly

good interlingua. "We take you to the Highland nation. You live. You no longer EASU."

Jaws dropped. The techs stared, utterly dumbfounded.

31

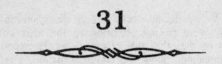

THE BALLOONS WERE LATE. AT THE DROP SITE, ON A CHOPPER PAD atop the Xanadu dome, Martin Overed waited with mounting anxiety. Above his head blinked the big red X that crowned the dome, proudly proclaiming it to be the biggest, newest dome on the coast.

Around it were other new domes, giants standing on sites that EASU had cleared by tearing down entire neighborhoods of older, smaller structures built by the first colony.

The problem was the damned onshore night wind. It was too strong, exactly as Martin had feared it would be from the moment this plan was first broached to him. In fact, the wind was unusually strong. The breakers were thundering on the beach while spray soared into the air, flashing in the bright lights from the beachfront restaurants and nightclubs.

Martin shivered in the warm breeze. This was the most dangerous time, the time when things could go seriously wrong. The other part of the operation was already in motion; alarms would be blaring here in a moment.

Mari tugged at his sleeve. "Look," she whispered, handing him the binocs. The light enhancer picked them out: a cluster of small, black sausage shapes, creeping along just above the buildings about two kilometers distant.

"Shit!" Martin snarled. "They're much too close. They're bound to be picked up on the perimeter screen."

Mari took back the binocs with an eloquent shrug. Mari and the other Roiders had been against this idea. Fair Fundan had persuaded them eventually, but they still had misgivings. The Roiders had wanted to simply blow the dome, making sure of annihilating the whole EASU top tier in one go. Fair had insisted on capturing the Big Man.

The attack had only been possible because of a stroke of good luck brought by a man seeking revenge on EASU. Security was normally tight—EASU was what it was, because it took care of such things, and always had. But EASU had its weak points. The building manager of the Xanadu was in love with a Hakka girl. The girl was beautiful and she had run afoul of an EASU enforcer, who'd had her abducted for the use of the Big Man. The girl was sensible, she had kept her mouth shut and endured it all, and she was released after a week. But then she had demanded revenge. The manager of the Xanadu had friends among the Roiders. He went to them, was interrogated carefully, and eventually was passed along to Mari and Uncle Ho.

With his help they'd been able to get inside the security net and hide the decapitation team in a room blocked off between two suites on a high floor.

The balloons were coming, but, oh, so slowly, it seemed to Martin. When they were still five hundred meters away, floating in across the beach, some people walking in the surfline looked up and saw them. The people had been to a party and they laughed and pointed at the odd black balloons. Martin felt his bowels turn to ice. Seconds ticked by, the laughter continued, but no guards had shown themselves down there, no guns were firing yet. Martin found himself praying to a god he hardly even knew of. Just another thirty seconds were all they needed.

But his prayers went unanswered. An alarm began wailing somewhere in the city. Lights were going on down by the airstrip. The attack over on the peninsula had been reported.

The wind gusted and the balloons lost formation and drifted in. One was caught on a projecting airduct on the top of the nearest dome to the east. Fein spilled out of it and slid down the outer skin of the dome. They missed the balconies lower down and fell the last hundred feet to their deaths.

By then there were alarms ringing inside the Xanadu dome itself. The rest of the balloons were laboring in the wind. Martin felt a sense of doom enfolding him.

There was a shot. People in the next dome had spotted the balloons and were shouting and pointing. A guard was out in the street below with his sidearm raised. He fired again. Mechanically Martin targeted him and fired. The guard was knocked down by the impact, rolled, and tried to get up. Martin fired again. The guard stayed down.

The alarms intensified. Mari gave him a vicious look. A searchlight came on somewhere down the beach and swung around to the area above the Xanadu.

At last the first balloons were close enough for Martin to clearly see the figures hanging in the cradles beneath them. Another EASU guard had entered the street and was firing upward. The nearest balloon was hit, and it emitted hydrogen gas with a scream as the self-repairing material struggled to close the hole. It wobbled, lost height, and was hit again. The Fein twisted around beneath it, their feet reaching out for the edge of the helicopter pad.

"Shit!" Martin moaned as he leaned over and fired down at the guard, who crouched behind some shrub tubs near the entrance to the Xanadu dome. More people were pouring out into the street. Concrete splintered off the tubs and the people fled back inside screaming.

The Fein got their feet on the pad and a moment later had slipped free of the harness. They turned to aid the next balloon, which dropped another Fein and a man, a familiar face—Elgin Fundan.

For a moment they were face-to-face. Elgin's expression was unreadable; then suddenly he put out a hand.

"Messire Overed, it turns out I was wrong about you. Congratulations, you're going into the history books."

Martin shook his hand. "Welcome back to the old colony, Fundan."

Elgin said nothing to that. Another balloon was coming in, but the gunfire from down below had increased. One of the men on the last balloon was hit. Then the balloon itself exploded, hit by three rounds at once. Both men fell to their deaths. The operation was turning out to be just as lethal as Elgin had always thought it would be. But there was no going back now—the die was well and truly cast.

The door on the roof of the dome cracked open and the Roider inside signaled that someone was coming.

Martin crouched inside the door with the man, listening to footsteps coming up the maintenance well. Someone wanted to know why the elevator to this helicopter pad was stuck at the top. That someone hadn't heard the commotion outside, either, and had no idea what he or she was walking into.

A moment later, a man in building uniform came up the stairs, puffing hard from the unaccustomed exertion. At the top he paused for a few deep breaths, then turned off the stairwell into the space surrounding the elevator mechanism. As Martin Overed slid in behind him, the man sensed something, and spun around too soon.

"Who the fuck are you?" he demanded.

"Shut it, if you want to live," Martin said, holding his gun to the man's head.

The man's eyes bulged. A funkshun user, addicted to heavy stimulants and built like a rock, he didn't take well to this treatment. His head jerked back and he lashed out and struck Martin's gun away as it fired. The bullet ricocheted around the place and finally exited into the stairwell. By a miracle, it hadn't hit either of them.

The man screamed a battle cry and tried to put his fist through Martin's solar plexus. Martin evaded and whacked the man across the side of the head with the sidearm. With a thud, the building worker fell to the concrete

The damage was done. Martin whirled back to the roof. Elgin was watching him with those critical eyes. "Hurry," Martin said. "We've had an accident."

"I noticed."

They jammed into the elevator, the big Fein alive with curiosity about the weird alien place they were in. Martin suddenly got the sense that the Fein were enjoying this hugely, like overgrown children out on a wild adventure. He wished he could be so blithe about the dangers they faced. The risk of failure was high. He was aware that the sweat was running off his body.

Every second was precious now. The Big Man could leave the building as soon as the alarm went up. He could be out of the building in thirty seconds, if he chose.

The elevator stopped and opened on the floor above the EASU headquarters. A couple of EASU guards blinked in astonishment and went for their sidearms. Elgin and Martin cut them down. The Fein followed the techs into the section at a lope, down a corridor with a beige floor motif, then left into a section with green tones on the floor. Finally the techs broke the door to a big suite of luxury rooms, decorated in Xanadu hypermod decadence.

A stunned resident, a woman in her middle years, appeared from a bedroom in a white towel robe. She held out a handgun, a small white plastic thing that might well have insured her death. Then she saw the looming figures of the Fein and fainted before they had to kill her. The Fein found this very amusing. One of them picked her up and laid her out on her bed while another took her weapon, which seemed toylike in the huge Fein paw.

The techs were already laying explosive charges in a square in the middle of her living-room floor. A few seconds later the charges blew and the floor fell. They were looking down right into the middle of an EASU High Security Suite, the Big Man's very own.

The Fein didn't hesitate, nor did Elgin. They sprang down into the room below and went into action. A moment later Martin, Uncle Ho, and Mari jumped down, too.

The guards were still picking themselves up from the art deco floor tiles when they found the Fein standing over them. These were the pride of the EASU Security Forces, and they didn't give up easily. The Fein killed them if they had to, stunned them if they didn't. One man escaped, bolting out the front door of the suite and diving out of sight down the corridor.

Then they crashed through another door and into a corridor. A guard was firing from the next doorway along, so they ducked back. The techs had been close in their estimates, but not quite close enough. They had to get into the next room to capture Erst. Bullets chewed up the molding around the door. They crouched down along the wall.

"Have to rush it," Elgin said calmly. He looked over to Martin. "We don't have time, right?"

Alarms were shrieking throughout the dome. More rounds were digging into the wall behind which they sheltered.

"I'll go," Martin said, instantly regretting the impulse.

N'ka smiled that huge, ferocious Fein smile and clapped him on the shoulder. "What good is life if it has to be held close like an infant all the time? You lead, N'ka follow."

Martin swallowed heavily and turned to go. He crouched there as more bullets hammered around the doorway. This was just monstrously stupid. He couldn't believe it—this was going to get him killed.

He tried, he tried to will himself onward, but he just couldn't do it. He'd risked his life for the cause for months, but this was too damn much. Sweat ran off his temples, and more bullets hammered the wall. The ceram wall was cracking up. It was now or never.

He couldn't go—his legs wouldn't move. "Oh, fuck," he wailed. "I can't."

Elgin shoved past him, followed by N'ka. By the edge of the door, Elgin launched himself, elbow and knee into the corridor. N'ka was right behind him. A big green-eyed Fein named Itupa leaned out and emptied a clip across the passage to the other door.

They made it to the doorway. Elgin thrust his gun around the door and fired, then scrambled in. The Fein was behind him. Martin was behind N'ka.

Bullets smacked into the wall just above Elgin's head. He kept moving. Bullets smacked into his shoulders, lifting him and throwing him against the wall with the impacts. N'ka was at the door. He shot the guard, but the guard shot first and Elgin was hit again, through the chest, through the face, through the skull.

Itupu joined N'ka at the door to the next room. Martin was close behind, his gorge rising. Elgin's head, blown like that, was the worst thing he'd ever seen, and Martin had seen many evil things.

And, of course, he knew that could've been him and not Elgin Fundan. He was still alive.

And yet the joy he ought to have felt was absent, replaced with a bitterness, a sense of loss. He should have gone; his manhood had failed him at the crisis. How would he ever face himself in a mirror again?

They looked in on a lavish bedroom packed with laboratory equipment and tables.

A voice stopped them, a big voice, sputtering with rage and fear. A screen, inset into the entrance to the room, blinked on.

"Stop right there, Fundan! You and the fur rugs. Not one fucking inch!"

Arvin Erst's face bloated on the screen. He was holding a button box. He waved it at the camera.

"Don't move or I blow the whole place. This is a live warhead I have here. I put it here just in case something like this happened." The Big Man was recovering a little of his poise. "Seven-kiloton yield on this one. It'll take out the whole fuckin' colony. You understand?"

There was a long silence. Martin sucked in a breath. The Big Man smiled through the perspiration on his face.

"You see, I respected you enough to think that you might not only try something like this, but also come damn close to succeeding. And you did! I hand it to you. But now it's over. You back off or you're gonna be radioactive dust."

Martin stared at the screen. The Big Man was hidden in there somewhere, behind the tables and equipment. The Fein were looking at him expectantly. He was in command. What the hell was he going to do?

32

MARTIN STARED BLINDLY BACK AT THE FACES BEHIND HIM, FEIN and techs. The alarms in the building were going like mad. EASU troopers were coming. The first shots were being exchanged in the outer part of the suite.

Uncle Ho held up a slice of what looked like clear plastic about the size of a playing card. There was a black button imbedded in the plastic surface. Uncle Ho's eyes were brown and absent of malice. Indeed, Martin saw a surpassing sadness there. Uncle Ho had liked this young man.

So it came around again. This was what they'd saved him for.

"Right," he said, and felt better at once, although more terrified than he'd ever been in his life. But he was clean, now, and he'd be able to forget Elgin Fundan forever.

Uncle Ho nodded and smiled. Mari simply stared. He blew her a kiss, then stood up and went around the edge of the door into the room, his hands held up and empty.

"All right, Big Man, we have to negotiate. Have to cut a deal, you know what I mean? You and me, otherwise we're all going to die, right?"

The Big Man was standing behind a barricade of lab equipment. The warhead was on a table behind him. Little green lights were winking on the outer surface.

"Overed!" he roared, and his face split into a horrid grin. "Well, well, well, at last I've got you, eh? Negotiate? You must be out of your fuckin' mind. Why should I negotiate with you? You're trapped, you and your fur rugs."

"We'll make you hit that button, Big Man. I think we'd all rather go that way than die on the hotbed."

"You little prick, I should have made sure of you when I had the chance."

"But you didn't, and you didn't give me justice, Big Man. So, here we are. And you do have to negotiate, or blow yourself to atoms along with the rest of us."

Erst stared at him, bug-eyed. A dynamo whirled inside him, and rage and fear surged to the surface.

"I will, I'll do it if you make me!"

"Go ahead, if that's what you want. Get rid of the whole EASU in one go. Solve everybody's problem."

"Fuck you, Overed."

"Negotiate. You can cut a deal. We'll let you live, up on one of the orbiting ships. It won't be so bad."

Martin was close now. There was another man there, a tall, pale fellow Martin knew, but not very well. Then it came to him—one of the Hamburgs, named Trockenbauer. He had to be the replacement for Slovo.

"'Lo, Trocky," Martin said. "You in at the death, too?"

Trockenbauer looked scared shitless; the sidearm in his hands was wobbling. Martin laughed. "Come on, Trocky, it won't be so bad. We'll never know what hit us, right?" Martin turned back to the Big Man.

"Do it, Big Man, pull the trigger, kill yourself, or we'll kill you instead."

The Big Man hesitated, on the defensive for once and hating it. The truth was, he didn't want to die. He wanted very badly to live. After all, right there in the safe he had enough pharamol to live in luxury for centuries, perhaps millennia.

"What choice do I have?" he asked.

Martin spread his hands. "All right, you want to cut a deal."

"Cut that, talk to me."

Martin edged closer, inside the ring of tables. He was within ten feet of the Big Man. Trockenbauer kept the sidearm trained on him, and the Big Man kept the hot button under his thumb.

"Keep your hands up."

The sound of gunfire from the outer suite was getting deafeningly loud. The Fein and the techs were enormously outnumbered and EASU would eventually send in men in battle armor. The time for negotiating was running out, and then Erst would hold all the cards again. The Big Man would be on top.

Martin could see that Erst was thinking the same thing. The Big Man's eyes were staring, as if pushed out by the force of the calculations the brain behind them was making. The big red moon face split open. "Negotiation is a two-way street, Overed. You say I should surrender, I dunno about that. I mean, I'm no more vulnerable than you are. Maybe you should surrender to me."

Martin had heard this sort of talk before. "Shut it, Erst. We don't have long, so put down the box and take the offer I'm giving you. Your life, and a comfortable future up on one of the orbiting ships."

Erst would never take it, Martin knew. There was only one way to do this. In his right hand he had the slice of plastique, wedged between index and middle fingers. His thumb came over and rested on the detonator button. The shaking Hamburg missed the motion.

A grenade exploded outside. No time, no time to waste.

"Hey, Big Man, first time for everything, you know that? Even for death."

The Big Man's eyes went wide.

Martin's thumb squeezed. There was a flash and then no more.

EPILOGUE

FAIR FLEW DOWN TO THE COAST. THERE WAS A LOT TO DO. UNCLE Ho and Mari and the other Roiders had set up a skeleton administration, but there was a lot of chaos in the domes and streets, a lot of revenge to be taken. It was a somber time. She listened to Wassenstein's "Death Masque" over and over. For some inexplicable reason the dark, doom-laden music made things more bearable.

The days of the EASU were over. All over the New Essex Coast the lampposts were decorated with the bodies of EASU enforcers strung up by enraged mobs. Looting was still going on.

Fair ignored it all. She knew the nightmare was coming true; there would be endless war, war for eternity. EASU would be replaced with some other organization, and there would be no escape. Her bleak vision chilled her, but her resolve remained. She and hers had discovered the chitin and their drugs; she and hers would hold them fast.

Elgin was unrecognizable. They had him in the morgue at the big old hospital in the center of the old colony. The bullets had ruined his face. Of course, they never found anything whatsoever of Martin Overed, or of the Big Man. They did find Trockenbauer's legs and shoes, but that was all. The plastique was very strong. The nuclear warhead had been destroyed as well, but without setting it off. No radiation had escaped to poison the air of ancient Fenrille. Martin Overed had more than made amends with his last act; he would join the list of martyrs to the cause.

They had a simple ceremony for Martin down on the ocean beach at sunset. Uncle Ho and Mari officiated, and Fair was there to read a short eulogy. About fifty others were on hand, including a few Fein who had stayed over to guard the Xanadu dome, which was now temporarily their headquarters.

To end it, Uncle Ho fired a gunpowder rocket out to sea. It

burst in a flower of green lights against the oncoming night, then slowly faded and went out.

The next day she went in Uncle Ho's boat over to the mainland, to Elbow Creek, to the site of the farm where Elgin had been born and raised. She felt impelled to search for a place that Elgin would have wanted. She knew he had had complicated feelings about the farm and his youth. Once he had spoken of his mother and her grave there.

But there was nothing left of the farm. In fact, it was only recognizable by the small size of the young *Esperm Gigans* trees that were now growing over the fields. They were all about seventy feet high, with their branches and vegetation clumped around the tops like huge balls. Farther away loomed the mighty giants of the old forest, some of them more than a thousand feet tall, the largest living things ever discovered by humanity.

Along the bank of the estuary the vegetation moved and Fair glimpsed the turretlike head of a woodwose peering out at the boat in the channel. For a moment there was a still silence. Then the engines coughed into life. Uncle Ho had seen it, too, and he turned the boat and drifted back down the inlet to broader waters.

Fair decided that she would take Elgin's body back to the Highlands. That was where he belonged, in the mountains he had loved, among the Highland nation.

ABOUT THE AUTHOR

CHRISTOPHER ROWLEY was born in Massachusetts in 1948 to an American mother and an English father. Soon afterward he began traversing the Atlantic Ocean, a practice that has continued relentlessly ever since. Educated in the U.S., Canada, and for the most part at Brentwood School, Essex, England, he became a London-based journalist in the 1970s. In 1977 he moved to New York and began work on *The War for Eternity*, his first science-fiction novel. Published by Del Rey Books in 1983, it won him the Compton Crook/Stephen Tall Memorial Award for best first novel. *To a Highland Nation* is Rowley's eighth novel.